THE SEX LIFE OF A KITCHEN GODDESS

Dear Madeleine,
Best wishes for a
lovely summer
from Walter and

Izinda

June '07
Brisbane

ISBN: 1-4196-5995-2
ISBN-13: 978-1419659959

Visit www.booksurge.com to order additional copies.

THE SEX LIFE OF A KITCHEN GODDESS

Ilinda Markova

2007

THE SEX LIFE OF A KITCHEN GODDESS

ONE

'Death is a hooker.'

I hate to imagine losing my mother Margherita to a hooker. But rely on Marylin to be sensitive. Her voice continues chopping the words like parsley. 'Death *is* a hooker. She's everyone's companion.'

'Hookers do it for money.'

'Well then it makes death a promiscuous bitch. Just like you, Sandy *Cornelius*!' Marylin's laugh sounds scary, bubbly and sad like a documentary about bleached coral.

I also smile, sparingly, unaware that I am hours away from becoming death's greediest pimp.

We are in a small shaggy den between the ocean and the lake where the tortoises stretch their necks for a piece of shepherd's pie. They make it best here in *Café on the Park,* which is also famous for its decadent poetry evenings. Two girls shuttle between the tables stitching up wounds with comfort food.

The blue-painted walls are decorated with posters and sepia photos from the time when cane-cutting in the region was booming: barefooted young men in dark suit trousers, naked from the waist up, dancing in couples on the beach, looking over their shoulders. Hungry migrants of post-war Europe: Greeks, Italians, Germans. Broken dreams, broken English, never enough money for a two-month voyage back to *mamma* from the backside of the world Australia.

In the mouldy air around us yellow balloons dance apathetically over our heads in the company of paper fish and sea horses. A jukebox offers Pat Boone's *April Love,*

Love Letters in the Sand and other evergreens. Next to it, a *Mignon* piano is squashed under a massive Chinese vase stuffed with plastic poppies, blackened by greasy smoke from the kitchen. On one side of the piano a telephone hangs over a sign—*Fire Extinguisher*. The fire extinguisher is on the other side of the piano next to a thin book on display: Norm Sherman's poetry *Voodoo Visions*.

Sitting on my right, Norm has just taken Marylin off my neck by reciting softly into her ear. Grateful, I pretend I don't notice his leg, casually rubbing mine like a stray cat.

Norm has the stocky torso of a rice-cooker and grace to go with. His flour-coloured face and dough-coloured eyes are half-hidden in Marylin's chilli-red Irish curls. His inspirational whisper is about stars and cosmic serpent.

'The usual crap.' Marylin winks at me behind his back.

She wears a multi-layer outfit, a sign of surrender in her ongoing war with the bulge. Tin and copper bangles clink with her every movement, temple bells sending prayers to the gods.

It's Friday night.

Behind us spread the city and the sky, bruised by needle-like buildings.

We feel like a pack of dingoes. Marylin is a single mum. Norm, single with a dog. I, single with...Ah well, more about this later.

The long-necked tortoises in the lake continue to stretch their heads in the dusk, a tribe of homeless penises walking on water.

The puddle of a lake, though, is in Brisbane. We are not by Beijing's West Lake, where I might have to slurp from a hotpot in the famous Guolizhuang restaurant offering *bian,* a concoction of the male organs of six animals—including snake's—boiled in chicken stock. A sought-after Chinese dish known to enhance men's virility and give women silk-like skin.

Nor have I to mix and prepare the pot in front of a TV audience. For I am a show chef. A kitchen goddess, a cooking guru, a gourmet initiator, a keeper of palate secrets, an academician of culinary art. A nutrition witch.

Laugh, but it requires a certain amount of witchcraft to conjure a heart-and-soul nourishing meal that fills the body and the aura, creating vibes that are good for you, the planet and humanity.

What we are having tonight is a simple meal of fish and chips. Something to go with the ocean view and my time off from the strenuous pretence that cooking is an extravagant occupation, a pastime for select adventurers in tastes, aromas and rare ingredients.

Even so, I keep my sunglasses on. It would be bad for my reputation as a sophisticated presenter of palate ticklers to be spotted at a place with one person in the kitchen fussing around two cauldrons of boiling oil. Sometimes the kitchen worker forgets where to throw the chips and where the fish. It doesn't matter. It's cheap and the customers keep coming back.

They might be sneered at but junk food places possess the energy to attract, not unlike brothels. They are on the winning end against organic shops selling carrots like arthritic fingers.

The sight of myself on the TV screen, standing by a traditional *umu* oven sizzling with food wrapped in leaves under a layer of earth and surrounded by rocks heated red-hot, makes me famous and desirable; the same scene makes my friend Marylin miserable. The blue lagoon behind me (is it on the tropical island of Vanuatu or Bora-Bora?), the cocktail served in a beheaded coconut, so hairy it looks obscene, make my best friend stew in her own bile juices.

Marylin takes my success as a personal offence. She suspects I am out there to seduce.

She might be right: food is the new sex.

'Here, gorgeous.' Norm transfers some octopus rings onto my plate.

My tongue whirls inside the tiny holes. Food has *always* been sex.

The cell phone rings.

I don't answer, the reception in the *Café on the Park* is no good. The ring tones fill the bellows of my bag somewhere around my feet, breaking away through seams and zips. For a while the first scores of Beethoven's piano sonata *Fur Elise* merge with the smoky smell of over-fried fish. The invasive combination brings tears to my eyes.

My bet is, it's Beverley ringing, she must be desperate to know where we are.

Lately Beverley has started to copycat me, which could have been flattering if it wasn't annoying. She compiles recipes for wedding cakes and has been trying to sell them to my publisher along with photos of the wedding gowns she stitches at home.

'Sorry Beverley,' I say in the direction of the bag. 'Marylin will never call *you* a promiscuous bitch under cover of a cookbook writer.'

These days I am suspicious that Beverley targets even Marylin, trying to snitch her away from me.

Beverley must be nuts to think she can come between us.

Marylin and I, we know each other from the time when I was cleaning old Greek ladies' houses for a living. The time when I'd rather scrub toilet than refrigerator where one could find anything between yellow cheese turning green, chunks of rotten cabbage, jars of home-made jam with a thick jellyfish-like layer of mould as topping, sprouted garlic, all drowned in brown marinate formed by the dripping water from the icicles and anything that they would meet on their way like a fleshed bone that even a dog would not consider appetizing or disintegrating leftovers of moussaka. I needed a welder's mask to clean those bacteria-breeding germ-friendly monsters of refrigerators exuding stench and sticky spores of bouillon where life was first conceived.

We know each other from the time when Marylin moved opposite the town cemetery stretching all along the horizon of Marylin's shabby, flaked, dirty house like a chicken-coop given to her by the House Commissioning in a doubtful fit of generosity.

Now times have changed. Marylin has also succeeded but only in finally convincing the House Commissioning to paint her house so it doesn't look like a bad case of dandruff.

Suddenly everybody in the cafe looks at the door, and I know who's coming.

Tamati, an ex-rugby player from the kiwi *All Blacks,* carries his body like Michelangelo's Moses. His Maori heritage: a striped green tattoo on a smooth glossy muscle on his upper arm, a green stone figurine *tiki* on a black leather string around his neck. Black singlet, black board shorts, black sandals, black baseball cap.

The heavy testosterone cloud preceding Tamati pushes its way in. The girls' voices become high pitched, their laughter fretting.

Tamati, a doctor, or as Marylin might put it, a temptation under cover of a medical practitioner, is also single. With housemates.

'Ah, fish,' says Tamati in disgust after a look at our plates.

He takes a seat a bit too close to me. His body heat brushes against mine.

In his shiny coffee-beans eyes I see my mirror reflection: healthy, juicy, fuckable material with protruding, gentle breasts, bee-sting lips and a genuine fair Alpine complexion courtesy of my yodelling ancestors. My glossy hair has that equestrian thing about it.

What men comment most on, though, doesn't show in Tamati's eyes. I am an owner of a rare, shamelessly quivering bum that sprays hormone sap in its wake and makes people primary and silly.

I feel sandwiched between the two men.

As a filling they find me as exquisite as veal Wagyu or Kobe, so tender it melts. This most expensive meat originates from happy Japanese calves that live in separate compounds and are fed on selected grains, which they swallow with the help of good beer.

'Hi, Tamati,' I purr, my hand feeling the texture of his chocolate mousse skin. Everything's right there, no granules. Smooth.

The phone kicks off again; my bag could be a tummy stuffed with Lima beans. *Easy, Beverley! You are not on my good books these days!*

Besides Beverley doesn't go well with us. She is *married*.

Tamati gobbles some of my chips. I stop eating, contemplating the sensual film of grease they leave on his lips.

'Go on, Sandy. You'll still be beautiful dying from food poisoning.' Tamati licks his lips. 'The fish is stocked with mercury.'

'Shut up, Mr Tonsils-cutter!' Marylin's vibrant freckles make her look like strawberry pulp. She fans herself with a stack of paper napkins. The oldest among us, heading for her forties, she is entitled to authority.

Norm's face starts to bake in the dim light. Relaxed in his baggy T-shirt, baggy jeans, baggy shoes, Norm doesn't like fights.

A waitress with zucchini green eyes takes Tamati's order. I can tell he finds her attractive.

This makes me unhappy and I wonder why. What's been between Tamati and me looks like a distant past, now that I have a long-distant passionate affair with a Norwegian lover.

Never love a Norwegian, Marylin spoils it for me, *they are born liars.*

Yet I am single with a lover. Married lover.

I got him three years ago when I went reviewing the magical, hot and dirty, cheap and sexy, city of Bangkok as an enormous food bazaar. Drugging myself on tantalizing aromas along *Khao San Road*, a real kitchen in the open, I kept away from the skyscrapers, the sky train, dodgy corrugated houses along stinky channels, where mangy balding dogs would approach you waiting for a pat, away from markets where raw silk and red corals were sold along butcher displays and fish stalls unfamiliar to ice. Taking pictures of a woman with a wok bigger than her (she kept juggling prawns, noodles, and pieces of vegetables on the gas burner), I saw a blond giant in his early forties standing in front of her. His saffron hair fascinated me, his leg muscles moving seductively under smooth, creamy skin.

Then I spotted the plain, horseradish-faced lady next to him paying for the meal. 'Come on, Frank,' she said with that unmistakable authority of a spouse and I was still crazy enough to follow them. Booking a room next to theirs in *Buddy Boutique Hotel* by the Canal was easy.

What happened in that room and in the massage cabin for lovers later could feed a sizzling bestseller.

The waitress leaves, and again I feel Tamati's eyes like potato-peelers on me. They remove my scarce attire, my sunglasses, my newly acquired celebrity confidence, my yearning to see Frank soon, listen to his *Sandy, scavenger of old books, tell me about that love concoction of pigeon's poo in coconut milk*.

For a while we listen in silence to the piano player, a bony Englishman, chiselled by frostbites and glass wool fogs. The piano hasn't been tuned for ages and the horrendous Chinese vase doesn't give much of a chance for good acoustics. But it's nice and homely and we give him a round of applause to honour the artist.

Later we go bar-hopping and mingle with other singles who have nothing better to kill than time in search of a sex partner. We spice ourselves up: I am on cosmopolitans with coriander, Marilyn downs martinis with dill; Norm dries up daiquiris with cardamom. Tamati cruises with stubbis in each hand around pool tables with girls stretching over their cues to show off the latest in knickers fashion.

Yet the glances Tamati casts at me could ovulate a crocodile egg.

TWO

Back home I sink into a religious rite. I prepare hot, black, healing ambrosia, mixing tastes and aromas. It has to erase the blur in my mind induced by the cosmopolitans, and make me work.

The house, every piece of fabric and furniture, are soaked in the rich, almost palpable smell of coffee. I smell of coffee, the best perfume I know.

I live with a jar full of it next to me, vapours filling my cavities with bliss. If they put me through a juicing machine they'll get a pure beverage of black blood smelling of death and enchanted love.

I put on Bach's *Coffee Cantata.* As a person who has never known her father I find the fight between a daughter and her father over coffee quite disturbing. For a moment I imagine paying for the knowledge of who my father was by giving up my favourite hot drink. Quickly I chase the thought away.

I look at my small oriental brass pot with a long handle called *djezve,* especially designed for this type of heavy body coffee. It's a real art to brew it so it forms an even thicker surface layer the colour of a hazelnut. Some add a pinch of ground rye to achieve that highly desirable effect. This thicker surface layer is called *cream* and may even protect the tongue, spreading over it before being washed away by burning-hot gritty liquid released by the black residue at the bottom of the cup.

I am on the deck of my suburban Brisbane *queenslander*, a wooden structure on stilts, not unlike the second pig's house blown away by the Big Bad Wolf in *The Three Little Pigs*. The breeze coming from the ocean some five k's away where I left *Café on the Park* and the tortoises is not the culprit for my gooseflesh. Tonight it feels spooky in the garden. For the first time I don't feel comfortable about living alone.

Yet coffee relaxes me.

I indulge in the sweet black sin, my tongue dips and whirls not unlike a devil's trident. The coffee spreads inside me like octopus ink.

It's pity there's no one to read my coffee grounds. I turn the cup upside down after shaking it around gently and make the sign of the cross over it.

I know my future; I need no one to read it. I have everything: good looks, a blooming career that starts to bring me money, fame and envy; good friends to hang out with; a Norwegian lover. Still married and on the other side of the globe, but this is not the Middle Ages. Ah well, he hasn't got immediate plans for one of our escapades, meeting secretly somewhere in the world when I even have no time to eat during a week or two.

The telephone must have been ringing for a while before I answer it, dredged as I am in my own thoughts.

'Sandy!'

'Frank! Tell me you're at the airport. Coming to see me.'

My stomach reels. The line turns into a groove carrying lust and care, cravings for another body, hands that make me scream in near death experiences.

There's no reply. It's only the stethoscope pounding of my heart inside the receiver.

I wait. Time becomes solid, a marble statue of Penelope with Odysseus prowling around disguised as an old beggar.

'No, Sandy.' His sigh can rekindle dead embers under scone-topped beef casserole. 'You haven't been answering your cell phone.' Cautious, tone-measuring, anything between question, scrutiny and accusation.

'Sorry.' What the fuss! Coffee is an aphrodisiac, I already feel it travelling from my lips to his. Italian telephone sex priestesses make me laugh when saying theirs is a terrible profession. I love doing it.

'Sandy, I need your help!'

Getting in the mood, I giggle, murmuring *sure, honey, sure*, looking for cushions to recline on for a better performance. My guttural syllables oscillating between purring and small teasing moans.

I realize I am alone in it.

'Frank?'

Another sigh. Suppressed frustration reaches me like steam escaping a heavy lid.

'What do you need my help for, Frank?' It's not a flattering moment for me, rather embarrassing in fact, yet there's no time to get hurt with my curiosity taking over.

An expert on ancient Scandinavian runes, the occult and the mystical, a reviewer of best-selling thrillers—needs help from a laid-back cookbook writer who right now has a problem convincing her publisher that a *Gastronomy in Art* will sell like hot cakes. (I can see the cover: *Gluttony* from Hieronymus Bosch's *Table of the Seven Deadly Sins.* A fat man sprawled on a chair, a fat child looking up at him, the wife bringing in a corn-fed chicken, marinated in wine and white pepper. The chicken looks succulent, at least more than the wife; both need more roasting.)

'Are you there?' His voice is spiced with fear. 'Sandy?' Panic, sheer panic is coming from the pit of his stomach.

My mind is racing.

What could have happened? His wife has found out about us and killed herself, leaving a suicide note? He has killed her over a refusal to give him a divorce? *Crime de passion.* In France he might get away with it. I don't know how it is in Norway.

Suddenly I don't want to know what his problem is. There must be a way out. Something to prevent me from facing a drama, a frightful situation, a complication. I am not ashamed of feeling cowardly, slimy.

He senses what's going on in my head and waits. His reverse psychology gets the better of me.

'Frank,' I say, exasperated, 'what happened?'

'Another cult killing. In New York.'

I freeze. I hold my breath and chew on it.

'When?'

'Watch the news.' He says curtly, exhaustion crawling out of his voice.

Then he hangs up.

I feel vaguely guilty as dread leaves me, giving way to relief. Frank takes this cult thing close to heart, and I am ready to help him whatever it takes. Yet there's no any immediate danger, not to him, anyway. I go inside, switch the TV on, still early for the news. A former president is reading from his book about death being like going home.

In New York someone has gone home prematurely, helped by a cannibalistic cult. Ritual killings are on the rise. What I already know is that Frank is somehow involved in tracking down the hair-raising criminals behind them.

I sag onto my mat in front of the TV, the place where I sleep, eat, and write, and wait for the news on CNN.

My laptop is open in front of me. I have been working on a chapter about Manet's *Le Dejeuner sur l'Herbe (Luncheon on the Grass).* The French impressionist conveys a secret cannibalistic message, serving the naked courtesan on the grass as a meal. She relates to the still life of bread and fruit around her, edible little thing about to be consumed by the two men dressed in ritualistic black. The garment under her looks like a tablecloth. Her left foot faces the viewer, appearing totally dismembered, confined in an imaginary triangle. Her breasts caged in another triangle.

Triangles, well-known symbols for fangs.

The second courtesan bathes in the background on the canvas, ready to replace her naked sister once she has been devoured.

But I'm uninspired, wondering whether this work is a precursor to a publisher's rejection.

Half-closed, my eyes brood over the floor-to-ceiling bookcase full of shabby, stained books passed down from hand to hand, soul to soul. Pages ripped off, words floating loose, authorless, titleless, dusty, pale, chapters swapped with a happy end or an appendix, epilogues disclosing ghost writers. Fragile edges crumble at a touch, going to ashes. Books like fjord coastlines, rolled, folded up, swollen like an old woman's ankles, dog-eared. The fate of books that weren't rejected, books that made it.

I read them, sniff them, lick them, listen to the rustling of their crispy bodies, feeling their skin eroded like the surface of the moon. I make shelves in my heart for these books, they come with wheelchairs, walkers, crutches, sticks or ebony, gold-encrusted canes. I don't want them to feel crippled. I comfort them the way they comfort me now when I mourn the death of an unknown human being somewhere in New York.

The bang of a door startles me awake. I look inside the room that used to be my mother's studio, where the piano stands like a coffin. It's only the breeze gaining power.

The telephone rings. I hope I haven't dozed off through the news.

'Sandy, it's David.'

I lift my eyes to the grandfather clock with a pendulum like a ladle scooping time. It's almost midnight. I don't know what to make of a publisher's call at this hour. My uneasiness returns.

'Listen, I know it's late but I just come out of a meeting.'

Life must be hard everywhere these days.

'Yes David?' There's not much encouragement in my voice, but I go out onto the deck to hear better, since on CNN they start to read the headlines.

'Sandy, grab a chair, old girl, so you don't topple over. I have good news: the publishing house is ready to give you a chance.'

'A chance?' A fire-cracker exploding in my brain illuminates big, thick, hardcover books splashed in rangy bookstore windows: *Gastronomy in Art*, *by Sandy Cornelius*. 'Fantastic!'

'We have a last-minute rejection that opens a crack for you,' David continues. 'When can you submit the complete manuscript?'

I resist jumping into the air—Tamati's mates, all ex-rugby players, built the deck snitching timber from old demolished fences.

'David! I am finishing a chapter on Jesus presiding over some tables. Caravaggio's *Supper at Emmaus*. Simple food: bread, wine, apples. *Marriage of Cana,* a roasted boar's head, a swan. Bosch, the sneaky bastard, was a member of *The Brotherhood of Swan*. I'll find their extravagant menus!'

'Well, bring the manuscript in! You don't have much time!' He hangs up.

I utter the old Indian war cry, answered by some frog-mouth owls, and do some improvised dancing, partnered by the swaying deck. Then I run inside to open a bottle of vodka, which I pour over ice and top with cold espresso from the jar on the kitchen bench. I skip the sugar syrup and the Toissant liqueur. That will do for my version of a Vodka Espresso.

I deserve every bit of it!

Going back into the living room, I catch the end of the news on CNN. They are showing footage on a story that began in 1998 in Nigeria where the beheaded body of a teenage boy was found. The chest ripped open, the heart missing. My heart almost stops, my excitement crashing down around me.

Within the last few years similar cannibalistic rituals have taken place in Oregon, the state of Virginia, somewhere in Quebec, in Bogotá, Columbia. Not long ago in Warsaw, in a café where the great Polish composer Chopin wrote some of his piano works, a velvet bag containing two hands chopped off the wrists was found.

I switch off the television, feeling sick, trying not to look at the bookcase beside me. But I know I won't be able to ignore it.

One night, feeling nostalgic for my mother, I started to open books one by one in frenzy. I must have been caught in a bibliomancy deviation perhaps. A booklet bound together with a thick pompous novel gave me the fright of my life. The more I read the more I got scared.

Years ago someone had gone to lots of trouble to verify that over the centuries high profile personalities and dignitaries have been familiar with the taste of human flesh. Not only that—they commissioned art to express their gastronomic preferences, for those who can read the symbols and coded messages.

I showed the text to Frank. His opinion was it was bogus, one of those cheap sensation-seekers trying to make a point. I thought Frank was right, yet I started to look through different eyes at the canvases of the old masters. I was stunned by some astonishing findings and decided to build my new manuscript around the outrageous idea.

Now I search through the shelves, looking for the camouflaged booklet. When I find it, I hold it close to my chest like a poker player holding her cards. Then I open it at random.

Left page, third paragraph, second line.

Man's an orchestra, I read, *his head a drum, his heart a fiddle*.

I close the booklet and go back to the deck to get the phone receiver. Gazing at the Southern Cross, I remember Frank and the earnestness in his voice, his ongoing worries that the cult is recruiting young rebelling people sick of Buddha and drugs, offering an aggressive, gut-wrenching challenge to a civilisation out of answers. Civilisation turning its own planet into a grave.

The phone rings and I answer it eagerly. I don't feel alone any longer. Frank is with me thanks to a small satellite somewhere above us where Norm sees his stars and cosmic serpent.

'You are dead, bitch!'

I scream dropping the receiver like a poisonous scorpion.

Sobering on the spot, I rush inside and lock the deck door. If I call the police, there's not much they can do about a telephone threat. The voice was completely unfamiliar to me, and I can't think of any enemies I might have, other than Marylin, occasionally. I try to trace a number on the display of the telephone. It doesn't show any data.

My heart keeps whip-cracking.

Don't dramatise, I repeat to myself. *Breathe, keep your head cool. Use your head, Sandy Cornelius. You are beautiful, successful. It's just a prank, an envious competition, trying a psycho attack on you.*

When Frank rings I make sure it's actually him on the caller ID, then I answer.

'They want my book,' I start, the enthusiasm still there.

'They want your head.'

My ribs feel like icicles. It's not a threat; he sounds like stating a fact.

'Frank,' I gasp. 'What are you saying?'

'The cult has found out about your manuscript. You are not safe remaining in Australia. Tomorrow you are flying to Vienna. I'll meet you at the cafe opposite St Stephen's cathedral on Sunday. Then I'll take you...' He abruptly cuts himself short.

I can hear the anxiety in his voice. 'Just get on that plane, Sandy. And don't contact me before you get to Vienna. It's not safe.' He pauses. 'Love you.'

Tears the smell of coriander and coffee flood my face and my short-lived writer's joy. 'Frank, don't go!'

The line goes dead.

THREE

Flying economy stuck in the middle of a middle row is an additional reminder that I am running out of luck. I hope my bladder won't be overly active.

I unpack my laptop and try some writing, remembering the urgency in David's voice. When I see I can't spell *meal* properly, I give up.

I recline my seat back as far as possible, ignoring some Korean kids who protest by kicking from behind, and close my eyes. Late last night Frank gave me another telephone call, provoked by my insistent ringing. Details from out conversation start to unroll in my mind.

Two weeks ago a young man from Nigeria whose name was kept secret for security reasons arrived in Oslo seeking asylum. He told the Norwegian authorities that as a boy he had been initiated into a cult practising cannibalistic rituals. Once part of this macabre society, the only way out is a death penalty exercised by the brotherhood: the betraying member is sacrificed.

The Norwegian authorities decided that the young man's life was in danger so he was granted a temporary visa.

Frank received a phone call from detective Jacob Jacobsen inviting him for a meeting. The Interpol officer shared with him intelligence indicating that the cult had started to infiltrate other countries, aggressively building up a network. A website called LongPig.com is operating under a humoristic pseudo male chauvinistic profile, rapidly recruiting young people for their chat-rooms.

No one questioned the real meaning of *long pig*, which stands for *man* in the languages of some tribes with man-eating history in the Pacific.

Jacobsen said that the Nigerian refugee had been closely monitored under the suspicion that he might be a Trojan horse for the expansion of the brotherhood into Norway. Jacobsen also thought it was a good idea to attract experts outside the national security department, like Frank, whose occult knowledge might be useful to decode ritualistic prop and symbols.

This is the big picture.

The little picture is a question yet to be answered. Where do I stand in all this?

Who would want the head of a kitchen goddess and why? Over a manuscript? It's somehow hard to believe.

After Frank I resort to the bottle of vodka without bothering to top it off with espresso. Later on I continue drinking whatever liqueur comes my way until I knock myself unconscious.

It might be a turbulence or the Korean kids kicking the back of my seat with a renewed vigour. Whatever, it brings me back to reality inside the belly of the plane and I order a glass of orange juice. Then I let myself drift back to how in the morning I use all my will to pull myself together, get up and shower.

From the airport they confirm a ticket to Vienna on my name for mid-afternoon.

I'd better stay home, I think, then I remember the voice of the telephone threat.

Why would they want my head? It is not of much use right now. I have my worst ever hangover. The aspirin I took is starting to wear off, and the headache is splitting my brain apart, starting between the eyes and sawing its way out at the dome.

When I called my producer Janette van Haren to tell her of my departure. I found her in Fiji where she was with the cameraman taking footage for our new series, *The Eyes of Coconut*, due to enter in active shooting in a fortnight.

'Something's wrong?' Janette tried to read my voice for a cold, hangover or PMS.

'Nothing's wrong,' I assured her.

'Then you're love-sick, am I right?'

Janette knew about Frank, so I left her to believe it. Actually I *am* love-sick.

'That's great,' Janette quickly took over leading me as if we were on a shooting location. 'Try more blow-jobs. That will tighten your face muscles and perk your boobs. Don't forget: sexier kitchen goddess, more chances for prime time.'

I was happy she couldn't see what I looked like.

Yet I went to my lecture at the Juvenile Correction Centre. I had to see Norm, so I decided I better go.

It's not a charity thing. Recommended by Norm, my floury faithful friend, I started my job there as part of a City Council project, securing a fat paycheck for me and the possible chef profession for some boys of good behaviour. But honestly, who would want to hire young criminals to slice ham or bone chicken?

Protected by the thick walls and rigid rules of the institution, I like to tease and mock the boys during my classes. I don't go out of my way this Saturday morning.

'Forget about restaurants, finding a job there, guys. They might think you are going to poison clients for fun.'

I can feel eyes burning holes in my back, some lashing glances like cat o' nine tails flogging my bare flesh. The boys' sneers tell they know I have had a wild night. I know I drive them mad, and I get a kick out of it because I hate them. Fifteen or sixteen, edgy, hostile, they've seen more blood than a battlefield surgeon.

I consult my watch: twenty minutes to eight.

'As for original sin, it is not what you think.' I begin my lecture. 'The original sin is the act of eating.'

Their smiles widen: *she's gone bananas*.

'Eating an apple,' I continue. 'And not a Granny Smith, but a nice red apple from the Garden of Eden.'

'Bullshit! It was bananas Eva ate!'

Roars of laughter.

His name is Michael. His gaze smashes into mine like a bull bar. Nasty little shit. I see into his future: killer, rapist, robber, drug dealer. He's already done at least one of the four. Anything but a chef.

'So says the Bible, Michael. Eve ate the apple and troubles kicked off.'

'Bananas,' he insists among approving shouts. 'She liked bananas.'

His hair is bleached by the sun in contrast with a dark face where a scar divides his left brow. The eye underneath also looks bleached, a reminder of what happened when Michael got into a fight with his father, eventually killing him over booze or petrol to sniff, I am not sure.

I decide to ignore him. The effort brings a dizzy spell and I lean against the podium.

'If eating a tantalizing, crispy apple has brought about the original sin, it shows the power of gastronomic cravings, doesn't it? I'll be talking about cooking as a healing power.'

I have them under control as I start to reveal the secret of the *Home for Rice Children*. A green or red crispy home which has to be cleaned first, sweeping all seeds away before letting the rice children in.

'Some would call it a stuffed capsicum,' I note bitterly. 'Yet it's a Home for Rice Children,'

'The way stars are scattered bones of Maya gods,' says Michael, unexpectedly showing a good deal of missing teeth.

We are all into that star and cosmic thing thanks to Norm, who has perhaps taken up astronomy as a hobby. Or it's just a poet's thing? Obviously Norm is not happy to be only a carpenter instructor at the Centre.

I find Norm covered in sawdust and shavings, showing boys of good behaviour how to carve souvenirs: crocodiles, koalas, wombats.

Soon we are sipping hot transparent coffee in the cantina.

'Black holes are whores for stars.' Says Norm dreamingly. 'They swallow them whole or slit them into pieces kicking them back into other galaxies.'

Listening to him, I think I am an idiot. Stars or not stars, life is simple around Norm. Why am I with Frank, who takes me three times a year to bed for a week; the rest is telephone bills and complications.

'Sandy.' Norm puts his flabby hand over mine. 'You look a wreck. What's wrong?'

There's so much care and worry in his voice that I break down. Tears stream down my face. I spill my coffee and end up with my head buried in Norm's rice-cooker torso in search of comfort and a non-existent shoulder. We are alone in the cantina; only a lady behind the counter keeps tinkling with glasses she washes.

'Come on, Sandy, you're a big girl,' Norm comforts me.

I sob and sniffle while he produces a crumpled handkerchief. Then I tell him everything. Well, almost.

Norm abruptly pulls away.

'You're not going to mess with psychos! Sandy, promise! That son of a bitch drags you into it!'

'It's the other way around,' I say feebly.

'What do you mean the other way around?' Norm looks suspiciously at me and flaps his moth-like eyes.

'Frank has information that they are after me and he is trying to help,' I blabber and immediately feel sorry. Up to now I've been dancing around, peppering words sparingly on what happened last night and what I saw on the news.

Norm looks flabbergasted. 'Can't believe it, Sandy: a young lovely woman like you...' He stops. 'Sandy, I hope it's not so serious as it sounds. If there's something I can do, you can rely on me.' He squeezes my hand. Then, as if ashamed of his momentary weakness, he finishes: 'Give them turkeys the fuck-off sign.'

'Actually I might be only needed as a consultant for the team that Interpol guy Jacobsen sets up.'

'Consultant? On what? Tomatoes filled with mushrooms? Sorry, Sandy.' And he laughs spilling sawdust.

It's ten when I drive home. There's still time before I head for the airport. That makes me nervous.

I check the locks and do the only thing that can keep me sane: work on the manuscript.

I focus on the culinary delirium of Salvador Dali: fried eggs as a chain of agnostic symbols, dreams of runny Camembert cheese turned into soft runny watches. I ponder on *Anthropomorphic Bread—Catalonian Bread*; the painting is stuffed with phallic, mammal suggestions and riddles like a homeless snail, an injured thumb, a writer's metier. I finish with the third of the *Anthropomorphic Bread* series, spending more time on this cheeky painting since it falls into the flow of my major pursuit: to trace hidden cannibalistic messages in masterpieces as part of my research for *Gastronomy in Art*.

For a moment I consider sending the unfinished manuscript to David before I fly. Soon I shake the idea off as born from fear.

I decide to cheer up and take care of my hangover. For the 'hair of the dog that bit you' recipe, I grind and brew freshly roasted coffee beans, pick a big mug, and fill it with the filtered black liquid and a splash of whisky.

The potion burns my mouth, it has a quick effect. My brain gets clear; unfortunately so does my sight. Looking at the big mirror opposite the piano, I get a shock. When Norm called me a wreck he must have put it mildly.

My survival instinct gives way to vanity. After all I am going to see Frank, whatever the reason. I resort to quick fix tools, which I find in the kitchen. What you put into your stomach is good for your face. Skin has its own way to digest and absorb valuable nutrition.

I grate potatoes and thicken them with a teaspoon of rice flour. Undressed down to my waist I scrub my face vigorously with a mixture of fine sea salt and olive oil, rinse and apply the potato mask. It should take away the puffiness. With my head tilted back, I sit in my mother's rocking chair by the piano and continue to look over the manuscript. My eyes, though, occasionally go back to the mirror, indulging in the spectacular view of my bared breasts.

I hope one day they will serve their real purpose. Breastfeeding fascinates me. Giorgione's *The Tempest* can't be only a sad story about Adam and Eve falling out of God's mercy. Little Cain is performing the most innocent act of cannibalism, satisfying his hunger with mother's milk, the way he had sucked not long ago on the blood in her womb. Nature has coded these mild acceptable forms of cannibalism as natural things, which no one questions.

To round up a paragraph, I find an original Catalonian recipe for *escudella i carn d'olla.* It needs impressive ingredients like ham hock or lamb, pig's ear or cheek, chicken, Catalan sausage, fatty bacon, lean pork, beef bones, pig's trotter and some vegetables. A hearty winter meal high in saturated fat and cholesterol, perhaps one that made Dali say, 'I know what I am eating. I don't know what I'm doing.'

Then I rinse my face profusely and apply another appearance-saving food: honey. I add several drops of lemon so it's even more astringent and supposedly able to pull my features back together where they belong by nature.

The potatoes have done their job, as they always do. In cooking I consider them the working horses among the rest of the vegetables.

With my mind clearing and my disturbed vanity at bay, I close my eyes and think how much I miss my mother in moments like this. Her portrait sits on the shelf next to my cookbooks. She's pregnant with me. The picture has been taken two months after she moved from Switzerland to Australia and two months before I was born. I have put an inscription under it: me inside my mother. After all, I have been a cannibal in my prenatal life.

Marylin usually waters my indoor plants when I go *Frank-ing*, as she puts it, but when I call her she is not at home. Her fourteen-year-old daughter Wendy is.

'Oh mum is at the Uni, a chronic student, you know.'

Yes we all know the word *job* has fallen out of Marylin's vocabulary of life never to be retrieved. Now and then, though, she goes back to the University pretending she is doing courses, actually harassing the lecturers.

Quickly running out of options, I try Beverley.

'Let me guess: Mauritius?' she says when I ask her to plant-sit for a week. 'You haven't been only to Mauritius, have you? Paradise on earth, old Ernest called it. Hemingway, of course. What are you going to show from there: lemon-placing? In the muzzle of the wild boar and in the grill of the baked fish. If you put it the other way around it would be catastrophe!'

'No, darling,' I say as peacefully as I can. 'This time I go *Frank-ing*.'

It becomes worse.

'Just like this? Suddenly? How come? He hasn't got his divorce. Or you keep it a secret?'

'Beverley, please! Can you or not water my pots? That's all.'

'Sorry,' she says suddenly in a small voice. 'It's just that Paul and I had a fight. I feel trapped.'

I imagine her sitting by the telephone, a woman of a rare, a bit dried up beauty, eyes the colour of lapis lazuli, the dark blue stone with golden specks the ancient Egyptian priests believed would bring them prophetic abilities. A wasp-body, lovely hair, not unlike mine. When in a good mood Marylin likes to say that Beverley and I can always find a job as pole-dancers.

Beverley promises to water the African violets. She is allergic to geranium and I can't do much to change that. Still she is surprised that I take off so unexpectedly. Perhaps she suspects that I am keeping her in the dark about every aspect of my life these days, which is true. Anyway, she wishes me a great journey.

A really great one, I think nervously, no doubt about it.

'And Sandy...'

'Yes, Beverley?'

'Trap the guy, give up on the pill!'

I don't see anything but spite behind her advice. For sure she fantasises that I get pregnant, look after a child, hopefully twins, and clear out of the competition in cookbook compilation.

Because that's what Beverley thinks, a recipe from here, another from your granny, a third from an old forgotten book or the Internet and *voila*. She would never go beyond ingredients in grams and spoons, not even scratching the surface of what the philosophy behind cooking is.

'Thank you! I'll give it some thought!' I say, and get off the phone as quickly as I can.

I take out my travel bag and check on what they call the most important achievements of our civilisation: tooth- and hairbrushes to start with. When the bag is organised I go to the floor-to-ceiling bookcase. I hesitate for a moment, then pick up the booklet that has prompted me the idea of my latest manuscript.

No longer bound with that pompous novel, it has life of its own. It burns my hands. I quickly carry it to the travel bag and thrust it inside under some seductive lingerie I have carefully selected.

The sensation of burning is strong, though; I almost see holes in the laced silk. I retrieve the book and insert it inside my hand luggage along with my laptop. They somehow belong together.

Keep yourself busy, don't think, I repeat to myself.

I fret around and start to do stupid things like plucking my eyebrows. I desperately look for something to pluck on my chin.

The bikini waxing is still holding.

I file my nails. I file my toenails.

I apply several layers of mascara to my lashes, which end up looking like witches' brooms.

I virtually bathe myself in Frank's favourite perfume turning me into a nutmeg to be gently probed and grated with a tongue during our nights of celebrated intimacy. As a kitchen goddess I don't need much convincing to pick among *kitchen* perfumes varying in magic fragrances like cinnamon, caramel, almond, vanilla, nutmeg. Frank went crazy for the nutmeg one. The flacon never leaves an inner pocket of my travel back. I check that it is well secured.

I even bring myself to answer the telephone when Norm rings. In the background I hear Billie barking. They are so tight up together, they look like each other; that is, Billie looks nerdy and baggy, too. Perhaps she has to: huskies are polar dogs, I wonder how she copes with the Brisbane heat.

Norm asks whether I need anything. I assure him I don't, which is a lie. I need someone to hold my hand and kick me in the ass at the same time.

I might even know who this someone is.

FOUR

I have a vision of a man around a barbecue busy handling mountains of sizzling sausages, pork chops, beefsteaks, meatballs, bacon. The only thing that looks like salad is the chicken wings. Lovely marinated chicken wings, honey melting out of big feather pores, caramelising everything it touches.

Every man looks like a shaman around a barbeque fire half hidden in capricious curls of smoke, the tongs in his hand like ritual sticks. In Brisbane BBQ is a strictly man's business, irresistibly sexy in a deep, primitive way. For a couple of hours the man goes back a million years in time to catch up with the archetype of the savage. He devours and is devoured. The miracle of the fire mesmerizes him while he watches the dance of the flames.

The man is Tamati. The vision of five years ago.

It's close to eleven when I give Tamati a ring. Mimi answers, saying Tamati is busy, but invites me over. She's Chinese, one of the five doctors from the Overseas program who share a house tilted to one side like the tower of Pisa. Recently they open a surgery in the kitchen, and once a week they hire a hospital theatre to cut the tonsils of some unlucky patients.

The hunk of the group Tamati introduced me to old songs honouring the spirits of his ancestors. The cry of the volcanic wilderness, the dark passion of the ocean—that is the sound of his Maori mates for whom the culinary definition of man was *long pig*.

Thinking about it I get gooseflesh.

Now Tamati and I are in the kitchen-turned-surgery, and I follow his expert movements around the stove. He is not stingy with sesame oil, soy sauce and brandy while he is tossing vegetables into the wok, along with something that looks like giblets. We listen to Maori music. The kitchen is my temple and the sacred ritual of cooking cleanses my aura. The aroma of basmati rice fills my nostrils and I can feel the tiny hairs inside getting heavy with sticky moisture. The vegetables are boc choy, onion, carrots, ginger, mushrooms and eggplant. Tamati cooks a Chinese dish on Mimi's request. Incredible. No, annoying.

A tall, dishevelled blonde walks in from the direction of Tamati's room, sails through the kitchen and leaves the house after giving Tamati a wet conspiring glance. He responds with a last minute spank on her backside, his eyes following her, a sleazy smile on his face not unlike the proverbial cat that has eaten the cream. Early this morning the five doctors cut a few tonsils and then relaxed, some with a nap, Tamati with sex. Annoying. No, credible.

'Come on, gorgeous, let's clean up your emotional clutter.' He gives me a pat on the hand, the smell of unfamiliar perfume (persimmon scent based) and lovemaking still lingering around him resisting the smells of cooking and disinfectants.

Next I am sobbing quietly sitting on his familiar room-size bed still preserving a stranger's warmth and blond hairs—bleached!—pouring out dread and fears, excitement and insecurities.

Tamati looks bored and sleepy. Perhaps he is. He remains standing, leaning against the door, his arms crossed in front of him.

Words like tsunami debris clog my throat, finally the uncontrolled emotions ebb and I find myself wracked but safe clutching a pillow, the indentation of the blonde's head still on it.

The healing process is powerful. I start to feel cocky and finish: 'How about if it has nothing to do with somebody called Jacobsen, if it's Frank's prank all along, his weird idea of sexual seduction, of spicing up our stretched-thin relationship. After all, he reviews thrillers, doesn't he?'

Saying this I realize I might have overdone it with *my* perfume. Nutmeg is an aphrodisiac. In large quantities, though, it produces hallucinogenic confusion.

Tamati's eyes widen. His brows arch. 'How about the news?'

'They don't say anything about me.' I am a kitchen goddess after all, a contemporary Hestia, the ancient Greek goddess of the Hearth. Why shouldn't I make real news, for a change? 'My manuscript has just got accepted, how would anyone know about it?'

I gaze into Tamati's eyes, feeling the comforting, protecting shield of his physical strength. In the back of my mind I wish Tamati could go back to his rugby days and tackle my problems, casually breaking their necks.

'After all, Tamati, I heard about the *long pig* from you first!'

He doesn't take it as a friendly teasing.

'Stupid woman,' he finally concludes, some loose boards screeching when he changes his posture, pulling, cracking his fingers, shifting his weight form foot to foot. 'As if you have nothing better to do but dig up lethal secrets! What more do you want? Money, success, you've got it all coming, now you are going to lose it over your big mouth, trying to impress someone who's already in the shit working for the police.'

This someone is Frank, and Tamati, a reformed ex-street kid, feels genuine hatred for anyone who works for the police. He is also known to easily fly off the handle in a big way so I prepare myself for more.

I am not disappointed.

Suddenly I can explain my overwhelming urge to see Tamati. As a child grown without any father-figure around, I have always missed this physical—in a way brutal—masculine authority as a corrector in my life. Something or someone reading and stating the obvious in facts, not interpreting words and emotions. Funnily enough, I feel good about being told off, verbally abused. Perhaps it wouldn't be a bad idea if he slapped me, a well-proven medicine against hysterics.

When Tamati and I were an item, it quickly ended when I understood that for him I was just a number. I didn't take it personally. For Tamati all women are numbers. He has neither time nor intention to change it. At least he was honest in his approach and did not pretend that there would be anything more than mutual sexual pleasure until the appetite was no longer there.

'...drama queen!' finishes Tamati and goes back to the kitchen.

I look at my watch. It's almost noon. Shortly I should be on my way to the airport. There's no reason to believe that I am heading for a week of carnal titbits behind the door of a four-star hotel room somewhere around the Belvedere palace in the city of Mozart.

Tamati comes back with a plate and insists that I try his cooking. I quickly agree, hunger keeps filing my nerves. Besides the meal is good and comforting. I start to gobble it and manage through full mouth: 'Where do you buy these fantastic giblets?'

Tamati doesn't answer, instead he asks. 'Are you sure you don't want me to come to the airport?' Now his voice is all coconut shavings in melted chocolate.

'Tamati,' I say reluctantly, 'it's not a good time. There are too many skeletons in my closet.'

'You haven't seen them all, baby.'

Friends.

FIVE

The plane stops in Bangkok for three hours, enough for a walk around the biggest airport in this part of the world. Gazing at shops and picturesque, sometimes scary figurines revealing the local religious culture, I buy Frank a souvenir—a teaspoon with an elephant. Frank collects elephants.

It's not so long ago when I was eating my days away on the streets of Bangkok, falling in love with banana pancakes soaked in melted chocolate, with exotic fruit salads decorated with purple lotus flowers. When red curry paste made of dried chilli, cumin and coriander seeds, peppercorn, chopped garlic, shallot, galangal, lemongrass, kaffir lime rind and shrimp paste was unsuccessfully trying to compete with the fire Frank was igniting in my poor dehydrating body. When after being pounded with compress bags soaked in herbal tea, or pampered with coconut oil gently massaged into our bodies, we headed back for a clandestine love session, we felt cleansed, all impurities like food and thought toxins expelled from our bodies leaving us pristine for a new fresh start with our lives, sinning.

Ah well, it hasn't been so bad until now. But as my mother used to say: *You are tough Aussie stock, Sandy, you are a survivor*. Needless to say it was at her death bed when she said it.

I urgently make a mental survey of a list of things I have to do and switch my cell phone on. The first number I dial rewards me with a lazy, cranky, belligerent answer: 'Marylin speaking.'

Actually she is munching and swallows noisily.

'Hi Marylin.'

'Oh somebody is having a good time, leaving the rejected lovers to me.'

So the cat is out of the bag.

'Marylin, I wanted to talk to you first but...' I start to explain myself. She always succeeds in making me feel guilty. 'Marylin, listen, I am in a big shit. It's a long story...'

'What's so long about it? It took Norm five minutes to fill me in.' I hear her stuffing something in her mouth and churning it around.

'Marylin, what *you* make of all this?'

'It's death that we live, kid, the real shit starts later when one dies.'

'What should I do?'

A fit of cough reaches me across continents.

'Eat pumpkin seeds.' She finally wheezes. 'It's good for your prostate.'

I leave the airport newsagency where I have secluded myself for the call between stacks of glossy women magazines all of them telling *what's good for you*. Not eat, diet; not move, exercise; not enjoy life, detoxify; not indulge, count calories; even the mere act of fucking is advertised as a slimming workout.

That's where we *clicked* with Janette. Our cooking series are about celebrating life through real juicy food conjured with wild fantasy and libido on the rise. Rolling in aromas of modest and decadent edible things within different cultures, climates, languages, races, geographical venues, projecting these aromas from the TV screen onto the viewer, teasing her eyes, her palate, her dormant adventure drive.

That's exactly what they say in one of these magazines praising me, adding that more men start to watch my show of a kitchen goddess hoping that I'll appear in bikinis shaking coconut trees or on my fours catching jumping salmons like an Alaskan bear.

The article is enough to bring my self-confidence back. I feel every bit important. Even danger starts to look like an ardent flirting fan. Then I remember where this danger comes from and cringe. A cannibalistic cult, for sure, can turn any food guru into ragout.

Back in the plane I fight again my fears with work and offer all my mental energy to the laptop.

I love Salvador Dali because of his obsession with food, especially bread. He used loaves of Catalonian bread for wallpaper in his museum in Figueras and could be heard repeating: '*Bread, bread and more bread. Nothing but bread.*' The Catalonian loaves could have been round, but his bread images are loaded with phallic symbolism. Dali prefers the stick-like shape of the French baguette, as in his painting with that improbable, long title *Average French Bread with Two Fried Eggs without the Plate, on Horseback, Trying to Sodomize a Heel of Portuguese Bread*. Of course, the series with fried eggs always in a pair induces associations from succulent, ready-to-eat breasts to eyeballs. It's another loaded cannibalistic suggestion that sticks nicely to my theme. I haven't yet included the most straightforward opus in my manuscript: in 1933 Dali paints his partner, devoted muse and model Gala, with two lamb chops balanced on her shoulder, suggesting he wanted to eat her up. And how about his *Nostalgia of the Cannibal*?

I interrupt my writing to see the film *Girl with a Pearl Earring* and enjoy the baroque approach to culinary activities at a time when there was no such thing as fast food. Then I crawl over a honeymoon couple sleeping in a tight knot and walk up and down the aisle working on my blood circulation. I compromise on a cup of disinfectant-like coffee served by a boyish Thai host who also insists on serving me cognac.

'French, French,' he repeats, waving the bottle under my nose.

He is disappointed at my indifference and takes it personally that I turn him down. Toying with the idea of including a chapter on *The Raft Medusa,* a gruesome canvas of shipwrecked sailors eating corpses for survival, I try another bibliomancy with my booklet.

This time it reads: *holy sound.*

SIX

Vienna, the birthplace of Marie-Antoinette, the French queen. I've always adored her suggestion, mythical or not, to those too poor to afford bread for their table: *Let them eat cake.*

That's exactly what I do now sitting at a table outside a cafe amidst a colourful crowd of tourists enjoying the pleasant weather. Despite my best intentions, I have a third serving of the famous Viennese patisserie (including strudel, the local pride, its sheets of pastry thinner than cigarette paper), trying different coffees: chocolate laced with heavy body wood notes, cinnamon flavoured, rich but delicate, sticky sweet vanilla one to match the big juicy éclair in front of me.

I love Vienna, the coffee capital of the world. Nowhere else has the preparation of coffee been turned into virtuosity a la Mozart like here. There's no limit to the varieties of tastes, aromas, texture, shades and mixtures. Highly trained coffee sommeliers work subtly for the clients of more than six hundred Viennese cafes. They are guardians of all secrets of how to grind and brew it so that the aromatic substances don't fly away. Yet the grounds do otherwise; there's no other explanation as to why I float in the coffee molecules saturating the air around me.

I breathe deeply in and think of my mother's idol Beethoven. I've just been to visit his grave in Vienna's Central Cemetery known as the final resting place of some of the greatest musicians.

Beethoven was known to be one of the most famous sommeliers of coffee. He had a very strict idea about what the real beverage should be, and he counted the sixty grains himself for the preparation of his cup. Of course, it made all the difference if the grains were ground in front of him and he could start drinking with fierce eyes, flared nostrils, deaf ears before the coffee boiled.

I order myself a fourth treat, a huge cone glass in which the coffee, elegant and classy as fragrance, is mixed with whipped cream. It makes the whole extravaganza look like a living thing in rhythm, a Brazilian samba dancer.

Risking unwanted attention I use my fingers to scoop it. For a moment I even forget why I am here. It's enough that I can indulge and pursue my black obsession.

When I look up at St Stephen's cathedral, however, I don't feel good. All these mammoth religious structures are built to make me feel insignificant and small. I remember the panic attack that overwhelmed me when I first saw the cathedral in the German city of Cologne. I got out of the taxi, raised my head, and there it was, a monstrous mince machine for my fragile human ego. I had this sudden urge to run, to hide, to scream.

With time I was able to overcome my barbaric pagan fear in the face of man's architectural idea of God's punitive power. But still, I feel more comfortable at a small home Buddha shrine in Thailand or in a tiny chapel somewhere in Northern Greece, near Pela, the native town of Alexander the Great.

Alexander the Great is, according to Frank, the most odious personality from history because the young aggressor used to kill elephants in battle. War elephants met the perky Greek, stamping on his archers, destroying his cavalry, covering with bodies what should have been his glorious road to India. I can see the confusion of the cavalry. I know horses can smell fear. They smell the adrenaline in the blood of a nervous rider. They sense fear travelling down their reins.

Sitting outside the cafe, watching the stone-laced relief of St Stephen's cathedral against the sage-coloured sky, I look at my small pendant watch, which my late mother used to wear, proud of all the tiny rubies incorporated in its mechanism. It's now well after six p.m., and there's no sign of Frank.

Fuckable, non-fuckable, I try to beat my worry resorting to the usual judgement, which comes to my mind when I eye up people passing by. Elegant, well-groomed, stylish manners, that's the locals. Viennese. Rowdy, shabby, bad dressed if at all, that's tourists. Backpackers carry what might be folded stretchers on their backs occasionally delivering uppercuts to inattentive pedestrians.

Hoping to overwhelm the smell of fear with that of cacao, I indulge in my double cream *Mozart* coffee and take some notes on the theoretical chapter of my manuscript. I find Claude Levi-Strauss' postulate about the raw/cooked axis in human culture, raw being of natural origin and cooked being of cultural origin, quite limited from a cannibalistic point of view.

I finish my coffee-cream-chocolate extravaganza and head for the entrance of the cathedral.

At seven p.m. there's an organ concert open to the public. The organist is young and looks more like a DJ. He plays Bach's *Toccata and Fuga* a bit like a rap recitative. Halfway through my cell phone rings and a hundred or so heads turn to me. I run outside to take the call, feeling like an idiot.

'Are you coming for dinner?' my Aunty Susan asks. 'You can still catch a plane to Milan and board a speed train to Lugano.'

That's what I like best about Europe. Attending a concert in Vienna and then having dinner on the top of a posh hotel overlooking the breathtaking lake of Lugano in Switzerland.

'It will be quite a late dinner,' I laugh, happy to hear the voice of my mother's sister. 'Anyway, how come you know I'm on your soil?'

'Jesus came into my dream and told me to be good to you.'

'Jesus talks to you?' I know Aunty Susan is overly religious, yet this is not to be easily believed.

'Sometimes.' She makes it sound as a confession.

It's sweet of Aunty Susan to invite me. Last time I saw her and Uncle Willie was on the occasion of fifteen years since my mother Margherita passed away, that is three years ago. At that time they invited me for a week and again popped up an invitation to remain and live with them. It was a crucial time for me, my first cookbook was taking off in sales, I was contacted by Janette and her TV channel for a project that later became a hot product. Although single and with no immediate family, forced to write the name of Marylin Nolan in the forms reserved for contacting people in case of emergency, I didn't know anything but Australia and that laid-back out-door way of life. Switzerland looked scary with so much formality and strictness, control and preciseness, a culture of *always* doing things right. I didn't say no to Aunty Susan, rather thanked her and promised to give her invitation a thought.

Marylin called me an idiot. 'Rich, childless auntie wants you to live with her what you can't say about any of your men over the years.'

'I want to do something with my life, Marylin.' I sounded like a character from a Chekhov's play, perhaps *Three sisters* or *The Seagull*.

'Every day through my window I see people buried. Some of them perhaps have done something with their lives, as you put it. I don't know what so bad with letting life go by, not disturbing it, just letting it run and flow if we all know the end is the same and there's no warranty that Hamlet will visit your tomb and talk to you calling you Yorick.'

That's a major difference between Marylin and me. She is more into Shakespeare shuttling between *MacBeth* and *Midsummer Night Dream*.

I have started to jot down pros and cons about moving to Switzerland, when a simple question ruined my good intentions to think objectively. It was Tamati who asked me: 'Who are you going to hang out with among the glaciers?'

Then things started to happen quickly. First Uncle Willie dumped Auntie Susan over...Ah well, more about this later. Then I met Frank and although Switzerland is way closer to Norway than Australia, I somehow knew that becoming a career woman I have more chances with him rather than being somebody on her auntie's paycheque. Not that Frank thinks highly of kitchen goddesses as a career.

All this flashes on subconscious level through my head.

'Sandy! What takes you so long to answer?'

Overwhelmed with embarrassment I quickly say: 'I'll see what I can do. You just rang me amidst a concert.'

'You're lucky I wasn't in the audience,' snaps Aunty Susan and I can't help thinking that Uncle Willie is the lucky one; he no longer has her snapping at him like well-honed scissors for boning chickens.

Suddenly she adds gently: 'Come home, kid.'

That's the straw that breaks the camel's back. In my case I break down. I sob and wheeze, fight runny eyes, nose and voice and suddenly realise that Frank, Jacobsen—whoever he is, and the Brotherhood are on the same side of the scale. On the other side is a home welcoming me and a mother figure cooking a meal for me. *Cooking a meal for me*—the highest expression of love and care, of compassion and understanding.

Of protection.

'Coming,' I answer, my voice like a sushi train bar moist with soy sauce.

The overwhelming emotions bouncing around inside me are scary. Dear old Aunty Susan makes me melt like one of Dali's watches. Soon someone will have to come and mop me up: a slippery spill of insecurities.

Where is Marylin to tell me off or Tamati to call me something nasty? I feel stronger met by friendly fire. Now, showered with acceptance and care, I collapse emotionally. For a moment I'm aware of the cost of mobilising myself always to be alert, competitive, daring, a go-getter. It wears me out, makes me edgy, confrontational, aggressive.

Forcing myself to remember my envious status as a single, independent, ambitious, successful, promiscuous woman and how proud anyone could be with half of my achievements, I start to come around. I straighten my back, my stooping shoulders and hunched head. I fish out of my bag and open a powder compact mirror. I look at myself. I talk to myself.

Sandy Cornelius, you are saucy and jazzy, you have beautiful eyes, right now they look like a pair of that tropical fruit rambutan, red and prickly. Eyes that can be any colour. Frank finds it disturbing.

Not now.

Frank still hasn't shown up. His telephone is still not answering. I think to leave a message, but I am so mad I just take off in a taxi back to the airport.

While the Yugoslav driver tries to chat me up I get Frank's call. He is at Frankfurt airport, his plane not leaving due to some trade union squabbles: demands for more money against less work, the modern dream. He confesses that it's his idea that Auntie Susan invites me. He promises to catch up with me in Lugano as soon as possible. That's all for Jesus coming into my auntie's dreams.

On the plane to Milan I treat myself to a good cry. That's all I have time for.

Before boarding the train I buy a bottle of Peroni beer to fool my hunger in anticipation of Aunty Susan's culinary exercises. She will prepare either fondue or raclette—her way to welcome me to Switzerland. I adore cheese.

'Lugano, *signorina,* Lugano.' Someone is shaking me gently and I open my eyes, fighting like a chick to come out of the shell of the dream.

An old, rather fat *signor* shakes me gently repeating, 'Lugano, Lugano.' His smile is disarming as he helps me with my travel bag. His baby smooth cheeks reveal a history of expensive facials, creams and moisturisers. The feminine touch of his baby smooth hands and manicured nails doesn't interfere with masculine accessories such as a leering, seductive smile, big greying teeth. And a moustache.

Uncle Willie used to have one. Perhaps he still does.

SEVEN

Lately I have this dream over and over again.

It came to me in the train to Lugano, too.

I feel light, almost immaterial, while I see myself in previous reincarnations.

During my last reincarnation I also was a woman.

A woman in love.

There's nothing more fragile or vulnerable than a woman in love. We are married and he adores me: my small feet, my fluffy hair, my overlapping teeth. He is crazy about me and he insists on feeding me with a spoon like a little girl. He cooks my meals and sprinkles salt on them, and love, always love with a dash of olive oil like drops of earthy perfume. The rest of the ingredients wouldn't matter, as he is good at mixing different cuisine styles: African with Asian, Mediterranean with Siberian.

His favourite dish is venison with berries and Chinese cabbage, cooked in lots of garlic, turmeric, soy sauce and brandy. On the side red caviar on buttered toasts of onion bread and Ethiopian honey wine *Tej*.

His food gives me love and protection. I come to know physical sensation is possible from inside my heart, from inside my aura. My perspiration smells of love, my tears smell of love, my laughter is an echo of love.

Then he leaves me over my red eyes. My irises are green, but I tend to weep late in night seized by fear that I am doomed to lose him. One day he says that I remind him of an Easter rabbit. It's Easter and he's feeding me with chocolate eggs wrapped in the saliva of his love as precious as swallows' saliva used in Chinese bird's nest soup.

He takes me to see those men who risk their lives descending down into a huge grotto where thousands of birds are busy weaving their nests. The men balance on bamboo rope ladders, swinging dangerously with every breath of wind over sharp-pointed rocks washed by high waves dying in bubbling foam. Occasionally a man drops down like a ripe mangosteen. No one looks for him. They know after centuries of experience that the man is dead the moment he hits the rocks. It's a hell of a risky way of earning a living, but one can see that they love it. Inside the grotto they start to shake their rope ladders; by turning them into pendulums they can reach the nests on the remote walls of the grotto. Fighting the agitated birds, the men quickly grasp their nests, tearing them off.

I wonder why he takes me there. He gives me a simple answer: 'If you love a certain dish, you must know where all the ingredients come from. You should get acquainted with the story behind the meal. That's how you establish a close relationship with it before you merge with the food on physical and spiritual level.'

As I listen to him I am holding his hand, loving him, knowing he is in possession of energies that nourish my life.

We have hired a boat that approaches the grotto and stays at a reasonable distance. It's still a dangerous adventure. We are at the mercy of the winds. He gives me a pair of opera glasses to watch the activity of these men. As I watch I become aware that he is walking out of my life, taking away all his nourishing energies, dooming me to starvation, turning me into a zombie. *Don't leave me! I can't live without you*, I want to shout at him. I can't. I'd rather jump into the sea and offer my transitional body to the powerful elements. One moment you're clinging to that swinging rope ladder, the next falling down into the abyss to embrace death.

I open my eyes, still dizzy with sleep. I want to return to my dream. Dreams with him have compensated his absence in my physical time. Stirring in bed, I feel him and I am soaked in love. I leave eye-prints, thought-prints all over him. I am sick with love, an omnivorous cannibalistic monster.

We are together. Somewhere in the world, we are together.

It was a surprise getting off the train to spot the silhouette of a blond giant. Surprise to fall into his arms and forget the world that dealt hurts and danger in the cards for me. Surprise leaning on him to walk into Aunty Susan's hotel in the middle of the night, legs lead-heavy, brain on autopilot from exhaustion.

His flight changed to Milan outside the trade union parameters of strike and he was lucky to board a plane about to leave. He hired a car and drove madly up to Lugano only to beat my arrival by fifteen minutes.

He feels me moving.

We don't talk. We leave our bodies to roll in lust like clandestine travellers into another world. He's breathing heavily, exhaustion and fatigue streaming out of him for me to absorb. Frustrated by our failure to achieve oneness, we break apart with a scary velocity.

I still feel cannibalistic; lovemaking induces a black-widow urge in me and now I am angry that the catch is making his way out of the cobweb, alive.

Consumed, but alive.

'Frank.'

'Tell me.'

I take my time. I look around the impressive hotel dwelling. A king-size bed where people have slept, made love, talked, read, watched TV, eaten food. Chairs used more for clothes hangers than anything else. A table with an ashtray, ads and a menu for room service. A TV set, a refrigerator, a bar. On the floor a tray with leftovers of a cheese plateau, Hungarian salami with lots of paprika (I hope it doesn't have horse meat in it, as the rumour goes), butter, crusty Swiss bread that's crustier now, a glass half full of white wine and another half empty.

I touch his shoulder with my lips. We are a pair of hermit crabs borrowing each other's shell.

'I forgive you, Frank.'

He strokes my hair. 'I am so sorry I missed you in Vienna.'

'I forgive you also for the maso-sado-psycho way to lure me in your bed across the ocean, you wonderful lover, Frank Magnar Syversen!'

He looks perplexed.

'What do you mean exactly, Sandy Cornelius, you wild lover?' He continues rubbing my back, strangely enough my most erogenous zone.

I relax further. 'You know, all this circus about somebody wanting my head and an anonymous telephone threat to go with like in one of those hard-boiled detective stories you review...'

He lifts himself on his elbow and looks at me in a genuine wonder, then in terror. 'What telephone threat?'

I stiffen. Fear comes creeping back to me.

'Frank, why don't you tell me what's *really* going on?'

With our appetites satisfied, we are strangers.

'Sandy, I know what you want to hear.' His voice suddenly lost, a cat beneath an earthquake rubble.

'I don't want to hear what you know I want to hear. What's going on? Why all this secrecy? Holding back the truth from me, why?' Anger is a dangerous thing. It brings the illusive feeling of importance.

'Sandy, no one knows what's going on. What I can tell you is a lousy cocktail: drops of facts and rocks of suppositions.' He's picked up my cuisine-speak.

'Let's start with the facts.'

He disconnects physically from me, breaks away taking his touch, his love, his warmth. Leaving me with a hollow feeling and a veil of nutmeg scent.

We go through the cult killings. He gives me more details about the man from Nigeria who is seeking asylum in Norway because he could not stomach, literally, what his family members were doing. Jacobsen's department has been tipped off to fresh evidence of activity of a similar nature, brotherhoods recruiting young rebellious people who despise the society choosing *shopping* as a sacred mantra.

'Tell me where I come in,' I demand, my body sober and cold, a piece of leg pork out of the freezer.

'You have landed in a hornet's nest by expressing an idea that cannibalism never ceased to be part of the civilised world, opposing the general belief that cannibalism could be only attributed to distant, in time and geography, tribal cultures. Something more, you have stepped on some very highly positioned toes by opening your mouth...'

'My big mouth?'

'Your big mouth,' continues Frank, undisturbed by my defensive-sarcastic interruption, 'involving a religious cult figure into your amateur suppositions.'

'You mean Jesus?'

'I mean Jesus.'

'He can't be an object of protection for the cannibalistic brotherhoods you are talking about,' I protest. 'Some of them come from outside the Christian world.'

'That's the problem, Sandy. You have made enemies on a front so wide you are not aware of the proportions of the danger. All this because you want to be *an art critic*. My Goodness, Sandy, come to your senses! I like you the way you are.'

'I know.' I feel pathetic. 'It's still only a manuscript, it's not even published.' It sounds as stupid as it can get.

Frank draws all the pillows behind his back, takes my head across his chest and strokes my hair in such despair that I slowly find my way back to intimacy again.

'Secret societies are overprotective of their activities. They have eyes and ears everywhere. That ritual killing in New York was wisely calculated to generate publicity and draw attention to the fact that *they* exist. It's only the tip of the iceberg. We can be never sure what to attribute to them. People disappear in thousands every year throughout the world. What we can keep track of more or less is in Europe, USA, Canada, Australia, and a few other countries. The rest of the world is a haven for criminal brotherhoods that can practice their bloodthirsty activities unpunished. The other day there was another report from Africa. A wide-scale tribal war that resorts to cannibalism as part of the inflicted death and routine destruction.'

I notice that he has a gold elephant on a chain around his neck. I don't remember seeing this elephant. Feeling a pang of jealousy, I regret buying him the souvenir spoon from Kuala Lumpur. I don't think he paid much attention to it.

I lift my eyes to meet his. 'Frank.'

'Tell me, gorgeous.' He strokes my hair passionately, almost causing me pain.

'What will become of us?'

He is not prepared to answer and I don't like it. There's an awkward pause, which no one enthuses to fill in. We stay silent for a while.

'I love you,' he says feebly.

'Then tell me where do *you* come in?' I ask briskly although I have no right to voice this question.

'I have been asked to help, you know this.'

'Now through your relationship with me you can be even more helpful. Can't you?' I casually dig my nails between his shoulder blades. The involuntary spasm on his face is the only expression of the pain I inflict.

'Well, the answer is yes and no.' I can tell he feels guilty at being evasive. 'It's not a betrayal to put the security of your country and perhaps humanity above a sex affair...'

'You bastard!' I pull abruptly away and slap him across the face.

He doesn't react. A glow of moisture appears in his eyes as he finishes: 'Yet I have my own tools to expose the culprits.'

'Have you? Don't tell me that Jacobsen and the like believe in your occult escapades as *reliable* sources of information.' I want to hurt him.

'Sandy.' He moves away from my claws. 'Our conversation is taking a dangerous course. What we have is special, we don't want to trash it.'

'I am not the one trashing it. I'm sorry I find you irresistible. I hope this will change soon.'

'Don't say it. We want this to work, don't we?'

'Frank,' I draw out my all-time favourite trump, 'don't forget you are married, dear.'

'Not for long.'

'We've heard this before.'

'We?' He gently places his hand on my belly, his ears straining as if to hear enigmatic sounds. 'Are you...?'

He looks searchingly at me.

His hope is so genuine that it makes my heart bleed. His handsome face beams as if painted by Vermeer, elusive yet defining light building seductive intimacy. Too much light. I know, whatever the reason, he hasn't got children.

I close my eyes. He takes it for a negative answer to his silent question. When I open them the light is gone.

He squeezes my hand. 'Perhaps when the time comes we can make our little baby. It doesn't require much.'

'Why don't you say, when it suits *you*, Frank Magnar?'

I slide behind his back. There are three bright red streaks between his blades. Wet, pulsating with his breathing, with the movement of his muscles. The smell, the pungent bittersweet smell of blood enters my nostrils, getting me high. I rest my forehead on his nape, then slowly lick the deeply scratched skin. I go after each drop.

His beautiful creamy cock, a giant nipple providing food for comfort.

I pray Aunty Susan is not snooping around, eavesdropping. Or maybe she's given up on old habits, I wouldn't know, haven't seen her for a while. Anyway, her flat is way up on the top floor of her four star hotel, where we are staying for free. It's good to know that sometimes it doesn't cost anything to indulge in sinful bliss. Did I say sinful bliss? Like preparing white cherry jam? There's nothing like hovering over a pot with bubbles surfacing in syrup congealing around the fleshy fruit, the natural aroma of vanilla wafting up your nostrils.

Frank moves under my lips.

'You are safe with me. Sandy? You hear me? You are safe with me.'

'How do you know?' I let bloodstained words roll down my tongue. 'It's not your life after all.'

'You are my life, Sandy.' His voice does the stroking.

I am under his spell.

EIGHT

When we get up, it's late morning. We go to Aunty Susan's place, on the top floor.

She gives me a peck on the nose and goes back to her raclette. Nothing in her behaviour shows that it's been quite a while since we've been together.

'Sandy, grab a glass, dear! You too, Frank.'

The cats Tiger and Chita are purring around her feet.

Aunty Susan is of small stature, stiff and dry, with thick, rimless glasses over a smooth, recently reconstructed face. The skin around her nose is still raw, the eyelids stretched nearly to non-existence. She has tried to beat time—successfully, in the case of her face, which looks like a well-preserved forty—but her hands are affected by arthritis and each looks like a mud crab, fingers determined to follow their own direction.

'The hotel is sucking the last drop of energy out of me,' she says dramatically. 'Perhaps I'll be wise enough to sell it one day and the next lie down cosily in a hammock swaying between two coconut trees.'

She might know more than necessary about my arrival in Europe, but she tries not to show it, keeping herself busy. She arranges little plates full of yummy things around the electric tabletop raclette grill already positioned in the centre of the table.

'Frank, you should have turned up in Vienna, darling,' I mumble casually winking behind Aunty Susan's back. 'We could have found a better hotel there.'

'Got sick of Mozartomania.' His smile comes out crook. 'Besides what's wrong with being among family?'

There's nothing wrong, of course. Aunty Susan ignores us totally. Is her hearing no good these days or is it the magic of the raclette that keeps her blind and deaf to the surrounding world?

Frank is holding my hand; I am holding his leg between mine under the table. I am suspicious of his luggage-handler story. One should be, with a married man. Not to mention, as Marylin says, that Scandinavian men are notorious liars. Where does she get her information, I wonder.

I watch Aunty Susan for a while. She has boiled potatoes and arranged bowls with gherkins, mushrooms, tiny corncobs, red capsicums, ham and sausages on the table. Soon she starts to melt the raclette cheese on the small pans meant to go inside the grill.

Frank pours the wine, *Fendant*, a dry white from the Valais region. Everything is delicious.

Suddenly I feel weak. I want to lie down, bury my head in his shoulder, breathe the smell of his healthy Northerly fresh body, and fall asleep. I feel myself being carried away from the table.

Then it's dark and nice.

When I open my eyes it's morning again. A relatively early morning. I must have slept twenty or so hours.

Nursing a terrible headache I make my way to Aunty Susan's bathroom and take a shower.

Did I say bathroom? I rest my eyes on the triangular Jacuzzi, the foot spa, the massage table with all the gadgets to send your blood running and your mind relaxing, the shelves with green tea scented bubble bath and body treatment crystals, bath fizzies and foot soak and different massagers along with a whole range of natural oils health shops would kill for: rosehip, avocado, almond, shea, coconut. And just not to give the impression that Aunty

Susan's skin is a vegetarian, there are also emu oil, tiger balm, and—wow—*placenta* cream! Her skin must be cannibalistic!

It's half past eight, the usual time when she attends a morning meeting with the staff.

I go to apartment number 8, which was Frank's and my love nest the previous night. The apartment is immaculately neat and ready for guests. There's no one there.

I run back to Aunty Susan's apartment and put the espresso machine on. I need a coffee to function and overcome my disappointment. I can't blame him; who wants to sleep with a woman with drunken blackouts?

Then I see it.

It's there on the table where the raclette grill has been a day ago, waiting for me.

A small note: '*Amore mio*, don't use your cell phone or any other telephone, don't use the Internet, don't go out. Be back soon. Love you. Frank.'

I am more thrilled than scared. I kiss the note all over before I finally focus on the name: Frank. And a funny scribble underneath it:

A leg of pork, fumed
For an egg extravaganza
Cut the Holy sound

As always, my monkey mind jumps around, but fails to make sense out of the funny scribble. Ah well, perhaps more games. I start to like the way his kinky side is progressing.

Then I pause. *Holy sound*. It does sound familiar.

The bibliomancy in the plane.

I've never seen Frank's handwriting, have I? Our only correspondence in these three years has been through telephone, e-mail and numberless text messages.

I know his kiss and laughter, his overtones during hours of telephone sex. I know his eyes look like two gall bladder stones in the darkness, I even know his fantasy to chase me in a hunter's outfit. I know all about his occult occupations, his ritualistic readings of the runes, those ancient Scandinavian stones with engraved symbols.

I have never known his handwriting.

Sitting there in Aunty Susan's hotel apartment, drinking her coffee, listening to her Beethoven albums and looking at one of her Renoirs—a certain *Nude*—I realize that I have to blindly trust this note or...do exactly the opposite of what it suggests.

Graphology is no longer a reliable science. It can't help me read Frank's character when he tries to convince me that he doesn't get a kick by reducing me to a cornered animal, my back against the wall, begging for my life, a trembling victim at the mercy of a hunter.

Ants crawl up my back. Fear or arousal?

I live a dream. Good hotel, good food, good lover. Happiness doesn't go much further.

I realise I have drifted away when my lips touch the cold coffee. I prefer it hot, like in that famous film with my idol, Marilyn Monroe. Speaking of my Marylin, though, I have left five text messages on her telephone to call me, which has not happened. I need her rough raw attitude, her bulldozer approach, her *memento mori*, the Latin for *remember death*.

Outside the window the skin of the lake goes into goose bumps under the fondling fingers of the gentle breeze. It's late spring, my favourite season for Europe. I inspect the note again. The suspicion that it's not authentic makes me look paranoid in my own eyes.

I plant a kiss on the scribbled name again. Of course, Frank has written the note, who else?

The kinky bastard. Disappearing like this, to make me feel weak, inferior.

It's not time to feel horny. I decide to have a look at Aunty Susan's other collection instead. She has a thing for shoes. Mules, wedges, slides, platforms, sandals, pumps, lots and lots of boots. It's time I tell her that the Chinese once had coins in the shape of shoes.

The shoes Aunty Susan possesses all look new, as if recently purchased. Maybe they are. Anyway, they have nothing in common with the ones in Van Gogh's *Three Pairs of Shoes*, worn-out, battered, snarling like beasts, carrying around the smell of cheap wine, bad temper and depressing labour.

Aunty Susan's shoes are more like Cinderella's glass slippers or Mercury's winged sandals. Her boots are annoyingly expensive.

I sigh.

The size of her foot is smaller than mine—a generational difference.

I look at the time. Aunty Susan is due back in about fifteen minutes, but I can't wait for her. I feel like moving around, producing action no matter how pointless, just not sitting and waiting. She might give me some explanation as to why Frank has disappeared leaving me sick with emotional and physical exhaustion.

I still feel giddy. Marylin might suggest it's too much drinking but who wants to know what she thinks.

I slide into a dress, tight and red, no underwear—with or without Frank, at least my fantasies are still there—and run down the stairs, ignoring the lift.

I trip on the last step and lose balance on the landing to the amusement of a young fellow behind the receptionist desk. He smiles at me, letting me know he thinks I am cheeky. I wouldn't mind deepening his impression when my eyes fall on the European edition of *The Times* next to him.

My heart jumps in my chest.

I grab a copy with shaking hands, only to be politely asked by the young man to pay for the newspaper. His fear of breaking Aunty Susan's stingy rules is bigger than his sexual interest in me, which is not flattering (but is very Swiss). Of course, I haven't got money on me.

'A quick look at the horse races.' Pulling gently on the newspaper I give him a wink and a better look at my cleavage, which must be trampolining under his nose if my pounding heart is any indication. His hand stays determined on the newspaper.

'I might even be generous with my tips.' I use my honey-marinated voice.

His telephone rings. He takes the newspaper away.

'The old witch will grill your arse before she fires you, you stupid prickholder!' I yell at him. Taking advantage of his shock, I toss myself across the desk and snatch *The Times*.

It catches him off guard. First he can't believe what's happening. That makes him delay his answer to the call. Then he briefly reports.

'Yes, Mrs Kretz, I'll call the security. I would say no, Mrs Kretz, the lady doesn't look under drug or alcohol influence, she rather looks, well, I would say *excitable*.'

Anybody who sees herself dead making headlines on a front page would look excitable, that's for sure.

I run back up the stairs and into Mrs Kretz's a.k.a. Aunty Susan's flat. I have enough common sense left to immediately get rid of the red dress, stuff it into my luggage, and get into a bathrobe I find hanging in the closet. I start reading.

'A young Australian tourist has been found dead at Beethoven's grave site in Vienna's Central Cemetery, famous for being the last dwelling of geniuses like Mozart.' The text begins under a big photo of me lying sprawled on my back half naked.

'Sandy Cornelius, an Australian cookbook writer, was found dead around seven last night at the foot of the composer's grave. The autopsy showed that the young woman had swallowed a cocktail of tablets, causing her own death. The police spoke to tourists who saw Sandy while she was laying flowers honouring Beethoven. "She looked sad and thoughtful," said one of the tourists. A couple of telephone calls placed to Sandy's home in Brisbane revealed that she had come to Europe on her usual annual pilgrimage to the composer's burial site, following her late mother's deathbed wish. Sandy's mother, Margherita Cornelius, was a music teacher before she died of cancer at the age of thirty-nine, never revealing the identity of her only child's father. "Sandy was always a bit of psycho over it," said her best friend, Marylin Nolan, for the newspaper.'

My first impulse is to call Marylin and let her know I'll strangle her. This, however, gives way to a deeper and creepier feeling, something like walking into a billabong full of crocodiles.

I camped once some fifty metres away from such a place, and it wasn't funny. It was Marylin's idea. She was fancying a crocodile hunter who finally told Marylin he was *scared of her*.

I am shaky but I swagger towards the full-length mirror. I look quite alive.

I pinch myself.

It hurts.

I even try to look on the flattering side of it. Calling me young twice is not bad for a girl leaving the comfort zone of her mid-thirties.

Then there's the advertising effect.

I see big headlines: Author Resurrected from Beethoven's Grave — Gives her vision of cannibalism in the works of the masters.

David would love it. I have to call him. I reach for my cell phone, which happens to be lying next to the note left by Frank.

Don't go near your phone.

Well, there should be some sense in it after my so-called suicide making headlines. I didn't know I was a figure of such importance.

I search for my hairbrush. Brushing my hair makes me feel alive.

I might be in shock. I am in shock.

The more I reflect, the more I get confused.

Why this set up?

Who, and why go to so much trouble to pick up a woman approximately my age and my height, who looks like me, kill her, and arrange the body sprawled over a grave among hideous flowers? Who bribed the police, or arranged for the false identification? My heart is bleeding for a life sacrificed to send a message.

I feel paralysed with fear. My hair responds with static electricity sparks. Cold sweat trickles out of my pores.

It isn't a joke, it isn't a kinky game.

Frank wants to protect me. I hear the lift stop outside the apartment and run to open the door for him.

It's not Frank.

NINE

The Little Italy of Switzerland, Lugano, fills the window with blue: blue lake, blue sky, blue white-capped mountains. I have all the reasons to feel blue, too.

Jacob Jacobsen gives me a long stare.

He is a tall blond bear who carries his weight with business-like dignity. The chair underneath him gives warning sounds.

'For security reasons, Ms Cornelius, you are not supposed to meet Frank until the problem is cleared. We had to *advise* him to immediately leave the premises of the hotel.'

'What do you mean by problem? Until they track down who splashed me in a second degree *rigor mortis* across the grave of Beethoven?'

Jacobsen's meagre intelligence has provided facts without who and why. 'Our sources point to swelling evidence of a proactive cannibalistic cult, a brotherhood cultivating a root system in Scandinavia.'

'Why Scandinavia? Have they been pissed off by the scorching temperatures in Central Africa?' I can be an arrogant bitch, can't I?

Jacobsen is patient and understanding. 'We *advise* that you should go underground, Ms Cornelius, into hiding until we get to the bottom of this.'

I translate his words as a threat—not being able to make love to Frank for another indefinite time. The scene of our previous night drops in front of my mind's eye and refuses to go. I almost physically feel the small bites Frank gave me, and it makes my blood rush.

It has a certain effect on Jacob Jacobsen for the wrong reason.

His breathing quickens and a film of perspiration forms a circle around his lips, two fat silk worms munching on mulberry leaves. Come to think: silk is also of animal origin, like fur. I smile.

'Can't I be of any help? I want to participate in any *possible* way. Please!'

Jacob Jacobsen shifts in his chair. The screeching is nerve-racking. The chair is part of a set of furniture so antique it could have been made by Jesus' father. It sits under the tapestry, displaying horsemen and hounds occupied in one of those boring sports which no one but royalty with nothing better on their hands cares to pursue.

'I am afraid this will only complicate things. I understand you, Ms Cornelius, I can see how much involved you are,' says Jacobsen and perhaps he means it. 'But we have already made all the necessary arrangements for you to feel protected. At three this afternoon one of my detectives will come to take you to a place where you'll be safe and guarded under surveillance twenty-four hours. There you'll be free to do anything except contact the world under your real name, appearance and voice.'

It sounds scary.

'I hope you're not going to perform one of those weird plastic surgeries on my face and thumbs to give me a new identity,' I say, feebly attempting a joke.

He is silent for a moment. It's obvious that he is trying to be honest with me.

'We don't think it's necessary. For now.'

I find this less than reassuring. 'It sounds as attractive as a lottery holiday, all expenses paid. I might even be able to finish my manuscript.'

'By all means.' Jacob Jacobsen smiles, his teeth two rows of Italian tiles run over by a Formula One racer. 'I am sure you'll eventually be able to write some new chapters.' Again a meaningful stare.

I hate him.

He must be a mind reader. He blushes. The deep violet redness engulfs his generously tailored nostrils.

I nod hastily in agreement. Or in surrender.

'I'll be ready by three.'

I realise there are not many options for me to keep myself alive and in one piece for Frank's fantasies of chasing me in a hunter's outfit.

For a while I still listen to Jacobsen's findings that tons of presumably human meat find their way into Norway smuggled along with illegal immigrants, drugs, dried adders, crocodile heads and a number of potions into the country. All in the name of health, he says, but no imagination there: you eat human brain to be brainy, genitals, to obtain virility.

Then Jacob Jacobsen goes and Aunty Susan returns mumbling excuses that she had been kept downstairs by some errors in the computer entries of hotel guests. But I know that she has been told by JJ—that's what I decide to call Jacobsen—not to interfere with our conversation.

Seeing the newspaper ripped by my scuffle with the receptionist boy, she gives me a puzzled look.

TEN

I've drunk quite a bit of wine, yet I need a lot more to knock myself unconscious. Occasionally I ask Aunty Susan whether I can fill her Jacuzzi with wine and soak myself.

'Everything can happen in life,' Aunty Susan says pouring herself a generous slurp of good red, ignoring my empty glass.

She must know what she is talking about. Her husband left her over a small difference. Aunty Susan was convinced that people of good taste over seventy don't think of, or have, sex. Uncle Willie was of the opinion that people over seventy know better. He ditched his holy wife for a girl half his age.

Well, my age.

It was quite banal and honestly I wondered what kept him for so long around Aunty Susan, who is snappy, moody, conceited and totally unbearable—like now, when she pretends she doesn't see my empty glass.

It must have been the hotel. The hotel they built together and made money on kept him home. Not any longer.

Taking a bank loan of thirteen million against a mortgage on their four star beauty, he went to live like a real homeless squatter on a yacht somewhere in the Mediterranean.

Aunty Susan was quickly over the shock. In no time she started running the hotel by herself, imposing her rigid demands on the staff, who found her a bit nutty.

I get up and make a clumsy remark about how hungry the cats look. That activates Aunty Susan. The well being of the cats are her priority these days. She scurries to the kitchen box to open a can of the finest pussy food and I get hold of the bottle.

'It's good for you,' notes Aunty Susan with her back to me. 'It's nice to have two, three glasses. Not *more*.'

That's what Uncle Willie thought: she's got eyes on her back.

I lift my glass and silently say cheers to the *Renoir* next to the humming TV set the size of a four-wheel drive. Original, nude, plump and curvy, charcoal. The *Renoir*, not the TV. The other original *Renoir*, oil, represents an orchard garden in his typical apple green and pinkish orange pastel colours. In between hang a series of Swiss masters—Hodler, Anker, Klee. I like them, but I am most happy about the *Renoirs*, that Uncle Willie didn't manage to take for the interior of his yacht. The seventeenth century tapestry sits well with the antique furniture. It's good to have rich relatives.

I watch Aunty Susan feeding the cats and think of a next project, a less dangerous one, like *Cookbook for Pussies*. Ah well, again, it doesn't sound right.

'Money, money,' drones Aunty Susan from the kitchen box amidst the delicate munching sounds of Tiger and Chita. 'All my life I have struggled for money and it's never enough.'

She should instead tell me more about what exactly Frank let her know about my coming to Europe.

'Money is everything,' concludes Aunty Susan when my cell rings.

Seeing the number, I'd prefer to have some privacy for the conversation, but the whole apartment is one open space stuffed with Persian rugs, sofas and lots of candles in unexpected places. It reflects Aunty Susan's personality in that it looks like a bat cave.

'I don't hear after the second glass,' snaps Aunty Susan, annoyed with the ringing.

It's Frank.

He knows he's in trouble. 'I love you,' he begins.

'You love me, shit! If you love me, where are you to hold my hand, or you don't feel necrophilic?'

'Sandy, it's a temporary setback, stay positive! Think of all the beautiful things we are going to share together once we are over it.'

I love him and I want to believe him; things, however, turn more and more macabre. I keep looking at my portrait taken at the grave of Beethoven. Perhaps it *is* my portrait, after all. From the future.

'I hate you,' I whimper.

'Please don't do something stupid! Everything will be over in no time, I promise.'

It sounds naïve and he knows it. When I insist on unravelling the newspaper *thing* using my Macbeth-drama voice, he is not the same self-composed, aloof, detached, academician-type of a man with Nordic fish blood in his veins.

He comes to life abruptly, his voice breaking the chains of imposed restrictions.

'Oh, baby, you shouldn't be put through all this! If I only knew...'

Here the connection is cut leaving me to wonder what he didn't know and what he actually *knew*.

I am sure about one thing: he sounds even more distressed than me. He sounds *guilty*.

That doesn't make sense. Or does it? I get more and more confused.

Slowly inside me the sprouting decision takes shape.

Instead of waiting for people like Jacobsen to do the job I have to do something myself.

After all, *my* life is on the line.

I disappear into the bathroom and place a call. It's based on pure hunch, yet it makes me feel better. I am going to use my head this time. I fire myself up, taking the time to refresh myself in front of the mirror. Soon I feel tough and aggressive like a Zulu warrior.

When I go back to Aunty Susan she is talking to her cats. I assume she is well informed about my troublesome situation but has been forced to promise not to say anything to me. Her pretended innocence is not normal.

I challenge it. 'You may be amazed, but I have mentioned you in my will. Actually I have left everything to you.'

'You what?' Her face flashes as she looks at me, suddenly interested.

'Instead of reading my face read the paper.' I make an effort to look sardonic, but before I know it I am crying. This time the tears are accompanied by cramps in my lower abdomen, faithful signs that my period is around the corner. Bad things don't come alone, do they? I am one of those women who, when they bleed, bleed to death. With or without a composer's grave in the background.

'What are you talking about, Sandy?' Aunty Susan is holding me. We sit on the sofa. She brushes away my tears and kisses me on the cheek. 'Come, come, you have your aunty to talk to.'

I feel like a small kid who all the adults love and hence gladly lie to.

'It's weird. Who would want to set all this up and why?'

She doesn't pretend any more. She heaves an enormous sigh. Then she seems to remember her iron-lady approach, which has helped her through rough times and says, 'Everything will be all right.'

She kisses me on the forehead. Now I feel dead. A kiss on the forehead always makes me feel dead.

'Why don't we make our ritual?' I ask. Each time I stay with Aunty Susan we follow our ritual of calling the spirit of the dead by cooking their favourite meal. I grieve over my mother and Aunty Susan adds her parents and some cousins unknown to me. Being Swiss, small wonder that the meal that linked our beloved dead is fondue.

In my cooking show I used to talk about my experience in an orphanage where I had instructed young women, voluntary workers, to take over in the kitchen. One of the children at the orphanage had his mind set on finding the lost smell of mother. I tried to remember the smell of my mother. She smelled of music. The kid in the orphanage didn't believe me. He said food is the smell of *every* mother.

History can be written through food. I know this. What I still don't understand, despite Frank's explanation, is why my humble culinary knowledge and occupation presents a threat to such an extent that they have opened a hunting season for my head.

ELEVEN

We prepare for the ceremony.

Thinking Switzerland, my mother's birthplace, it's easy to imagine matchless mouth-watering chocolates with their own museum in Vevey. Then, of course, banks, watches, cows decorated like young brides on their way up or down the Alps full of *edelweiss*, castles like Chillon. Neatness, orderliness, boredom are also part of the vision. Aunt Susan's husband, my Uncle Willie, says that it's the biggest country in the whole world, if you flatten the Alps with all their glaciers.

Nothing beats the Swiss train-coach system. I've seen big yellow buses climbing heavenwards in mid-winter to reach small villages like Spruga of fifty or so people, high up in the Alps next to the border with Italy, six times a day. The drivers follow the narrow serpentine road, chasing away imprudent drivers of sedans, calling them *porco cane, porca madonna* and other Italian pleasantries, the road squashed between icy rocks and an appalling abyss. I've even seen coach drivers turn their heads back, talking to friendly passengers while flying their jolly vehicles down towards civilisation.

In towns like Bern some streets and houses still look like life-size decor for *Cavalleria Rusticana*. But it's mostly steep mountain countryside, where cows look more privileged than their Indian cousins.

And the cheese, of course.

Actually, fondue originated in Switzerland as a way of using up hardened cheese, *fondre* meaning 'to melt' in French.

It's a classic peasant dish, though nowadays a touristy one, too. It can be prepared with varieties of melted cheese. *Gruyere* is probably the tastiest, *Emmenthaler* too. Kirsch, is served in small cups for everyone to dunk a piece of crusty bread into before dipping it into the pot. The cheese is melted with lots and lots of white wine and dashed with kirsch. So small wonder many Swiss start yodelling long before they shine the bottom of the pot. And poor you if your piece of bread gets lost in the pot. If you're a woman you have to kiss all the men at the table. If you're a man, you kiss all the women present.

Aunty Susan and I, we don't kiss each other.

An hour later we are sitting around the small elaborate pot.

'This is the traditional food of our bloodline,' starts Aunty Susan ceremonially, the long fork in her hand like a ward. 'We eat and drink to honour and remember the dead and call on their spirits to share this simple meal with us.'

I remain silent, emotions constricting my throat. With Aunty Susan as my only family, I don't have much choice but to love her. We hold hands for a moment and each say a prayer. Mine is simple: 'Mother, please, watch over me!'

With Margherita in mind I can't but think of the cauliflower with semolina soup, my mother's *favourite* meal. I don't know whether it was the fine grain texture of the semolina to match the soft grainy texture of the cauliflower, this middle-class cousin of the squatter cabbage, yet still light years away from the sophisticated and haughty broccoli, the prince of the cabbage family, the aristocrat with green blood. What Margherita managed to do with this cauliflower/semolina bland liquid and turn it into something that one's body and mind remembered through the day in an elevated state was partly explained by the fact that she grated two or three cloves of garlic, pasted them with a bit of crystal salt and pepper. She added the mixture into the pot amidst an elegant scoop of good quality butter. Butter is responsible for the flavour and the mild slippery touch to this soup so close to the French *potage*.

A piercing reverberating bang makes us both jerk in our chairs. Aunty Susan jumps onto her feet with a little sway and looks around, I have a look out of the window. Nothing. Then we realize it's Chita playing with a metal hanger.

Cautiously, we return to the ceremony, the rest of which is spent in silence.

I have my own interpretation for Chita's antics. My mother has just let me know that we have connected and she approves of my decision. I will follow her guidance.

The fondue is delicious; as lousy a cook my aunty is, she can't put a foot wrong when it comes to fondue.

After scraping the last thready bits from the pot, I get up and leave Aunty Susan without a word. She looks absorbed in her spiritual interior. I go to her bedroom, dragging my laptop with me, and try not to notice the offending difference between this palace and my small bedroom in Brisbane. Aunty Susan still keeps her huge double bed in hopes that Uncle Willie will get sick of his young concubine and return to his legitimate home.

I sit on the floor and open my laptop, another ritual act: the moment I perform it, the world around me stops.

Disregarding Frank's warning about connecting to the Internet, I just do it downloading the infamous web page LongPig.com. Cherubs with piggy faces float around and suggest holy carnal (or is it carnal holy) knowledge to share and entertainment to offer. It's friendly, that's the first thing that strikes me about it. There are a couple of chat rooms and I join one in the middle of an ardent discussion about global warming, the planet turning into a Noah's Arch amidst floods caused by melting Polar caps. How are we going to survive?

I am about to leave the chat room when a line catches my eye, saying *How about ancient Sparta they used to get rid of all their weak mentally or physically burdening the society There are too many people on this planet causing the chaos why not cut the sick half save the healthy.* Signed *Nelly*.

There is an immediate response, fully negative. I can imagine. Who can be sure that he or she won't be labelled weak (who hasn't had at least one *mental* crisis) and eventually disposed of by some computerised authority. The massive objection doesn't stop *Nelly* from throwing in another question of dubious innocence: *How about the Druids guys those smartasses living around Stonehenge They loved to slay a fellow eat flesh drink blood make a musical instrument or a bit of crockery of his bone material.*

I remain put. Soon *Nelly* is back: *Has anyone tried the blood brotherhood?? I did it cutting my own wrist sucking my own blood Awesome!*

Nelly is disturbingly close to my mental disposition right now, yet she gives me an idea.

Soon I return to the search engine and type *rare make musical instruments*. More than ten thousand hits there, yet I quickly trace down what I am interested in. My next typing reads *private detective* and I specify the region: Lugano and neighbourhood. Finally I put some telephone calls through.

All the ingredients are in the pot, let's the cooking begin.

People might say there's nothing creative in writing cookbooks, but these are the same people who wrongly assume that eating is a mechanical act of shovelling food down your throat to keep you going.

The act of writing has never been an easy job, and to save my back I sit with my legs crossed under me like that *Seated Scribe from Saquarra* from 2400 BC now displayed in the Louvre. He looks slightly cross-eyed into your eyes as if waiting for you to scratch your words of wisdom on his table. I have always liked him. I think he is still layable even in light of present standards of male beauty. His ears are perhaps too flashy, contradicting the firm chiselled features and suggesting balance between the earthly and the spiritual pleasures. I shrug my shoulders to settle in more comfortably, start to put in some notes. Soon I forget that I am in Lugano, having theatrically committed suicide at the grave of Beethoven. What I am engrossed in are the masters.

The wine still lavishly mixed with my blood liberates me from any form of self-censorship.

I start with apples (not the green Granny Smith ones).

Apple, the forbidden fruit Eve offered to her rib shareholder, the poisoned apple the stepmother gave to Snow White, the apple Newton saw falling on the ground in his orchard. William Tell was forced to shoot an apple off his son's head with a crossbow; witches say the apple has magic powers to bring love, procure healing and immortality; two apples are the inevitable dessert of the one-dollar dinner at the Brisbane men's hostel where they fight over fags and sickly whores. Don't upset Bernard Shaw's *Apple Cart*. Aphrodite received the apple from Paris prince of Troy, apple the symbol of New York, birds drunk on fermented apples, the Apple Market of Amsterdam where

Rembrandt loved to linger before or after a self-portrait. Apple Computer system, dishes full of apple offerings to the gods in Egypt, Apfel Strudel, cider applejack, calvados the favourite disinfectant of Dr Ravick and the lost generation of perpetual emigrants, love apples—Cezanne painted them green—Henri Matisse painted *Still Life with Apples* leaving a discordant feeling of imbalance.

You're the apple of my eye, Frank.

The call I am waiting for comes through.

Before I leave I can't resist. I grab one of Auntie Susan's cookbook for a quick bibliomancy.

Toad in the Hole, it says. Cooking 35 minutes, use plain flour.

TWELVE

On board the small ship crossing Lake Lugano, I spot a man reminding me of the *signor* who woke me up on the train urging me to get off. Yet I am not sure. Elegant, well-groomed middle-aged men are no rarity in this part of the world.

I get off the ship at Campione d'Italia and visit the Casino. It's empty or nearly so. In the middle of the day there are few people willing to lose money in a relatively painless way. A broad-shouldered blonde woman presses the buttons of a poker machine like an arthritic pianist in the rainy season. A couple of rows further up a man perches on his chair like a bored bonsai tree in an oversized pot, just where he said he would be.

A glass wall separates these legal robbers from a restaurant where the solitary figure of a waitress moves in circles like a fish in an aquarium. She is young, yet looks tired. Dull skin, unwashed hair, all the signs of a family life that takes its toll on her. I think what it would be for her to have a night off, a long and lovely sleep without being interrupted by a toddler's whinge or a horny husband.

As I go nearer to the glass wall, attracted by my favourite poker machine, I notice that the waitress has long lashes and a tender vulnerable nape; and I think that beauty is a question of arrangement and *mis en scene*, a question of impression that some achieve and others fail to do. I think of the latest fad for cosmetic surgery as panacea for a happy life and I thank heaven that I have no need to resort to it.

Ah well, you never know. Old age is always around the corner in one way or the other. Even Marylin was shocked when she found a white hair.

'Not on my head,' she raved. 'But down *there*, you know where I mean!'

This is Marylin who went under the knife to diminish her boobs at a time when breast augmentation is a household topic. Marylin, a belligerent feminist who was arrested ten years ago for kicking a police officer in the balls at a peaceful demonstration.

Beauty, as everything else in this world, is a personal decision to which you have to stick twenty-four hours a day. I remember deciding I was beautiful at the age of eight after one of the girls at school, a certain Tilly, called me fatzy. She was a skinny thing with four amazingly similar limbs, big lips and even bigger eyes. However she had one weak spot. Her hair was thin and slack. My hair has been always glossy, thick, with a life of its own. It was an object of widespread envy among female teachers. One day while discussing our career dreams in class, I stated humbly, 'I'll be a hairdresser model and every year cut some of my hair to make natural wigs so I can help girls like Tilly to be happy and attractive like me.'

It was a bombshell. I had just uttered the unthinkable, presuming that I was happier and more attractive than Tilly with only my hair as a backup. I could hear my classmates' brains buzzing, weighting against and in favour of my words. That was the moment when I got it: words are power. Gradually the truth sunk in—my truth. Tilly was no longer just lippy and leggy; she was also *bald*. I was no longer fatzy; I had a mane. Finally every boy wanted to take me to a party.

I leave the casino 200 CHF richer. The receptionist thanks me before I tip her, so I don't. I walk along the deserted lakeside alley and to a café where I see the bonsai man from the casino. In the corner next to the entrance there is a group of several men who look like regulars. One is holding the key to a Mercedes, mentioning casually that it's his son-in-law's birthday present. His friends try to look impressed, here my Italian fails me to pick what exactly they say.

I sit on the bench at a small, unoccupied table and the bartender, a typical Latin lover type, is already standing in wait. I have the hots for Latin lover types, but this one's brows are too bushy so I don't give him my usual let's-screw-around look. He also looks more interested in reviving his slack business. To his credit, he shows enthusiasm when I order my espresso and takes his time preparing it. I have drunk my best espresso in Naples, but this one is not bad either.

I sip on it, keeping an eye on the group next to the entrance. They are in their mid-sixties, well off, well groomed, and well fed. I can see them enjoying good meals and exclusive wine, raising secure families, visiting a mistress or an occasional girlfriend in between buying a villa or a new Ferrari. It's relaxing to be in this part of the world, where life looks like a well negotiated, profitable deal.

Out of the corner of my eye I see the bonsai man fold his paper and get up, tossing a bill onto the table.

I leave the cafe reluctantly, accompanied by the nostalgic looks of the gentlemen by the entrance. Each of them considers me a missed opportunity. That's the way life is, full of missed opportunities.

I love Italy and this patch of her surrounded by Switzerland, protected the way the Pope is by his Swiss guards.

I follow the bonsai man from the casino. We walk up a steep, narrow street flanked by two-story houses in warm colours. A Thai woman is cleaning the entrance to one of them with soapy water and I wonder why she is scrubbing so vigorously. To me it looks clean and neat without her effort.

The bonsai man slows down in front of a yellow house and turns around to meet my eyes, then disappears behind the corner. Everything has a price, and so does he. But he brings me here, which should serve me as a random start. Very random, I must confess, but there are not other ideas right now in my head so I follow what might be a disturbingly long shot.

The bonsai man is a private detective whose telephone number I find on the Internet. He tracked down for me the person whom I am going to pay a visit, a well-known collector surprisingly found on a cannibals-related web-page.

I take a deep breath and approach the yellow house. Entering the small foyer is like entering a big, waxed cake of parmeggiano-reggiano cheese.

There are two doors. The one on the right has a plate with the name Dott. B. Nicholas on it. In Italia almost everybody is *dottore*, but I know this is a real one.

I press the bell, producing strange, creepy sounds not unlike vulture's wings flapping over a freshly ripped carcass, Tasmanian devils in flight, or the materialised scream of the famous Edvard Munk painting.

I shiver and try to calm my heartbeat.

I have the feeling I am watched. A home surveillance camera, of course. I lift my head and smile in as friendly a manner as possible. Soon I hear shuffling behind the door and it opens a crack. When the door finally opens fully, a small fragile figure emerges from the dark.

Dr Nicholas is wearing a pure wool dressing gown over an immaculate white shirt, trousers and a bow tie. His golden-rimmed glasses contain heavy lenses. His skin is strikingly smooth, soaked with cream. The perfume he's wearing could be Bulgari.

'Ms Cornelius?' he croaks, giving me an overall glance. What he sees makes him happy; his behaviour changes abruptly. 'Of course, of course, Ms Cornelius, I've been expecting you. Please come in.'

His English is old-fashioned Oxford that hasn't been maintained properly. Dr Nicholas could have been one of those men sitting in the café down by the lake. Wealth is written all over his face.

He steps aside, an invitation to go in. As I pass him in the dark, narrow space my bust line brushes lightly against his nose. He shuts the door behind me and finds a light switch, but it's still semi-dark. The vicinity of his physical presence bothers me. He is violating my personal space and it makes me edgy.

He opens a door and suddenly we are showered by sunlight so intense that I squint to prevent being blinded.

'Follow me, Ms Cornelius.'

When my eyes adjust, it's postcard beautiful. The room has a full view of the lake, and the atmosphere inside is also a snapshot frozen in time. The room is full of glass cubes of display cabinets. A small blue sofa and tiny padded chairs frame a coffee table. There's also a fine china coffee set and I can smell premium Italian espresso. That makes me relax.

Coffee makes me feel at home, even here in the presence of Dr Nicholas, from whom you can order any musical instrument you want. Any musical instrument made of a human body part.

The eerie silence around me prompts that the room might be sound-proofed.

Coffee, coffee, I keep repeating to myself like a mantra. Like a clutch word.

Dr Nicholas turns to me with a smile. 'Now, where to begin?'

THIRTEEN

Man's an orchestra.

I walk past Dr Nicholas into the room where glass boxes shelter musical instruments of an unusual nature. They look like your ordinary trumpet and drum, but they are not. These musical instruments are made of human parts. The glass boxes could as well be sarcophagi. Looking at this bleak exposition I feel rooted in the middle of the room. My own body strikes out in reaction to what has happened to these other bodies and I don't blame it.

'Oh, I see, a girl in style.' Dr Nicholas smacks his lips behind me. I turn to see him admiring my shoes.

'Paying a visit to a surgeon in stilettos! That's what I call a personal touch.' He chuckles happily and waves me to a chair.

The moment I take a seat he kneels on the floor near me with a surprising agility and comments, 'A good pair of stilettos are able to perforate the skull of an old Caucasian man whose calcium has fled the bones leaving them like Brussels' lace.'

'Well,' I say, embarrassed, 'they are just shoes.'

'If you say so.' He sounds cranky now. It takes him some effort to raise himself off the floor.

I anticipate him offering me coffee and am prepared to say yes, please, black, but he has other things in mind.

Staring at my legs, he exclaims again: 'Unbelievable! The longest femur I've ever seen.'

I feel chill creeping up my back. He goes to the tallest glass box and points inside.

'What you see behind this glass, Ms Cornelius, is a femur. Actually it's a rare musical instrument called *rkang-gling*. A Tibetan trumpet made of male femur, the thighbone. You want to hold it, perhaps play a tune?'

I don't know what to say. I want to please him and eventually gain his confidence; on the other hand I don't want to slobber a male bone.

'Can I serve us some coffee?' I try a question instead of an answer. Sometimes it works.

'Of course, of course. You'll excuse your old host. Please, by all means.'

I pour and swallow mine like medicine. It's not as good as the one I just had down by the lake, but it charges my batteries and gives me strength to take in more of this bizarre conversation.

I look at the *rkang-gling*; he looks at my face through his fat lenses.

'What a nice skin you've got, Ms Cornelius, faultless! Do you mind following me to my other room, I want to show you something.'

I mind, but I follow, to where an even bigger room overlooks the lake. The light falls at such an angle that the first thing I notice is a samurai sword hanging over a king-size bed. A trolley with surgical instruments on display is positioned as a bedside table. The stainless steel of scalpels and scissors exudes a cold and menacing glow. I feel hypnotised. Dr Nicholas startles me from behind. He is carrying a volume from the wall-to-wall bookcase. Silently he offers me the book, making it appear a rare gesture. Perhaps it is.

I take the book and feel the smoothness of its surface.

'Bound in human skin,' he explains, sounding like a guru descending to earth to initiate an ignorant.

Instantly I drop the volume, scoring bad points. I see the hospitable disposition melt away from his face, replaced by a cold mask of contempt.

I want to pick up the opened book whose pages flap softly in the air like the limbs of a newly-born. I bend and take a glimpse of the word orchestra and I wonder whether it is a message from my mother that I shouldn't play this game solo but stick to the group, *the orchestra*. But my host is so quick, our heads meet midway down and his gold-rimmed glasses scratch my forehead, which doesn't improve things. He takes hold of the book as if he is dealing with a crystal object and inspects it for damage. I feel stupid, my head hurts.

'I am sorry, *dottore*.' It's all I can manage. I am thinking I should come to terms with my visit as a fiasco, when he suddenly smiles.

'No worries, as you say in Australia. Nothing can stand between friends. We better go back and finish our coffee. And our conversation.'

I am no happier with this outcome because it still sounds creepy. But I am not here to judge, rather to achieve what might be a contact with a group plotting to wipe me out.

'I saw that you finished yours; you may have another one,' he continues. 'I use fresh coffee beans. They look like adrenal glands ready to produce hormones for a flight or fight situation.' He puts the book back on a shelf. 'It's funny the way people react; really it's just another artefact.' And he escorts me outside the room.

Still feeling clumsy from the head-on ramming, I step away from the rug and knock into something that falls all over me like a plastic octopus. It's actually a skeleton and this time I scream my head off.

Dr Nicholas is disapproving but amused.

'Come on, Ms Cornelius, you are a big girl. It's just the old Giaccomo back to his old tricks. He used to be the most inventive womaniser among us. Not like me anyway.'

I calm down and we go back to the first room. As the sun starts to exit the stage, it's even less cheerful in this house.

'Perhaps you'd like a cup of chocolate. Women love chocolate. When you open a female skull you can always see that she has indulged in chocolate. The chemistry of the brain is different.'

'No thanks,' I say and pour myself another coffee. This time he drinks his with me and doesn't show any annoyance that it's cold.

'Talking about skulls, I'd like to show you, young lady, one of the jewels in my collection: the *damaru* drum.' He gets up and goes to another glass box. What you see is two joined human skulls and monkey skin attached with human hair. The skulls are first smeared with virgin menstrual blood. You see?'

I hold my breath and force myself not to avert my eyes. 'Interesting,' I sieve through clenched teeth, shaking my head as if in amazement.

He gets more and more enthusiastic. 'I am a collector, you know; these are priceless objects of art, and I was glad to know that you wanted to write an article on these...let's call them unusual musical instruments.' His telephone rings somewhere in the guts of the apartment, but he ignores it, continuing his lecture. 'And I assure you, each of these instruments is tuned and fit to produce the music you want to play. You see here? This drum is also decorated with a lotus. Another Tibetan musical instrument. Man's an orchestra, as you see, Ms Cornelius.'

'He, she is,' I agree.

'Now, I will tell you something that you can't probably hear anywhere else.'

He comes near me with the drum, holding it with such a necrophilic tenderness that I want to puke.

Dr Nicholas lowers his voice to a reverent whisper. 'The spirit, or rather, the energy field of a man remains in his skull forever. That's the reason the Vikings once drank from the skulls of their enemies. To obtain their power.' He brings the double drum almost to his face as if to show me how easy it is to turn the two skulls into grails. Then he pulls it away and starts to softly drum on it instead.

'The Maori tribal chiefs also drank from the skulls of other chiefs they killed in battle and ate in peace. To obtain their power. However, if you handle the skull of a weak insignificant person, you weaken your own energy field, which can lead to your downfall.'

He stops for a moment to enjoy the effect of his drumming. I have to admit that he does it quite artistically. I give him a reassuring smile, trying to think of a way to interrupt his verbal diarrhea and get to the point of why I am actually here. But Dr Nicholas carries on.

'Let's take for an example that unhappy jerk Hamlet. He mucks around with the skull of Yorick, some insignificant jester, long enough to catch profanity like the flu. Profanity and an urge to fall out of his royal level. Weakness of the spirit is contagious, as is greatness. Shakespeare knew that. Hamlet was contaminated and unfit to be a king.'

I should find the artistic references interesting and probably memorize the Shakespeare part and pass it down to Marylin, but I feel sleepy and can't suppress a yawn.

Dr. Nicholas shakes his head. 'Not very polite, young lady. Aren't you going to take some notes for your writing? I am trying to give a lecture here.'

He tries a louder drumming next to my ear, in a joking way as if to wake me. Then he puts the weird instrument away and returns to the trumpet, which he holds loosely by his side, almost casually, swaying it a little. Nonetheless, I am aware of what he is doing. He is comparing the size of the femur trumpet with the length of my thigh. I find this annoying and want to strangle him with his own bow tie but retain control of myself.

'This femur or *rkang-gling* turns air into music to accompany chanting and rituals. The human bone cavity modulates unique sounds.' Dr Nicholas returns the trumpet to the glass box and shows me another example. 'This gourd is threaded around with human vertebrae. You can see it in the hands of a shaman with human teeth in his necklace. He rattles it to induce a trance and conjure magic.'

He starts to rattle the gourd and despite my skepticism I feel the drowsiness coming back.

It might not be a bad idea to rest a little.

I sit on the sofa and lean back, a silly smile lingering on my mouth, when I detect triumph in Dr Nicholas eyes. That activates me. I grab the coffee pot and hurl it against the glass box. The noise sobers me, or maybe it's just that Dr Nicholas has stopped rattling.

I haven't done much. Only the pot lies in pieces. The glass box is as sound as before. I should have known that it's a special make.

Hatred makes his eyes change colour. 'I know why you are here,' he says matter-of-factly. 'They expected you to try to reach them.'

'Them? Who are they? What have I done to them?'

'They are exactly who you think they are. The Brotherhood of the Cannibals that has existed throughout the centuries in Europe. They have nothing to do with the primitive tribal man-eaters. Humans are not physical, but spiritual food for them. It's difficult to explain in brief.'

I am not here for a verification of something I already know. 'Why are they after me?'

'Because you are stupid. I apologise for being rude but that's not only my opinion. I quote. Nobody before you has tried to publicly expose their continuous existence. Many have guessed, speculated, theorized but preferred to remain quiet. And here you come, greedy for fame. It's stupid, and it's a waste, because you are a beautiful specimen, Ms Cornelius.' He allows himself a small pause and shrugs his shoulders. 'Perhaps it won't be a total waste, bearing in mind your phenomenal femur size.' He takes the gourd again and starts rattling it gently.

I feel the drowsiness again and in a desperate attempt, I pretend I can't keep myself straight, letting my head fall.

Just before it hits the coffee table, I grab my shoe, wrench it off my foot, and launch myself towards him. I stab at him with the stiletto, backing the blow with half my weight. It gets stuck in his ear and he drops to the floor, lifeless enough for me to figure a way out of the house.

'Sorry for the mess,' I say while retrieving my shoe. In a fit of anger I spit on him. 'You bloody shearer!'

Mostly, I am disappointed.

I shouldn't be because I sniffed a probable trace and it paid off. But I have only come into contact with something peripheral because from what I know about the Brotherhood, its members wouldn't be so talkative.

The secrecy that surrounds their practice has proved to be efficient and has ensured their survival. Dr Nicholas is a buffoon. Perhaps, like me, he is only interested in cannibalistic related themes and thinks that this is enough to proclaim himself one of the selected. We were two amateurs attempting to claim the other's life to prove something to ourselves.

FOURTEEN

On my way back to the ferry, I touch my thighs; the flesh is healthy, bouncy, my femurs are still in place, supporting me along my way to discover a long kept secret. It might cost my life, but I am so carried away, I don't give a shit. That's it; I don't give a shit!

The dying sun is playing with me, its rays sending hot breath into my hair, my ears, my nape. The sun is covering me with kisses, impersonal kisses, more like an echo of kisses.

The esoterics have a saying: the angle of deviation is equal to the angle of suffering. More we try to escape from our initial make coded on all levels, more we subject ourselves to failures. If we dare to swim against the trend, we have to be ready to accept the consequences. I know it, I know the urge to be different, noticeable, reckless, crazy.

I think of my manuscript, perhaps already doomed.

A tide of hesitation threatens to drown me. What's the purpose of my persistence? If God came down to earth he might not recognise man, and it's not because man's an orchestra as Dr Nicolas also affirms.

The question is why should I, of all people, make it my business?

I can't help it.

That's it: I can't help it. I am obsessed by forces that spin around me and turn me into a tool, a mere tool for weaving cannibalistic yarns.

Pieter Aertsen's *The Meat Stall* kept in Upsala University, Sweden, makes every vegetarian head for the bathroom. Among plucked chooks, pig's and cow's heads, hanging sausages and cuts of meat is a tiny, hidden landscape with a humble religious plot: the Virgin in the flight into Egypt giving bread to the poor. Yeah, the poor are vegetarians, aren't they, though not by choice. Around this holy subject the stall with its articles of flesh appears too naturalistic, shameless.

I can't stomach it, and I see how my carnal and mental preferences clash. I am a meat lover when it comes to a good meal, but it's not my idea of good taste to turn chunks of raw meat into objects of art. Does it mean that I am a hypocrite or that I am afraid to look at it because of my deeply hidden fear that I might find it appealing as a display of cannibalistic craziness?

Still, there is nothing hypocritical about the fact I find it more aesthetic to observe a still life entirely composed of vegetarian objects, like Juan Sanchez Cotan's *Quince, Cabbage, Melon, and Cucumber*. I'd rather write about paintings like Pieter Bruegel the Elder's *Peasant Wedding,* which makes you wonder whether people live to eat or eat to live

While sexual pleasure can't do much to feed you, gastronomic pleasure can bring you to an orgasm even more multifaceted than a sexual one. It's not by chance that I am in the culinary business. This is the only way for me to get off, to dispose of an excess of sexual energy before it clogs me or explodes the world around me.

In this aspect I prefer to ponder over Jan den Heem's *Still Life with Parrots.* It's full of vanitas symbols, a profusion of objects, food and food-related, of higher, more exquisite value. It's a playground of extravaganza in tastes both of palate and genitals. The grapes stand for the Eucharistic wine, hence human blood for cannibalistic blending with the divine.

As an opposite line Vincent van Gogh's *The Potato Eaters* has no equal. The man holding a cold potato—the potato must be cold by the way he is holding it confidently between his fingers, letting it rest on his palm on its way to his mouth—is literally eating it with eyes; ogling it, rather, as the sensual enthusiasm on his face at the sight and handling of this simple food tells all.

Food orgasm is not a class thing.

Isn't a potato so much like a human heart ready to pulsate, to imitate life? A potato soup could be rhythmic, intriguing, full of metaphors and flavour assonance, of hidden messages and subtle glamour, seductive, overwhelming, inspirational, written with the heart.

Years ago I cooked one such a soup on a desert island in the Great Barrier Reef, inviting the spirit of Nature to sit on the stump in front of my tent overlooking the coral beach. The back door of the tent was also open overlooking the forest where colonies of terns were nesting.

I put some water into a shabby aluminium can and added a cube of beef bouillon. I peeled two potatoes, washed them in the sea, cut them into non-existent geometrical shapes, and threw them into the water to boil together and exchange vows for everlasting friendship.

Soon the soup was ready. I offered some to the spirit of Nature who gobbled them up with the help of a cranky seagull.

That was how I got the idea of my first culinary book, which I entitled *Cooking with Spirituality*. It was my own spiritual journey that paved the road to success and insight into ancient life-supporting art of cooking.

A sudden bout of jealousy caused by the fierce competition in the fork-and-knife field makes me call Beverley. Besides I desperately need any link to the outer world that might suggest that I am still sane and that what's going on is a bad dream caused by indigestion.

Beverley swears that she has been looking after my African violet, which means not watering it because the last thing an African plant wants is plenty of water. She never mentions the geranium, caught up in a long story about calling spirits the previous night.

'It really works, Sandy,' she says in a strange voice. 'Your telephone call is proof.'

I try to tell her I am not dead.

'I know, I know,' she continues in the same deep, husky voice. 'We don't die; we assume different energy outfit.'

'Something like an energy wedding gown.' I can't help it. 'What about Marylin? Where is she?'

'Catching up with her love life,' says Beverley mysteriously. 'Actually she is crying her head off for you. But she doesn't mind making a profit out of it.'

'I know,' I say gloomily.

'Of course you know, dear. You know everything there, don't you?'

I ask her to take over the exhibition *Eating the Old Masters.* It's a project I spent half a year convincing the Brisbane City Council to organise.

There's nothing cannibalistic here, however.

The idea was to *recreate* some of the old masters' *nature morts* excelling in things to eat. By *recreate* we meant to substitute the artistic images with real objects of the same sort juxtaposed in the same manner. The exhibition, of course, had to be short-lived, otherwise the *art* would start to rot.

'I've already taken over, Sandy,' Beverley assures me, and I think, *The bitch!* She continues, 'After they heard about you the sponsors summoned me and, since you are...well, busy travelling to outer spiritual planes, they asked me to give the speech at the opening. I hope you don't mind?'

'See bloody well that it doesn't start to stink like an abattoir,' I croak.

'Sandy? Are you okay?'

The stupid cow.

'Of course I am. And very happy for you.'

'Thank you. It's such a relief to know. Yesterday when I tried this séance I wasn't sure whether it would work, it usually takes nine days for the dead to reach their finalised verdict. But I see that's not the case. You've always have been an exceptional lady. I love you.'

'Same here.' What else can I say?

'By the way, Sandy,' says Beverley casually. 'I was just cooking eggplants to honour and celebrate you with your favourite meal.'

'No,' I yell. 'Don't do this! Eggplants are my territory! Don't go anywhere near them!'

The eggplant is not so called by accident. Its shape always tends to induce philosophical pondering in me. I like to touch its smooth, almost perfect surface, oval and complete like the universe itself. It's like a semi-precious stone, an amethyst shell about to give birth to something conceived in the twilight of the subconscious mind—something of a great importance, so I am alert not to miss the message if the semi-precious shell cracks open and the message breaks out.

The spirit of this message will be written in feelings and telepathically transported to me from the very depth of death. Death is the other side of life and spells its purpose. We all are born with death sentences hanging over our heads; *memento mori* is the great teaching of how to live. Most of the evil comes from when we forget that we are mortal, transitory, and must concentrate on what's necessary for us to do. That doesn't mean that we'll live like we're in the army with a mission to accomplish. It doesn't mean that we are not supposed to be lazy and artistic, absent-minded and flirtatious, to enjoy the hedonistic side of life. To live for pleasure is also spiritual, because you are free. Free to make your choice, as Beverley is free, in this mild afternoon, to make her choice of what to do with the amethyst egg in her hand, cool and fresh and little bit astringent to smell.

If I am the one cooking it, I usually start by talking to it, telling the eggplant that it's my favourite veggie. I thank it for being my cooking companion over the years. I thank it for the life force all the eggplants have nourished, for its vibrant colour, which intensifies the colour of my seventh chakra, supposedly the most spiritual one, the link between me and the universe. I tell the eggplant of my tendency to like plants of this colour, no matter how intense or pale. I describe the jacaranda trees in blossom in October and the purple-mauve carpet on the street where I step and breathe the scent, or sit and touch the fallen flowers.

I show the eggplant my collection of amethyst jewelry, which is not big, just a few pieces I love to wear: a ring for my little finger made of fifteen tiny beads on an elastic thread, the amethyst heart my mother gave me, the deep purple amethyst stone I bought one day on impulse from a spiritual shop in Brisbane. I touch the eggplant with the stone and let it know what it is to be a real amethyst.

Then I heat the oven and put the eggplant on a tray inside. I know it's quite hot there, but the eggplant likes it hot in order to give me the best part of itself, so I leave it there for about half an hour or forty minutes, depending on how large it is. I put on music from the Pacific; the vibes make it easier for me to communicate with the eggplant.

When I take it out of the oven it's brownish, looking ruffled and cocky with its stem burnt. Some of the juices have come spilling out into the tray like a halo, sticky and appealing. I know that they are bitter so I discard them and cut open the skin to scrape the pulp out with a spoon. It's fleshy, it's submissive, it's beautiful. I peel quite a few cloves of garlic. A girlfriend of mine who lived in India for years feasts every day on garlic and is as healthy as ever. A good head of garlic is as white as a bride and as hard as a bridegroom. I press the cloves into the eggplant and wish them happiness together.

FIFTEEN

I get off the boat at Lugano and fish in my purse. Frank's note is there. This time I reflect on what he has written under his signature.

A leg of pork, fumed
For an egg extravaganza
Cut the Holy sound

It looks like a haiku. It also looks like a poetry wink to a lover up to her ears in gastronomic spurs.

But I want to believe it's more than this.

I want to believe that Frank loves me and has something in mind, that he wants me to find him beating Jacob Jacobsen on his own field: intelligence.

The mere thought of Frank makes my starving body feel sharp pangs of sexual hunger. My lips swell and I feel moist in my ears. I must be really fuming from every aperture in my physical compound.

Then I get really hungry. I don't mind an eggy thing in white and yellow, something suggesting prenatal journeys of culinary nature. I've read somewhere that Churchill used to have twelve eggs for breakfast, twelve packages of life sustaining nutritious, presumably the best feed. I have no idea how he had preferred them but I can tell heaps about a person by the way this person cooks the morning eggs.

Strict perfectionists or cranky people would usually go for soft snotty egg, which they would slurp like cough syrup in a discipline masochistic way.

Bohemians love them boiled medium, the yolk silky solid with a tiny dent of over-softness like a jelly puddle.

Reckless people like them hard-boiled like a detective story with an unhappy ending.

I like to peel my hard-boiled egg and split the white so that the yolk can roll out mossy and freely like a planet, let's say Jupiter.

I have often snitched eggs from hotel buffet breakfasts. They are easy to hide and carry in purses or shorts. It's fun and I hone my deceiving skills because I know from Aunty Susan that her hotel staff is instructed to never leave the guests alone with the eggs, buns and other easy to tuck away goodies.

Frank is not into it. He is too serious.

'Never love a Norwegian,' I say to myself, I repeat to myself, I chant to myself like a mantra.

It never helps. I've done it for three years already, my most celibate years, salivating over him. Abstention is not for me. Yet I don't know what he's got to hold me so tight to him, denying me consummation of my sexual interest in him. Perhaps, as he says, he has raped my mind.

Frank read the runes for me when we were in Athens once and said that my mother had one wish for me: to go to a nunnery. I couldn't believe my ears. 'Wasn't this the wish Hamlet expressed for Ophelia?'

Frank looked cross and disappointed with me. 'I am not reading the runes for Hamlet, I am reading them for your mother, Margherita Cornelius.'

'Are you sure?' I persisted, since Frank sometimes reads the runes for Don Quixote and Gulliver, too.

Right now I wonder whether my mother had foreseen the events of the last few days and had suggested that I should hide in a nunnery.

I miss Frank. My body aches for him. Memories flood me.

He says my bottom looks like a heart turned upside down. He gives my cheeks little exploring bites. The feeling is on the fine line between pleasure and pain, and I python-slide under him to ease my breathing. The sensation inside me creates a pulsating path between my throat stuck with tonsils and my other throat swallowing him in a cannibalistic frenzy. My moans are rooted deeply. We shed our egos and for one long moment perform in an achieved oneness. I feel the Buddhist term of emptiness in practice. My head is a vault, there's not a single thought to chase, not even with a fly-killer. I am a knot of sensations that change in colour and intensity, spinning within and around my physical field. I could be energy, animal, hieroglyph for madness.

I remember our tryst in Athens, the white city made of ruins. Everywhere skeletons of once glamorous buildings, temples, marble chunks and slivers. A graveyard used by living people on the presumption of a social life with the dead, titbits of glorious history, bear traps for gullible archaeologists, taxi drivers ripping you off—a distant cry from *peripatos*, the covered walk where Aristotle lectured while strolling to and fro with his students. Waiters entice tourists on the sidewalks, noisily praising their *moussaka*, Macedonian wine, *zhaziki*, marinated sardines. Oh, these marinated sardines—first charcoal grilled, then soaked in olive oil, vinegar, parsley, pepper and salt. The olive oil is a medicine itself, drops of melted sun heavily swaying like a line of *sirtaki* dancers ready to break plates till the cows come home. Old Greek men sip sweet Greek coffee brewed in hot sand, slow, slow, with thick cream, return it three times back when it starts to overflow the metal *djezve*. They sit in a *cafenio* on the Manastiraki Square nourishing a necrophilic tenderness for the ruins. Their ancestors had invested wisely in ruins for centuries to come.

I go back to what happened in the train on my way to Lugano and try to remember the face of the fat *signor* that woke me at the Lugano station. I have no name for him so I call him *il signor*. I don't know why that signor sticks to me like a flea to a mongrel. A picture of a well-fed, well-groomed man who's old but can't be called such because of the baby fat showing on his cheeks and hands. A metrosexual man, one in touch with his feminine side.

For a moment I wonder: being in touch with the masculine side of me as a sexual preference or life-saving behaviour, shall I think of myself as subwaysexual? *Subway*sexual sounds a good version of *metro*sexual for women.

I return to Frank's note. There's nothing to unravel there. Even God is an omelette lover—I can bet on it even though I haven't died properly, as my friend Beverley thinks, and I can't have a glimpse on God's menu.

I swirl the word *omelette/omelet/om-e-let/om-let* around my mouth, feeling hungry. That's all I get from this mind-cracking exercise.

I find a small cafe by the lake where they serve breakfast all day long. It's nice to know that places like this exist. It means I am not limited in space and time, I have the capacity to rearrange the order of the earth, spinning around the sun, and this gives me a feeling of power. I sit and order ham-and-eggs. Chewing like a lion with the help of my three-teeth lower partial denture complimenting my prone-to-rot natural whites, I give a sigh of relief.

It sounds like OM, the holiest Buddhist sound believed to be the most harmonious link to the universe. I feel happy which is weird given the situation.

Suddenly struck by an idea, I visit the toilet carrying my glass of Sprite, and squirt liquid soap into the glass before returning to the table. With the help of a straw I start to make bubbles and watch them float around me. It fills me with excitement. I have always loved to blow soap bubbles; I remember sitting with Uncle Willie and trying to catch them.

Uncle Willie, *homo bulla*, man the bubble, that's what he is, I think. Aunty Susan has always stressed that Uncle Willie is *homo ludens*, man the game. Actually, what's the difference? The attitude? Life's a bubble. Life's a game.

My fellow diners watch in amusement, and the waiter brings me another glass of Sprite, on the house. They all like what I do. For a moment we have this collective perception of life as a bubble. A brief moment of floating existence, a sweet carefree bubble that we try to load with a ballast of emotional rubbish.

Never love a Norwegian, I repeat to myself, looking at the *Paradiso* suburb and Aunty Susan's hotel, where I left my virginity as a law-abiding person.

Ham. Om(e)let. Om.

Ham-let.

SIXTEEN

The next morning I am in Elsinore, on the eastern coast of Denmark looking at the stretch of land across the briny blue Nordic sea, a lace of fjords that makes it nice and easy for the water to copulate with land. The reason of me being here is the stupid culinary riddle giving the answer *Hamlet*. A riddle written by an expert on ancient Scandinavian runes, the occult and the mystical, a reviewer of best-selling thrillers, getting down from his high-fly realms to please his profane *mistress in distress*.

I am kind of allergic to trivia stuff from the time when a TV smartass told Janette that our show shouldn't stay at a primitive stomach level like all the other cooking shows, there are buckets of them these days, but offer some food for brain, too. That meant ask smart riddles.

'If you want to stay in the show, you should come up with a nice cooking riddle each time,' said Janette friendly. She didn't like the fact that our cameraman who she was bedding was all eyes for me. 'Besides *sex* and cooking tricks you are supposed to appear also intellectual, if it's not too much for you.'

That's how trivia gems found their way to our prime time show and I started to ask questions like:

Is it true or false that pizzicato means small pizza in Italian? Answer: false. (Pizzicato is a playing technique that involves plucking the strings of an instrument.)

What was *Doctor Zhivago's* favourite vegetable? Answer: Parsnip. (That was the literary translation from Russian of *Doctor Zhivago's* author's name Pasternak.)

What is this favourite snack whose name consists of two words meaning a. a beach commodity; b. a woman who uses supernatural powers and conjures magic to influence events—take a letter off? Answer: sandwich. (a. sand; b. witch—letter *t* taken off.)

Soon I was running out of ideas. Luckily the rating of the *Kitchen Goddess* started to plummet. Nobody wanted to hear anything about *pizzicato*, they had difficulties pronouncing it and almost noone remembered the novel or the movie with that sixties heartthrob Omar Sharif who openly sneered at women 'always cooking'. Finally the TV smartass gave it a miss and we went back to give people what they like best, a friendly sensual nurturing pastime. Anyway, I wonder what will happen if all of a sudden there's no TV any longer? Would people start to jump out of their windows as they did during that Black Friday in 1929 when the New York Stock Exchange crashed?

I also had my Black Friday back in Brisbane when it all kicked off.

Here in Elsinore if I am lucky I might find Frank, or at least a clue as to who wants to wipe me off the face of the earth and why. Too much of Hamlet floating in the air makes me feel psycho like him, that's for sure, following another hunch that might or might not result in anything.

To fool Jacob Jacobsen is another priority. To see whether *I* can do something about solving the enigma of the cannibalistic rituals and killings and save my own skin. Then perhaps buy one of those grass-thatched roof houses in Odenze and call it a day with Frank by my side, watching a Woody Allen movie. When it comes to Frank, JJ is also *a rival*. I am too territorial to let him have a say on whether Frank should stay or not with me, especially after we've been separated for months that looked years. Still fuming about Jacobsen *advising* Frank to stay away from me in Lugano, I manifest tolerance of a control freak. It's a question of power, power over Frank and I am a bit touchy there. No need of another spouse-figure. Now that I am declared dead I am going to appear in Jacobsen dreams as a ghost and *fry* his wits! My hands are itchy, haven't done cooking for a while.

For a moment I wonder what David thinks of the newspapers that have surely reached his desk. He's probably already giving a call to a desperate author who has a lucky morning invited to submit a manuscript. I dread this author is Beverley. What about if David solicits a manuscript on the theme I so generously shared with him?

I feel cold. The weather is horrible; it stirs my marrow with ice in a cocktail cylinder. Yet there are other reasons for me to shiver.

Running down the millennium-old steps back to a small kiosk outside the castle I buy a newspaper. There is a short coverage on the mysterious suicide at the graveside of Beethoven. My publisher is quoted as being extremely surprised at the events, calling them tragic. He says that he lifted my spirits by inviting me to submit my manuscript. Then he blurs what I was writing about, calling it an inspirational insight and a new look into the works of titans of the brush and the conspiracy of the Brotherhood of the Cannibals. He says he had discovered me through a woman's magazine where I had published a surprisingly spiritual recipe entitled *Potato Soup as Poetry*.

David admits he was emotionally bribed by my comparison between potato and human heart. He knew my new book would be another overnight bestseller, and only death could have prevented it, which unfortunately was the case. He continues that, luckily, Beverley Jones, a renowned cookbook illustrator (Holy shit, now she's also an illustrator!) and confidant of *poor Sandy* is ready to fill my shoes and finish the writing after some legal formalities.

Damn it.

At least I have Frank, Norm and Aunty Susan to back me up.

Not to forget Marylin.

I ring her number.

There she is. Her deep burly voice, her spinning vocal energy breaks distance, hostility, fear.

'Marylin.' I utter and it's like going home, hanging my hat on her solid, a bit vulgar, loveable head.

'Where are you, bitch?'

It *is* like going home!

'Here...' I start.

'Heaven or hell?'

'Denmark.'

'Bedlam. Give my regards to Christiania people. I admire them.'

'Marylin, listen...' But she wouldn't.

'What idiot gave you the idea to start advertising your *cooking* profile from Europe?' She is panting and pronounces cooking to sound like fucking.

'I am not doing any advertising!' The pattern: I start to explain myself, feeling guilty.

'Then why all this crap about you in the newspapers?'

'How about all this rubbish in the newspaper about my private life, everything you said?' I remember I hate her.

'Sandy, you old drama-queen! I wanted to help.'

'To help.' I repeat bitterly. 'You call this help?'

'Sandy, I never knew you were ready to go to such a length to obtain popularity. But believe me, I was crying my eyes out only at the thought that it might not, you know, be the case, that you have kicked the bucket for real...Tamati is also worried.'

'Marylin, it's not what you think. But I have no time to explain, just keep your mouth shut!' I start to get impatient.

'But you tricked even me and it's not fair. When for a change life starts to look promising.'

'Tell me! You've been up to some dirty things?'

'Hunting crocodile hunters!' And she laughs. I can see her freckles like strawberry seeds, her sleazy smile. She laughs so happily that for a moment I am under her spell and feel happy and carefree. For a moment I ride the illusionary foamy wave of wellness. Then I get cranky. They are having all the fun there in Brisbane: Marylin, Tamati, Norm, even Beverley. Mostly Beverley, wasting no time to hop into my shoes. I miss out on a good quality, laid-back, out-doors Aussie life-style and my heart is full of envy.

I spit, 'Terrific!'

There's a pause. Marylin works on her compassion.

'Don't forget I am your friend.'

'How come I can forget it?' I say without much irony because I understand it's easier for her to love me *now*.

'Marylin, I am in a big shit.'

'Join the club, baby, I've been there all my life. I'll tell Tamati you are all right.'

The connection is lost and I am not sure whether Marylin did it or the satellite had enough of us.

I feel hesitant about ringing David. He served me the most exciting chance on a tray and I am going to blow it. Unless I manage to track down and fight back a deadly cult. Am I so stupid or crazy to believe I can do this? Perhaps both.

After queuing for a program for the Hamlet Festival, which starts tomorrow, I cross the bridge and head back up the stairs of the wall. A downy touch in the air shows summer is not far away. Meteorology, like graphology, is a doomed science. The planet has its own way to rebel against man's ruthless invasion. Climate is no longer built up around equinoxes and comfortable predictable periods. These days the Tarot readers can't look into its future, neither can planet shrinks explain its bizarre behaviour. Nobody can predict small periods like this one within a gloomy day when the sun decides to pierce the layer of woolly clouds and say hello. It's a couple of hours of summer.

At least this looks like a good omen to me.

Keeping a low profile, flying under the radar could be good for me, and I hope that Frank will make the contact.

Standing by an ancient rusty gun pointing at an imaginary enemy invading Denmark from the sea, leaning against the castle wall of Elsinore in the cold, wet morning, I recite: *To be or not to be*; I see Ophelia running mad and naming flowers, Hamlet talking to the skull of a jester called Yorick; and I remember what Dr Nicholas told me about the danger of mucking around with a skull of a inferior being.

I look again at the coast of Norway rising from the sea fog into the sunrays. What they have there is ice, oil and herrings. All of them slippery with a dangerous charisma.

'*Jei elske dei*,' I whisper to the sea. *I love you.*

I have made love to the sea so many times, or rather, let it make love to me, its waves engulfing me, smothering me, penetrating me in the tiniest of holes, my pores, cleansing them, rubbing my nose in its salty realm with the aroma of Neptune's armpits.

Never love a Norwegian. I hear the voice of Marylin in the back of my mind. She is desperate to spoil it for me.

Why not love a Norwegian? The Norwegian men are handsome. Soft creamy skin, trolls living in their smiles. They are raised as amphibians or terrapins, their land is smaller than a raft, bigger than a coffin, a tiger-shaped peninsular. The sea is where they belong; they build their churches the way they build their boats, masts support the roof. Odin, their god of poetry, knows the magic of the runes; he can wake the dead and learn secret things from them, then turn those secrets into poetry.

Who reads poetry these days?

Norm does, for sure. My dear faithful friend, solid as a rock in his feelings. Always there for me.

I merge with the slender silhouette of Elsinore against the bleached Nordic sea, succumbing to the golden gilding of the unexpected sun. The waves reflect the rays like fish scales. I go down back to the cobblestone courtyard, wondering if the place is haunted, and a Japanese couple in their early twenties ask me to take a photo of them.

Normally this annoys me, but the sun has put me in a good mood so I position the camera in front of my eyes and have to suppress a cry. On the screen the couple appears accompanied by the father of Hamlet. The Ghost has spread his arms around the young people's shoulders, his fingers like talons fighting the gravity.

The couple looks at me expectantly.

'Sorry,' I say. 'It's just a funny shadow.'

They smile with sympathy and are quick in retrieving the camera. Long after they are gone I am still shivering.

Finding a motel by the sea is easy. I get into the mood looking through the window at the grey foamy waves against the grey foamy sky.

But then, I get into the mood because of a fluffy cat, a crystal ball, a crispy apple, the shadow of a passing cloud, the warmth of the sun, a cushion with a dent of someone's head.

My idea of a threesome is going to bed with *The Dying Slave* of Michelangelo and *La Fornarina* of Raphael. When I look at her curvy lips and huge egg-like eyes; when I contemplate the way she touches herself, her fingers fondling her left nipple, her other hand casually resting on her lap; when I feel like exploring her belly button shamelessly exposed like an additional sex organ, along with her deeply channelled ear, I think of the human body as of a set of pleasure points. I think that her occupation as a baker is obviously ambiguous; I think that *Fornarina* comes from *fornicare* (fornicate) rather than from *fornare* (bake).

As for the provocative yet matter-of-fact posture of Michaelangelo's young man, his most seductive pleasure points is his armpit, bared against the onlooker as he peels off his flimsy top. Imagine marble and flimsy, but that's the effect, because the young man is stripping off what little garments he's got on. A lover in wait.

La Fornarina is teasing, suggesting, attracting, there is a hint of a premeditated, calculated show off, not aggressive yet little bit noisy, laced with humour, irresistibility, presavoured victory. She'll give and take herself and guide you if necessary in a wicked, perhaps even an intelligent way. Her mind will be watchful and alert for better options and surprises. Nothing can be too much or too little in her instrumental hands, the fingers like strings, the thick heavy hair suggesting the glossy turf around her vagina, which I bet is a replica of one of her egg-shaped eyes.

I can feel the prickle touch in her private folds because she plucks what's excessive there, embarrassed by its abundance. She's a fleshy, healthy Mediterranean woman, a good cook and a great fuck.

So is *The Dying Slave*, but for different reasons. Made submissive by nature and social use, he is a personification of self-unawareness. Sensuality drips out of him, bringing fantasies of human moisture and wetness. He's there, no effort, no initiative, no suggestions. Passiveness that drives the willing crazy, floating deprived of judgement and opinions, elusive and unattached—the ultimate specimen of conquistadors. He is an instrument for pleasure. He is pleasure with no form, shape, dimension, an unidentified fluctuating warm and subtle energy field charged with hormones. No brain challenges there.

She's the brainy one. She has to be because she's lazy, deceiving and foxy; she demands to be spoiled and introduced to luxury, the transparent veil around her shoulders is silk and the heavy brocade cloth around her hip woven in gold. But *The Slave* has a simple life. Passing away he takes nothing with him, as any of the human tribe.

I finish writing.

Outside it's dark and the moon licks the moisture of the rocks along the beach like a buffalo caught in a long drought season.

The last chapters of *Gastronomy in Art* are coming out nicely. Hopefully, after all, the manuscript will be on its way to David's desk.

Shutting down the program and the laptop I leave the room and head for a well-deserved dinner.

SEVENTEEN

In the restaurant next to my motel the owner, a plump motherly woman, serves me the ox-tail soup. She can't guess my omnisexual (*subway*sexual) dreams. That keeps me in her good books.

The crockery she uses is of those rare sets of porcelain bowls and adjoining saucers created as one piece. The spoon is neither big nor small. A real soupspoon, not just something to scoop with, oval and deep enough to keep the thick liquid warm while travelling between the bowl and my mouth.

The ox-tail soup tastes delicious, no wonder it puts me on the mood, and I tell the owner what I think about her culinary skills.

She blushes slightly and openly watches me as I wolf down the portion. I order a second one almost immediately and she serves it under my nose.

It's the most amazing steam bath I have pampered my face with. I feel the disintegrating carrots go inside my pores and do their cleansing job, helped by celery and potato molecules before the lightly greasy film of the meat bouillon seals the pores into a smooth relief. The smell crawls inside my sinus cavities and decorates them with primitive paintings, something like big oxen by a water hole.

Soup makes me relax, and this ox-tail soup makes me forget for a moment about my situation as a fugitive with many unanswered questions. For a moment I feel guilty; I can't wipe the smile out of my face.

I feel soup. I act soup.

Ox-tail soup meant to give warmth and comfort. I love that woman, the owner, for providing it, and my smile hangs out there for her, a smile gurgling with soup. She returns the smile, then casts a glance at a small TV screen showing an ancient reel, perhaps one from the First World War. It's black-and-white and people move funny, kind of hopping around.

It would have been comical if the people weren't solders falling like dead autumn leaves on the ground.

It happens suddenly. My lips are still sliding apart, but the smile is gone. This reflects on the owner. She backs off, covering her uneasiness with a plain gesture: wiping her hands on a piece of cloth.

I can't believe my eyes.

The desert animal, the cats' throat's slitter, the petrol sniffer, the car-snitch-and-crash bastard who was bullshitting me in Brisbane, the father killer Michael with the bleached eye is standing at the entrance.

Michael from the Brisbane Juvenile Centre, of all people, is making his way to a table on which, I now notice, there are two sets for dinner.

I remain numb.

He takes a seat with his back to me. The landscape of his back scares me stiff.

How come? It looks unreal.

I want to run, but I have to pass by him to leave. I remember that voice which now reverberates in my ears: 'You are dead, bitch!'

His voice!

I can hear it now as he orders his meal.

For a moment I feel schizophrenic. I can't take my eyes off him; at the same time I am drawn to the TV screen where they now show a flick with three deserted solders on a battlefield covered with corpses. Blood drops down their chins, but they are not wounded. They crouch over an enemy solder, tearing flesh from his body, digging their teeth greedily into the blooded pieces.

I hyperventilate from the voltage passing through me, then try to breathe deeply as I watch the owner transfer her attention to Michael. There's something really good about her motherly radiance. But I have stopped feeling a kid.

I feel like a trapped animal.

I watch Michael's bulky shoulders, his thick hair almost alive, so glossy, so full of primary life force. He'll become a heartthrob if he's not already, I think, and can't believe that I can find the courage to produce such a thought.

The ox-tail soup, suddenly greasy and cold stretches my stomach to the limits. I want to puke.

The door opens again to let Michael's companion in.

Against all sensibility I expose myself by giving away a cry of joy, surprise and readiness to face my fate, whatever it has in store for me.

Norm, because it's Norm who is about to join Michael, is happy and no less surprised.

Soon I find myself in his strangely stiff arms, which sprout out of the trunk of his body. I feel like I'm clinging to a bottle tree.

'Sandy! What are you doing here?'

I find this rather aggressive, but I might be becoming paranoiac.

'What are *you* doing here?'

'Let me introduce us.' Norm makes a bow and I see that Michael has sprung to his feet, watching us with amusement. 'Your faithful servants, ma'am: the young Hamlet and the old rat Polonius.'

They lose me for a moment.

'Norm, you never mentioned you were coming here!' Not an accusation, rather a statement.

'Neither did you, Sandy.'

He has a point there.

Norm smiles teasingly and his arms drop by his sides. 'A last minute decision to participate in the Hamlet Festival. The money was found and here we are; a bit of a coloured Hamlet is Michael but it doesn't steal our hopes for a prize. Is that right, Michael?'

I want to say that Hamlet wants the killer of his father brought to justice, he doesn't kill his father. Instead I mumble something like: 'Norm, I never knew you were into theatre as well. I mean stars, furniture, now theatre.' I continue to ignore Michael, who sits back in his chair.

The owner is a silent witness to our exuberance. She waits for their order with the innocent curiosity of a stranger given the opportunity to peep into someone else's life. She stares at us, a strange composition of chaotic emotions inside this ordinary regular place.

'Why don't you join us?' asks Norm.

I hesitate.

'I've eaten already and I feel tired. I better leave you to your dinner. The ox-tail soup here is delicious.'
Perhaps Norm thinks that I owe him an explanation because he seems to be waiting for one. I don't volunteer, I look at the small TV screen instead. The deserted solders are no longer there, exposing their secret.

'Tomorrow morning we are first to perform after the opening of the Festival,' says Norm. 'The crown princess, our own Aussie Mary, is going to open it. That's why they put us on immediately after her speech, so she can watch us. This puts pressure on me.'

Norm scans my face and speaks in a low voice as if to prevent Michael and the owner from overhearing. 'Don't tell me you are still in trouble? Where is Frank?'

That's a good one, I also want to know where Frank is.

Obviously Norm hasn't seen the newspaper and I leave it like that.

'Not really in big trouble,' I say, not very convincingly. 'Things are quieting down.' Then I crack. 'Norm, I am in big shit!'

He dumps Michael and his meal and accompanies me to my motel room. He wants to stay and keep me company, but I am afraid that if I have him stay for the night I won't be able to restrain myself and will spill the beans again.

Besides, he might get ideas and this is that last thing I need.

'Don't hesitate to call me, if you need me, whatever the reason.' He gives me the number of his room. 'I don't want to steal the surprise, but I'll tell you anyway. We interpret Hamlet as a young delinquent; after all, he is a killer, isn't he? He takes law and order in his own hands and they get bloodstained in no time. Of course he pays with his own life and it's such a waste. If he had been sent to a Juvenile Correction Centre his destiny could have been quite different.'

Poor sweet Norm. That's him in this presumption. Norm is kind of a legend among the staff in the Juvenile Correction Centre. The story goes that a young Aboriginal boy, someone like Michael, was having fits because he was the only one with no visitors. One day Norm arranged for his dog Billie to come as an official visitor for the kid. There is a photo in one of the classrooms: a grey-white husky with Arctic-blue eyes and the black boy with his arms like a collar around the dog's neck, both slobbering with pleasure.

'Norm.' I yawn. 'Who is looking after Billie?'

Norm's face lightens. 'Beverley.'

I hope it doesn't get too much for Beverley these days. As if I am in a position to pity other people.

Finally Norm says good-bye and I promise not to be rowdy and yell *Aussie, Aussie, Aussie* tomorrow at their performance. I know I'll stick to it; I don't want unnecessary attention.

At the door Norm tries to kiss me, but I play it down to a touch of a nose a la Maori greeting, a heritage of Tamati, the spunky, sexy Tamati.

I sigh and lock the door after Norm. I still don't know what to make out of all this.

Coincidence?

Instead of brooding uselessly, I open my laptop.

I hate how quickly David and Beverley have moved on, marauders of my manuscript, my idea. Tearing pieces of flesh still warm and bloody. But there's nothing I can do.

Nothing, but write and wait for Frank.

So I do both.

Being on Scandinavian soil I decide to open a chapter about Claes Oldenburg, an American of Swedish origin. His pursuit in chain fast food products brings him fame. His sculpture *Floorberger 1962* looks like a sick by-product, an ice bag on a meaty head, bursting with high blood pressure. It shows the reduction of world's multicultural cuisine down to a burger, the standardisation of food cravings and satisfaction of appetite. Just another commodity.

I hear a tap at the door. I expect this and quickly rehearse what to say to Norm to send him away without offending him.

'Norm, you need to get some sleep,' I start, opening the door an inch.

I look into Michael's fierce eyes.

EIGHTEEN

I slam the door in Michael's face.

'Ms Cornelius, I want to talk to you,' he pleads from outside in a strange, soft voice.

'Talk,' I say, weighting my chances of grabbing something as a weapon in case he starts to ram the door.

'Can I buy you a coffee in the bar downstairs?'

I fail to recognise his language and manners. Boys like him are perhaps afraid to behave normally when they are among other boys with long records, afraid to be singled out as softies and subjected to bullying.

I am ready to say that I don't mind; then I have second thoughts. Still I open the door and stand there gazing at him, trying to read his intentions.

'Please.' He chooses a word that is unlikely to be heard at the Centre, and it works. On my way out I grab a purse; after all, I am not going to let him pay for my coffee.

That's exactly what happens. I produce money, but the bartender takes Michael's and it would look silly to raise hell over it.

Besides the money is stolen.

Leaving Aunty Susan's apartment I borrowed a jacket from the many hanging in her closet. One of those black fine wool things that keep you warm and at the same time make you look classy anywhere. A jacket with a pocket. A pocket with a purse. A purse with money. It makes me a good company for Michael.

We sit at a small table and I let myself be steamed in the chocolate flavour coming out of the mug full of black coffee in front of me. He has ordered the opposite: chocolate with a coffee flavour.

I find it disarmingly childish. He is sixteen. An age that can be anything.

'About this chef training,' he starts, looking somewhere between my eyes. 'It will be good if I do it.'

'You want to hear my opinion?'

He seems enthusiastic. 'I've seen some of your TV shows, they're great! All this juggling with bottles: spices, cooking oil, vinegar, all this chopping on the board: onion, garlic, parsley—'

This *chopping* word makes me shift uneasily in my chair. After all, reformed or not, I have a killer sitting opposite me across a glass-top round table with a heavy marble ashtray.

'Well, I can share a thing or two with you, if you are so interested,' I offer reluctantly.

'It's really exciting. It's more like a game and the smells, oh, I can feel them from the TV...'

I am flattered, but I purse my lips to show I don't like to be interrupted—there is a pattern of a teacher-student relationship between us.

'...And these couple of things might hook you on the chef profession or might turn you off for good.' I allow a pause for suspense, meeting his eyes, which go inside my skull like corkscrews. I add casually, 'Honestly, I don't care either way.'

He keeps a poker face while I cross my legs under the table for more confidence before continuing.

'Statistics in the United Kingdom show that chefs are among the happiest people, along with hairdressers. The best chefs are men. Some are rumoured to be paid in gold by Arab royalties, or celebrities and socialites who know that the success of a party of any sort relies entirely on the chef. Here we finish with the good sides. Ah well, let's not forget that the French philosopher Voltaire says that the good chef is a divine creature.'

Michael doesn't know about Voltaire but is quick to say: 'The gentleman must have you in mind, Ms Cornelius.'

He looks at me with the interest of a consumer, as if he is going to eat me but has no idea how to start. I shake my hair; actually I want to shake off the persisting thought.

I might really be getting nutty.

His good eye is suddenly yellow like a burning ember among piles of smothering brackets—that's what his face looks like in the artificial light of the bar.

I start pelvic exercises in order to ground myself.

'Statistics in Australia, however, show that young people are not keen to work long hours under pressure, sizzling over hot plates and pots among overwhelming aromas that clash most of the time, like garlic, stewed cabbage and strawberries frappe. This is not a social occupation; your faithful friends would be the chopping board and the ladle. As for salary, gold comes later in life if ever. On the other hand you know that you'll never be hungry and can get titbits if you are clever and not greedy.'

I sound like a Protestant preacher, severe, lashing words stripped to the point. It's outrageous. My conscience is not holy at all.

When I sip on my coffee it's cold. Michael has finished his chocolate drink. Somehow, I feel we have reached an ice-breaking moment and I relax. I forget that he might be the author of that telephone threat back in Brisbane, that he is a physical menace to me.

That he is a killer.

I tell him that, like those artists who can paint not only what they see but also what they think and feel, in the studio of your kitchen you can express your thoughts and emotions along with your optic perceptions. Cooking is an available creativity and a rewarding one. Through preparing food like a sacred ritual you'll put power into your life, gain health and spiritual growth.

Around us the bar is quiet. Dim light, soft music, sweetish sticky bouquet of aromas coming from mixing cocktails, occasional clink of ice.

I tell Michael that salt is a natural purifier, basil a heart opener; olive oil, after the ancient symbol of the olive twig, is believed to bring peace in discordant families. Rosemary is for lasting love, passion and protection; sugar is crystals you can transfer your dreams into—many clairvoyants use sugar for their divination; tomatoes are for inspiring new love, in some parts of the world called *pommes d'amour*, love apples. Garlic is a cleansing powerhouse and a repellent for negative energies. Onion is the apple of the poor. As an 'apple' it is still considered to symbolise love, but there's something more to it; it is said that onion brings about sexual potency.

I talk again about salt, in a different aspect. In the Voodoo religion the mysterious powers of the sorcerer turn people into the living dead known as zombies, mindless creatures that hang in the narrow twilight zone between life and death. It is known that if a zombie eats salt it becomes instantly aware of its condition, with disastrous consequences. It becomes possessed with a terrible desire for revenge, killing its master and destroying his property before going in search of its grave. I've learnt all this reading Norm's poetry book *Voodoo Visions*.

'The spirit of the earth is angry and fiercely volcanic, it shivers, shakes, moans, roars, rattles, rages like Papa Legba, the god of communication between the spirits and the living. We have turned the Earth into a zombie, Michael, and now it has eaten salt and strikes back. In a place stricken by salinity, like the Australian outback, if you touch the bark of a tree, it turns into grey dust under your fingers. If you lick the dust, the taste is that of a dying light. The taste of Death. In a place eroded by salinity the trees are twisted, with stunted trunks, roots and branches, abandoned like corpses under the merciless sun.'

I see his dark face turn even darker. 'I come from Cunnamulla,' he says solemnly and I remember the name as a small town way in the Outback where drought can turn life unbearable and people have to resort to oversized beefsteaks to keep themselves happy. 'The mother earth is barren, arid, cracked and itchy; skeletons of cattle lie in the scrub, feral cats and foxes snoop on each other, roads are graveyards of run-over kangaroos. My people reach for booze or petrol to breathe.'

I am put off guard by his burning passion.

'I know,' I say, helpless to make things look prettier, at least in words. 'I've been travelling there.' The red heart of our green continent, Uluru, and Cunnamalla, her liver, processing toxins like drought and salinity. And no matter what you eat, bread or grey dust, you always incorporate it into your personality. This gives me an idea. 'By the way, Michael, what is your favourite meal?'

He shifts uncomfortably. Either he doesn't know or is shy to say it. Finally he arches his brows and smiles: 'Possum pie.'

'Possum pie?'

He nods and swallows and I realise that he might be still hungry. 'You want to eat something?'

'Not really,' he answers, but his body language tells another story. He eyes the bar stall for any sign of food, but it's not very encouraging.

We order peanuts.

A rowdy group of festival people invade the bar breaking up the intimacy of dim light and soft music.

Weariness overcomes me.

'Aren't you sleepy? You don't want Norm to be angry with me because I kept you up. It was nice talking to you.'

Then I remember to whom I am talking.

I must feel really lonely to go for a late night conversation like this. I try to challenge myself by thinking that here he is, Michael, the offspring of Aboriginal tribes that have supposedly snatched Chinese workers from the mine fields centuries ago and broken their legs so they couldn't run, handy for a meal. At least, that is what some people say.

Again I remember Cunnamulla, the liver of Australia but the arse of the world. I remember the Aboriginal community, life on the dole, physical and sexual abuse, alcohol, kids inhaling petrol, stealing fruit, girls who never reach their teens as virgins, old women collecting berries in the desert, men hunting snakes, tribal healers chasing evil spirits out of the sick. Their white and ochre-smeared dancers spell life in rhythm and music, dancers telling stories from the Dreamtime, stories about the land, their mother. A man wipes his mouth with the back of his hand and starts playing the didgeridoo. The phallic instrument sucks in his voice, whirls it around, pushing it down, turning it into bass rumbling sounds forming twenty words for sand of different consistency, colour, pelt.

I wonder when I'll get the courage to confront him about the telephone call. Instead I ask him whether he finds it interesting interpreting Hamlet.

'Yes,' says Michael, 'I know what it is having a *bitch* for a mother.'

I shiver.

'How about your father? What happened?'

He backs off as if receiving a heavyweight punch.

'He was screwing my baby sister.'

Nausea adds to tiredness.

There's nothing I can say any more to him.

He has. 'I am sorry.'

'You mean this annoying banana stuff during the last lecture?'

'Ms Cornelius, I want to tell you something. I did that call.'

'You mean *that* call?'

'Yes, Ms Cornelius.'

'Calling me dead bitch?'

He wants to tell me more but a shadow passes over his face and I am not sure whether it's grief for being nasty or a real shadow from an object or figure suddenly between two lights reflecting on him.

The moment is gone. He stops his confession the way he starts it. Abruptly. Emotionally charging, daring.

He is withdrawn again. I am shocked. His words change again the picture of the whole situation I am in. What if my dead portrait on the grave of Beethoven is another prank while I am the one visiting collectors of weird musical instruments, stirring unwanted attention to myself thanks to Jacobsen and Frank who might be using me to smoke the fox out of the hole.

'It's nothing,' I say, 'teacher-student relations are always complicated. But it's all right. It's all right, Michael.'

He nods and animation surfaces again on his face, his sun-bleached hair like a halo against the flickering lights of some musical system that starts to blast deafening decibels.

It's not all right.

Back to my room I find it ransacked and my laptop missing.

At least I have to thank my absent-mindedness. In the rush I have forgotten my precious booklet on secret cannibal societies at Aunty Susan's place. Otherwise it could have gone missing, too.

My first impulse is to run to the owner or call the police myself. Then I remember: police at this latitude means alerting Jacobsen.

I feel stupid.

Obviously Michael invited and kept me downstairs so somebody could go into my room undisturbed and get what he wanted. I want to shout, to kick the furniture, to smash the window. Instead I rush into the bathroom and fully clothed stand under a cold shower.

When I go back to the room, dripping wet, leaving puddles in my wake, there is another tap on the door.

'I am fucking sick and tired of you bloody jerks taking me for a ride!' I snap open the door brandishing the bedside lamp.

'It's not a Neptune carnival I expected for a welcome,' says Frank and I fall in his arms sobbing.

He is angry with me for leaving Aunty Susan's hotel against his will but he has no chance to express it. I muffle his words with biting kisses sautéed in tears and snots and he looks quite confused.

That makes him also quite fuckable.

NINETEEN

We don't *make* love.

We hold hands and we talk love.

It's intense. It's like ongoing orgasm, exchange of energies that rattle us, words suck on us like vampires, unearthing fresh or forgotten traumas, voicing accusations, hatred, suspicions, hopes.

Voicing love.

Love is a sound cushion we roll in naked, shameless, greedy for attention. Egos circling, eyeing each other like fighting roosters, striking with the razors attached to their feet, blood spurring everywhere.

Our voices clashing inside us.

I've been followed, Frank admits. They call it protected after my reckless escape.

I am sick of being something somewhere in other people's games, completely losing touch with my life. That's the worst: it's not *my* life anymore. It's not what I conjure, I live, I control. It's something I endure, suffer, run from.

Right now I am in Frank's arms and that's all what matters for this stolen moment of eternity or infinity. For we remember our first day in Bangkok, the Reclining Buddha, the Tiger Cave. We know that we are together because of the subtle energies generated around those spiritual shrines.

Subtle energies helped us to communicate on a different level. Three years ago we discovered each other through unsuspected dimensions of our beings.

I feel multifaceted.

My hair dries slowly and due to the air-conditioner feels cold against my shoulders. My head is well tucked in his armpit. I can't have enough of his creamy skin.

Another anonymous hotel room with impersonal furnishing. Again I wonder how many people have been here before us. How many prints of characters, destinies, words, dreams, room-service meals, passion, movie channels still linger in the corners in spite the efforts of the cleaning ladies.

There are two porno channels. Sometimes we pay for a film or two.

Not now.

We are into a more exciting thing.

We are talking cannibals.

Frank, who throws the runes for Gulliver, tells me about Jonathan Swift's *A Modest Proposal*. Written in 1729, it is a satirical pamphlet proposing that poor Irish families sell their children to be eaten, thus bringing some money into the family.

I silently wonder how Marylin's Irish blood would react to this. Perhaps in the same way as Swift's contemporaries. *A Modest Proposal* cooked a big scandal. For a moment I'd like to know whether it was bigger or smaller scandal that the one produced by Manet's *Luncheon on the Grass*.

Frank has no idea.

He gets out of the bed, sheets twisted as if ready to facilitate an escape from a high window. Opening his shoulder bag he produces four pieces of a big coconut shell, the husk stripped off, the meat scraped. Soon a half of a smaller coconut shell joins them. It's covered in white scrolls. He places it like a dome among the other pieces. A black candle appears from one of the bag's pockets. He uses the match courtesy of the hotel to light it and stick it in the ashtray close to the shells.

Mesmerised I watch him from the foot of the bed sipping on a cup of instant coffee from the courtesy basket and the electric jar on the bench.

I have an idea of Frank's occult practice. It's not the first time I've witnessed him or through him other mediums who try to go beyond cognitive receptions and establish a contact with those four-fifths of the existing matter declared invisible by the scientist.

I can hear him whispering under his breath: 'Obinu ku obinu ano obinu ofo obinu ayo.'

His torso sways while he kneels continuing to chant: 'Obinu ku obinu bia obinu tutu ana tutu.' The rhythm of his chanting faster and faster: 'Tutu ana tutu ana obinu.' He grabs the coconut shells, rubs them between his palms, then gently throws them over his shoulder. Three land on the carpet their hollow side up, the half falls on its side inside Frank's shoe, the last piece reaches the bed, hiding among the twisted sheets. When we discover it it's lying with its humped back up.

Frank doesn't talk but keeps looking at the configuration and the position of each piece, mumbling something.

Quite suddenly he interrupts his occupation, collects the pieces and goes back to the candle. He quickly smudges the pieces over it then blows it out.

'You can now read what the Coconut Oracle had to say,' he turns to me handing me a small notebook out of the pocket of his jacket.

I take the notebook and open it. It contains drawings and descriptions of possible positions of the shells after being thrown and their interpretations as an answer to unspoken questions. I have difficulty finding a description of a similar outlay as the one in front of us. Frank finds it. When I want to read it he pulls the notebook away from me, a grimace of disquiet on his face. I have to wait until he uses the bathroom. My photographic memory is not bad and I soon find the page he silently read from.

Death. Stop consulting the shells, rinse them in river water.

If this is the answer I wonder what the question is that Frank has asked. He wouldn't tell me, of course. At least I don't see any similarities between a Coconut Oracle and a plainclothes cop like Jacobsen.

When he returns we resume our talk about cannibals. I idly mention the Bible and the story about the two women making a pact to eat their children during the siege of Samaria. Then we go into a lengthy discussion about bread and wine transubstantiated into the real flesh and blood of Jesus. I recite: 'While they were eating he took a loaf of bread, and after blessing it he broke it, gave it to them, and said, "Take it; this is my body."

That what Frank does. He takes my body.

We make love and I drink. A white blood drink. Cannibalistic.

A drink you can also have after cutting the eyes of the coconut.

A fruit, a one-seeded drupe. A renowned sailor travelling from island to island, from coastline to another, making friends with the cool sea water, storms, tide waves, eruptions, preserving its embryo for a coconut palm known on every continent as a tree you should be careful about. The *stone* of this drupe has eyes. The shell has two dark spots that make it look like a skull with hollow eye-sockets.

Coconut milk is not the juice found inside the shell. It's a derivate from the cream made from the grated white part.

My mind conjures up jumbled images of me scooping coconut milk from a can, mixing it with sweet chilli sauce, fish sauce and lime juice, leaving it to boil while cutting a nice butter pumpkin in small cubes. The orange colour, the slimy seeds. I usually don't peel the pumpkin and since I don't like coriander much, I decorate with fresh chives.

Suddenly I miss my culinary activities. Leaving without any notice is not good in the TV business. It's true the crew has a break between series of shows. Still, they always need me for the script. For cooking is like jazz. Improvisation is the main ingredient.

Lecturing, cooking classes, magazine columns, occasional articles, my book, all jeopardized. I can't afford it.

I simply can't. Even over existentialistic reasons.

Frank comes from money.

His mother has a big farm in Loeten, somewhere near Lillehamer. He can spend as much time as he likes on doing nothing. Ah well, I am not sure; he might be on a payroll with Jacobsen, too.

It's his business.

My business, though, is sinking. I have to earn my money to pay my bills. In a way it's a good motivation on the road to success. I realize how lucky I've been.

'Frank,' I say rubbing more nutmeg scent behind my ears. 'Please, help me to meet the Nigerian refugee. Actually I should have been in Oslo right now looking for him if it wasn't for that culinary haiku-riddle you left for me in Lugano to suggest that we meet in secret here when this control freak Jacobsen...'

'What riddle? What are you saying, Sandy?'

'When this control freak Jacobsen...'

'Stop for a moment. I don't follow.' He has started shaving himself and now stands there his face half foamed in white like those funny birthday cakes ordered half lemon cheese, half meringue.

That's what I like about him most. Frank would shave himself in the middle of the night for me. And he would never ever consider composing weird riddles.

But then who wanted me in Elsinore?

TWENTY

I wake up the next morning to hear Frank talking on the phone in Norwegian. That's dent in my ego, but there's not much I can do.

We go to the same restaurant for breakfast. I am ready to order an ox-tail soup, but Frank gives me a surprised look so I choose a continental, which usually I can't stand. The coffee is something muddy, hot enough to burn all my taste buds and thus put them under anaesthetic. I sip on it sparingly while waiting for the breakfast and fantasize about café latte. The *latte* or the milk is what makes or breaks it. Organic, non-homogenised, full-cream milk, warmed under boiling point, mixed with sugar, preferably raw cane.

The breakfast arrives. Bread, butter and strawberry jam with a cup of black tea. Hot for Frank, cold for me. If I drink a hot tea in the morning I feel sleepy afterwards. It might have something to do with my low blood pressure.

The owner, the same plump, motherly lady, is serving us with increased politeness, which I attribute to Frank addressing her in her own language.

Soon we are outside and I notice with relief that the weather is passable. No sign of rain. This, however, is not enough to improve my mood. I miss my laptop and Frank promises to buy me another one, but I want my files too.

'That's what they are after,' says Frank. 'Your files.'

As if I don't know. I still feel devastated but try to put on a brave face.

There's still time before the opening of the festival where Frank will accompany me so we can applaud the performance staged by Norm and his weird Hamlet boy, number one suspect on my list for the theft. There's no need to report it to the police. Frank has informed Jacobsen. Jacobsen, the Polar bear, the king of these Northern latitudes.

'I'll show you around,' says Frank, as if we are here on one of our usual sex tourism adventures.

He takes me for a drive along the coast. Chalk white cliffs rise vertically from the sea and fall onto us or at least that's the impression. A shock from an almost palatable massive crash from above cleanses me. The feeling of an immediate physical danger pushes away from my paranoiac fears of unknown nemesis I have to fight or flee from. Somehow the feeling is not unlike the one I had in front of the cathedral in Cologne.

I look up. The cliffs are over a hundred meters high crowned with trees, a green ribbon to seal them off from the sky. I feel dizzy and fall in Frank's arms.

'It's all right, it's all right.' He rocks me gently against his body of a Viking while I cry at the thought that even in his arms I am alone with no one to call me their first and only priority in life. That unique feeling I had only with my mother Margherita, and perhaps I could have had it with my unknown father. Now I have to pretend I am happy to be self-sufficient, self-contained. That silly woman Sandy Cornelius being my one and only priority in life.

The princess is a pretty little thing. I admire her delicacy and way of being royal without being imposing or looking stuffed.

She speaks perfect Danish according to Frank and uses all her charm to turn the routine opening ceremony of the Hamlet Festival into a cosy, guild-family thing.

People like her.

We wait for the first performance, the Australian one with Norm and Michael. I still don't know what to make out of my conversation with the controversial young man.

I look around.

We are in the cobblestone yard of the Elsinore castle, sitting on cushions in circular rows. There's no stage, just an empty space in the middle.

I remember my scary experience with taking the photo of the young Japanese couple and shiver.

The Kronborg castle looks sombre—a blow-up of Pandora's box. Holger Danske, the warrior who sleeps underground in the labyrinth, is supposed to wake if an enemy attacks Denmark, but who will protect me if an enemy strikes?

I push myself against Frank's warm body. He's always like a heater even in a cold weather. I close my eyes and try to relax, to no avail. The words of Hamlet burn my mind: *now could I drink hot blood*.

The art of drinking to quench the thirst caused by too much salted herring. The daily portion of wine for the nuns once here was three litres and for the solders, five. Not bad.

A presenter comes forward to make an announcement. The Australian performance of *Hamlet* has been taken off the programme. He doesn't specify why. Instead he announces a theatrical group from Gotteborg with 'Being Gay Hamlet's Way.'

Frank and I exchange glances and leave the venue. Frank tries to contact the organisers and see what's happening. Somebody suggests that we contact the police.

I freak out. 'The police? Why the police?'

Nobody knows the answer.

Frank takes me to the police station in his hired car. We find Norm crying, nervously flapping with his moth-like eyes.

'Michael,' he howls, getting up to embrace me, then collapses back into his chair with uncontrolled sobs.

An officer explains.

A road patrol has found Michael in the early hours of the morning, his bike smashed against the trunk of a tree. Michael was declared dead by the paramedics called to the scene. The backward prognosis is that he had died instantaneously.

My brain is like scrambled eggs.

I don't know what to think. I don't know what to feel. I want to hate Michael for luring me away from my room in the night but I can't. I want to be suspicious about Norm because he could have been the one ransacking my room, but I can't.

I stand there feeling empty. After all, Michael was just a boy curious about a universal profession in order to build up a future and bring pride to his people. I forget to worry about myself, seeing death hit so close.

Someone has to identify Michael. We have to go to the morgue. We take Frank's car and Norm holds my hand, reaching out from the back seat.

Frank is not happy of this display of what he takes for intimacy. I don't give a shit. Norm and I, we are part of a pack of dingoes and we go by our own rules.

At the morgue they make us wait. A lady in a white coat comes and invites us to follow her. We enter the autopsy theatre and Norm identifies Michael.

'There's something that perhaps you should know.' She addresses Frank, obviously aware of his position as a hot link between the police and us. 'The boy's heart is missing.' She waits for us to sink in the bombshell before throwing the next. 'There's no wound or incision on his body suggesting how the heart has been removed.'

I look at the stranger on the gurney. A shell, a body of what has been Michael. The difference between life and death is simple: a bolt of energy has shot out, leaving behind the ballast. Unlike what Dr Nicholas tried to tell me.

At least I know Michael's favourite meal.

Possum pie.

TWENTY-ONE

We leave Norm still sobbing.

I worry over his immediate future in connection with Michael's death. Back in Australia Norm might face serious charges for neglecting his responsibilities as a supervisor, mentor or whatever he appears to be in this strange theatrical tandem miles away from the Centre.

To me it's more than obvious Michael was killed first, then the accident set up; but Jacobsen and the like need proof and let the investigation take its normal course.

Yes, Jacobsen. He's here, contacted by Frank, and Frank sides with him, forgetting all about me. They talk in half tones, exchanging words and phrases that should mean something more than the usual semantic load. At least they do it in English, acknowledging I am there, so I don't feel excluded.

My impatience grows by the minute.

I have had enough of being pushed around when it comes to my own life and now to the life of people around me. I know that Michael's killing is connected with me and the situation of threat and persecution I am in.

But Jacobsen needs proof. I find him quite strange actually. That is he is normal. Nothing of the features of your usual cranky cop dwelling books and movies. Jacobsen's language is not dirty as if he has mopped the streets of Calcutta with it, nor his clothes have shrunk on him after a night of chasing drug killers in pouring rain. He hasn't got stooping shoulders, drooping eye-lids, bad breath, dysfunctional family, secret AA meetings. He is not delusional, paranoiac, he hasn't got GSOH expressed by calling his partner *a shit up to its neck in the dung*. Jaobsen hasn't got bad habits like eating junk food while cruising the streets or pissing in kids' sand pits, nor has he been unjustly removed from his favourite job to scare people with his gun so he is not motivated to prove himself at any cost; he doesn't behave recklessly putting on the line his life and the lives of those around him. He doesn't believe in the existence of a universal conspiracy against him nor is he the best cop among all backyard jazz musicians and, note, chefs.

When I discussed this once with Frank, though, I was surprised to know that Jacobsen is interested in archaeology and spends his holidays scratching with a spoon for delicate digging works on sites in progress.

'You mean that funny science that gets a hard-on at the sight of an inch-sized piece of a plate that's been broken against the head of some neolith man who failed to provide?' I knew that Jacobsen couldn't be clean and not hide shameful facts about himself.

So now he doesn't impress me when he says, 'Before we jump to conclusions, Ms Cornelius, we need to investigate what and who caused Michael's death. Let the forensics do their job first. Frank will explain to you perhaps what track we want to follow here.'

'Frank is not my nanny,' I snap and they exchange glances over me. Frank remains cool as a cucumber.

That's what annoys me most about him. Composed, classy (needless to say he would never consider cookbook writing as an option), smooth, a fly will slip down from his façade of Mr Imperturbable. Letting me be the one emotional, irritated, profane, consumed by outbursts of anger and frustration.

Jacobsen matches him. Bastards. I wonder if I could marinate them for twenty-four hours, whether they'd lose some of their toughness.

'Well, Ms Cornelius, I didn't raise the question of your violations of the orders I prescribed. We had an appointment, hadn't we? Three o'clock that afternoon in Lugano. You should be in hiding by now, not strolling the streets of a town where every second man is disguised as Hamlet and sporting a dagger.' Jacobsen is nasty. Surprise, surprise. He can be even nastier. 'By disappearing you have jeopardised our operation and probably facilitated the death of the poor boy.'

'So you admit that it's linked!' I am like an eagle, all over him, hoping to peck out his eyes if not his fleshy ears. Bing Crosby allegedly said once that his ears made him look like a taxi with both front doors open. Jacobson is not far off.

He says nothing in response and leaves us to attend a telephone call.

Frank takes over.

'This time I am not taking my eyes off you, Sandy. I have to escort you in the car that is due any moment. And be with you as your personal guard while things cool down and Jacobsen scores some progress.'

Progress, shit. I am fed up with orders meant to immobilise me.

Who is Jacobsen to give me orders anyway? Who is that hunky man standing by me right now, talking seductively to me? I think of him as a foxy married man out for a sex spree that costs him nothing, all expenses paid by the secret services he obviously is involved with.

'How about taking me to the Nigerian refugee? You promised!'

'I've never made such a promise!' He gives me a bad eye.

'I'll tell Jacobsen that you promised.'

'You're irresistible when you are angry. It's amazing how irresistible you are at all times. I am looking forward to be with you, believe me. We are together in this.'

I give Frank a smile with a tag: 'I can't wait.'

He pats me on the shoulder. His tag reads, 'I know how to make my woman happy.'

I touch his arm. 'I'll quickly go to the ladies. I am not used to drinking tea.'

'Sure. I'll wait for you with a cup of good coffee.'

He must be mad to think he can find good coffee in a police station. But it makes my task easier.

I head for the toilets, called thunderboxes by some authentic Aussies. Thank God, they are always situated at the end of a corridor not much in use. I take off my trench coat revealing black tights and a pullover. I bless my taste for black. Does it have to do with hanging out with Tamati? Or it's perhaps the idea that black makes me look slimmer? Whatever, it pays off in an unexpected way.

I tuck my hair under a small shawl I have tucked into the pocket in my trench coat. Next I wipe out my lipstick and smear a blotch of concealer over my face.

What was it that Jacobsen said about every second man in this town right now walking around disguised like Hamlet? I walk right out the front door of the station without anybody noticing me.

I put a good ten minutes between me and Frank, and Jacobsen, of course. I presume they'll look for me at ferry ports, bus and train stations; they'll stop cars although they have no legitimate right to do so.

I am not a criminal.

I run from criminals. Or perhaps getting high on danger, I am on a hunt for criminals. Poor reckless Sandy!

For Jacobsen, though, I am only a segment they need to put their puzzle right.

Now that I am saturated with Frank I can afford to hate him. I leave him, hopefully for good. And she who leaves takes the energy along; that's why no one wants to be dumped.

Eh well, Frank Magnar Syversen, *I* have dumped you.

I return to the castle where the festival is in full swing. I find a cushion to sit on and watch the old game of killing and getting killed played by people of all colours and cultural traditions.

Here I am as safe as I can get.

I wait for the night.

There's no sign of Frank, or of Jacobsen. They both try to reach me on my cell phone but I don't answer. The only thing I read is a message from Tamati asking me how I am doing. 'Can't be better.' I text back to him.

When I get hungry, I snitch a McDonald's burger. My reputation as a kitchen goddess is again on the line with the burger in my mouth but who cares. Janette is not around to take a compromising footage of me. Perhaps she is still in Fiji eating cassava and coconut chutney. I remember her advice for tightening up my facial muscles. Ah well, bad luck, I am not seeing Frank any more.

I wonder whether Janette would know that, *The reports of my death are greatly exaggerated*, as Mark Twain would say.

Munching on the burger, I think of cooking a possum pie. For filling: a farmed possum, can be from Tasmania, cut in pieces, left to boil with celery, onion, bush resins, salt bush, tomatoes. I can use it one day as a ritual to call the spirit of Michael.

And it appears. Right then.

I give away a scream of terror.

Michael's spirit snarls at me. The last thing I see is a dagger pointed at my throat.

I slowly regain senses. Someone sprinkles cold water on me, another slaps me gently on both cheeks.

'Too much forbidden sex,' says a Shakespeare, an actor dressed as the ancient bard. I remember him as one of the rowdy group that came late into the hotel bar where I was in what might have looked a cosy if not intimate chat with Michael.

Michael! The boy's death takes toll on my nerves. He wanted to tell me more about this telephone threat. Now something important has been lost with him. Perhaps an important clue or even name. I blame myself for not being more persistent. But then I am not the pushy type.

I look around.

On the improvised stage Hamlet is a front man who has LSD induced visions of killing his mother and sodomizing his uncle. The actor is damn good with the electrical guitar.

The audience likes it.

There's no one with the slightest resemblance to Michael.

I feel weak, my heart barely pumps.

For a moment I consider going back to Frank.

Then I imagine the triumphant face of Jacobsen and the things he is ready to put me through in order to secure my safety. The thought is enough to put me in gear.

TWENTY-TWO

A friendly Bulgarian group of actors agrees to help me reach Copenhagen. They haven't got money to sleep in a motel, so they travel at night and occasionally park their old rattling minibus off the road when they need some sleep.

I like their interpretation of Hamlet as a pawn in the hands of invisible forces; there's lots of magic and spiritual séances to suggest the idea that no one is in control of their fate.

The Bulgarians make their Hamlet dance over fire, and it's for real. They bring a bucket of burning embers and the actor gives a performance that sends the public raving for half an hour. The actress playing both Gertrude and Ophelia changes her 14C bra to show which character she's playing. It's a metal mesh bra for Gertrude and white lace for Ophelia.

I give them some money, no guilty conscious there by now, and they all kiss me because they say they haven't eaten a proper meal for days.

Soon they return with a chicken dinner from the *Colonel*—my second fast food meal in a row. I feel appalled with myself, yet I gobble some spicy wings.

The kids love the meal and I hardly see any bones left. We all burp happily and top it off with a complimentary cheese cake.

A real *proper* meal.

Other people have different ideas about what a proper meal is, though. *The body was cooked, as pigs now are, in an oven specially set apart, red-hot basaltic stones, wrapped in leaves, being placed inside to insure its being equally done. The best joint was the thigh.* That's a cannibal recipe reported by the pioneering missionary William Wyatt Gill.

The Bulgarian actors are a nice bunch and I promise to do something to get them to Australia. They ask me whether they'd see crocodiles in the streets. I don't promise.

We spend half of the night crumpled over each other in the narrow space of the minibus, keeping each other warm. Impersonal, healing human warmth.

Gratitude overwhelms me. I pay the thespians with a story remembering the story of Hamlet directing the actors into performing the scene of the usurper administering poison into the ear of Hamlet's father.

During the story I keep repeating Frank's name, which is a bonus. I even imagine I am talking to him.

Amore mio.

Rome was another of our sex-tourism escapes.

Rome, founded by two brothers who had suckled the she-wolf, hence were not cannibals.

Frnak gave me coins and I threw them in the *Fontana di Trevi* over my shoulder. A spell for returning back to Rome.

Rome.

Rich, vibrant, sensual, surprising, nutritious for mind, spirit, soul, body, name it. Frank took me to *Piazza di Spagna* and I had my portrait drawn by a street artist waiting in ambush for passing gullible visitors. I kept the portrait although I didn't like it.

Frank and I spent an afternoon with a prima ballerina, a friend of Frank's at the famous cafe *San Eustachio,* notorious for its espresso: short, strong, kick in the mouth with fantastic aroma. The Lamborghini of the coffee world.

Frank ordered coffee and *gelato,* the ballerina kept talking as if in need of compensating for her silent art. We heard the story of the English ballerina Alicia Marks, who changed her name to Markova after joining the Diaghilev's *Ballet Russes*. 'The best interpreter of *Giselle*.'

The coffee was so good it was a crime to drink it.

Frank looked at my portrait made by the street artist.

'I've always thought of you as beautiful, Sandy, but artists know better. Perhaps he has drawn your inner portrait, he made you look like a witch.' He was happy to make the ballerina laugh.

'What are you thinking about?' The Bulgarian girl playing Ophelia and Gertrude by changing bras is looking at me attentively.

I am still on this Rome-Frank wave, so I tell her about my favourite pasta. *Pasta puttanesca* is something unique to Italian cuisine. I haven't heard of another dish named likewise in any other culinary culture. *The whore pasta*, the literal translation, is made of olive oil, olives, anchovies, garlic sauce and pasta. The pasta should be *al dente,* which doesn't mean toothy, but just little bit on the harder side. I love *pasta puttanesca*, I might as well have been a night priestess or a sexual slave in a harem, or travelled around with the Mongolian army of Genghis Khan to entertain his generals and keep their beds warm in the severe night cold of the Gobi Desert. Or perhaps I've been a hetera in Ancient Greece, choosing my own lovers.

The girl continues listening to me. There's something sisterly about how we click and share things. There's something of Marylin in her. I show her a copy of the portrait of me inside my mother. Also a photo of Brisbane, with Everton Heights covered in a mauve-lilac carpet, so beautiful and unreal when the jacaranda trees start to shed their blossoms.

There's no city like Brisbane, I tell the girl, where the sun shines 360 days out of 365 only to witness the marathon coitus of the river and the ocean. I miss Brisbane the way I miss my mother.

I don't have a photo of Frank. I have a picture of Jesus, though, a detail from the Tintoreto's *Last Supper* where Jesus quite aggressively offers his body and blood, in the form of bread and wine, to his disciples. The miracle of Eucharist—the transubstantiation of earthly into divine food. I am happy to know that it's easy, so easy, to turn divine into earthly food.

The girl gets excited. 'If Jesus was around he would have said to his gang, "Give yourselves the needle with my blood, it's the best quality heroin you can lay your hands on, sniff and lick on my flesh, it's the purest cocaine you can find, getting high will make you stand close to me, you rotting pricks."'

Early in the morning they leave me at the outskirts of Copenhagen, giving me a padded waistcoat belonging to Polonius. It has holes from Hamlet's dagger but protects me against the cold and the famous wind of this flat landscape, a wind that makes old grannies grasp at street trees for balance.

It's nice of the Bulgarians, since I can't use my credit card out of fear of being tracked down and I am starting to run out of my found-not-reported cash.

For a moment I fight a bout of depression. It will be a long journey.

TWENTY-THREE

Soon I am doing well in Copenhagen, even manage to find a better gender for myself.

Never Mind is a club on Norre Voldgade 2. It's a friendly joint, full of gay men with a dash of lesbian and transgender folk. That's what I need: to lose myself in the brother/sisterhood of a minority well known as highly protective of its members.

It's not easy when you are an endowed female specimen, but I follow Shakespeare's lead in *Twelfth Night*; it's one of his favourite deceiving modes.

I go into the *Rainbow Hotel* and lock myself in the ladies. I put on a wig: dishevelled short black locks with purple highlights.

Looking in the mirror, I start to enjoy using disguise. Where is Marylin to call me *a promiscuous bitch under cover of a cookbook writer*.

Cookbook writer? Sounds familiar. When was it?

With the help of toilet paper I accentuate my boobs in a way that they look absolutely artificial. If I don't shave my legs for a couple of days and wear fishnet stockings I'll be taken for the real thing. I can't grow stubble, but I can use some greyish shade on my lower face so the effect will be that of makeup plastered over stubble.

When I finally emerge from the ladies the receptionist gives me a popping-eyes look. I am wearing a bright yellow pair of shorts, black stockings, high-heeled shoes and an orange-red blouse that shows off a Pamela Anderson's chest. All the gear has been previously purchased in a cheap-o shop.

I hope I am not overdoing it. My sporadic visits to Sydney's Mardi Gras might pay off. Marylin would usually drag me there, saying it's better than a Rio de Janeiro carnival, and I have to agree perhaps because I've never been to a carnival in Rio. Attending Sydney's Mardi Gras for Marylin is also a question of expression of liberty, for me it's just good time, lot's of costumes and colours, decadent conversations, plenty of sex facets to relate mine to. My, how did I call it, subwaysexuality. Once there Marylin is more drawn to the lesbian lot while I cruise and feel at home everywhere, my favourites the travesties.

I hail a taxi and order in a mixture of perfect Italian and broken English to be taken to *Never Mind*. The taxi driver is not surprised by the destination. He drops me there and wishes me good luck, giving me a wink.

I don't give him a tip so he takes his wink back, so to speak.

I feel at home in the joint. The smells coming from the kitchen could make a hard-fasting hermit sin and break his one-to-one prayer-talk with God.

I talk Italian, repeat things in broken German and finally in even more broken English. I speak perfect Italian thanks to my mother who, coming from the Italian-speaking part of Switzerland and being into music, made me learn the language. These days it comes in handy. As it is for opera singers, Italian is a compulsory language for culinary gurus. Some will say French, others Greek or Chinese, even Japanese, since Okinawa is the place with most centagenarians per capita on earth. It goes that their centagenarians look like people in their seventies.

It's hard to continue with my culinary linguistic gerontologist pondering, not only because my meal arrives, but also because there a quite a few fellows making signs to me. Among them there are some young oldies, too. Good lean muscles, flat tummies, good tan, black leather trousers and vests (I might suggest Frank to buy himself such an outfit, I find it extremely sexy), an impressive chain around their necks or a massive bracelet either in gold or in sterling silver. That's all they wear along with sexy boots and a matching belt. Slick hair, faces well groomed, the wrinkles more like tribal decoration that signs of old age. For a moment I have the weird feeling that I might meet Uncle Willie here and reveal another streak of his secret life. Thanks God, that's not the case.

Some of the fellows get aggressive and I think that it was easier to get away from the iron grip of Tamati.

Here I have to pretend I play along. The atmosphere, however, is cosy, predisposing and friendly. I soak in it. Having a thing about transvestites I chat one up and buy him/her a drink. He says his name is Fernando, Brazilian, something I already suspected, given his shameless beauty, black ropy hair, long in a ponytail, skin the colour of a Milo drink with a bit too much whipped cream in it, grey eyes perched on high cheekbones, legs out of a stocking commercial, great arse. Ah well, he also complimented mine adding that it's just a friendly observation. Back home in Brazil Fernando is *normal* with a girlfriend. It's just that he's working to afford a wedding and a house.

Introducing myself as Sandy, after all I am not here a hundred percent phoney, I feel like on a blind date. I know that there should be something, yet I have no idea what to expect. My overdeveloped hearing (Marylin says I could hear grasshoppers mating from miles) rewards me with a cut from a brisk conversation between Frank and Jacobsen in the station. Jacobsen was telling Frank that they had secured surveillance on this *Never Mind* joint following a signal that it's been frequented by a suspect related to the cannibal case.

Fernando and I watch the 'girls' dancing around the pole on the stage. After all, it's not a cooking show. I wonder whether Beverley and I could qualify for pole-dancers despite Marylin's opinion on the matter. Fernando tells me the names of the *artists* while I start to ponder on a next culinary, less dangerous manuscript titled *Discovered by Captain Cook*, only to remember that allegedly he was also cooked and eaten by certain natives.

'That's the only luxury I allowed myself,' my new friend says showing me a massive golden chain bracelet with *Fernando* inscribed on a plate along the chain. 'I save everything.'

'How about this, Fernando?' I am mesmerised by a big blood-coloured ruby imbedded in 22-carat gold ring he wears on his little finger.

'Here I am Nanda,' whispers Fernando, 'and this ring is a gift from a very rich client.'

'Would I know him?' I start to congratulate myself for deciding to come here.

'No way,' answers Fernando. 'He is not a regular and he wouldn't show himself around here for months.'

'Sounds interesting.'

'Yes, it actually is. His profession is well, kind of weird.'

'You think so?' Looking around it's hard for me to believe that there could be heaps of professions more weird than those of nice blokes polishing metal poles, penises hanging like panting dogs' tongues, arses like sea anemones. Seductive dancing bodies for the entertainment of other blokes as if we are back to the time of the Druids when women were cut out of that in-and-out fun. 'They (men) longed instead for the embrace of one of their own sex, lying on animal skins and tumbling around with a lover on each side.' As one historian wrote.

Reminding myself that I am kind of a man right now, I return some wet looks to a couple of admirers. 'What do you mean weird?' I also remind Fernando that he hasn't explained himself.

'He is into musical instruments.' He makes a pause. 'Musical instruments made of...'

'Human bones.' I finish shooting at random.

Fernando spills his drink and abruptly backs off.

'Why should you say so? It's not what you think.'

'What you think I think, Fernando?'

'Nanda, please.' He offers the next drink and looks like he wants to talk with me but is not in a hurry to start. I let him take his time, which later I would consider a huge mistake.

Continuing to admire his physical beauty I take mental notes on a future class in cooking as part of anthropology. I am not kidding. Looking at Fernando, I know that he hasn't been raised on dishes like Chicken Kiev or cucumber soups. His exquisite beauty incorporating long limbs, lean muscles, unexpected facial features and dripping sensuality is vastly based on samba cuisine, a mix of bean protein, occasional starvation, manioc, churrasco—the wood fire grilled meats, long grain rice sautéed in garlic, cheese cakes, bolinhos de bakalhau (codfish balls).

My greedy eyes can't have enough of Fernando's beauty nor of his jewellery. I almost start to weight my chances if I stay with Fernando/Nanda in this business, when he leans over to me and says softly: 'I feel you are a *real* woman, Sandy and beautiful at that. Don't know what your game is but don't make a wrong move, there are lots of hysterics going on here.'

Not knowing whether I should be happy or sad, I prefer to remain silent. He obviously doesn't want to answer my question and I don't want to push him.

Fernando produces a long brown cigarette and a loosely made sachet. He lights the cigarette without offering me one and drags a long lungful of it. Next he mixes the powder contents of the sachet with his drink and sips on it.

'You said you save everything, how about this?' I point at the sachet. 'Don't tell me it's another present.'

'I have my own cheap ways,' Fernando says enigmatically and I start to dislike him. 'I crack up if you crack up and tell me why are you here. I can smell cunt from miles, you don't deceive me.'

'A writer,' I say. 'A cookbook writer. Need some characters to go with *proscutto con melone, deer with rosemary and honey, truffles with sauce of wild pears*, *tea salad*, *swallow's nests,* the usual.'

He likes it. He chuckles and his chuckle comes soaked in fragrant phlegm specked with carnival flamboyance. 'You kill me. A cookbook writer? I always thought of them being double-chinned fat grannies brandishing ladles.'

My genuine laughter wraps around his words. I tell him how once stranded with my TV producer and the cameraman on a tiny island east of Belize, we were met by an enormous Negro woman, almost twice the size of the island, its owner and only inhabitant. She cooked for us black beans and rice, occasionally lobsters, the white delicious meat with tender fibre melting in its own red crustacean pot.

'Yes,' I say. 'She was that type of a cook that gives you more than meal, gives you back a childhood and wards off death for you.'

'Have you got a website where I can learn more about you?'

Of course, I have one created what Janette van Haren has in mind how it should be: a filed of sliced ripe figs as a background and then me naked down to my waist, for breasts two drawers with knobs and signs *spices*. Janette didn't even want to put my book titles. She said it would be enough to generate impressive amount of hits and make our show *Kitchen Goddess* popular. She was right.

'No, I haven't got one,' I say to Fernando blushing. 'Perhaps one day when I become popular.'

'You kind of do look familiar to me,' he gives me a scrutinising glance, drags another powerful puff from the cigarette and finishes his drink.

'Perhaps I have something Brazilian in me,' Flirting at a free fall speed. 'I've drunk so much Brazilian coffee, that it has become the better part of my blood.'

'You need a transfusion?' He orders two Brazilian black and turns back to me. 'We'll drink it like two real sloths.' Then he tells me how coffee first reached Brazil and the story of a man in love a certain Lieutenant Colonel Fransisco de Melo Palheta who returned from French Guiana with a bouquet from his lover in which cuttings and fertile coffee seeds were hidden.

'I like you,' says Fernando. 'Why don't you come again tomorrow night. I might have something equally exciting for you.'

Wrapping myself in the familiar aroma of wildness, a real aficionado I drink my coffee like a death-bed wish.

TWENTY-FOUR

The sky is acting like someone with a prostate problem: pouring, pause, drizzling, pause, dripping, pouring, pause. The sky should be put on a diet of pumpkin seeds. The winds are at bay, though, so I am having a stroll along the city.

Copenhagen is not only the Little Mermaid, *den lille Havfrue*, in the Castellet Park by the harbour. Yet it attracts me like a magnet. Perhaps the macabre history of this petit bronze sculpture makes me feel it as a sister in fate. Nearly. Hans Christian Andersen's fairy tale says about a little mermaid who came out of the depths of the sea because she was in love with a prince but the bastard didn't return her love and she went back to her sea, leaving this wonderful world of humans. Ah well, also of cannibals. In April 1964 the mermaid's head was sawn off and the whole of Copenhagen was in shock. I wonder who will mourn me if *they* do get my head? Anyway, the old moulds had been preserved and it was a happy ending because the little one got herself a new head. It won't be the case, I think sadly, if something similar happens to me.

Through my profession of a chef I have learnt that little gastronomic joys consumed daily can keep me happy, so I try to taste Copenhagen. There is something elusive about the city, like in an Indian coffee with aromatic wood notes and a whiff of bitter walnut tones. Or like a metaphor in a clumsy translation of a Pablo Neruda poem, as Norm would say if he was not still in the shit I left him in.

Copenhagen is life sizzling with vitality, café culture and strange, defiantly protected concepts of individual liberty and social comfort. A city where I would love to live if I ever get sick of sunny Brisbane. Copenhagen has the ability to make your spirit feel at ease on all levels; it's neither big nor small and travels with the flow of modern life like an inspiring Heraklite river.

The famous hippy enclave Christiania is kind of an equivalent of the Australian town of Nimban where a colony of *different* people have embraced hemp culture, non-violence attitude, nature-friendly life, freedom to have goals outside of making money. They are a bit passé for me. A passive contemplating style of existence? Not for me.

I manage to find a cheap hotel not far from the statue of Andersen, Hans Christian, that is. I am trying to save as much money as I can; I dread that Aunty Susan has realized about her missing jacket with the purse.

I do feel uneasy.

Andersen is considered the Danish Shakespeare and the country's best export product. Every kid has grown up with his fairy tales: *Thumbelina, The Princess and the Pea, The Little Mermaid, The Ugly Ducking, The Little Match Girl* and my all time favourite, *The Emperor's New Clothes.*

Though he is a household name all over the world, few people know about his ambiguous sexual preferences. Sometimes I think it's really sad that Lewis Carrol was a sleazy paedophile, the brothers Grimm cheap cannibalistic propagandists, and Hans Christian Andersen a visitor of red-light districts and dukes' bedchambers.

To put Michael out of my mind is hard. And I can't wait for my next step to discover the Nigerian refugee in Oslo and hopefully have some first-hand information about the cult or at least about one of its branches. Yet I promise Fernando to meet him again tonight trusting my gut instinct that there will be something worth the sacrifice of another day.

The Museum Erotica is a famous venue offering a rich sophisticated collection of erotic paintings, films, and magazines as well as photos and postcards.

I am its first visitor for the day, followed by many more.

Swimming in familiar waters, I relax. The Museum is far more than an institutionalised adult shop. It makes you feel you are out on a cultural expedition not a voyeuristic one.

I stand in front of a blow-up of three Hollywood legends exuding sex appeal to kill. It's Humphrey Bogart sandwiched between his wife Loren Bacall and Marilyn Monroe. The photo is extremely interesting in how it shows Bogart ogling Marilyn's cleavage. Mankind sometimes produces a specimen to die for.

I feel someone standing too close behind me, breathing down my neck. I don't turn immediately. There are lots of people around me by now, so it might be innocent. Somehow I know it's not. I take a quick step backwards and my heel goes right into a foot.

'Ow, shit!'

A man's voice, throaty, educated, like silk velvet with golden threads, smooth and scratchy at the same time. And familiar.

Uncle Willie!

'Sorry,' he says, his eyes still on the blow-up. There's envy for Bogart in those eyes.

Filthy old man! I want to shout at him, because that's exactly what his intentions are. But my relief to see someone so close, a family member, is so big that it drowns my indignation.

'Uncle Willie,' I exclaim instead and slide my hand under his arm.

'Sandy! You look terrific! What are you doing here?'

'What are *you* doing here?' Again I resort to one of the postulates in the Chinese tract *Art of War*. The only disturbing thing is that I am falling in a pattern of asking back *this* question.

'Having a break, what you think? Women your age can be quite exhausting.' He is referring to his girlfriend Lilly. 'As you know I am not one bit interested in this sort of thing. Have you been to the Rick's Cafe?'

'Rick's Cafe? The one from the movie *Casablanca*?'

It's Uncle Willie's all time favourite flick; he must have seen it hundreds of times, ten of these hundreds times with me in his company. He says that one movie is enough for such a short time as a life span.

Now he takes me by the hand and leads me along to a small staircase. To the right there is a corner reconstructed as the *Rick's Cafe* with Ingrid Bergman and Humphrey Bogart discussing their doomed love affair, and Sam, the Negro piano player ready to sing their favourite song.

Uncle Willie pushes a button and the show starts.

'Play it again, Sam,' says Ingrid in her casual voice, loaded with nicotine and love nostalgia. A line which isn't actually in the movie.

Sam sings: *'A kiss is just a kiss...'*

Uncle Willie is mesmerised. He stands quietly, then takes me in his arms and leads me in a dance on the landing of the staircase, pulling me close to him.

I submit to his impulsive behaviour, feeling protected, wrapped in him. It's like being home.

We dance to the song that has nourished the decadent feeling of post-war generations.

Uncle Willie hums the tune in my ear.

Soon I hear people giving us a round of applause. Forming a circle up the steps we are blocking, they don't show impatience.

The magic, however, is broken and Uncle Willie whisks me away and out of the museum.

TWENTY-FIVE

Uncle Willie doesn't read papers so he doesn't know he is treating a ghost in a friendly joint near Charlottenborg, a seventeenth century baroque palace housing the Royal Academy of Arts. I don't realise how hungry I am until I wolf down the sausages I've ordered. Uncle Willie watches me fascinated; he likes any display of appetite.

'You are a healthy little thing,' he comments between two sips of his French coffee with a shot of expensive congnac in it. That's him; he always surprises me with his changing taste when it comes to women and cuisine. I don't mind a coffee myself and I order one when I feel I am full enough. I also order one of those Danish bakes with two apricot halves popped in the pastry like two Brisbane suns.

Suddenly I feel nostalgic about Brisbane. I want to be home in my quiet residential suburb with the lorikeets the only noise-raisers in the absence of crows. I feel like a slow walk down at the old wharf along the river, sitting on the steps near the Customs House, watching the Story Bridge buzzing with traffic, the cars looking like mechanical toys in the hands of God.

Around me now it's full of young seventy-ish ladies; they seem to be everywhere these days, sporting knife-reconstructed faces, glossy-glassy in the mixed day and artificial light, rehearsed naive-seductive smiles, eyes like prison security projectors scanning the area for prospective fugitives. Heavy eyelashes flap on ice slab faces painted in subtle natural shades. The expensive jobs on their pretty heads, the bodies trim and fragile, achieved through workout, wellness retreats and a balanced diet. Fur coats, their faithful lovers, embracing them gently.

And then, the betrayal.

One of their hands pops out of the hollow of the fur sleeve, looks around like a snout of a mink ready to hunt after a day's sleep.

The hand! The tell-all. Deformed finger joints, protruding veins, age spots like woodcocks' eggs. The cosmetic industry still doesn't bother to do much about hands. Aunty Susan's problem.

It's sad to look at pairs of hands mismatched with the faultless beauty of their owners. I only hope when I get old (if I get the chance, with all the events crashing like an avalanche against me) that cosmetic surgery will be advanced enough to cover my worn-out from typing and chopping onions fingers.

'You look beautiful.' That's Uncle Willie. This time not to me, but to one of these ladies, dolled up and shiny. She flashes a smile and reluctantly pulls her hand out of the cosy hollow to be kissed on the snout.

'And you, Willie, you look cool.' The rhythm is rap. She updates not only her face but also her vocabulary and mode of speech.

Uncle Willie gives her a smooch and they both giggle with that specific trained cooing that could make all pigeons ashamed of poor performance.

I remain forgotten for a long moment.

Uncle Willie comes back to our table and pinches my cheek. I feel five years old.

'I'll tell you a secret,' he says. 'This Willie name kind of makes me stand out in a crowd of all those men sporting nice names like Joshua, Craig, Jonathan, Matt or Darryl.

Women can feel that there is a shortcut to bed with a man named Willie.'

'I don't like Sandy,' I complain. 'There's nothing outstanding in a name like Sandy. I wouldn't have anything against being named Pamela, Jennifer or even Courtney. It could have a different impact on my personality.'

'I didn't want to call you Sandy, but your mother was so insistent.'

I trace a strange echo in his usually well-modulated voice. Something cautious, I can't be sure.

I look at him for more clues, like I do any time I sniff that there is an indirect implication about my parents' history, but Uncle Willie is already busy kissing another mink hand, splashing an abundant amount of compliments.

I wonder where his girlfriend is, the concubine as Aunty Susan calls her. I met her only once and I kind of liked her. Lilly looks one of those immature creatures that at thirty-something still carries a baby bottle to suckle on their water and sits in a puddle 'to splash around' in the hot weather. It's kind of inevitable for her to end up with an older gentleman, a father figure, wiping or smacking her bottom depending on the occasion.

Lilly, a simple name for a simple child.

Turning to me, Uncle Willie proves to be a mind reader.

'Lilly is at home with a cold.'

I don't know whether by home he means the yacht, but I don't ask. Instead I say, 'When the cat's away, the mice dance.'

He ignores this. 'Tell me, what are you doing? Still filling the bookstore shelves with cookbooks?'

He pronounces *cookbooks* with a frank sneer and I wonder why; he is not your reader of Seneca or Kierkegaard either. I wonder whether he has read anything besides manuals in poker, a game he passionately loves and the only thing that can take his mind off women.

I brief him on my latest project, telling him that I feel signs and omens that cannibals are coming back and that I can read in the paintings of the old masters that they have always been around.

He listens attentively and doesn't even get distracted by one of the hand-minks who desperately wants to arrange something with him before leaving. He looks a different man now, his eyes down, fixed on his empty plate.

When I finish he reaches across the table and grabs my hand. His palm is hot and moist. I wonder whether he is also coming down with a cold. His voice is feverish, a croak full of syncope.

'Kid, you are sitting on a golden egg. Have you told anyone else about this?'

'Oh, yes,' I start casually, despite the uneasiness climbing up my throat like a Sherpa lost in a blizzard, the last member of an expedition he is guiding up Everest.

Willie's face, usually frozen in a Mona Lisa mask of omni-meaningful smile, now distorts in a grimace of displeasure.

'For your sake, Sandy, I hope it's only Susan you have shared your ideas with. If so we can remain calm, she's a tomb.' After a small pause he adds, spreading his arms dramatically, 'In so many ways Susan is like a tomb—or at least a tomb statue.'

It sounds like an excuse for leaving her, substituting her with a young, childlike woman who doesn't mind playing in puddles. I don't feel like discussing family matters; however, I can't help it.

'Why didn't *you* want to name me Sandy?'

He looks now like a kid caught in a candy shop with loot in his pocket.

Suddenly he becomes rude.

'Sandy, you better tell me who knows about your project.'

I answer: everybody from my closest circle. Marylin and her daughter Wendy, Beverley and her husband Paul, my publisher David, Norm and of course Aunty Susan and Frank and even a special detective of a more special department of the Norwegian security services named Jacob Jacobsen.

Also Mimi and Tamati; we have discussed it in their kitchen turned surgery.

Hearing that list of names Uncle Willie becomes upset. Declaring he needs a good drink to keep his brain ticking, he orders a glass of Courvoisier I don't know how many years old; but by the price appearing later on the bill, the cognac must have been around at the time of Cleopatra and her notorious Caesar sex life.

Aphrodite also comes to my mind. Aphrodite, a dish, the way she's believed to have come out of a shell as in the famous Botticelli painting. The god of sex in the Greek mythology should be Zeus. He didn't muck around but fucked everything within reach, turning himself even into golden rain to penetrate Io. I love this. I think of Zeus as a soul mate, the way I feel about Cleo. That is that promiscuous bitch Cleopatra.

The cognac has the same effect on Uncle Willie as coffee has on me. I order another one with a hazelnut flavour.

We remain silent for a while. I feel that not only is my life in danger, but also my manuscript.

I have to admit that I am an ambitious person, something I inherited from my mother, who ended up as a piano teacher for gifted brats, occasionally playing in the Sandgate community orchestra in Brisbane after giving up a brilliant career over...what? I've never known. Well, while we're on the subject...

'Uncle Willie, why did Margherita give up her career as a soloist?'

I have disturbed his train of thought. He reaches out again for my hand, patting it gently.

'Your mum was an extraordinary woman, Sandy. She gave up her career so she could look after you and—' He stops and suddenly he is in a hurry.

He scribbles down a telephone and tells me to join him for lunch. Then he walks away, bowing his head left and right for the delight of the girls.

Aunty Susan answers the cell phone number given to me by Uncle Willie, leaving me flabbergasted.

'What are you doing here? Or you are not *here*, he is *there*?' It slips out of my mouth, much to my regret, because she snaps viciously at me.

'This is a free Europe and I am where I want to be, by the side of my husband wherever he is.'

'Isn't he with another woman?' I still can't believe it. For a moment I think that the behaviour of the people I know is influenced by the recent increased activity of the sun.

'And this lady happens to be sick so there's no one to make your uncle breakfast or to make her a cup of tea.'

'Haven't you got your own hotel to bother about? The tourist season has been disappointing for Switzerland, or at least that's what they write in the newspapers.'

'I thought that you, of all people, would have reason not to believe what they write in the papers. Now I'll call Willie.

No, actually I'll bring the phone to him. He is soaking in the bathtub. I just added some more hot water.'

And she's off.

I remain speechless. Soon I hear the purring voice of Uncle Willie.

'Darling,' he starts, 'your unsubstitutable aunty filled me further in. I have some ideas. W*e* wait for you. The yacht is next to the mermaid. You can't miss her. I mean the yacht. Her name is *Margherita*. Take care, Sandy. We, I mean Lilly and me, well, and your aunty, of course, we love you.'

The line goes dead, but not before I hear Uncle Willie giggle as if being tickled. I could have sworn that my aunt has given him a shove in the ribs, standing there, towering over him, letting more hot water run into the tub.

TWENTY-SIX

I hire a taxi to the mermaid statue. It makes me remember the mermaid cocktail I once drank in Redcliffe. It was a smoothie with top-secret ingredients. With a little sniffing and a lot of imagination I detected the presence of coconut milk as a base, custard apple, pear, vanilla, lemon zest and a few drops of *Bailey*.

I have a head full of questions about life and death.

Poussin's *A Dance to the Music of Time* is a jolly, macabre thing. A winged old man is playing the music while three women and a man dance with their backs to each other in a weird circle.

An hourglass in the hands of a putto still explains what it is all about, as if the symbols are not enough.

Gruesome.

I have seen myself dead on the front page of a newspaper and still can't come to terms with the idea that one day it might really happen.

One of the women dancing in Poussin's painting has a sensual expression on her face like a cat that has drunk the Irish cream *Bailey*. She parades her satisfaction, and I want to rub her nose in the fact that I happen to be a totally satisfied woman, too.

My thoughts turn to Frank. After my wild-weird *Franking* the other night, I have been walking around with Frank's breath and juices altering the contents of my cells. I feel cannibalistic. I feel his fingernails grow inside my heart. I feel his words resonate inside my nostrils.

The sensual fumes he releases still hang in my hair. I have delayed taking a shower and can feel his sweat blending with mine. I am wrapped in him and he is wrapped in me. I swallow. He is part of my saliva. Gorging on his smell, semen, saliva, sweat, skin, senses—those molecules are now mine. Sensual spirituality or spiritual sensuality?

It's all in the old books where cooking, witchery and cannibalism go hand in hand.

'Sandy, you know your life is in danger, please, listen carefully.'

I strain my hearing, but his words get sucked in a vortex, a black hole. We float, gravity-free objects in space, occasionally passing each other, occasionally touching each other.

'Frank!'

I pay the driver and follow how the car makes its way away from the water like someone who can never learn swimming. It takes me a couple of minutes to spot the yacht. She's not a monster, but neither is she a baby. One can comfortably cruise the ocean in her.

Margherita. It hits me in the pit of the stomach. *Margherita.*

On the yacht it's quiet.

Uncle Willie is reading. Lilly is sick and puking. Aunty Susan is busy cleaning around her bed and cooking muesli for her. I like muesli. It's quite creamy and I shouldn't eat it regarding my butt, which is voluminous or voluptuous depending on your point of view. However people watching what they eat deprive themselves of freedom and pleasure. And what is life without freedom and pleasure? One big shit. Which is my life right now.

Uncle Willie leaves the book and joins me for the muesli, which I snitch from Lilly. Aunty Susan rushes in and out as if she were in charge of a Red Cross field hospital. She brings Uncle Willie a spoon of flaxseed oil for boosting the immune system and a small bowl with soft-boiled eggs. Light lunch for people over seventy. For me there is a steak, which I refuse.

For a moment it starts to look like a preparation for Titian's painting session: 1 part egg yolk, 1 part linseed oil, 1 part water, all this vigorously shaken for the emulsion called tempera used before oil paints were introduced.

Uncle Willie and I finish the muesli and engage in small talk about the weather, Lilly's persistent cold, Aunty Susan's gold heart and the 'homeless' status of Uncle Willie after their separation.

He wants me to feel sorry for him.

I can't. Especially as I look around the artistic luxury of the yacht. It's quite bohemian actually, and the only object that sits awkwardly is a big filigree silver cross between two bottles of cognac, brown like caramelised sugar. I can bet my last penny Aunty Susan has sneaked the cross in, a naïve attempt to retrieve her husband by imposing moral standards.

'Sandy, you know I love you. I want to show you things I've never talked about to anybody, not even to your aunt.'

He leads me to a small dark room in the back of the yacht prepared for watching movies. I squirm, knowing his passion for the cult film *Casablanca,* and dig deep inside my mind for an excuse to disappear.

'Have you been to *Frihedsmuseet*?' he asks casually while making himself comfortable in a padded armchair next to me, remote control in hand.

I admit I haven't visited the museum telling the story of Danish resistance during Nazi occupation in the early forties. I even don't know anything about it.

'Well, well, well,' he sneers mockingly at me. 'Don't tell me sex museums are the only ones you visit.'

I bite back my frustration. With so many things to do, figuring out how to survive, how to beat an unknown invisible enemy, I am stuck here with a nice but obviously not very right in the head relative who has nothing better to do but watch old black-and-whites.

Uncle Willie flicks the remote and on the big screen in front of us appears something that blows my mind.

There are plenty of films showing what Hitler did to the Jews, but I have never seen such terrible atrocities as the one I watch on a yacht called *Margherita* rocking gently by the mermaid.

It begins with a huge mountain, a sad mountain with no trees, no streams, no birds flying around or wild animals hiding among the bushes.

It's a mountain made of bones.

Human bones.

A pyramid polished by the sun and the southern winds, where only snakes could survive. Watching these bones sculpting the most horrendous mountain I've ever seen is a painful experience.

I am sitting there, my elbow touching Uncle Willie's arm, and all I can feel is a knot somewhere inside my body, pulsating with the rhythm of death.

We are ten terrifying minutes into the film when he clicks the remote and the screen goes blank, still soaked in dread by the thousands disappearing into gas chambers and dying in so-called scientific experiments.

Uncle Willie turns towards me and I see for the first time his real age, down to the last minute, digging itself up in the shallow trachea of his wrinkles. His skin is the bark of an old tree, dry, easy to peel off, with invisible life underneath.

'Sandy, we are in Denmark, a country where the King himself put the yellow star of David on his jacket and marched the streets protesting against what Hitler was doing to the Jews, who have genetically inherited pain from the times of the pharaohs and even earlier. There were few countries in Europe like Denmark, where they managed to save the Jews and prevent the Nazis from sending them to slaughter mills like Auschwitz and Buchenwald.'

I can't help thinking that the English word *war* is identical to the past tense of the German verb to be: *war*. *Ich war*: I was.

War takes your life away and you become part of the past.

The history of mankind is the history of its wars, made by men for men. Men are addicted to war. Even their lovemaking is like making war.

'The Germans grew up with the brothers Grimm and their gruesome tale about Hansel and Gretel being shovelled into the oven by the old witch to satisfy her hunger,' I say cautiously. 'Small wonder that the Nazis sprang up easily among them.'

Uncle Willie eyes me thoughtfully.

'You are not aware of what you are saying, kid. I can see now that weird ideas come naturally to you. You aren't responsible for the chaos they throw you in.'

I don't know what to make out of it: rebuke or compliment? I remain silent.

'My father's family is in that mountain, Sandy. Only my father survived. He was the youngest witness. Death was everywhere around him. There are no records of it, but he witnessed how they gave the prisoners food made of other prisoners' bodies. A Herr Tommler, the Drummer as they called him, was the man who supervised, making sure they ate it. A mother forced to eat her child in watery soup, a husband his wife. Whoever refused was shot in the head by this same Herr Tommler.'

His Adam's apple starts to jump and he has difficulty clearing his throat. There are no tears in his cognac brown eyes.

'I can't stand brown,' he whispers between two coughs. 'Nazi brown.'

'I'm sorry,' I say, 'I didn't know this part of your family history. You always look so cheerful and relaxed; one can hardly suspect the burden you carry.'

'At night I often think of fire,' says Uncle Willie, and now there are tears in his eyes. 'Fire, the ardent lover of the virgin Joan of Arc; the fire in the lantern Diogenes carried in search for an honest man; *agni*, the animated fiery energy; spontaneous human combustion; *auto da fe* the Nazis borrowed from the Inquisition; Pompeii erased, buried under liquid fire pouring down from Vesuvius; Giordano Bruno burnt alive.... You must have seen some of these things in the books I left to your mother.'

'All those shabby old books at home come from you? My mother never mentioned it to me. Some of them are responsible for me being in the snake pit now. Borrowing wrong ideas.'

'So at the end of the day it's my fault, isn't it?' He looks sad. But I am not deceived. His sadness comes from his vision of the bone mountain.

'Uncle Willie.' I touch his hand to prevent him of going into self-inflicted pain. 'Are you all right?'

He looks through me and utters, 'Jupiter is a gas planet. You think *he* would have turned it into a gas chamber, if he could?'

I know to whom Uncle Willie refers but I don't feel like discussing a failure artist like Hitler, nor a successful artist like Dali with his canvas *Hitler Masturbating*, so I ask again, 'How about a nice, tar-like coffee that can raise the dead out of a coffin?'

Even this doesn't rouse him from that semi-stupor; he blabbers, 'Alotrifagia, that's what they call this disease for pervert appetite. Some people develop a physical or psychic need to eat chalk, glass, paper, dirt, human flesh.

'Uncle Willie, how about—' I start only to be interrupted by a rowdy announcement.

'Here's the coffee!'

My earthly aunty appears with a tray. I smell Gevalia brand and small lemon-cheese cakes. I presume Dali wouldn't be in Aunty Susan's good books with his words, 'Jesus is cheese. Mountains of cheese.'

Uncle Willie shifts in his chair, giving her a gentle stroke on her backside.

Soon she leaves us alone.

His grieving is genuine, but his hedonistic nature makes it short-lived.

'My father was a jolly fellow; I wish he had been around when you were born, Sandy. He was a fiddler.'

'Like Nero?' I want to provoke him and hear his chuckle. It just doesn't suit Uncle Willie to be sad. 'You know, fiddling nicely while Rome, which he allegedly put to fire, was burning away, as if feeding lions with Christians wasn't fun enough.'

But Uncle Willie is still serious. 'No,' he says solemnly. 'My father was more like Chagall's fiddler, a sad nostalgic Jew seeking refuge in the shell of his fiddle mingling with music, turning into music.' He sighs deeply, then abruptly lifts his head and goes into a fit of operatic chuckles. 'Even

Nostradamus predicted the bastard and they couldn't stop him, could they? Hitler came to power in the most democratic way, by being voted in.'

'Nostradamus?' I think I know what he is referring to.

I explored the idea of feeding the beasts in my first book *Cooking with Spirituality*. It says that you should feed the evil deities, giving them offerings like compliments, gifts, and food. I have even designed special meals to turn people who want to harm you into well-wishers.

'Yes, Nostradamus.' says Uncle Willie. 'Second century, quatrain twenty-four. "Beasts ferocious from hunger will swim across rivers / The greater part of the region will be against the Hister."'

'Well, you know the dispute: Does Hister stand for Hitler or for the Danube river?'

'I don't give a shit what it stands for. I want to erase the tragedy of my people, but I can't. Minced and eaten or forced into cannibalistic acts like my father. That brought about a hideous trauma along with the rest of the routine Nazi cruelties like gassing and melting body fat for soap.'

I have nothing to say. This is an Uncle Willie I am not familiar with, that I am not prepared to get familiar with.

Perhaps it's time for me to go.

But I have a soft spot for Marc Chagall.

My uncle's description does the famous painting justice. I close my eyes and imagine the small canvas: earthy colours, an earthly landscape and figures, and the fiddler, gravity-free, flying in mid-air, the fiddle in his arms a beloved home, a piece of land made of music.

'Thank you,' I say to my uncle and give him a peck on the chin. 'It's so nice that you want to help and give me a lead. I have to move on my own and not to involve all you guys in this mess.'

He grabs my hand and brings it to his expert lips.

Aunty Susan bursts in and the magic is gone.

At least she doesn't mention anything about a missing jacket.

TWENTY-SEVEN

I wonder whether I should visit this Christiania area and see how's life outside the square. See whether the people there really believe that they make the difference in a world dying in a mudslide of greed, orchestrated poverty, or soulless material satisfaction. Then I realize I am not far away from *Never Mind*.

It's late afternoon and perhaps the place is still closed but I might be able to talk to somebody from the staff before meeting Fernando for a night chat and see what he has for me. Normally dressed and without the disguise, I doubt about my chances to be served even a Brazilian coffee. But then you never know.

I advance slowly along the streets of this flat country, quite the opposite of Switzerland as a geographic relief, feeling the wind as a living thing with its own moods. It touches me gently, next pokes into my back only to quickly jump in front of me and try to punch me to the ground. The wind stops so abruptly as it starts, then whirls in my hair and massages my temples still throbbing heavily after my conversation on the yacht. My simply constructed Aussie mind fed with healthy physical things has a problem digesting everything Uncle Willie says to me. It's like being on bread, fruit and water for days and then gorging on half-cooked chunks of meat in a saucy puddle of spiced blood, so highly appreciated in some Northern countries. A climate thing.

Soon I can see that there won't be any Brazilian coffee for me in *Never Mind* and this not because I am not in disguise but because the sidewalk around the club is sealed off.

A couple of police cars are parked by the yellow tape, some uniformed and some plainclothes work on the scene walking in and out of the entrance. My first reaction is to turn away, catch the first ferry and go to Oslo in search of the Nigerian refugee, forgetting about Fernando. Then I see him. They escort him out of *Never Mind,* handcuffed and beautiful, a wild animal with lean muscles and face like a crystal of magnetic sensuality. A policewoman in front of him is leading the way to one of the police cars. Two other cops side him. The policewoman bends to open the door and then it happens. First I hear a sound similar to that of a champagne cork pop and Fernando falls, a slow motion like the dance of a heavy bird in a mating season. Then the two cops start running after a fast moving target, a figure in black, which quickly disappears behind a corner. The policewoman squats next to Fernando pressing one hand to his neck while calling the Central.

A crowd quickly gathers. Some sparing comments can be heard. *It's a gay thing. They are a jealous lot.*

I stand some twenty metres away torn by the impulse to reach for Fernando giving him some of my strength and the screaming warning inside me to clear out as soon as possible. Then I see him and take cover behind a broad-shouldered man. Jacobsen comes out of *Never Mind* and an archaeologist won't need to dig deep to find spikes of anger all over his face.

An ambulance arrives and the paramedics fuss around Fernando. The policewoman takes the manacles off his hands. I hope he is still alive.

There's nothing I can do. It's time to move on.

I scramble back to the hotel. I need to think and let what I just witness sink in, refresh myself and get information about ferries crossing to Oslo. I think of Fernando and the way he talked to me about that famous giant statue of Christ the Redeemer standing with stretched welcoming arms on a vantage point overlooking the city of Rio de Janeiro. 'You have to see it,' he said to me, 'to feel it. Jesus died for us on the cross.'

'But then he got himself back to life, Fernando. Perhaps he knew there wasn't much of a risk involved in him dying.'

Teasing, teasing. Why I just can't get rid of this bad habit? Or is it what makes me tick. Teasing. Teasing the Cult of the Cannibals, what a misery!

When I let myself in the hotel room there is something waiting for me.

My laptop on the corner of the bed like a lap dog.

I forget everything. Hilarious, I grab the laptop and open it.

My manuscript file is named *Frank*.

I go back to the menu and see that all my files, old and new, are named Frank and numbered from one to over forty.

This makes me uneasy.

I open at random file *Frank38* and read: 'The secret is in the fire. Fire should be neither too brisk, nor too weak. It has to have a steady, persistently engulfing flame that turns logs and branches into long-lasting embers transmitting their heat into the stones, covering the cuts of the long pig. Moderation is essential; forcing is non-recommendable, as is slack burning that leaves the meat tough, even stringy.'

I stop reading over a dizzy spell.

A quick inspectional look at the laptop confirms it's my laptop all right. Mine has specific scratches and a sticker *I am a bugger* borrowed from Marylin and another one *The world is a ship in an ocean of shit*, from Norm's poem. They are placed at a certain awkward angle and I have drawn a doodle where they overlap. It's my doodle and I can swear on it. Then there are those small signs—a bit of dirt here and a coffee stain there.

I continue to open files.

Frank23 starts: 'When cutting the long pig use all the necessary tools. Failing to do so may spoil the integrity, the shape and taste of morsels like liver, heart, Venus mount on the palm or pieces of the thighs, separated along the muscle's fibre and never across it.'

Frank 8 says: 'Human flesh *bokola* is eaten with fingers while multipronged wooden forks *iculanibokola* were used to pass the flesh into the priest's mouth so god within him could swallow it.'

Frank13 recommends: 'If you want to use some material from the long pig like hair, knuckles, skull, skin, teeth for shamanic or decorative purposes, be sure that they come from a healthy specimen, since they preserve the energy of the long pig and can be destructive having lived in a sick body.'

Each file is accompanied by Hans Staden's drawings. Hans Staden, a solder and a sailor who allegedly escaped from being cooked and eaten experience in Brazil in the middle of the sixteenth century. His drawings, appallingly detailed as barbeques with human parts on the grill or big pots boiling people for an impatient cannibal tribe, made him famous.

My scream bursts inside me. Finally I have opened the file *Frank1*. It reads: 'Cooking instructions for roasting the long pig Sandy Cornelius.'

Numbness is like a heavy blanket.

I can't move but a funny creature within me starts to walk slowly like an Indian villager determinedly to reach to the Ganges river for her annual pilgrimage thousands of miles away.

TWENTY-EIGHT

My first geographic love was Calcutta, where Uncle Willie took me at the age of eight. He was paid to give a concert before a few people of the highest caste, very rich people. And being rich in India was something impressive.

We arrived in Mumbai and were taken to a party in the inner garden of the *Taj Mahal* Hotel. I couldn't take my eyes off the women, who looked like they had stepped down from a fairy tale, wrapped in strange, shiny clothes leaving one shoulder bare. The cloth was woven with golden threads, and diamonds sparkled in the women's noses. I was amazed to see that some of the women had rings with precious stones on their toes too.

Uncle Willie, who was never a pianist for big concert halls, but rather a camera performer for selected cosmopolitan elite, whispered in my ear that some of these people had rooms in their houses full of emeralds and rubies, sapphires and diamonds. They were so rich that they couldn't tell what their fortunes were worth.

Then the dances began. Young girls wrapped in ephemeral costumes followed the rhythm of a subtle, magic musical like small beams of light falling down from the stars. The dancers movements symbolised various messages, Uncle Willie told me. I was fascinated by this bewitching language.

There, I realised what real poverty was, too.

They drove us around the town and we climbed to the panoramic restaurant towering over the enormous Mumbai port, which hosted thousands of ships flying different flags.

On our way back the host proposed that I wait in the car while he walked off with Uncle Willie to a small wood. But I followed them, and what I saw made my heart sink.

There were dead bodies hanging from the branches of the trees. Our host was explaining to Uncle Willie that it was one of the local rituals for burying the dead. For the first time I heard of the Parsis.

A vulture was having a lavish feast with one of the bodies and I began to feel sick. Then a strange feeling overcame me. There were no heights below me because I was on the ground. But an abyss was descending down from the sky and at the bottom there was the vulture recycling the expired human body. I was afraid to look up into the abyss of the sky because it invited me to jump into it.

I gave a small cry; it was the host who reached me first and carried me in his arms back to the car. He whispered words of comfort to me and I relaxed, my eyes fixed on his. There was another abyss down there, the abyss of his eyes leading to a scary unknown world. An abyss that also invited me to jump.

Then we arrived in Calcutta.

A saying goes: 'If you've been to India and never been to Calcutta, never say you've been to India.'

Everywhere was overcrowded. People lying on the streets along with lazy, sanctimonious cows, busy rats stirring around them.

There was no sewerage system or at least not a functioning one; stinking waters poured out of the houses and ran freely, flooding the sidewalks undisturbed. Small white lizards crossed the walls of our apartment in the best hotel. Being that I lived in Australia, they didn't bother me, but Uncle Willie was annoyed.

In the evening Uncle Willie dressed in his coattails and myself in a beautiful white dress were driven to a marvellous marble house surrounded by blooming gardens.

There was a special reception in which we were decorated with long flower garlands in vivid colours. I soon felt dizzy from the strong aroma of the heavy garland around my neck, and it was a relief when I could get rid of it.

Strong tasting chai (cardamom, ginger root, cinnamon bark, nutmeg, black pepper, and clove steeped in hot milk) was served in the musical room, which was decorated with hand carved pieces of pink tree, and incense burned, creating an atmosphere of sanctity.

The piano Uncle Willie was to play was made out of pink tree, too, and here where the elephants were as common as the humans, I was not surprised to see that the keyboard had an ivory covering. A mosaic of semi-precious stones decorated the lid over the keys, and there was another frieze on the upper part of the instrument.

I wondered what my mother would say about this. She was never a show-off person and her beauty used to glow in the subdued shades of beige prevailing in her wardrobe. Classical simplicity shared all the things that surrounded her.

Nobody was in a hurry. As if they had all the time in the world. While the people around us chatted and sipped at their chai, a strange musical instrument began to play.

If I hadn't seen the man singing, I wouldn't have realised it was his voice and not an instrument. The singing possessed the same enchanting quality as the dancing of the girls. It sounded like part of the holy silence, part of the prayer of the universe.

I could feel another abyss in this singing—a good one, inviting me not to jump but to slide, to float like a cloud, not outwards but inside myself, my own space. Later the voice was accompanied by a sitar and a tabla.

The host was saying, 'In music, like in poetry, there are closed societies with a taste of their own who enjoy the beauty no matter what its form is...'

He was standing there looking into my eyes and I realised I couldn't tell his age. He could have been anything between thirty and seventy. Letting myself sink into the abyss of his eyes, I was not aware of when exactly the concert began. All I knew was that it was the best sound I had ever heard and for sure Uncle Willie's best performance.

On the following day we were shown around that remarkable town. First we visited a Buddhist temple. We took our shoes off, went in barefooted, and on the stone floor I could feel no cold.

The air was wrapped in the sweet, somewhat heavy scent of flowers. A monk with a shaved head came over to me and whispered something. I couldn't understand the words, but there was no need. I comprehended the meaning, or rather, the message. He welcomed us to the spiritual home of an ancient philosophy that preached peace of mind and oneness with the universe.

Towards the evening, when it was beginning to grow dark, our host took us to the Ganges river, one of whose hundred and eight names is *svarga-sopana-sarani*. That means 'following like a staircase to heaven.' Like so many other things in India, the waters of the Ganges had that hypnotising effect on me, another abyss that invited me to jump. I was aware of our host's eyes on me as I let my arm sink in up to my elbow.

I felt I *was* water, moving like water, thinking like water, loving like water.

When we went back to the bank our host helped me out of the boat, holding me by that very hand that had made me feel part of the world's water body.

While Uncle Willie and the other two men were slowly climbing the steep bank heading the alley, our host took me into one of those covered boats along the bank, most of them already occupied by lovers. I could distinguish the unmistakable giggle of the girls and that gentle rocking that made the boats look like cradles, cradles of love.

He kissed me there in the dark of the covered boat; but it was not a kiss, it was an abyss of a feeling.

I knew I was no more alone, all by myself; now there was another creature inside my own abyss, taking care of me.

Forever.

Times change quickly. The same newspaper announcing my suicide covered a strange story from India. Dead bodies still hanging outside Mumbai. Vultures, for centuries faithful undertakers, recycling death-life-death, are failing to turn up in the city's forest. It's against nature that vultures refuse to feast on dead bodies any longer.

People, however, refuse to believe it and continue to bury their dead high up in the trees, waiting for the vultures to return.

TWENTY-NINE

I am sailing to meet the refugee from Nigeria whatever it costs me. Lately I am allergic to newspapers, but on the ferry to Oslo I keep a low profile behind one.

I read about a Danish artist Marco Evaristti (Italian name) using a giant iceberg off the western coast of Greenland as a canvas, splashing three thousand litres of red paint on it. Fire hoses were used by a twenty-person crew. The artist, they say, used the same dye they use to tint meat. They don't specify what meat. With global warming, however, I dare to think that this kind of art might be doomed.

The second story that attracts my attention is about a snowmobile drive-in theatre built from snow for a film festival in Norway's far north. The event is being hosted by Sami reindeer herders who also built the movie screen from snow. I'll have to remember this and challenge Uncle Willie and his old-fashioned yacht movie theatre.

Last but not least, I try to memorise a report about recent evidence of cannibalism in the northern corner of the Congo, where warlords cut off heads, then chop the bodies into pieces and throw them into a drum to cook.

Simple.

Then it's time for me to chuck the paper. We are entering a fjord, and it's breathtaking.

Oslo has always been the imaginary home of Frank and me, a future in which we are married and live happily ever after. I cook for him, he initiates me in the occult power of the runes, and in between we fuck our heads off. I want to forget that on paper Frank is still married.

It hurts.

It's painful when you know the person with whom you share your man. Frank's wife is not a beauty but she has an authority that pulls the energy field towards her somehow.

I don't like my train of thought. The weather doesn't cheer me up, either. Even so, I like Oslo at first glance. It's peaceful, subtle, clean. I easily blend with the people, who look neat, purified and balanced by an environment that excels in cleanness, pristine snow, and fjords, where the only negative things are the ions. Ah well. If you live here, my bet is you can always find something to nag about. The world is not meant to be perfect.

I don't hail a taxi. I walk, feeling the liberating sense of anonymity of being in a foreign country and city, at a longitude where no one knows me, where no one cares whether I am happy, miserable, or both.

In the Viking Ship Museum they show the ships that were used as tombs for the nobility. Vanity has no limits.

The ships contained, beside the noble, lots of jewellery, food, furniture and servants. Archaeologists found them buried in blue clay that had preserved them well.

I start to toy with the idea that the servants were not only for performing everyday chores but also for satisfying carnal needs of different profiles, I mean, real food for the palate. Skull-cups were in use.

While admiring the royal tombs I try to do some planning. I have to find a hotel; I have to establish a contact with the refugee from Nigeria as a short cut to the source of my troubles. I don't know which task is more difficult. I've never been a fugitive before, and I can't see myself earning a living as one.

If I go to a youth hostel or to a five star hotel the chances are equal that some of my persecutors will find me. The only thing I carry in a backpack is my laptop with the instructions on how a certain person is to be cooked and eaten.

A person bearing my name.

I hope to merge with the crowd of backpackers. If you have a backpack, you're not a single person anymore; you form a couple, a team, a crew. The backpack protects you from winds and rain. It can be used as an umbrella, a vest or a brace. It's a pillow, a tent for freezing hands, a kitchen, purse, treasury safe, and hump full of invitations for partying on the beach.

Wendy told Marylin once, 'I want my backpack for a tomb stone.' Living opposite a cemetery can influence one's wishes.

I hope I can use the laptop and write the sequel to my interrupted manuscript, a chapter about the head of King Herod, steamed in Salome's dancing-heated breath, or a recipe for a Gadarene swine in brine. Gadarene swine is a euphemism for mankind in the vocabulary of the UFO believers who usually predict a sad end for the intelligent collective being.

On Scandinavian soil I can't but think of Svedenborg and his dreams and angels. I can't but think of the mysticism of the North, so different from the dramatic mysticism cradled in Spain. What I feel, however, deep in my heart is that there are no other entities but us operating on different planes.

Each of us is many persons. We spend lifetimes suppressing most of them, letting surface only what we rationally decide is good to be shown. But we can be on any one of these planes, transforming ourselves into energies of different properties and qualities, oscillating in different worlds, generating different shapes and experiences.

Because as much as *I am God* I know I am also Lucifer. I am an angel of Light and an angel of Darkness. I love people unconditionally because they make a good menu. I understand the cannibals. They want to maintain a level of acceptance, to grow higher and higher in the eyes of God. I can trace this through man's artistic display as one of his most sacred confessions.

Man has never stopped being cannibalistic.

Since cannibalism was banned by the so called civilised society, man has learned to give way to his cannibalistic urges through art, and last but not least, through endless, useless wars. That makes me think that man was not designed for peace, but for slaughter. Man's a killing machine.

Kill and be killed.

Trying to lighten my thoughts, I decide to visit the famous Vigeland Park.

The park is lined with life-sized statues created by Gustav Vigeland. I number two hundred of them in granite and bronze. The range of feelings is amazing; I like best a screaming pot-bellied baby on the bridge and a couple of entwined lovers.

I remember Frank describing some of his favourite statues and that he likes to spend time with them whenever the weather permits. I have always thought that I would see these stone and metal figures with him. I know that his occult occupations have led him to freakish interpretations of the figures' inner lives; he has a story to go with each of them, a long fleshy story, and he reckons the models for the figures have left part of their essence to follow its own way.

I miss Frank.

It starts to get dark, an early procedure at this latitude. I put some speed in my walk. Suddenly I hear steps behind me. Cautious, rubber-soles walking lightly. The noise of a broken branch finds me hesitating whether to turn and look over my shoulder or not.

Panic takes over. I start running towards the bridge. I pant and my feet pound heavily, my heart trying to leave the rib cage on its own will.

I don't turn but I see moving people all around me.

A scream scrambles out from my constricted throat.

'What's happening? Has someone attacked you?'

A police officer asks me first in Norwegian, then in English. His face is the colour of a tender freshly peeled banana. He is so young I wonder whether he shaves. His blue eyes concerned, his chunky reliable hands supporting me.

By now I know I am a psycho, still I look around.

No one's there.

Only the Vigeland's master figures closing down on us in the falling darkness.

'Bad nerves.' I smile.

He escorts me out of the park from where I reluctantly go on alone. He is really lovely.

The reason I am in Oslo, though, is another young man.

I continue to have lower abdominal cramps to go with my PMS hysterics. I can't think straight. Sometimes I love to be woman. Sometimes I hate it. Sometimes I love to be single and think of all gorgeous fuckable lays out there. Sometimes I bet I'd be better off saddled with someone like Norm or Paul and stitch wedding gowns. I doubt whether I would be having so many strange things happening to me like creating a bond with that Dutch painter Abraham Mignon and his *Still Life with Fruit, Oysters and a Porcelain Bowl.* The Dutch have invented the still life genre along with the flower studies, which I find so boring. But this still life is openly promiscuous, with the pomegranate ripped in the middle, the oysters shamelessly naked, the grapes heavy with juice exploding against the transparent skin and the silly China porcelain bowl open like a nymphomaniac pussy.

Finally deciding against a youth hostel (I'd hate everyone to find me old there), I check for the night in a modest cosy looking hotel near the central railway station.

By the time I fall asleep I have worked out a plan how to try to establish a contact with the Nigerian refugee.

Silly me. Who sang that life is all but a plan about life?

THIRTY

My sixth sense perceives something weird going on around me. I squint in the flood of strong artificial light meant to help the stingy daylight filtered through the big windows of the breakfast area of the hotel restaurant.

Jesus! Am I becoming a schizophrenic or what?

What I see in front of me is me, Sandy Cornelius, standing by my table, looking at me, smiling at me! Or perhaps it's an out-of-body experience. After all, I might not be alive.

Then I squint again and pick eyes of lapis lazuli colour staring boldly at me.

Beverley!

Beverley of all people. I want to cry and I scramble out of my chair to embrace her. I must feel really nostalgic to do this. We must look like identical twins and that makes me sick. Oh yes, the perfume. The nutmeg scent she must have washed herself with.

I pull away.

I get angry. I get furious! 'How about my pots? How about the African violet?'

'The African violet is half dead because I over watered it and the geranium is half dead because I never watered it.' Beverley takes a seat opposite me creating a mirror effect for both of us.

'Two halves make one dead.' I am getting madder and madder now that I continue to smell *her* nutmeg perfume across the table.

'I am really happy that you are not dead,' says Beverley, smudging the lipstick on her upper and lower lips. 'After all, I was absolutely sure I was having an extrasensory experience talking with you on the phone last time.'

'You look disappointed.' I give her a searching look.

'Not at all,' says Beverley casually, taking care of the excess of lipstick in the corners of her mouth. 'Even if you manage to convince David that you're alive and able to present the manuscript although you are running out of time, he still has a project for me.'

'Has he?' I clutch my hands together so I don't strangle her.

'Come on, Sandy, don't be mean; you of all people know that I have talents. David thinks so, too.'

'What else does David think?'

'That it's pathetic the way you pronounce *Last Supper.* In your mouth it sounds something like *La Salsa*.' She giggles, covering her freshly painted mouth with a hand, a habit from the time when her teeth looked like a replica of the *moai*, the famous giants of Easter Island. Now they look like mine, needless to say.

I don't laugh; I don't like the intimacy I detect in her voice every time she pronounces David's name either, but I have better questions to ask.

'Beverley, what's going on? How come you know where to find me?'

'Oh, I have my own sources. And, Sandy, don't get worked up about it, but it's in your interest to remain dead.' Beverley tells me very casually that David has paid for her trip to Oslo. She was supposed to use my contacts and even present herself as me to obtain valuable information in order to finish the manuscript.

'Why Oslo?'

'Because of Frank. I have always been intrigued by him since the time you showed him for five minutes in Brisbane before taking off to Uluru or was it the Kakadoo National Park or the Great Barrier Reef, impressing with Aussie icons.'

I remember that old French trick used by Madam Pompadour or whatever highly-placed courtesan in the French court. The easiest way to snitch another woman's lover is to find out the name of her perfume. To steal her fragrance means to steal her spirit and empty this same woman of her sacred core substance. They say perfumes are the easiest tools when it comes to manipulating men's sexual desires.

Beverley has actually washed herself in nutmeg scent.

I look full blast into Beverley lapis lazuli eyes. 'How could you?' I hiss killing her with a glance.

'It was a collective decision, Sandy, that we come and join you here.' She trades a direct answer with something next relevant not unlike a sport personality cornered to have used forbidden drugs.

Who are they? David? I don't believe it. He has better things to do then travel around in search of a dead author.

She tries to play it down but somehow I know it. I've been followed again. At least she's admitting it while refusing to tell me who's with her.

We cross the restaurant to the buffet, walking side by side, occasionally touching each other. Eskimos rubbing noses or touching noses like Maoris.

It's very *in* to talk against the Maoris, but I've been among them and I find that they are the most genuine tribe on earth. Aggressive, hostile, angry, warsome. That's what the real warrior is, and life is war, that's for sure.

A la guerre comme a la guerre.

The Maoris don't pretend; they don't deceive you with lullaby talk saying how mankind should be loving and gentle. Good can't prevail over evil the same way evil can't prevail over good; they are like yin and yang, like day and night; they are heads and tails on a coin, tails perhaps belonging to the devils. Good and evil are judgmental.

Beverley has a full plate in front of her nose. Rolls with vanilla cream, with honey and nuts, sweets with dried and preserved fruit, chocolate biscuits. The beverages show a total lack of style: half a cup of tea, cold milk, water, juice—pineapple, by the colour.

She casts funny looks at me, saying something patronising like, 'I started to enjoy being in your shoes, Sandy.'

I am not happy that she takes it seriously being me. It starts to go too far.

Yes, too far.

When Frank appears and exchanges warm greetings with Beverley I don't know what to think. He gives me a kiss, though, and that helps a bit.

Frank is having black coffee and a roll splashed with butter. He eats so much butter, I worry about his heart being clogged. I might pretend I can do without him. But that's not true.

Jacob Jacobsen appears soon after I have finished my second coffee. He gives me a fierce look and grumbles something that should pass for a greeting.

'Ms Cornelius, I have arranged a meeting between you and the Nigerian asylum seeker,' he says blandly.

I stiffen. I didn't expect this. He has started to predict my moves and intercept them. Right now I have no choice but to play along with him.

I hate to leave Frank with Beverley but I shouldn't forget that I am here to solve a mystery and not on a sex tourism trip.

As I get up to leave, I can feel Beverley's eyes burning holes into my back. It is getting worse than in the Brisbane Juvenile Correction Centre.

We reach Jacobsen's office, which turns to be just around the corner from the hotel, and I am invited to take a seat. Jacobsen excuses himself for a moment, and I take the opportunity to ask a passing policewoman for directions to the toilet. My bladder is about to burst. It's my bladder that reacts directly to tension, fear, sex drive, name it. As if my little heart is in there swimming in prenatal waters of lemon piss.

When I come back Jacobsen is waiting for me, and he is not alone.

I jump in exaltation, but Tamati's eyes freeze my enthusiasm.

'This is Mr AbdulBilal from Nigeria.' Jacob Jacobsen starts the introducing.

'Hello, Ms...?' Tamati's voice carries warning and caution. His accent is unrecognisable.

'Cornelius,' I prompt mechanically.

It must be another charade. They are all taking me for a ride. I shift in my chair, about to say that for God's sake, I have fucked the guy and here he is now, pretending. I don't want to know whether Tamati is here with Beverley, whether he deceives Jacobsen or Jacobsen uses him without being aware of...Ah well.

What game is this and whose? One thing is sure, it's not my game. I quit.

'Mr Jacobsen,' I start, sombrely avoiding Tamati's eyes bulging at me across the table, 'I think I know who this—'

I can't finish because Jacobsen's cell phone starts to play *'Amor per me non ha'* from the Verdi's opera *Don Carlos*.

Archaeology and opera lover, the guy will kill me before the cult. Or perhaps the *words* are meaningful for him: 'There's no love for me,' sings the old king while his son fools around with his stepmother, the young queen.

Who would love Jacobsen?

It's neither the place nor the time to ask.

Jacobsen's face starts to look strained while taking the call. Tamati, on the other hand, relaxes. He even manages a wink. This time *I* pretend I don't know him.

There's something extremely tense in the air; it affects me on all levels. I keep my mouth shut and wait. That's the best strategy I can manage, and it proves rewarding.

Jacobsen clicks off the phone and puts it away in his pocket, then finds a glass of water and places it in front of me. 'Could you please drink it?' He looks humble.

I sip on the water.

'Ms Cornelius,' he starts in a trained for the occasion voice. 'Your friend Beverley Jones has just been killed.' While breaking the news Jacobsen keeps a close eye on me.

I don't faint.

I scream, 'Frank? Is Frank all right?'

'It's not Frank, it's Beverley,' Jacobsen repeats slowly.

Finally it penetrates my brain. 'Why Beverley?' There's sneer in my voice. Who would bother to kill Beverley? She must have done it herself to prove that she is equally important as I. Then I am aware of Jacobsen staring at me, reading me so I quickly add. 'Is it really poor Beverley?'

Jacobsen nods. 'Mrs Jones has been killed while finishing her coffee. No one saw the attacker.'

I remain mute.

Beverley! Coffee?

Meeting Jacobsen's eyes, I say dryly, 'Beverley wasn't a coffee drinker. She liked her cuppa.' Then I hide my face in my palms. 'Oh, no!' Actually I am hiding my relief and my joy that the little bitch who wanted to sneak into my personality and take over my life, my lover and my career as a cookbook writer has been taken care of.

It's all about friendship. I look up at Tamati. His face has contorted with pain.

Suddenly it sinks in that the attack was meant for me and I go into hysterics. I try to drink the rest of the water and end up splashing it all over me. I grab Tamati's hand and start to scratch it just to let out horror.

His reaction is predictable, he slaps me across the face and soon Jacobsen has to untangle us.

Tamati gets out of my grip with a bleeding hand and face and I get a good shake from him, which sends me almost comatose. But Jacobsen's bear-like, massive body is a match for Tamati's athletic rugby antics, to my advantage.

'I am sorry we have to interrupt the meeting between you and our Nigerian friend,' says Jacobsen thoughtfully. He thinks he has already had enough of me. But his mission needs me in the big picture so he continues to show politeness, which I suspect has a burning wire tied to an explosive.

Jacobsen and I leave together to return back to the hotel. I don't say good-bye to Tamati. He tries again to wink at me and I take a mental note to sue him for a sexual harassment.

Worried silly about me, Frank puts a protective arm around my shoulders because, like Jacobsen, Frank also thinks that I'll be shocked by the picture of Beverley lying in a puddle of blood and Italian coffee, Lavazza by the fragrance of it.

The only thing I feel is that I want a cup of this aromatic coffee, that I want to pee and then call Marylin to arrange someone to look after my geranium and African violet in Brisbane. Beverley can't be considered reliable for a task like this.

Nor for any task, now.

All eyes are on me so I summon my poor actor's skills and burst into loud sobs, hiding my face in Frank's handy shoulder. Having three quarters of my surface area stuck to him makes me horny, which results in a naughty display of my tongue probing through his shirt.

If he is shocked he doesn't show it. Instead he turns around, dragging me with him so he now shelters me with his body and I remain almost invisible to Jacobsen.

Suddenly I think of Norm and how our little pack of dingoes have to face brutal times. He is a real pal; he would have come up with an idea to outsmart the killers who are after me. Right now he has his own worries.

'I'll take her to her room,' declares Frank.

I continue to give a poor performance, asking with a weak and scratchy voice that is my idea of a devastated long-term friend, 'Who's going to break the news to her poor husband?'

'I'll do it myself, you shouldn't worry about it right now, Ms Cornelius. I'll break the news to Mr Jones.' This is Jacobsen.

I give him a sad shadow of a smile displaying appreciation.

As if I'll kill myself with worry.

Frank is anxious to take me upstairs, but I remain rooted to the floor.

The paramedics roll a stretcher in and load the shell of what had been Beverley less than an hour ago. She is still warm, and I am hypnotised by the miracle of death swapping different types of cosmic matter.

Death is a teacher. Never waste time on things that are not worthy of you. Death makes me alive as nothing else does.

Alive and horny.

Fuck, family, fun. The three pillars of my purpose in life. Since I am not lucky with family I have always tended to compensate with sex and sometimes with fun. Like writing a manuscript about the cannibalistic messages in the works of the old masters, a proof that the Brotherhood known also as the Order of Cannibals is still around reclaiming its right to rule the world.

Some plainclothes do their homework, outlining contours of the body with chalk. The breakfast area of the restaurant is already sealed off with a yellow tape. People from the forensic lab crawl around picking up visible and invisible things with pincers, placing them in plastic bags.

A doctor puts his fingers on Beverley's neck and nods to Jacobsen. All this reminds me of the crime scene with Fernando. I feel like walking on a mine field these days. Around me mines explode in a big way and I wait for my turn.

The manager of the hotel keeps at a certain distance, visibly upset, worrying about the reputation of the place, looking disapprovingly at the mess on the carpet under Beverley's body as if she had thrown up after a drinking binge. What I read on his face is that it's such a bad taste to get killed ruining an expensive carpet.

I hang on Frank's arm and slowly push him towards the lifts.

Jacobsen hurries after us.

'Frank, see that Ms Cornelius has a rest. I'll meet you both in a couple of hours.'

I close my eyes. That's my speciality. I pretend I am blind. Frank leads me by the hand. When you don't look you see more things with your inner eyes. Eyesight for a life on different planes. I see even into Frank's soul and feel filthy because he really loves me.

Soon we are in his room.

There's no need for him to draw the curtains. I still have my eyes closed and the darkness is like a black hole snacking on stars.

There's no need for him to blindfold me. I keep my eyes closed so he can follow freely his sensual whims. Tears stream down from my closed eyes.

While Frank tries to bury himself inside me I have time to focus on the manuscript.

I think of Manet's *A Bar at Folies-Bergere*. I scribble mental notes on *Feast of Herod* by Pilippo Luppi and one of my all time favourites: Renoir's *Luncheon of the Boating Party*. A quick parallel between Tintoretto's *Last Supper* and the more modern E. Nolde's *The Last Supper* sounds as tempting as Frank's sipping champagne from my belly button. He insists calling it *his holy grail*.

THIRTY-ONE

When I finally open my eyes it's so dark I am not sure whether I have opened them.

I flap my eyelashes, I squint, I rub my eyes.

It's still dark.

I get nervous.

Then I hear the scratchy sound of a matchstick being lit and a flickering light starts to dance over my head.

In a moment I see Frank busy lighting candles arranged in a circle on the round coffee table next to an armchair.

I count thirteen candles.

There's something strange about the way he moves, the way his lips move, the way he waits after lighting each candle as if for a permission to go on. The candles reflect in the mirror behind the armchair, a wreath of lights in the hair of darkness.

I am afraid to breathe. I am afraid to disturb him.

After lighting the last candle, he falls to his knees, puts his elbows on the coffee table, his head in his palms, and starts chanting a prayer. Almost soundlessly.

A couple of minutes go by and I start to feel funny.

His chanting penetrates my body and I can feel my blood follow the rhythm of his prayer.

Soon I have no control over myself.

I feel like an instrument in the hands of a force, superior and stronger. A vessel open for new, different energies to pass through, an empty vessel ready to be refilled with a different presence, borrowed existence.

I am not I.

No thoughts, no feelings, no fears.

I am not Sandy Cornelius, chased and threatened with death for enigmatic reasons.

I am a breath, a heartbeat. A breath and a heartbeat harmonised with the secret oscillation of different, invisible matter. Perhaps black matter. I have no voice, yet I hear with my inner ears how I tune along with the chanting into timelessness.

Then I see something moving above me. A clear crystal is suspended from the chandelier on a red cotton thread. It starts to move anticlockwise in bigger and bigger circles. Frank reduces his chanting to a single word: *Odin, Odin, Odin.*

Being in love with a Norwegian I know that in addition to being the god of poetry, Odin is the principle god in the Scandinavian mythology. His name means *wind and spirit* in Old Norse.

According to a legend Odin hung for nine nights on the Tree of the World, *Yggdrasil*, wounded by his own blade, suffering from hunger, thirst and excruciating pain. Before he fell from the tree he spotted the Runes and grabbed them in one last effort.

The chanting of Odin's name could have signified the invocation of Odin himself in Frank's quest for guidance. I notice that the crystal is catching and reflecting a tiny shard of sunshine, turning it into rainbow dots dancing around me. The rainbow, the heavenly sign that God made peace with mankind after the flood. That tells me it's still daytime and the heavy brocade curtains are drawn.

I wonder what has become of our promise to meet Jacobsen. The question seems irrelevant and offending in its concreteness, for an atmosphere of sanctity is established in the sacred space of the room.

I feel I should continue to withdraw into myself, turning into a subtle accompanying energy for Frank's doings. It comes to my head that in Greece, where the Oracle of Delphi is, it is written *Know Thyself*.

Somehow this simple invitation prepares me to sink even deeper into my own etheric juices, feeding on my own sensory system, on my own perception skills, feeling that questions and answers are made of the same matter in *coitus continuum,* generating each other. That perhaps the answer is a reverse hologram of the question, and the spirit of reading the unknown lies in knowing the self, lies in the flowing with the present; ears sealed with wax to prevent listening to the tempting songs of the sirens of future in disguise as past, past in disguise as future.

The deeper I sink into myself, the more I feel related to all the objects in the room.

Slowly the animated bubbly, chaotic, bouncy molecules of Frank blend with the non-animated bubbly, chaotic, bouncy molecules of the clear crystal, the chandelier, the coffee table, the bed I am lying on.

There's less and less difference between Frank's skin and the shirt he is wearing, between the air I breathe in and out and the tiny shaft of sunshine sneaking playfully into the room. I am no longer a solid object, but awareness and fluids that conduct life through.

Suddenly I feel immortal.

I know I have broken a taboo, messing with cannibalism, since it is the Alpha and Omega of the universe. The matter forming the universe feeds on itself, the only way for it to continue its existence.

This truth was known only to the initiated throughout the centuries. They have expressed it cautiously, honouring it and at the same time protecting its sacredness fiercely.

The idea of the cannibalistic messages has been somehow prompted to me. My brain, my metaphysical aerial has caught signals that it's time for this truth to be disclosed.

Perhaps the messenger Sandy Cornelius is supposed to be killed, as some messengers of bad news are. Perhaps mankind is not ripe, not mature enough for the truth about itself as part of a cannibalistic machine. Life and death as another form of life.

These are not thoughts, since I am as empty as I can be. These are voices filling this emptiness with another deeper, more profound emptiness. Emptiness sheltering occasional trees. Trees of major importance in various religious philosophies.

Buddha was sitting under a tree when he attained enlightenment. Odin was hanging from *Yggdrasil* the World Tree; Jesus died on a cross made of stone pine tree. Just before his birth Mohammed's father dreamt of a tree growing from his unborn son's back. I take a mental note to look into this further.

Frank turns abruptly to me. With my pondering on concrete things I have broken his cycle of meditation. But he doesn't look angry. There are no emotions in display when he addresses me almost formally and asks me to take part in his ritual.

I slowly get out of bed and sit naked on the floor with crossed legs, my favourite writing pose.

When Frank looks at me I don't see lust in his eyes, only spiritual comradeship. He asks me to put my hand in a turquoise velvet bag and draw a rune. The touch of the rustling pebbles is cool and reassuring. I come out with a stone that bears the symbol for Sun's energy, Wholeness, Life Force.

Frank is amused, almost happy.

'It is Love that loves through us and we are not creators of Love,' he half-chants, then takes me to bed.

'What happens is not empowered by us; we have embodied the occurring,' he whispers in my ear while entering me in the old-fashioned missionary way. 'This rune with the sign *Sowelu* counsels to let the light into a secret that has been kept for too long. Let the sun in, advises this rune. Sandy, this is the answer Odin gives to us. I am on your side in this battle. To hell with Jacobsen. I love you.'

I know he does, although he doesn't, since it's Love that loves through us.

'Frank.'

'Mmm?'

'You know what? I feel like taking you south where there's sun and sandy beaches and people walking half-naked around eating each other with eyes.'

'You don't mean taking me down under to Brisbane?'

'No, I feel like a closer place, Spain perhaps. Andalusia, a land hot like bread out of the oven, steamy, soaked in the blood of bulls and matadors. Matador is *killer* in Spanish. I want to take you there and share with you a cool Gazpacho soup. Frank, I love you.'

I rehearse in my mind the recipe of the soup: tomato, capsicum, cucumber, onion, garlic and bread worked through a processor, add water, mayo, vinegar, salt and pepper. This part is refrigerated. Meanwhile for the avocado salsa, stir together an avocado, a peeled tomato, chopped mint. The cold pulp goes in glassware, topped with avocado salsa and a drizzle of extra virgin olive oil.

It's delicious, it's *extra virgin*.

'Frank.'

'Mmm?'

'I'm concerned about Uncle Willie.'

'Really?'

'He might be undergoing personality changes. A couple of days ago he was crying about his family wiped out by the Nazis. Uncle Willie hasn't mentioned this before. It's strange.'

'He hasn't got time to do it, as busy as he is picking lilies.' An allusion to his girlfriend's name.

I don't like the irony in Frank's voice. It makes me feel less guilty, though, when I say, 'Uncle Willie's brain must look like a Faberge egg, smooth yet full of exotic designs.'

Frank thinks Faberge egg is something like a free-range egg and spanks me in approval.

'By the way, Aunty Susan never opens her mouth these days, it's unlike her,' I observe casually and Frank stirs in bed, stretching in a display of shameless bliss.

I feel heavy. His moisture is like the ointment of Mary Magdalena, soaking into my skin, impregnating it against the shower of poison-tipped arrows attacking me.

It requires effort to get grounded and remember that my life is hanging on a shoestring.

'Frank.'

'Yes, darling?'

'Who is behind this website LongPig?'

'I'd wish I knew.' He places his arm protectively around me and pulls me towards him.

'You think Jacobsen is working on this lead?'

'Ask him.' He sounds annoyed.

'Why don't you ask him?'

'I don't want to argue. I want to come inside you again and feel the core of you, Sandy-babe, soft, velvet, so different from the prickly wrapping of words you come in.'

I lift my head and look at him. He is a ripper, even wearing a five-day growth and an air of ennui.

'I want to read you something I found in an old cookbook.'

'A recipe for scrambled eggs? By the way, why don't you move a little bit away from my crotch? It hurts, you know.'

I move as told and quote:

Oh this skin with its magic glow of a pearl
Conceived from the thin thread life's woven of
Through it I can see the stars like through a telescope
Where the dead will come to life here
On this Earth to die again
The way you bury your phallus inside me
To die and die again.

Frank looks at me thoughtfully: 'It sounds necrophilic, you know. All this suicide bull must have gone deep into your frizzy brain. I wish I knew what for a cookbook was it from.'

'It's Norm's poem. Beautiful.'

THIRTY-TWO

Beverley's husband Paul doesn't take the news with dignity.

He smells either a rat or money. Or both.

That makes him nag on a television interview about his late wife's relationship with 'that opinionated cookbook writer, calling herself a kitchen goddess.' He pronounces *book* like he might pronounce *puke,* and sneers at *writer*, a profession that obviously has no higher place in his evaluation.

He talks more of me than of his deceased wife, and in terms that suggest I am a direct descendant of Satan. He also adds that the tragedy strikes at a very inappropriate time of their marriage, when they were looking for a conjugal identity.

'Come to think of it,' he adds, whingeing, 'in her short absence we've got two more orders for wedding gowns and now we won't be able to meet them. I've always pointed out to Beverley that I didn't like this Sandy Cornelius business. This Sandy, my wife's so-called best friend, has sexually harassed me by giving me wet looks and making ambiguous remarks about whether Beverley appreciates me enough in bed.'

That's all according to Marylin who sounds genuinely upset. 'You know what,' she starts to complain. 'I can't find even Tamati to hang out with these days.'

'How about crocodile hunters?'

But Marylin is not in the mood to make long stories and hangs up.

'After all, if I come to think it might have been that Beverley pinched my laptop from the motel room in Elsinore!' I say to Frank who lies in bed with all his gear on. He didn't have time to take it off.

'Really?' Frank is stunned. 'What makes you suspect her?'

A million dollar question. I also have one for him.

'How come nobody saw what happened to Beverly? After all you were sitting together.'

'Well, she said something about boiled eggs and you know to maintain conversation you have to ask how she likes her eggs boiled, and she's like: "Soft, please." She might have thought that I was going to bring her some.'

The bitch. She wanted not only my life, my career, and my manuscript; she was also after my lover. Small wonder she got my death.

'Did you bring her the bloody eggs?' My voice squeaky like the rubber toys with which toddlers drive their mummies mad.

'I didn't!'

I feel triumphant and wait for more.

Frank continues: 'She waited to be sure that I had no intention whatsoever. I don't know why actually. I like to please women, but I sat there as if nailed to the chair. She said she could understand why I was not bringing her soft-boiled eggs. I was feeling uneasy knowing you were with Jacobsen.'

'Thank you. What happened then?'

'She just got up and was a bit clumsy because she didn't notice her napkin fall off her lap and she stepped on it, entangling her high heel in it losing balance for a moment. I think she was annoyed with me.'

'What happened next?'

'Well, I watched Beverley move towards the egg basket past the coffee machine, along the plates of ham leg and turkey breast.'

'You were looking at her legs and breasts, you bastard!' I poke my elbow into his ribs.

'That's exactly why I didn't see what happened.' He doesn't mind driving me nuts. 'All I saw was that she swayed, and for a moment, I thought there was an earthquake or something. Then she just hit the floor, sprawling on her back. Her jacket was all stained in coffee before it turned red. We all ran to her side. What I could see was that the blood came from a wound where she had hit her head.'

'She didn't scream?'

'She didn't scream. Why are you asking?'

'Nothing.'

'Then don't pretend you're Miss Marple.'

'I can't. Remember, I am the target, inspector.'

He doesn't laugh. He is losing his sense of humour.

'How about Tamati?' I continue my attack.

'Well, I admit, Tamati was a silly idea. But not mine, Jacobsen's!'

'He doesn't seem to run out of them.'

'That's not fair. I know the guy, he's doing his best. He's probably working on a lead we have no clue about, right now.'

'If you say so.'

'Sandy, he wanted to confront you and Tamati.'

'What for?'

'Perhaps the idea was to make one of you confess.'

'Make one of us confess?' I can't believe it. 'Am I included in the suspects? Tell me!'

'Perhaps to the extent that you know more than you are willing to share with him.'

'Frank, I take this for another silly idea of your Jacobsen.'

'I don't like your tone, Sandy. The man is working like crazy to find the people behind the gut-wrenching rituals of a cannibalistic order.'

'He is paid to do it.' I snap. 'It's not that he is my protector from above.'

Frank ignores this. 'By the way, you shouldn't have visited Dr Nicolas in Campione d'Italia.'

'I don't like it when you spy on me. It puts me off and I can't make love to you more than five times a day.'

'I wasn't spying at you. Jacobsen told me.' He tries to play with my hand again, but I am too nervous for it.

'How come, then?'

'What how come?' His eyes are close to mine, and for the first time I see that they are so blue that even the white has blue reflections.

'I found you because your aunt told me you were there.'

'Aunty Susan?'

He nods.

I start to put two and two together. Is Aunty Susan of all people connected with all my troubles? How come she turned up where I am and why won't she speak to me now?

I go to the other side of the bed and open the laptop. These days it's not very healthy to be associated with Sandy Cornelius. Suddenly I experience fear for Frank. It's quite an egotistical fear. I start to cry, imagining he would not be there to make love to me any longer.

Frank pretends he doesn't notice I am crying and leaves me alone with the laptop. I open another file, *Frank16* and read: 'Scrub the skin with volcanic pumice or brick to obtain tender cracklings.'

I want to wail; instead I dig teeth in the heel of my palm and suck blood.

Death is casting dice too close to my liking. That's what I think while Frank quotes Emanuel Swedenborg at me: 'There are two worlds, a spiritual world where angels and spirits are and a natural world where men are.'

I can't but think of my dead mother and tell Frank all about her.

Margherita was a beautiful woman, one of those naturally pretty creatures who walk through life never imposing themselves or demanding more because of their special looks. She behaved as if she was just another plain, uninteresting woman, and I could never figure out why. I suspect that there was a traumatic event in her life before me that squashed her self-esteem down to invisibility. I didn't know much about her parents, besides the fact that my mother came as a surprise pregnancy when her mother was in her mid-forties.

Margherita was a gentle soul, very soft in speech and manners, and her piano students adored her. I remember I was jealous of them coming home, paying for her attention and squeezing the last obtainable drop of it. Some of them had to be dragged out of the house by their equally jealous mothers, who would never guess what it was about this quiet, refined piano teacher that made their kids want more and more of her.

That was what I felt around Margherita. I wanted more and more of her and could never get enough. An explanation for her enigmatic life as a single mother with considerable means. Hours to stare at her subtle beauty, occasionally enhanced with gloss on her lippy yet not vulgar mouth, curved upwards the way a toddler's would; her left dimple, not very pronounced, appearing and disappearing every time she got that look of a child lost in the woods.

I think that was what attracted children, aspiring concert pianists, to her. Another child was leading them to the secrets of the instrument with hidden strings. The piano looked like a gigantic comb. It was fun to listen to the variety of tones one could produce scraping along with fingernails, the back of the hand facing the teeth of the weird comb.

Some of her students rebelled; the piano looked too old-fashioned, like a black-and-white movie.

'Can't the piano come in colours?' they asked, and she smiled.

She loved them the way she loved me, and that was killing me. She taught them, knowingly or not, to play the piano not only in a digital way, but also by touching the keys and sending messages with their feelings. I remember a couple of those kids who were very good at tapping on the piano keys, fingers as extensions of their feelings, and they both are performing internationally these days.

I never knew what stopped my mother from achieving such success, and last, but not least, I never knew why she didn't try to lure me into piano playing as a major goal and occupation in my life. Instead she left me do what I wanted, and when, at the age of five, I produced my first pancakes out of flour, chicken bouillon, beach sand and apricot marmalade, she gave me a passionate kiss, a display of condensed feelings that was not characteristic of her.

It was my first lesson in living life from inside. Living life by being alive, alert, present in the present, living life with integrity and zest, living life enjoying what I was doing, thinking, talking, feeling my body and mind fully involved in what I had bitten into. I loved her for giving me that.

It was difficult not to love her, but I loved her for different reasons than the ones that made kids anticipate their piano lessons. From the distance of time I think my mother was the only creature I came to know who had no defined borders. She was more like a flow, a fluctuating roll of energy around me, reaching and withdrawing, sometimes at the same time. She cultivated me in this wrapping of non-intrusive yet unconditional love.

Words were a last resort for her to express things. Music and a communication soul-to-soul, mind-to-mind were her primary mode of conveying and receiving information on different levels.

Sometimes I would watch her in the early hours of the day, when the darkness of the night was dissipating, mixing, blending with light, creating a unique atmosphere of shared wholeness, something I would be searching for in sexual merging years later. I watched her face growing paler and paler with the descending of the day, as if she was a kind of light chameleon, absorbing and living on sun particles.

I could somehow feel the chemical reactions taking place in her body. I was learning to spell the word *love* in hieroglyphs of subtle energies, disappearing into an invisible world and coming back loaded with history that wasn't mine and a future that didn't exist.

I could hear her voice resembling a hesitant drizzle falling on the leaves of the big mango tree in the garden. Her voice, a shell for the quotation she loved to repeat at any and all times of day and night: 'For I am as a weed/ flung from the rock/ on ocean's foam to sail.'

She never told me it was by her favourite poet Lord Byron. I found it myself when he became kind of an icon for me, along with Virginia Wolf and Oscar Wilde, when it came to accepting my versatile sexual fantasies.

Frank listens to me without interrupting.

He knows without being a shrink that a regression into my childhood could bring me a relief I need desperately in order to continue across the swamp all around me.

Please God, don't let me sink!

THIRTY-THREE

Being aware of my poor psychological condition Frank decides to give me some space. He leaves the room, closing the door softly, and I love him for this. I take advantage and do what I do best: write about cooking and cooking-related things, in this case cannibalistic orgies and symbols.

With so much death around me I start to think of Harmen Steenwyck, one of my all time favourite Dutch painters. The work I have in front of my mind's eye now is *Vanitas*.

A simple still life with a skull resting on its upper jaw on a table, tilted between a flute and a book. Another book leaning against the crown, a smouldering lamp peeping from behind, a sword, a chronometre laid open to confirm that time has flown by—all the macabre paraphernalia, the sockets inviting another dimension. The swollen smoothness of the spherical crown corresponding to a shell, the brass lamp, the pitcher, the shawl, all pregnant with *nature mort* life that only *looks* still.

The painting was obviously meant to send a *mort* message but for me it's always been proof of coded cannibalistic belief that man is self-sufficient and self-contained, that he can recycle himself only through himself, that a skull, the presumed headquarters of mind, continues to carry knowledge after death.

Everything is worthless unless...Unless what? Suddenly I regress into a passive contemplating state of mind and existence. What has to come to me will come.

I no longer feel an urge to act. I lie back in my corner of the vast universe and wait for the inevitable.

All this talk about justice being done is irrelevant. Life is neither just nor unjust; it's people's limited concepts and beliefs that tint events and situations. I feel like a cosmic dust particle.

It's hard to believe that one is the master of one's fate if one is not master of one's death.

I think of Vincent van Gogh and his cut ear. Why would have he sent it to his mistress if not as a display of cannibalistic sacrifice? It's one of the most genuine declarations of love I have come across. In light of this ear, the letters of Napoleon to Josephine look like cat's piss.

I return to Renoir's *Luncheon of the Boating Party*. Everything is there, the leftover food just eaten, the fruit starting to ferment in the warm weather, exuding a sweetish aroma, the women themselves like ripe fruit to be consumed—that special ripe freshness, juiciness of youth, healthy females who don't mind being drunk, eaten, slurped, turned into another even more sensual form of life.

The sex life of cannibals is painted on this canvas. Hormones, elegant appetites, the casualness of pairing, ardent and ready to fluctuate at the same time, wine to wash down the sticky seductiveness.

With the sailing boats in the background, the suggestion is that the party might want to go on a cruise again—and then, you never know. With the weather turning nasty you might have as a result *The Raft of the Medusa* on which the discarded bloodstained axe is a reference to the horrific cannibalism described by the survivors.

Two worlds: one of the boating party that has not a single worry in the world, bubbly, spoiled with beauty, riches, available sex; and the other with the so-called *Pyramid of Hope* made of dead bodies to be finished off by the cannibal survivors, energetic enough to wave to a rescue ship on the horizon.

While Frank is away I ring Marylin. She has already heard about Beverley and asks whether it's true or another gimmick like my fake suicide. I tell her it's true this time.

'Sandy,' Marylin's voice gets deep and motherly, 'why don't you come home, kid?'

A good question. Didn't someone else asked me already?

'I have no answer to this, Marylin,' I say tearfully.

'Come back without one, what is so special about always having answers? Who cares?'

I sigh. That's so typical of Queensland that it makes my heart sink. *Who cares?* A password for a casual, laid-back way of life. A password for happiness.

'I care.' I don't want to be cross, but that is how it sounds and I immediately regret being rude to her. 'Marylin.'

But she's not offended. 'Yes?'

Her totally relaxed attitude does make me mad.

'Marylin, why don't you go and fuck yourself, you miserable bitch? Why don't you hang yourself upside down so your prolapsed vagina for once falls into place? Why don't you bury yourself in that cemetery across your street so the stink doesn't reach me here where only the herrings could...'

'Herrings? Don't tell me you're with Frank in Norway!'

That's Marylin, that's a friend. She'd always let me have my little fit, outburst or whatever, and even be happy for me. Ah well, everybody knows how difficult it is to be happy about somebody else's happiness.

I am about to say yes, then I have second thoughts. For Marylin's sake I don't want her to know for sure where I am. I change the subject, and then it's her turn for pouring out her soul.

'Sandy, you wouldn't believe how bad I feel since I discovered that white hair sticking out of my pelvis. It's grown again!'

'Oh Marylin, it's nothing.' I try to give her long-distant support. 'You can always pluck it. After all, you have some white in your head hair, so what's the difference?'

'Huge,' sobs Marylin on the other side of the world. 'It makes me feel ancient with my pussy going white, perhaps even bald. I want to hang myself, as you recommended, especially now when I finally met a decent bloke. We were in that pub, you know, and he came, a stubby in hand, and he is like: "I just come out of the grave, gorgeous, could you microwave me a bit?"

Ah well, finally somebody in her line of necrophilia.

After we're finished talking I put the receiver back and thank her silently for letting me have my outburst. My nerves needed to be attended to and she was there for me. Good old Marylin.

There's a knock at the door.

'You know it's open,' I hiss, but my emotional steam is not under such pressure so I sound almost friendly. Besides I am happy that Frank is already back.

The knock repeats and I realise that it comes from the window. I am ready to scream, but have no chance.

Someone quick as a bullet jumps into the room. I feel a hand over my mouth.

I could do with some oxygen so I dig my teeth in his palm.

Tamati!

'What are you doing here? Are you mad?' It seems that the people I associate with lately need to have an examination of their mental health.

Tamati has no intention of hiding that he finds me attractive. He eyes me up and down, breathing heavily.

It makes me more irritated. 'What was that performance with the detective? Why would you say you are a Nigerian refugee and how come he didn't know that you are not?'

Tamati is not impressed by my questions. He says nothing.

I rage, 'If you think that I am in a fucking mood you're deeply mistaken!'

'If you think you are not in a deep shit, *you* are deeply mistaken, lady!' he retorts. 'Now get off your butt and come with me.'

'I can't. I have to wait for Frank.'

'Not Frank, but Frankenstein, Sandy. You shouldn't trust the man!'

Right then there's another knock, this time at the door.

'Sandy, it's me, Frank. Are you ready for some company?'

I panic and show Tamati to hide under the bed, but he dashes across the room and locks the door.

'Don't open!' He hisses at me. 'The guy's dangerous.'

I feel cold sweat between my boobs. Might be suppressed sexual desire.

'Come with me. They are preparing to make an arrest!'

'They found Beverley's killer? So soon? Who's he?'

'You!'

'Are you gone crazy?'

'They found what caused her death. A small capsule with poison with your fingerprints on it.'

The shit gets deeper and deeper.

He already is leading me by the hand out through the window. I have a fear of heights so I start to pull back. I am not sure what's a better end—arrested and in the hands of Frank-enstein, or air-born, flying down to the sidewalk.

'Sandy, are you okay?'

Frank knocks, then tries to open the door, calling my name.

Frank is a big man and one attempt at ramming the door with his shoulder is enough. He bursts into the room, but we are out, creeping along the façade, and I thank God that there is a ridge wide enough for me to lie down and close my eyes.

I can hear the street noise coming from thirteen floors down and the breathing of Tamati who has his arm around my calves.

Lying there on the ledge I hope nobody will notice us and raise the alarm. Then I hope somebody *will* notice us and raise the alarm.

Then I remember that Tamati hasn't answered my questions and I tell him in a low voice that I want to return to the room, since I don't trust him.

'It can't be true what you told me. I haven't killed anyone. I'm the one they want dead!'

He doesn't talk, just lets go of my calves and I start to feel dizzy and disoriented. I shut my mouth.

There must be another, easier way to live this life.

Then I remember my previous state and I let myself be. Whatever comes, comes. I am not fussy any longer. After all, I have a history with Tamati and he is a doctor. As for Frank, our history is full of blank spots.

Tamati waits for Frank to leave the room after searching the bathroom and under the bed and talking to someone on the phone. I can hear when Frank says: 'She's not here. Hope she hasn't suspected something. I better go and see whether she's outside, bored of waiting for me. Tonight I'll be there. '

I try to interpret it all, but the only thing that comes to my head is that it sounds like betrayal, no matter to whom Frank is speaking. Why should he be so cryptic informing someone about my whereabouts? Why should I be suspicious of him? Could another woman be involved? I don't know. I almost wish it's another woman.

Unless they have to make the arrest.

Then it comes, the famous Danish wind. The gust shakes me and fills me with air like a balloon. It dries my tears and reminds me of the elements. My survival instinct gets a boost.

In a while I let Tamati drag me back to the room and out to the lifts and onto the roof of the building.

'We'll wait here till night,' he says, finding a cosy spot between two trolleys loaded with boxes full of detergents and varieties of cleaning materials. It smells of chemicals that kill cockroaches and ants and probably people if they are exposed too long.

'You owe me an explanation,' I confront Tamati just before he starts to rub my back. If he goes on like this I won't stay angry for long.

'I owe you nothing, Sandy. You owe me one.'

'What you mean?'

'One good fat fuck. But everything at its own time.' He continues with the massage.

'How come you know they want to arrest me? And why should they think it's me? For God's sake, I was in Jacobsen's office when poor Beverley got killed! You know this!'

'That's the smart thing about you, Sandy. You would never go for a banal thing!'

'Tamati!' I do want to kill *him*. 'You are a bloody liar. I am not a killer. I am the victim. Hello, remember me?'

'They reckon it's a different line. You are a target of an aggressive pursuit conducted by an outlaw organisation, while there's history between you and Beverley: jealousy, competition. You might have had enough of her pretending she's you, even trying to seduce Frank.'

'She tried to seduce Frank?' I fume. 'Tamati, I also want to find her killer only to thank him in every way he might be interested in.'

'Calm down, Sandy! You haven't heard half of it! They must be desperate by now to accuse anyone and feign success in tracking down the bad guys.'

Soon I purr under his expert hands that bring memories to my body.

'Don't hope for more.' Tamati enjoys his cruelty. 'Just relax.'

Strangely enough I manage to let it go. I float somewhere between earth and heaven, my head full of hot memories, my heart mercilessly pumping blood to my erogenous zones.

I remember Picton, New Zealand. Oh, I loved it there.

Tamati and I had a modest accommodation in a caravan park where we fucked our heads off. I have no idea how we managed to go for a cruise; time not spent in bed was almost unthinkable. But that was the bonus: the Queen Charlotte Sound, the fjords, the breathtaking beauty, land torn in pieces by the demanding aggressive passion of the sea.

The feeling is so strong that it brings me a headache. I try to think of something else.

'Tamati, tell me what were you doing with Jacobsen.'

'That was his way of telling you to trust me. He was afraid there might be a leak of information on a police level.'

I don't know what to think. Frank has just told me a different story. 'Tamati, tell me one reason why I should trust *you*.'

'Your pussy can't deceive you, can it?'

'But she craves Frank, honest!'

'She only thinks she craves Frank. Now shut up and have a sleep, because I promise you a long evening.'

I shift and moan for a while before I find a position comfortable for my aching body.

THIRTY-FOUR

In the dark on the roof I can feel all my senses alert. I am hungry. I haven't cooked my own food for a while.

Nothing is more nutritious and beneficial than cooking your own food. If people knew what they lose on health and energy when, in the name of sparing time, they buy food prepared by strangers! If they would just stop doing it and spend half an hour each day, no more, with all these modern facilities around, to prepare their own meal whether it's a sandwich, lemon chicken or *pasta puttanesca*.

'Tamati.' I touch his arm. 'Can you remember what meat we ate the other day at your place? I think you had done a good job of it. Giblets, I think?'

'Nobody could have said giblets, Sandy, and you know why?'

'Why?'

'Because they weren't giblets.'

I hate to be taken for a ride so cheaply. It's old bait for stupid fish. But let the guy have his fun at my expenses.

'Tamati, I am hungry. I actually think you've got yourselves a good deal with Mimi around teaching you cooking, washing...'

He pronounces 'fucking' to overlap with my 'washing.'

We both start to giggle and poke each other and end up rolling on the floor of the roof, bouncing against the trolleys.

Next, Tamati is holding me tight.

I have always have wondered how he can squash me in his arms yet I don't feel pain, only difficulty breathing.

His grip exercises a different kind of pressure on my body. Let's not forget as a rugby player he was not supposed to induce pain but to *tackle*.

Tamati *tackles* me.

Now that Frank is drifting away from my peripheral sight, I settle in Tamati's grip and relax.

His lips are making their way towards my ear. He likes these kinky kisses, half a kiss, half a bite, and I anticipate the pleasure.

'About those giblets you ate the other day, Sandy, they were nice saucy tonsils actually,' he purrs in my ear.

I freeze.

The only comment that comes to my mind is, 'Aren't they a bit toxic?'

With so many extreme situations like a loop around my neck it looks quite *normal* that I snack on tonsils.

'Not if you know how to deliver them. The trick is to make them release their toxins in the body just before you cut them, and *voila*. Yummy.'

'Yeah, it was yummy,' I confess, wondering what's next.

For a moment I feel queasy, then relived. After all, I write about cannibals, and the universe just provided me with firsthand experience. I am now absolutely sure that I was aware of the nature of the lunch provided by Tamati on that Black Friday. In a way, it was doomed to happen. Like attracts like, they say.

I might have developed a stupor or pathological apathy, so little I am impressed. Or I might have even liked the idea of walking around with tonsils sauté on a bed of rice in my system. I think there's more than a practical joke to it. I settle down to wait for the time to come so I can be taken away by Tamati.

Frank. I still can't believe it. The guy fucks me and participates in plots against me behind my back.

Appalling.

I am embarrassed to let my body change hands so quickly, so I am relieved when Tamati, obviously reading my mind, says, 'You had enough fucking for the day. I don't think I will squeeze any more juices out of you, and rubbing a dry pussy is the last pleasure on my list of earthly delights. Remember your all time favourite artist Hieronymus Bosch.'

'I can understand this,' I mumble sleepily, since Tamati has that effect on me, total relaxation to the point of drifting off in the realm of Morpheus.

'No offences meant.'

'No offences taken.'

'That's my girl.'

When Tamati wakes me I think it might be around midnight. It's not that I consult a watch; I usually don't wear mine. It's only the lazy, stifled noise I hear coming from the late working bar on the terrace that gives me the indication.

I'm sure I look a mess, probably because I haven't combed my hair since I went creeping out and in the window of the room I was sharing with Frank. I haven't brushed my teeth either.

My consolation is that Tamati's breath could also knock out a horse. Since I am the one close to him, it knocks me.

'It's time,' whispers Tamati carefully. 'It's not easy, we have to sneak out of the hotel and find my car.'

'Have you worked out how?' I feel uncomfortable. The best trick is to look at what happens to me as if it is happening to someone else. After all, why should I be Sandy Cornelius all the time?

Tamati takes my hand and, surprise, surprise, kisses it. I don't know where he's picked up these refined manners. Perhaps on the East Coast of the North Island, in his native New Zealand, but I doubt it.

Something strikes me—New Zealand, North Zealand. Elsinore is in North Zealand. My mind goes berserk, but I can't make anything definite out of this. It might only be a question of geography coincidence after all. Or conspiring of the universe. Or something to do with winds like those on the tower of the winds in the Roman Forum of Athens. There are eight of them, all blowing, all mischievous like naughty kids throwing pillows at each other, making authorities in New Zealand install rails along houses in Wellington so people can clutch onto them and resist the gusty currents that threatens to blow them away. Only very experienced pilots land there, most prefer the relatively calmer airport of Palmerston North. In Denmark or in North Zealand winds are also legendary. There are no mountains to stop them. One sees people grasping sign posts to anchor themselves on the streets, the ones with umbrellas open nearly taking off the ground. Poor Danes, they do need hot ox-tail soup to beat the cream-flambe-with-vodka-tasting winds here.

We take the emergency stairs, which is not a very bright idea, but there are not many options. Halfway down we hear noises and a door opens onto the flight of stairs below. Luckily it's only a night shift maid who lingers there for a while, smoking, and then disappears.

We advance down with care and proceed towards the underground parking lot, finding cover behind a column while two couples get into their cars.

One of the women is giggling drunkenly, hanging on her partner's shoulder, sweeping the floor with her feet. The other woman is tall and gawky; the man by her side reaches the level of her barely covered nipples, which he is following with the primal instinct of a bear cub.

My heart bursts with jealousy.

When was the last time I was partying?

There in the bowels of the hotel I still don't know what kind of a party I am going to attend.

A party sprinkled with ecstasy to exceed all my expectations, perhaps.

THIRTY-FIVE

The meeting takes place in a Mongolian restaurant. I have psyched myself up, rehearsed the right questions.

I am famished and order fried bananas.

One shouldn't order fried bananas in a Mongolian restaurant—rather, one should have something like lamb roast, Genghis Khan yurt cake or turnips stewed in blood at least—but it's not a good time for me to be stylish, even in my field of occupation. Anyway, fried bananas have to do as a logical transition between lovemaking and talking cannibalism.

The Nigerian refugee is a good-looking young man with casual rapper manners and shifty eyes. A naturally born athlete never to agonise over obesity problem. His fingers are slim and long like McDonald's chips. The whites of his eyes are the colour of *Peroni* beer and give the impression that the intense dark brown of his skin has leaked, tinting them.

Mr AbdulBilal is of perfect proportions, something I notice when he stands to greet us. With him and Tamati for company, I feel really lucky. I am tempted to find a way to take a picture of the three of us. One day I can send it to Frank and make him sick with jealousy.

Tamati watches me in amusement and ambiguously orders *chicken bang bang,* which I also like because of the tahini, a sesame paste used among the other ingredients: dried rice noodles, shallots, broccoli, garlic, red capsicums, Lebanese cucumbers and, of course, chicken—roasted, flesh shredded, plus the whole arsenal of powerful Chinese Szechwan seasoning.

I am slow to decide on my main meal. Then I have an inspiration. I order Beverley's favourite: *risotto ai fungi*. Suddenly I miss Beverley. I am appalled by the way I met the news of her death. I should learn to accept people the way they are. Unfortunately, sometimes it's too late.

I explain to the young waitress with banal blue eyes and a banal expression of interest in Tamati on her face that I want the risotto moist and juicy and the mushrooms cut in bigger wedges, not diced.

She looks at me as if I want entry to a party on Noah's Ark. She pretends to take notes, but I know she doesn't give a shit what I want. She hates me just because I am with two model-like men while she has to feed me.

I already know this risotto will make me sick. But I feel like a softy tonight, with Beverley dancing in front of my eyes, dressed like me, hair styled like mine, manners that start to make me nervous because I could see myself as if in a mirror.

I can't believe she's dead. I can't believe they want to pin it on me. Again who and why? I wouldn't cause death to anyone, not even to Beverley, although what's all that fuss about being dead?

In Santiago, Guatemala, on the first of November, they have a day for celebrating the dead. They prepare for this day, creating big kites with written messages. Then they fly the kites high up in the sky trying to reach heaven where all the dead are. If there's no wind to carry the kites up, they burn them so the ashes can still go up and deliver the messages.

AbdulBilal orders a vegetarian meal like me.

I don't know whether he is a genuine vegetarian or has to build up reputation. After all, with a family history like his, it's wise to prove perhaps that he has converted. I look at him and try to read what it is to be a boy growing up in a family practising cannibalistic cult rituals, ripping people open, pulling their hearts out.

Taking a bite of a still warm, pulsating heart.

I look at him, the way he handles the potatoes, savouring them slowly, and can't but think again that the potato looks like a human heart.

Ah well, meanwhile my meal has arrived. We still beat about the bush, engaging in a small talk as if we are here to hang out like a pack of dingoes. Tamati and I share a bottle of white wine. AbdulBilal doesn't take alcohol. We talk about the weather in Brisbane and Lagos.

The coffee arrives and we stop pretending we are at a social gathering.

It's then that I hear the names like *Ogboni, obeah, muti, sangoma*. It's then that I hear AbdulBilal's story.

'I come from a well-off family,' starts the young African man, looking at Tamati as if for an excuse for being rich on a continent where poverty continues to dig mass graves no matter how many concerts Sir Geldof organises. 'We are seven brothers and a sister. My father is a lawyer, my mother is a midwife. She works in a hospital. Since I can remember, once every month we travelled to a village where we attended a ritual. I grew up with the presumption that slaying a human being and filling jars with blood to pass around and drink from was as normal as going to school and playing cricket with my siblings.

'I learnt,' he continues, 'that if you open the rib cage and pull the beating heart it feels like a pet ready to nestle against your palm. I was taught that a morsel of this heart elevates you to the highest level of your ancestral warriors and that it is the way to preserve their winning spirit within the family. I also knew that if I broke the law of silence about our cult rituals the anger of our ancestors would find and punish me wherever I go. But I don't believe it. The world must know.'

The lights go off.

It's pitch dark in our corner away from the window through which the street lights filter.

I was enjoying the risotto, which surprisingly came the way I ordered it, and now I am annoyed.

One doesn't expect blackouts in Oslo.

It lasts three or four minutes. I feel Tamati's hand over mine while I try to orient myself in the dark.

What feels like a gust of wind sweeps by my ear booting the heavy menu book off the table. It falls with a thud and I bend to pick it up.

At this moment light floods the restaurant and I have no problem seeing where the menu book lies open to a page boasting the restaurant's special: turnips stewed in blood.

I have a problem, however; the menu is lying in a dark puddle of what looks like blood. Then I see a big bundle some two feet away from the menu book.

The bundle looks like a body.

The body looks like Mr AbdulBilal.

THIRTY-SIX

We disappear from the Mongolian restaurant before the cops arrive and go straight to the airport. We barely make the last flight to Venezuela. I had suggested leaving the country by private boat because we don't know how serious Jacobsen is pursuing me as a killer. But Tamati insists that we don't have time; we have to get to Venezuela in time for a medical congress that he says will get us a step closer to the Brotherhood. He has been tipped off by Mr. AbdulBilal about the existence of a *Promoting Centre* with an experimental laboratory there.

I still can't get over the death of Mr. AbdulBilal. 'At least I know I wasn't the target this time. Oh my God, I shouldn't feel that guilty! What do you think?' I produce a handkerchief and blow my nose, turning to Tamati while settling into the seat.

He is busy flirting with the hostess, asking for a spare blanket or something.

'Tamati.' I grab him by the arm.

The hostess extends her painted smile to me. She has seen them all: cranky jealous wives, girlfriends sickeningly territorial.

'Orange juice!' I shoot, and she disappears. 'Tamati, if you don't tell me what's going on, I'll start to scream.'

'Scream,' he says, shrugging his shoulders and eyeing me mockingly. 'The marshal on the board will take care of you. Don't forget these are terrorist times we live in.'

'Where's the marshal?' I pop my head up over the seats and look around. 'I'll tell him you are a dangerous suicide bomber with explosives strapped around your body.'

'Don't be pathetic, Sandy!' Tamati puts his fingers around my wrist and starts to shake his head with an unhappy expression on his face. 'Your heart is racing. You are the one that is going to explode. Calm down, girl.' And he shifts his fingers up my arm placing his thumb on the inside, finding the acupuncture point H6 and exercising gentle pressure.

I settle down in no time and even smile at the hostess who brings my orange juice with a packet of peanuts and a blanket for Tamati.

This time I love her. I love the big humming plane we are on. I touch the seat under me and feel my own warmth. It's reassuring beyond description.

I lean back and close my eyes. I feel safe. As safe as one can be flying ten thousand feet above the ocean.

I am collected and relaxed. I can even think of those unlucky football players caught in an air-crash somewhere over the Chilean Andes in freezing conditions for ten weeks. I remembered every detail of those young men's struggle to survive—including the use of human flesh as a source of energy. The poor guys learnt to axe skulls and suck on brains, salt came from the intestines of the perished passengers, their main menu frozen muscles. I always think of these courageous boys, who fought death on its own ground, as a reverse image of the sailors from *The Raft Medusa*. When I think of the survivors of the Fairchild F-227 of the Uruguayan Air Force chartered by an amateur rugby team on October 12, 1972, I think of them as heroes.

I also think of this big painting *Hannibal Crossing the Alps*. Turner succeeded in showing how helpless humans can be when exposed to the elements. The mountains, the blizzard, the threatening clouds, the avalanches accumulating to squash the Carthaginian warriors, victims of a bigger enemy than the Salassi tribesmen. Strangely enough, the real feeling of doom and despair comes from the sun, rolling over a cloud somewhere in the upper part of the painting. It's a sun in its negation. Cold, distant, impassive. Reduced to as equally vulnerable a presence as the humans below. More like a hole, the sun does not exude light but sucks back its remnants in a feeble attempt to survive.

I make a mental note to tell Frank about the elephants in the distance, those huge impressive animals, the terror of the Hannibal's advancing army bulldozing everything on its way. I miss my laptop.

I take Tamati's hand.

What I need most right now is a friend. He gets the message and remains still. I appreciate his understanding, then I catch him trying to establish an eye contact with the hostess.

Men!

But I am the last person on this planet to judge them because I myself know that sex is everything. Aunty Susan doesn't have to tell me it's money.

'Tamati.' I fill my voice with urgency so he slowly turns his head to me, his eyes keeping their initial position, his hungry gaze like an unrolling leash after a dog as he follows the movement of the pretty young girl.

It's annoying to see that the world is full of them but then I grow aware of how lucky I am to be liked and coveted by Frank.

I see why women embrace religions that are family oriented and proclaim that all adulterers will be burnt in hell, as Hieronymus Bosch painted them in his famous triptych. I see why women drag their husbands into practicing such religions. But I also see women demonstrating in defense of a woman stoned to death for adultery. Marylin one of them, of course.

'Tamati,' I say again when I finally catch his full attention. 'Why you think this Nigerian chump Mr AbdulBilal wanted to reveal things to you and not to Jacobsen?'

'Guess.'

'No idea.'

'Colour compatibility, Sandy. Simple. I am black, he is black; we don't pretend to be unaware that people are racially prejudiced. We trust each other for a backup when white people are involved.'

'I refuse to comment.'

'Don't be a bigot, Sandy, I love you.'

'And you're unbearable. How come you say you love me and can't take your eyes off that cheap girl carrying trays around?'

'Oh, that's interesting! Your reaction flatters me. Perhaps your darling Frank who was selling you cheap might object, don't you think?'

I want to smack him between the eyebrows or kick him in the teeth, but both actions require space, another thing I haven't got right now, along with life and love comfort.

'One thing is sure, the Nigerian guy wasn't a Trojan horse in Norway working for the expansion of his nutty family club of cannibals. He was a genuine repented boy, but they played too smart to believe him and that cost him his life. He wanted protection, he was killed instead.'

'I thought that the meeting with us, I mean with me, cost him his life, Tamati.'

'I wouldn't be too sure about it.'

'I don't know. Wherever I turn up these days, a mess follows. A bloody mess.'

'Have you heard of Ogboni? A murderous vampire cult in Nigeria. They control people through terrifying stories about cannibalistic sacrifices. It's a deep-rooted culture. People fear confronting it. Have you heard of sangomas, those traditional healers who use human remains in their *muti*—the curing process? The boy wanted to help you with his knowledge. He is aware of the fact that cannibalistic cults around the world differ as to their so-called spiritual pursuits supposed to justify human flesh-eating.'

I get the creepy feeling that Tamati is rehearsing a speech, but I am so cluttered with the thoughts and feelings of an oversensitive nervous system that I ignore this one.

I must be crazy.

I am cut off from the whole world in the belly of a jet galloping through the turbulent space over the ocean as if it was Phar Lap at Melbourne Cup Day, and I still have the guts to confront the only person I can rely on in this long crossing.

I didn't like how quickly Tamati produced my documents at the Oslo airport, mumbling something about how, *by pure chance*, he came across them. He must have picked them up from my hotel room in Elsinore after my escape. I was so happy to be a passport-holder again that I never asked the logical question: how come? On second thought, this wasn't on my priority list of looking for answers. I was so panicked that if Tamati had suggested that we board a space shuttle no doubt I would have done so.

Tamati is a happy combination of a born warrior, as all Maoris are, and a cultivated cynic, which most doctors are. He doesn't react to my open hostility because he is also a man of his own standards; he is not a person-echo but a person-voice that produces an echo of reactions in other people.

Right now he simply ignores my question with a gentle yet stinging smile that reads *women are all hysterical, but that's the way they are and that's the way I treat them, I simply put up with them or boot them out of my life by reading one of Norm's poems to them.*

I am angry. I have to do something physical to slow down the build-up of indignation inside me.

I crawl over his legs and get myself into the aisle. When I find myself over Tamati's remarkable *love pendulum*, I freeze for a split second. It's a nice stopover.

Once on the aisle I stretch and start walking toward the toilets.

The hostess intercepts me and shows the lit sign: fasten your belt. I should have known because the aircraft is already tossing its big body around, squeaking along the seams to match my stormy mood.

I try to pass by her, but she stands there like the Statue of Liberty and I wonder whether she is trained to tackle problem passengers. I tell her that I am going to piss in my panties, but she remains unimpressed.

Then comes Tamati. He smiles to the hostess, she smiles back and I run to the toilets where I lock myself in.

I am not feigning. My bladder isn't my bravest organ. Anger, cold weather, fear, hysterics—all seem to first affect my bladder. As if I open a leak in my body for all negative energies to be discharged. Sometimes I think of my bladder as the major detoxifier in my body, and I am thankful for it. I have a special relationship with my bladder. Bladder belongs as an organ to the spleen chakra, which, according to yoga, relates to the sexual appetite and the sense of taste—neither of which, of course, have *anything* to do with my vocation in life!

Turbulence or no turbulence, people have to be fed. Tamati chooses beef on mashed potatoes; I am stuffed with yin energy, so I opt for scrambled eggs, a good source of yang.

I love eggs. I can cook them in one hundred and one different ways.

Eggs are about conceiving life in pre-material form.

Eggs are the most spiritual food; they bring me curiosity about what it is like to be unborn. We wonder what it is like after death, but we hardly accept that after death it might be just what it is before birth.

The egg is part of this answer, the link between life and pre-life, which is perhaps death. Death is the bouillon of life. That's why there's nothing scary about death.

Death is as divine as life is because life and death are two sides of the same coin. I know all this, but right now I am scared stiff.

I think about Beverley. She liked her eggs soft, didn't she?

I poke into the scrambled eggs. They have the taste of smoked paper. I think with nostalgia about Brisbane and my small handy kitchen where I prepare my favourite omelet a la Pesho. Use ready croutons or toast a slice of bread and cut it into small cubes, or fry small pieces of old bread. Then take the eggs, beaten with one teaspoon of water, and splash them on top. Turn down the burner to low and wait until the magic creation starts to rise and it is no longer runny. My best achievement with omelets a la Pesho was when I tried it with cubes of garlic bread. Oh, my mouth waters. Decadent dreams!

THIRTY-SEVEN

The lights are on and I am dressed in a straight jacket, with two strong men standing on either side of me.

They must have gone all nutty.

It must be just another charade.

'Sandy, dear, you killed Michael and pulled out his heart to sustain your theory that the cannibals exist and have existed for centuries never, ceasing to promote their presence in the so called civilised world.'

It's Norm talking. I smile at him. He is such a good friend. Always there for me.

'Sandy, you orchestrated your own fake suicide at the grave of Beethoven. It wasn't fun to think you were dead, believe me.' It's Frank, but I ignore him. How can I believe a man who says he is going to divorce his estranged wife for me and then appears with her at a meeting of the Order of the Cannibals? But it is not what it seems. They are trying to tell me that there's no such thing, that it's all in my mind, fantasies, imagination, my sick mind. Something else is going on, they actually pin all those strange events on me. My fake suicide, Michael, Beverley.

'What about Beverley?' I ask hardly moving my lips.

'That was clever the way you killed your friend Beverley.' This is Jacobsen. Trust a cop to be nasty. He has abandoned his oily voice and sounds like ready-made paste of horseradish to squeeze out of a tiny hole. Sausage pieces decorate the grooves between his teeth. 'Noticing that she was excited to be in your shoes, you took advantage of this and lent her your jacket. In the front pocket of the jacket you put a small capsule of poison sensitive to heat. It was a long shot, but you calculated your chances. Beverley approached the big coffee machine, scorching hot, and the capsule burst, penetrating Beverley's skin while you were having the perfect alibi being with me.'

'On a false pretence,' I interrupt him, my speech gluey like overcooked ocra stew, 'that I will meet the refugee from Nigeria who tries to introduce the cannibalistic way of life to Norway.'

'Exactly. There's no such refugee and I was watching you, playing with you, to see what your reaction would be when you saw your old friend Tamati.'

'Ah, Tamati.' I smile widely and turn to Frank, 'You old, cold herring, you can bet that Tamati is a hell of a better bonk than you.'

I am avenged. Now they can do whatever they want with me. Turn me into sausage or whatever.

They accuse me of setting up the scene for the return of the cannibals. I laugh their words away. I know there's no need for them to return because they are already here. I didn't stage my fake suicide in Vienna just because I am a drama queen and I thought it would be good for advertising my manuscript. I didn't killed Michael, nor did I plant the capsule with poison in the pocket of that jacket Beverley borrowed from me. The capsule was meant for me, but Jacobsen is too limited to be persuaded to believe something opposite to his conclusion. I only wanted to wave the red flag, not expecting the mess I'll find myself in. I am lucky they don't pin on me the shootings of Fernando and Mr Abdul-whatever-his-name, the authentic refugee.

'Sandy! Are you okay?' It's the bloody imposer Tamati, shaking me gently. 'Are you having nightmares or what?'

'You can say so.' I am glad to open my eyes. He looks worried.

'You were tossing around, causing turbulence.'

Turbulence? Ah well, we are flying. Not to hell this time. 'Sorry,' I mumble and touch his chocolate mousse skin. I don't tell him I no longer have romantic dreams like Frank and me in a grotto full of birds, men ripping their nests for cooking soup. These days my dreams sprout from guilty consciousness. So many deaths. Life does start to look like a mine field, people around me getting blown up. I wonder when I will step on *my* mine. Or where?

'Venezuela.'

'Pardon?'

'Soon we'll be in Venezuela. Attending a medical congress on obesity.' Tamati tries to look important.

'You were better off taking Marylin with you then.'

Medical congress, shit! I want to be Brazil. To see the statue of Jesus the Redeemer overlooking Rio, the one Fernando was so proud of. Jesus offering his blood and flesh to the poor boys who have to earn a living as prostitutes. It's late for the carnival but there are plenty of samba clubs with their own dancing sprees, that's what I am told.

I want to walk around in a floss bikini on Copacabana, the world's most famous beach, rubbing shoulders with the world's most beautiful people. Like that hot Fernando from the Copenhagen gay club.

I want to soak myself in Brazilian coffee and paraphrase the great Brazilian author Jorge Amadu saying to myself: *Sandy, you can't sleep with all hot men in the town of Bahia, but you can try.*

Perhaps. In another life.

We land safely (Marylin says one should always count the numbers of the landings so they are equal to the numbers of take-offs) at Caracas airport near the ocean. I step out of the plane and squint against the blazing sun. The first gulp of air instead of supplying my lungs with oxygen, drowns me.

So high is the humidity I could as well breathe water.

The nasty experience lasts no longer than a few minutes. A black limousine is waiting for us at the exit and we sink into its relaxing, air-conditioned comfort.

'Are you sure they are meeting *us*?'

Tamati places his hand over mine, squeezing it reassuringly. He doesn't talk during the drive from the airport to the hotel. I also keep silent, looking through the windows of the car that slides like an anaconda along highways and streets stuffed with long, old models American cars that must have been popular around the time of Elvis. The driver of the limousine breaks all the rules by driving through parks or in the opposite lane to avoid being caught in congestions.

Caracas is an enormous city situated on several hills, each of them a different *barrio* with a different climate; the cooler ones are reserved for the rich (of course). Our accommodation is at Anauco Hilton, in one of its twin skyscrapers—unusual for this Latin American country where one-storey houses, whether poor corrugated shacks or rich haciendas, are part of the landscape.

Grills on the windows keep the thieves, who are also part of the landscape, away. On the haciendas, these are not ordinary grills; each one is a unique improvisation with an original style, often an imitation rococo pattern with plenty of curves and ornaments: leaves, flowers or miniature animals, mostly iguanas. All of them painted in flamboyant colours, blending into a landscape that itself offers a real colour feast.

At the hotel a man from the staff wants to know where our luggage is so he can organise it to be carried to our rooms.

'Lost,' says Tamati, ignoring me. He spreads his arms smiling. 'That gives my wife a good reason to go shopping.'

The short man of olive skin and curly, greasy as if treated with mayonnaise hair responds with a macho-to-macho smile, eyeing me with interest.

'I have to make some telephone calls.' Tamati says to me. 'Go upstairs and refresh yourself. We are going to attend the concert at the opening ceremony. The president will be there. It's always of use to be on good terms with the medical world. Meet you in an hour.' He gives me a wink and a friendly slap, which sends my bum quivering.

I am so submissive I can't recognise myself. I go to my room and take a shower scrubbing all of Europe off myself: killings, love-making, family histories. I scrub off also the weird nightmare I had in the plane.

I am tempted to call Marylin but then I calculate the difference in hours and drop the idea. Marylin should be a day ahead of me and it's silly to call someone from the future. Besides I am afraid that she might turn up nearby in the old pirate city of Maracaibo or along the Orinoco river where I've been told the sun falls like the guillotined head of Marie Antoinette, the queen who used to recommend cakes to be eaten in lieu of bread. Come to think, Marylin is the only one that hasn't joined me one way or the other. But then there are pots to be watered, crocodile hunters to be hunted, which might sound far more adventurous than hunting cannibals.

When Tamati comes to my room he finds me on the terrace gazing at the sky.

It's quite hectic up there.

The rich of this petrol country fly in their small planes, leaving the huge beaten sedans with leaking tanks to the poor.

The traffic is so congested that appointments here are fixed not for an exact hour, but for between three and five p.m., for example.

Tamati brings me an elegant white dress and a pair of high-heeled slippers. He hasn't bought them in an op-shop. I hope I am not going to blood-stain the white dress through exposing myself to an attempt on my life or through a banal female reason: my ovaries are soon going to produce the usual non-ovulated egg in spite the sizzling glances Tamati casts at me.

'You don't need much to be beautiful,' he says when I slip into the dress.

'How about a bag?'

'You can use my pockets.'

The concert we are attending, a kind of status symbol for the attendees of the massive event *Doctors Against Pandemic Obesity*, begins after a delay of more than an hour, but those who arrive on time show no sign of impatience. The President himself is present, after all the medical congress or whatever they call it, is under his patronage. He arrives accompanied by several bullet-proof cars and military jeeps with the doors removed. The soldiers are positioned with one foot inside, the other on the step of the vehicle; one hand in a tight grip around machine guns sprouting from their midriffs at an angle of forty five degrees and pointed upwards, the other hand clenched for support at the hood's edge.

It is a scary and impressive spectacle.

After the concert of top performers in ballet, opera, poetry, folklore singing and dancing, the participants in the congress are invited to the President's residence and driven there in a procession of shiny black limousines. It turns out to be a cocktail party in the open, even more exclusive than the concert itself. The illuminated garden is huge and skilfully designed among palms and exotic bushes.

I notice a number of strikingly beautiful women, each breathtaking in her own way. No other country has produced as many Miss Universes as Venezuela. Tamati is busy flirting so I leave him and go on my own to the table decorated with tantalizing bites.

I have lots of them, and they all are yummy.

I am crazy about papaya, also called paw-paw, and here, where the fruit seems to be extra rich and juicy, I can't have enough of it. Its taste gives me the sense of well being.

The abundance of freshly squeezed juices is appealing; so is the fruit cocktail bar. I grab a full, high-stalk glass. The liquid is oily and smooth with the fragrance of strawberries. I swallow it in one gulp.

Two minutes later I feel sick. I run and hide behind a coconut palm. I start to throw up and a frowning soldier appears out of the blue, his machine gun pointing at me.

His eyes bulge when I enrich the pattern of his khaki uniform with pieces of papaya, banana cake, chocolate mousse, lobster, enchiladas and fish pate, all lavishly syrupped in a strawberry champagne cocktail.

The expression on the soldier's face changes rapidly from utter disgust as he suppresses a burp, to a sure sign of his own upcoming spell of sickness. He manages to call out something like *mujer borracha*, a drunken woman, then bends over and throws up himself. The ricochet of what might have been partly digested baked beans reach the skirts of my brand-new white dress.

From a distance we must look like two kids having fun.

Soon two other soldiers appear on the scene, but a young woman with olive skin and beautiful small teeth has already taken care of me, helping me clean myself. I hope I am not attracting undesired attention. Soon I thank the girl and slip away.

I find Tamati involved in hot conversation with a tall blonde, her skin so smooth that it could have been the complexion of her early babyhood. I don't even try to interrupt them.

Next on the programme is the best guitar player in Latin America. For me it turns to be a lesson in perceiving Modigliani.

The best guitarist of Latin America has white shoes and an expensive black evening jacket. The whiteness of the collar makes him look beheaded in the night descending as a casual cloud of sepia ink. He touches the strings, plays with the tuning pegs, which seems obscene since the guitar looks like a woman.

At the beginning I don't find him very special. He looks kind of stiff and clumsy. But it is just a first impression. The moment I hear him touching the strings my skin explodes in goose bumps. The guitar in his hands promises to be not an instrument, but a voice.

The voice of the selva, the jungle, floats to us in a duet with the voice of the savannah. The rustle of the pampas grass where a jaguar is crawling low before its lethal jump, the whining of prey caught in deadly claws, condors circling, churning the air with heavy wings, waiting for their feast; the tantalising smell of blood, the cry of the coyote accompanied by a foolish parrot, the hiss of iguanas, the heavy slide of anacondas in a swamp. The wind howling against the stars, moonlight dripping down into the eyes of hyenas. The beheaded man in front of me is performing the prayer of the savannah out of seven strings, handmade white shoes, an evening jacket and a model of Modigliani, the poor handsome bastard, the bohemian artist, dying of tuberculosis, drugs and heavy drinking. I remember his painting *The Cellist*. It has the same compelling tenderness of handling the similar womanly-shaped instrument that I witness now.

In 1917 Modigliani hung his lush nudes to create his first and last one-man exhibition, which was closed down by the police for moral reasons. The naked women were called *filth*, but they were just food. Heavenly, delicious fruit on the canvas, like on a tray, turning the eyes of the viewer into two greedy mouths, devouring, sucking, munching, chewing, swallowing.

Yeah, it is the voice of the universe the man is plucking out of the seven strings. I can feel what *duende* is—the word with which Lorca described once the overwhelming performance of a female singer of flamenco.

The people around me all seem carried away with the guitarist's talent to create a voice and lead them to the only unknown place, the place where the dead lived.

I think of Frank. I miss him. I wish he were here.

I want to exfoliate myself of the recent spinning-out-of-control events and be my old self again, a humble cookbook writer with occasional big ambitions.

Wanting Frank back, thinking of him hurts.

Tears come into my eyes.

The bloody street musician!

It's beautiful, it's bloody beautiful, but I hate this.

It's not my life.

I want my life back.

Then I remember the mountain of danger and unanswered questions that stands between Frank and me; I remember that my life is on the line and I urgently have to do something about it.

I regret putting that much trust in Tamati, it's all I have right now.

Not a pleasant conclusion.

Long after the guitarist is finished nobody moves, and it is the President who goes and embraces him, followed by other people eager to express their wonder and admiration. I look thirstily at the fruit cocktails but am wise enough to keep away from them. For now.

In the late evening Tamati's blonde companion takes us to the beach where the sand is supposed to be a golden pink colour. I can only guess at it as we order drinks at the beach cafe. The moon is about to set behind the palms.

There are few people around and the ocean seems inviting. Leaving Tamati and his blonde engrossed in each other, I cross the strip of sand and soon the waves rub against my ankles like Aunty Susan's cats Tiger and Chita. When I look back Tamati and the woman are no longer there. Only drinks deserted on the table, along with my coffee cup.

Slowly I pull the frock up over my head. I toss it back on the sand and walk into the tepid water.

I swim for a while.

The body of the sea against mine is like a tender lover, penetrating me. It's such bliss: the moon like a greedy pimp watching us.

Then I hear people shouting. I recognise Tamati's voice and that of the woman.

I turn lazily and peer towards the beach, my eyes half blinded with the salty water. Time to leave; I swim back with mild strokes.

Closer to the beach I clearly see Tamati's face and know that something is wrong.

I have swum in waters full of fish that discharge enough electricity to kill me. My first thought is *thank you God, again.*

THIRTY-EIGHT

The next morning, a plane for nine passengers is ready for us at the airport for small aircraft in the middle of Caracas. It will take us sightseeing over the southern part of the country, down to the jungle of the Amazon river where the Brazilian border is.

The famous waterfall Salto Angel is there. It's the highest in the world; its waters do not rise from the earth, they collect from tropical rains on a huge plateau that pours them down into a *narrow* gap.

Narrow is an understatement. When we get there the pilot has to manoeuvre the plane and enter this needle ear with the left wing of the small aircraft pointing vertically up.

Gravity sends me all over Tamati. I grab hold of the seat arms, the buckled belt practically cutting me in two.

On our right a misty curtain appears.

The pilot is thickset with glasses and the manners of a man ready to play with fire. 'Look down,' he shouts joyfully at us while entering the mouth-trap of the abyss. 'You can see the skeletons of aircraft that weren't so lucky to be flown by me.'

Sure enough, there is a small macabre graveyard of sticking metal wreckages. I am distracted for a moment and a bit dizzy. When I look back at the misty scenery, the waterfall is no longer in sight.

My view is further restricted by the profile of Dr Andrew Anthony Belloc. His face is mostly nose, a massive, well-shaped, fleshy, smooth-skinned nose—a proud frigate crossing the turbulent channel of his bony, wrinkled face.

Dr Belloc is tall, slim, and wears Italian designer clothes, which puts him at the top of my rating. He has a deep, hoarse voice.

'Carlos,' Dr Belloc addresses the pilot, 'the young lady didn't have a good look at the panorama. Try to fly in one more time.'

I mumble something in order to prevent another dangerous dive into the needle of space between sharp protruding rocks. The pilot, though, is already making a turn, heading for the narrow gorge, lowering the right wing of the plane, holding it in a vertical position for twenty or more seconds.

Again I have toppled over Tamati and we all look through the huge front panoramic window of the cockpit. We hang like St Peter, head down, but it's rewarding. This time I really see the waterfall. It's more of a foggy steam than a cascade of water, something unreal, a heavenly veil. I can understand why it is called *Salto Angel—The Jump of an Angel.*

Besides us the sightseeing group consists of two more gentlemen, sombre and unreadable, both keeping to themselves, showing no enthusiasm. Looking more like government servants on a diplomatic mission. Dr Brankovic, a massive man with his belly floating around him under a light linen jacket, a badly dyed rusty-black sheaf of hair grown from one ear to reach the other across his dome, small eyes swimming in circles of solidified fats. And—surprise, surprise—my old friend Dr Nicholas. Apparently recovered from my stiletto he pretends to have never seen me before. Occasionally, however, I catch him giving me a bad eye. That makes me jittery.

And there is another young lady on board, Tamati's blonde companion at the party, who turned out to be

Dr Belloc's personal secretary. Laura, that's the blonde's name, juggles a computer notebook, a recorder, two cell phones, and passes coffee around. Not bad for the holder of Master's Degree in genetic engineering, as I am told by Tamati, who doesn't hide his interest in her.

We stop for lunch at an unexpectedly luxurious restaurant run by a middle aged German couple on the outskirts of the jungle. After landing the airplane on the short strip in a small clearing Carlos thanks us for giving him a round of applause. Producing a gallon of rum, he slurps at it repeatedly, then passes it around.

Tamati takes a mouthful, and some of the other men are mildly interested. I touch the bottle with my lips, but the exuberant pilot helps himself again, lavishly enough.

'Who is going to fly us back?' I ask only for Tamati's ears.

'Me, who else!' exclaims Carlos, overhearing me, and leads us out of the plane to the restaurant, which is situated on a lake whose crystal waters come from the waterfall.

Carlos orders lunch for everybody and jumps into the lake.

'*Venga, venga*, come, come,' he shouts to me. 'If you dive into these waters you remain young forever. *Joven para siempre*!'

I don't hesitate, not even for a moment. I jump. It feels like a machete cut into my oversensitive abdomen, so ferocious is the pain. The good thing is that it lasts a split second. Sometimes, I think, even Marylin is not happy to be a woman.

After my cool and refreshing swim, Carlos the pilot tells me that an old Indian legend claims the lake waters are a fountain of youth. We try to talk Tamati into having a bath in the lake, but he says he doesn't believe in Indian legends.

Anyway, he is engrossed in a heated conversation with Dr Belloc, Laura by their side taking notes.

The reason we are here in the gravity field of the lavish mysterious Amazon jungle has nothing to do with obesity. We have left behind well-known physicians discussing health-threatening weight issues with representatives of pharmaceutical companies who have invented multibillion-dollar *solutions* for weight-loss.

Carlos is emptying a second bottle of wine and chatting with the German lady. What menu has she to offer in a place so unusual for running a restaurant? I expect that the food she prepares is hardly different from the food available at any Munich *stubbe*. *Wurst,* sausages, potatoes, Apple Strudel.

Uncle Willie says that every country is good at one or two things only. Germany is good at classical music and philosophy. That's plenty, I think, and feel pretty snobbish.

Soon I have to change my attitude.

The restaurant owner is told that I am a TV and book culinary personality and has put much effort into making the cabbage look appetizing. She has prepared the potatoes baked in their jackets, a meal that under different circumstances would have made me scream with orgasmic delight. The sausages are barbequed. This makes me only more nostalgic.

I want to be home again.

Nobody can fix a BBQ the way we Aussies do. I break the rules of this traditionally male occupation and smudge myself in the most delicious smoke coming from healthy Australian beef marinated in mustard, soy sauce and honey, or sizzling pork steaks with the fat rind uncut to annoy all the self-proclaimed health gurus. I think pork is very good to eat because it's now official that pigs' IQs are next to those of humans, and pig's organs are a good transplant substitute for human ones. That tells something.

Man and pig are closest relatives in the animal kingdom whether people like it or not. Small wonder that man is called *long pig*.

The German lady, whose name is Ingrid, has fussed over a second dessert as well. Mechanically I swallow the bland lemon cream only to do something, my mind and hands occupied so I don't strangle Tamati, who keeps Laura giggling. Dr Belloc has transferred his attention to Dr Brankovic and Dr Nicholas. That leaves me with the pilot Carlos for company. He drinks like a sponge, treating the bottles with almost sensual love.

I feel totally out of place and after lunch try again to drown myself in the small lake, but they all keep an eye on me for various reasons. My revenge is that they have to wait until I dry in the sun.

During their discussion, Tamati, who is here known and addressed as Dr Whititika, and Dr Belloc cast thoughtful glances in my direction, something I try to ignore.

It's easy to do, given the lush surroundings.

Queensland is tropical enough, but still there is a hidden beauty for me to discover here in the Amazon jungle. It could have been the holiday of my life under different circumstances.

Yet I am not becoming complacent in the fact that nobody has tried to kill me or someone around me in the last couple days. I can feel something really massive coming my way and I am prepared for it.

I take a drink and walk around the pool to sit on a bench. Two huge parrots perch on either side of me, obviously waiting for me to give them some food. One is red and green, the other blue and yellow. I sit without moving, afraid to disturb them.

I repeat in my mind: Frank, Frank, Frank. Like a mantra, like a prayer, like a cry of a total despair. Then I think I might talk Janette into shooting a series here in the jungle with Ingrid by my side helping me with the potato jackets.

Dr Belloc and Tamati casually head in my direction, still conversing, still sipping at their glasses of wine. One would think it's just another party like the one at the President's palace. They both reach me at the same time and sit on either side of me, mimicking the parrots.

They both smile at me. The men, not the parrots, and I know it's starting.

'Sandy,' says Tamati, honey-voiced, 'Dr Belloc has invited us to see his rancho after lunch. It's a rare opportunity, you know; nobody is invited there.'

'Oh, really.' I have to play along, that's what my gut instinct says, so I also use my honey voice. 'How nice! And where is this?'

'It's twenty minutes' drive,' offers Dr Belloc, revealing that he is not to be outdone in the honey voice department. 'It will be my pleasure to show you around.'

'Here? In the jungle?' I squeak, forgetting the honey voice game.

'Actually it's more like a farm.' Dr Belloc kisses my free hand; the frigate of his nose crashing against my knuckles. Then he lifts his eyes, looking into mine. 'A human farm.'

THIRTY-NINE

Two jeeps with their hoods down are waiting for us.

Dr Belloc drives Tamati, Laura and me; Carlos drives the other two doctors.

Soon we come to the air strip, where three hours ago Carlos landed the plane, and head south, deeper into the jungle.

The rainy seasons haven't done the road much good. I feel my kidneys bouncing around my ears. The only comforting thing is knowing that the whole journey doesn't take more than twenty minutes. I have talked myself into switching onto autopilot, taking things as they happen.

Try to stay alive, Sandy, I say to myself. *Try to get out of this mess as soon as possible. Think of Frank as a source of a universal protection, tap on his occult energies for guidance, tune into his love as a source of power.*

Another voice screams in my head. *He betrayed you, you silly woman, he is a bitter memory of the past.*

Soon we stop in what might be an Indian village. Dr Belloc tells us that this is the last point of civilisation. A long-haired man comes out of a shop cluttered with handmade souvenirs; he spots Dr Belloc and disappears. The doctor gets out of the car and follows him into the shop.

He returns with a one-foot-long crocodile made of wood without pretence of perfection: carved with a pocketknife it possesses a genuine charm. Brown paint has been used for the inside of its gaping jaws, its back and the zigzag relief of its tail ridge. Around its neck the crocodile has a thin rope connected to its tail, so that this simple piece of art could be hung as a decoration.

I notice all this because Dr Belloc hands the crocodile to me—a present, it seems. That pleases me beyond any logic. I want to forget everything and give him a hug to show my gratitude.

'Thank you,' I breathe with such a passion that he melts. A big smile tsunami engulfs the frigate. He obviously considers this moment an icebreaker and touches my arm reassuringly.

'It's a connecting thing,' he says. 'Crocodile is as much an Amazonian thing, as it is Australian.'

When he resumes driving, his softly whistling 'Ode to Joy' from Beethoven's Ninth Symphony gains him another plus in my books until an uneasy thought comes to my mind: isn't the tune a blunt reminder of the front page coverage of me lying lifeless across the grave of Beethoven?

When we stop for a second time, it's really in the middle of nowhere.

The lavish plantation spreads its canopy between us and the sky. It's semi-dark, humid and hot like in a glasshouse; breathing is a hard job here. We have to walk for about ten minutes. Then there it is: a long, inconspicuous structure, one-story, L-shaped.

Laura swings into action, unlocking doors, making quick telephone calls, organizing coffee and cold drinks. She checks on the generator and the air-conditioning and then takes orders from Dr Belloc regarding some written materials, prints them.

Soon we are in a small office where we take seats around a table. The atmosphere turns solemn.

Dr Belloc clears his throat. When he speaks, the words come from somewhere deep inside his throat. He might not be a Demosten, but he knows the hypnotizing power of his voice.

'Distinguished guests, allow me to welcome you to our humble nest of research, a laboratory of the future where, we dare to think, we *create* that future.'

He makes a well-calculated pause and continues: 'Twenty-five years ago I was a dropout student in psychology from the University of Oklahoma. I envisioned myself as a writer. I published a poetry book and a review for it found its way to *The New Yorker*. I was anticipating a life bathed in glory and magnificence. Then for five years nothing happened. My attempts to attack publishers were met with blunt refusals. I continued, though, to work on my writing while becoming more and more active in the cause of the International P.E.N. in defense of writers around the globe. At that time a P.E.N. congress was held in New York and I took part in it. It was a memorable event.'

This time Dr Belloc stops, overwhelmed by emotion. He meets my eyes, sees my own emotional response in them, and a small, conceited smile betrays his subtle game with our feelings.

I hate him.

I hate myself for being sentimental and punished for it.

Dr Belloc becomes aware of my frustration and carries on.

'The mayor of New York gave a party for the participants in the Metropolitan Museum. In the Egyptian wing among sarcophagi, drinks and bites were served to guests sitting on mummies' tombs. Everyone was a name of success. There was Norman Mailer with his white mane and teasing manners, Kurt Vonnegut with his abnormally large blue eyes and silver-green velvet jeans. There was Arthur Miller, his skull that of an ivory deity, his metal-rimmed spectacles hiding knowledge of the all-time most beautiful woman, the great Marilyn Monroe. There were other living legends.

'It was decadent talking literature among the mummies of dead pharaohs. There was a necrophilic feeling in the air, a thrill that overwhelmed me. There was also a concentration of high quality brain material that was almost physically perceivable. I was sitting at the foot of an open casket with a bandaged mummy. Somebody was talking to Norman Mailer: "Have you ever played chess with only the white figures: four white officers, four white horses, two white kings?" I looked at the mummy. The corpse under the wrap was as small and delicate as a child's. The art of balsam had kept it throughout centuries. I had seen another method of preserving human bodies. Not dead, but live people petrified forever in Pompeii. The lava had granted them the same deathlessness.'

Suddenly the on and off cramps in my abdomen intensify, attacking me like vultures, tearing at my womb, my Fallopian tubes, making me feel sick and dizzy. Soon I'll be gushing blood like a sacrificed animal.

I'll have to talk to Laura. How stupid of me. With all this commotion I have forgotten that life is simple and consists of cycles commanded by nature, day and night, breathing in and out, menstruating, living, dying.

Dr Belloc follows the reflection of the pain on my face. I might as well have turned green, I don't know. He looks concerned for a moment, but either he thinks that I feign it to disturb his speech or he doesn't give a shit because he continues with the same elegance and enthusiasm.

'I saw the poet William Meredith approaching, supported by his lover. The elderly man was limping after a stroke. I told him I liked his poetry, and he seemed pleased. His speech has been affected by the stroke. His lover, a poet himself, was a younger man who had dedicated his life in service of the great poet. They both signed books for me. I was fascinated.‘

Dr Belloc stops again. I can see that his words have bored Dr Nicholas, animated Dr Brankovic, who starts to readjust his badly dyed hair touching it with his chunky ham-like hands, and have no effect on Tamati, who casts questioning glances at me. He is not sure what's going on with me and shows concern.

As if on cue, Laura brings a tray of cold drinks.

Dr Belloc smiles at her and continues. 'Dear friends, I am telling this long story because on that distant night I conceived the idea for the research we are doing these days in our human farm.'

I produce a spasmodic jerk, but Dr Belloc is either oblivious or he ignores me. 'My friends, as a young unknown poet in the presence of those megawatt power stations of talent I felt that the only way to achieve their level was to consume them the way the old Maori warrior chiefs ate the chiefs of their enemies. It's there, it's simple; it's been there for thousands of years. Of course, I couldn't formulate it in raw terms. I had to think of something else close to it, if not identical. With the help of Ms Laura Hay, my assistant and personal secretary, I will show you a short video covering some of our experiments. I have to admit that some of the material could be considered illegal and immoral, but we don't question Leonardo da Vinci's visits to the morgue, where he spent his nights cutting corpses for his studies.' He gives a thin smile. 'After my P.E.N. experience I went back to university and finished my studies in three disciplines: psychology, bionomics, and physics. I also came into a large inheritance which I invested wisely, and now I can introduce into the existence and the normal work of our research a new diet that will bring the coveted power to man—' He stops again, the bloody thespian, looks around and finishes in style, 'The cannibalistic diet.'

No one looks shocked. On the contrary, they look *conspiratorial*.

Dr Nicholas is cautious. 'How are you going to convince the public that what was good for the cannibals is good for them without drawing a sign of equation?'

'That's why I have invited two other lecturers today: Dr Tamati Whititika, to share with us some traditional tribe values in this respect, and the charming Ms Cornelius, a TV culinary guru and an author of highly praised cookbooks with fresh ideas on the subject. Perhaps she can suggest that the theme of our congress is very timely. We have to teach people to eat healthy and watch that their muscle mass is lean and tender. We don't want clog-arteries cholesterol freaks.'

The eyes of all turn instinctively towards the massive figure of Dr Brankovic.

Tamati produces notes out of his pocket and starts to arrange them, saying, 'Thank you, Dr Belloc. Ms Cornelius might also want to express her opinion on the matter.'

I have had enough. 'Ms Cornelius has one thing to say: fuck off!'

Now they are shocked. They look at me in bewilderment, even in horror.

Only Dr Belloc finds it funny. His pig-snort laugh actually makes me laugh. I feel hysterical. I want to punch, kick, scream. I want to strangle them all. I also want to remain alive, fuck Frank for the rest of my life and have thirteen babies with him.

'Women!' says Dr Belloc and shrugs shoulders.

'Men!' I say. 'Pigs! *Long pigs!*'

Dr Brancovic is choking with laughter. Laura and Dr Nicholas are hesitant for a moment, then also burst into chuckles. Tamati is serious, unsure what to make out of it; and I love him for it.

'Well, let's show you a video before we give the floor to Dr Whititaka.' Dr Belloc gives me a quick look to say, *You see, I don't mention you, happy?*

The efficient Laura draws the curtains behind a huge plasma TV set.

The video shows a sample of skin from a beautiful young girl and a 'product' charged with everlasting youth and beauty. Then a sample from a man whose identity Dr Belloc doesn't disclose. What he says is that the man is one of the most famous playwrights of our time and the sample was obtained bridging all moral rules. This 'product' is supposedly nourishing for flamboyant talent and creativity.

I am disappointed. When he said a human farm, I thought it was a place where they kept kidnapped people as a fresh supply for some sickos. Now he shows me cloned skin cells and cries that it's illegal. Cat's piss, that's what I call all this.

Then I get it.

The bugger has cloned Arthur Miller!

No kidding! In pills and powder for stimulating genius growths.

I can't believe it. He must have done it the night of that spooky party among the mummies, pinching away a hair perhaps...Wait a minute, what hair, the guy was totally bald. Maybe his spit, or sweat, or the young Belloc might have suggested something of a more intimate nature. I'll never know. But even if I knew, so what?

I hope the witches of Salem created by Miller will come to life and do their revenge on Dr Belloc, turn him into a he-goat or a creepy crawly.

It starts to get amusing. I better have some fun, but then again what fun can I have with a volcanic womb between my legs, rumbling, rattling, bubbling, fuming before a due explosion, tearing my gut apart.

Oh dear!

Laura seems to notice something is wrong; she comes over to me and whispers: 'Anything wrong, Ms Cornelius?'

I nod and say in a loud voice: 'My period is coming any moment.'

She blushes. Her efficiency is well trained, though, so she asks again in that same soft, impersonal tone and manner, 'Can I be of any help?'

'Yes,' I say loudly, further shocking the male presence. 'I need ten packs of tampons for a start.'

'I'll see what I can do,' she says embarrassed and disappears.

'Gentlemen, I think we can have a small rest until our ladies handle their little problem.' Dr Belloc smiles patronisingly, happy to see that the three other men relax and engage in small talk.

I want to kill him. Calling my package of PMS and geyser-like menstruation a little problem!

Laura returns and discreetly informs me that something that can do the job is available in the ladies. Meanwhile Tamati completely ignores me.

I expect this, but still it hits me hard.

He gets up and begins his speech. 'Tribes and societies throughout human history practice cannibalism as rituals. A religious, healing, magical quest for power is the bottom line. Power over the elements, enemies, disasters, diseases, evil forces. Blessing of a superior force, of deities can provide such power for a healthy, prosperous life. The belief that cannibalistic rituals are a short cut to such a blessing is enough to keep the tradition alive.'

Next Tamati resorts to namedropping, referring to Michel de Montaigne's *On Cannibals* and the 'noble sauvage' of Rousseau. Dr Nicholas suppresses a yawn and I don't blame him, but Dr Brankovic is soaking up every word. I can see him becoming a devoted follower of Dr Belloc.

For a moment I wonder where Carlos the pilot is. Not that I expect to see him among us, but it's interesting to know whether he's got himself another bottle to kill time.

I am distracted for a while, and when I resume listening, Tamati is onto a new chapter. Dr Belloc follows him carefully. I think Tamati has earned his commission as a consultant.

'I'd have to say I am an expert on cannibalism,' says Tamati and smiles, waiting for a reaction. He gets one of encouragement from Dr Belloc, who nods approvingly.

Tamati passes some photos around. 'I'd like you to have a look at some Maori combat weapons like *taiaha* or *patu rakan*, the one-handed club made of hardwood. Have a look at our man-eating tools: *maripi*, the shark-tooth knife or *kotate* used to rip open the body; that violin-like cutlery, *wakaka,* to extract the liver; a hook-shaped weapon used to break open the rib cage. My people are proud of their heritage.'

I can't believe it. Then I think, that's exactly what we *all* are, offspring of cannibals. They have even scientifically proven it by finding certain immunity in all of us to a disease transferred through brain eating. *Human* brain eating.

We can pretend as much as we want that we are appalled and squeamish and run to vomit at the mentioning of human flesh-eating, but it's there deep in the subconscious world, suppressed, rebellious, struggling to surface in one form or the other.

As always, art comes in handy and is therapeutic. That's my concept. The old masters weren't aware of what they were up to, at least not fully. Perhaps they were manipulated. Perhaps art was tapping on their pre-history, because we are not only what we are, but also carriers of information which one day will be read to an extent that the whole history of mankind will be rewritten with all the blanks filled in.

I now know that it's exactly what Dr Belloc wants to hear from me, but I am not going to give him the satisfaction.

Oh Frank, where are you? Your eyes are crescent cracks in the facade of your painted clown face. Through them I can see another, sadder clown. Here in the jungle, *amore mio*, the circus is in full swing. The thought of you is my sanity's only clutch.

I am with a bunch of perverts who want to profit from people's insecurities, from their desperate need to be loved and feel special. They soon will all be good-looking like Marilyn Monroe, Marlon Brando and Brat Pitt, overwhelmingly charming like Oprah and Humphrey Bogart, painfully young-looking like Lolita, bloody talented like Leonardo, ah well, perhaps, also like the new one, di Caprio.

The question is, are they going to be happier, more able to attract love? Or will they join the new fad just for the sake of wellness? The energy of happiness generates inside you and does not rely on external events. Happiness is a question of choice.

I have chosen to be happy and so I am now, with my life hanging on a shoestring, with my belly torn apart from piercing pain, with my love life in limbo and my sex life reduced to zero. I am happy, Dr Belloc, and you can fuck yourself, you old bloody vampire, vulture, marauder and psycho.

Nobody can hear me, only the wooden crocodile sitting on my lap.

FORTY

'The heart is the seat of the soul in the beliefs of ancient Egypt,' I hear Tamati say.

He is stirring his melting pot of ideas and Dr Belloc can't hide his delight.

Laura looks at Tamati with different eyes. His intelligence arouses her more than his looks. I bet my last penny that she is looking forward bedding him.

I love promiscuous women.

Think about how long you'll be dead and how other people in the world will have all the fun. I just love fucking and I don't mind doing it with only one person if the person's name right now is Frank.

Thinking of sex makes me hurt more. I make a pleading sign for an excuse to Tamati.

I get up and follow in the direction Laura disappeared not long ago, promising my goodies. She arcs her brows with a questioning look in her eyes, asking whether I need help. I make a gesture with my hand: stay where you are.

It's a bit of pantomime meant not to disturb the men, but it has the opposite effect. Tamati pauses and the other three shift uncomfortably or sympathetically in their chairs.

I get out of the room and come to a corridor that forks at the end. On an impulse I take the left wing.

There are two doors. Both black, both with no signs on them. Might as well be toilets.

I try to open the first one. It's locked.

The second is not. It opens revealing something I was dreading all the time.

I forget my excruciating pain. I stand numb, paralysed.

'Welcome, Ms Cornelius, I was expecting you,' says the man behind the desk.

The voice is familiar, so familiar. I knew he was somewhere around.

The puzzle was not complete without him.

The new scientific guru, the go-getter. We have all had a glimpse of him speaking from important tribunes, saying in the enigmatic voice of an initiate that the biotechnological revolution is around the corner, leaving you to wonder what it means—computerised cousins in the family, pre-programmed babies with an exterior and interior design on order, or Frank-ensteins for sexual toys?

His announcement makes me feel inferior as an ordinary human being conceived in an old-fashioned way by my mother Margherita. It will be a new world, promises the scientific guru, no sentiments, no emotions, only healthy feelings. Whatever that means.

His appearance is a perfect reflection of his beliefs. Young, early thirties, immaculate and handsome, tall, slim, fit, with strong facial features, and exuding health, self-confidence, and a will of steel. A cross between a Greek god and Einstein.

His emerald green eyes are two screens reflecting and entering the data of the person in front of him. I can see myself disintegrated down to a molecular level, analysed in a blink of an eye—an eye that knows not what tears, love or laughter are.

Yet he smiles and shows perfect teeth; a reptile's smile couldn't be friendlier. He emits an overwhelming animal magnetism, which is strange, bearing in mind what his goals are: to stray from the monkey story about creation of man and marry him with science, so to conceive the future generation of centaurs: half man, half computerised horsepower.

I hate him, but I find him irresistibly sexy. For a moment I don't even feel the first streaks of blood down my legs.

'Welcome,' he repeats, 'to the realm of human engineering eliminating poor impulse behaviour. Like yours, Sandy. I am Professor Enescu. You can call me Walter. You may have a seat.'

I don't move. Somehow the door behind me closes softly. This harmlessness in the air is far more menacing than open hostility.

I scream.

I scream so that my lungs burst, but to no effect. Nobody seems to hear me except Enescu, who looks at me with dismissive curiosity. He doesn't do anything to stop me but shifts in his chair and looks at some papers on his desk.

My screaming serves more to relieve my tension than to achieve anything else. When I have enough I stop.

'What do you want from me?' Given the failure of hysterics, negotiation is best. Bargaining for my life perhaps.

He doesn't answer, another psychological attack. He sits there bolt upright in his chair sporting a label suit as if he is in a high profile office in New York city not in the outskirts of the biggest jungle with parrots to meet over lunch. I feel my blood gushing between my legs, stimulated by the sounds gushed from my throat. I make a couple of steps and sit on a small elegant *leather* sofa, again totally out of place given where we are.

'Ms Cornelius,' he addresses me solemnly, 'you are an extremely well endowed person.'

I smile cynically. Men. They all notice my bum.

He continues, 'You are, without being aware of it I am afraid, one of those extremely rare species.' He makes a small pause. I bathe in his flattery. I have to buy my bum a pair of nice shorts one of these days. 'One of those extremely rare people who can tap into metaphysical information, reveal it and pass it down to us.'

I don't get it.

Poor impulsive behaviour follows. 'What do you mean by us, you cunt turned arsehole, snot-like sissy prick, cripple-brained idiot?' For the first time I am sorry I haven't learned street-wise language from the boys in the Juvenile Correction Centre. I am ashamed of how inadequate my abusive vocabulary is and take a mental note to do something about it once...

Once what?

'Ms Cornelius,' he carries on as if he's never been interrupted, his emerald green eyes sparkling behind the glasses, as if with a vision only he can enjoy but is now ready to share with me as a favour. 'There was a missionary man once. A missionary man who went fifty years ago to the cannibals of the Febu tribe, not to preach, but to be eaten. "If they eat me," he wrote to his wife from the ship taking him to the Pacific, "eat my body and drink my blood they will be closer to God and easier to convert into Christianity. With my flesh and blood they'll also consume my faith in God which will reach their consciousness. This will be my reward."

He keeps silent for a moment.

'He was also one of those rare people like you, Ms Cornelius. He was my mother's father.'

'That doesn't make you special, jerk!'

'You can consider this a business meeting, Ms Cornelius. I am offering you a highly paid job in our Institute for research on—'

'Or for your Brotherhood?'

He meets my eyes and studies me carefully.

'Yes, for the Brotherhood.'

I feel faint. I must be losing blood like a slain long pig.

'I have to urgently go to the toilet,' I say and stand up. I feel dizzy and sway for a moment.

'You want me to call Laura to accompany you?'

'No,' I say frantically. 'I am okay.'

'As you wish.' He sounds supportive.

He gets up and presses a button. The door opens.

Once I'm out I start crying.

That's the end of it. I can feel it.

There's no way out.

I go back along the corridor and this time take the other wing. Soon I find the toilet and the sanitary towels stacked for me by Laura along with a pair of brand-new undies. I'm starting to love the lady.

I wash myself, change, package and go out in the corridor. Then I see something that strikes me with what must be the extent of the monstrosity that is going on and my heart almost bursts.

'Abattoir' is written on one of the doors.

The noise of my heart is not enough to drown the sound of wheels behind me. I slowly turn, restraining my desire to flee.

He is ancient.

Ninety or over.

His eyes are the yellow-bluish transparent colour of egg whites. He looks at me or through me. I think once you are so ancient you have the ability to see things invisible for the others. He's leaning forward in his motorised computerised wheelchair, half curious, half cranky at seeing me.

'*Wer bist du? Die neue Laboratorium Assistentin?*' Who are you? The new laboratory assistant?

Having relatives in Zurich I understand a bit of German.

'*Ja*,' I reply. '*Ich bin die neue Laboratorium Assistentin.*'

He rolls his computerised wheelchair towards me in such a fit of anger I wonder for a moment if he is going to run me over. I back off against the wall behind me. But he doesn't crush against me, just violates my private space by parking at my feet and sticking a stack of papers into my face.

'*Xylographie! Schnell!*' Copy! Quick!

I grab the papers on the spot. 'Yes, sir!' I feel the spring in my back.

'*Was? English?*' Manoeuvring backwards, now he is ready to turn. He stops and looks at me.

'Herr Tommler?' A two-meter bimbo appears at the end of the corridor. The bastard must have touched his baby-sitter button. It takes her pretty head some time to sink in the situation.

It takes me some time, too.

Herr Tommler.

The old filthy bastard, uncle Willie told me about? Could it be him, his age looks right? The bone pyramid, the Nazi camp, forcing people to eat human flesh, the place here run by cannibalistic elements. Oh no! I want to punch him, kick him in the balls. Cook him and his balls and feed him to Norm's dog Billie.

I want to kill him.

He also scrutinise me before saying triumphantly, 'You are one very predictable young lady, Ms Cornelius. Sandy

Cornelius. I knew that sooner or later you'll come to visit me.'

'Visit you? You fucking fox fart. The monster, the scary messenger of death, the omnipotent Herr Tommler, shit! Look at you now, worms coming out of your ears, the bad breath of history coming out of your mouth where loose dentures dance like pirates on the coffin of a dead man. You are a dead man, I have a debt to score with you about what I just heard you did to my family, you old criminal bastard.'

He enjoys every minute of it, knowing he has me like a mouse in a trap. The bimbo bodyguard by his side ready for action and nowhere to escape. This time I had it.

'You are more good-looking, Ms Cornelius, than when you appear on those appalling shows where you chop carrots and onion and call yourself a kitchen goddess. Everybody starts to chop carrots and onion for a living these days, don't they? And I can easily accuse you of a crime against humanity, too. Half of the population in the world die from overeating and the other half of hunger. You tempt the first half to eat even more by creating tempting irresistible dishes, you lure them to their death.'

I don't know what to say, so I scream. My own head chimes with the scream and the professional blow the bimbo gives me with the side of her hand putting a lot of weight behind.

I curl in on myself like the crust of an old sandwich.

Herr Tommler watches me with sympathy.

'Maria, don't break her,' he says softly, 'I still need her in one piece for the ritual extraction of her heart.'

I start to cry. For myself, for Frank whom I still love, despite his betrayal, for my unborn child, always postponed. I cry for Marylin and Norm, for Tamati, the bastard that dragged me here, and my mother Margherita, for a father I will never know. For the good old days when I was cleaning refrigerators of old Greek ladies who always had jam of green figs for me or a half-rotten apple to share. I cry for a pack of dingoes hanging out in the night, sniffing each other, feeling good. I even cry for Beverley.

Feeling weaker by the minute, losing blood, losing my mind to fear, I sag on the floor and cover my face burning from the marshal art blow.

They finally got me. Who I think I am to outsmart them, to beat them on their own playground? Next I'll be a shell of rotting flesh, my heart *extracted*...Like a tooth, like a tonsil?

'You are a remarkable specie,' continues Herr Tommler as if I am here to be judged by a panel. 'You have zest for life to match your provocative beauty. Believe me, I hate to do it, at least I am sorry that it will soon finish because I was watching every step of your reckless bravery. My admirations.'

He hasn't moved while talking, still blocking my way. The bimbo next to him, athletic, menacing, ready to deliver.

For a moment I know what a pilot feels when seeing a mountain peak rushing towards his craft, what a scuba diver experiences at the shadow of a great white shark. What they feel is not unlike a broken beer bottle stuck against their throat.

'Please,' I say. 'Please, I don't want to die. You've caused so much death in your hay days. Perhaps you can spare me.'

The bimbo called Maria sneers. Herr Tommler has his eyes on me wide open like two Cunnamulla beefsteaks overflowing the plates.

He gently rolls his car towards me. 'It won't hurt, *Sandy*. Promise. I like your texts on Salvador Dali. I used to know the old he-goat. Yet you lack an insight about his fascination with *the Fuhrer*. Dali said he saw Hitler as a masochist obsessed with the *idée fixe* of starting a war and losing it in heroic style. You see, the war was never lost because *we* are here.'

'You are overdue,' I stop crying, feeling angry, regaining my confidence. 'It's a biological thing. You have to go. It's high time you died. It's a new millennium.'

'We have always been around, we will always be, Ms Cornelius, Sandy. You are right. The Last Supper was a plain pagan initiation, a cannibalistic orgy to show the profane plane of human existence Jesus was aware of. John the Baptist, the young eunuch castrate was the carrier of spirituality. The kiss the two of them shared sealed the duality of this cosmic message. Remember when Pilate asked Jesus whether he was the son of god, Jesus never answered walking away. Why? A good question for a cookbook writer, don't you think?'

A grimace that can mean anything surfaces on my face. I save energy. I am a cookbook writer! Then cook. Cook something smart. Smell, sniff, use your nose, your palate, your brain. Smell with the tips of your fingers, try your taste buds to define what's missing? What ingredient do I need to cook this meal to perfection?

'Don't worry, Sandy,' the old fellow drones. 'Maria has a black belt and she has mastered her blow of mercy. Then I see for the rest. As for the Last Supper it's a men's thing. The same men's thing that brought together Dali and Lorca and the other male genii of their circle. There weren't women elevated enough to keep them company. They had to keep company to each other in every way.'

'Don't tell me you hint that the Last Supper was a gay party?' One can hear any crazy interpretations.

'Perhaps as much gay as Fernando was.'

'Was?' I cringe.

Herr Tommler nods sadly.

And somehow this fresh grief triggers and carries out the reaction. I spring forward without exposing myself in height and grasp one of the wheels. They are blocked and don't budge but the impact is enough to overturn the monstrous robot of a chair, which hits the ground with a thud. Herr Tommler drives without a belt and pays for it. He flies out of the wheelchair and grabs Maria by her hair to stop himself in his fall as she bends to finish me off. He topples over her. Quick like a lightning, she handles the distraction and comes after me.

But by that time I'm already running.

The door with the sign *abattoir* abruptly opens and that causes a second setback for the marshal art bimbo who ends up hitting it with her pretty nose. And I know my mother Margherita must protect me from above.

FORTY-ONE

It might be our *Pastoral* time. Beethoven's Sixth Symphony played over and over again. The bucolic tunes chasing each other, a repetitive question, a tender, obsessed persistence equal to that of Rembrandt's churning self-portraits. The wind instruments take over, introducing the murmur of the leaves, the rippling of the brook ready to succumb to the approaching storm. *Allegro* amidst peals of thunder, *staccato* and *pianissimo* of the violins heralding the return of the rain tears shed by Chac, the Mayan god, bringing gentle rain to earth.

Silence.

Like a full stop before the madness of Nature flares up. The four elements fighting for dominion: water earth fire air, all in one, blasting, roaring, rotating, rolling, hissing, howling, shuddering. What is the colour of the storm arriving violently, forcing its way into the ear trumpets of the stone deaf composer?

The rain.

I don't know what they call it here. Monsoon, tropical storm, it doesn't matter. Water pours in buckets, a wall coming from the skies as if they've been ripped open.

I am having a rough time in a stolen jeep—the one the pilot was driving. He had conveniently left the keys on the dashboard, unless it was another trap.

The road is sinking under me and the jeep is bumping and tossing me around. I struggle to keep control of the steering wheel. I am dripping wet; the car fills with rain and the pedals respond like madmen, if at all. I start to doubt the wisdom of my impulse to run. I bet they won't be bothered to follow me, knowing that the rain and the road conditions will kill me anyway. I hope someone will be crazy enough to organise the pursuit. I consider stopping, turning back, asking for mercy.

I try, but I can't stop. The vehicle doesn't know whether it's a car or a pontoon. We could skid any moment. I can't even slow down. I pretend I am in control, but I might as well close my eyes. I can hardly see anything besides the tunnel between canopy and trees marking the blurred road. On top of it all I feel my blood sugar level dropping. If I don't eat something I'll faint and that will be the end.

The green eyes of Professor Enescu flash like lightning through my overworked brain, and I realise that they looked absolutely identical to Vincent van Gogh's eyes in *Self-portrait with Bandaged Ear*. Madness, crystallised madness in those glassy eyes. I would shiver with fear if I wasn't shivering with cold already.

I really might go back, but for Herr Tommler. The Drummer. That's what Tommler means. The Nazi war criminal from the pictures in that video Uncle Willie showed to me on the yacht.

Small wonder they have gathered together, the old icon pushing cannibalism in wartime and the young disciple armed with science and money to continue this crazy thing.

My only comfort is the documents stuck deep into my cleavage. The feeling is like when I had to make my boobs look artificial in Copenhagen. If they aren't ruined by the rain, they might be important enough to end all this. On a hunch I pull them out of my shirt and stick them in the glove compartment.

Then it happens. The engine coughs and stops abruptly. I am thrown out of the car to land face down in the muddy soup of rain and dirt. I lie there dizzy, without the energy to crawl off the road and into the dubious shelter of the jungle.

The impact of the water is like a power hammer. I'll soon be dead. The way I have heard it happens, patches of my life will start to emerge before my inner eyes. The waterfall of rain flattens me down like a butterfly and I can't do anything besides pray to stay conscious.

Slowly my fingers find the energy to grasp the slime in search of something hard, a rock perhaps, to motivate me into an attempt to move.

I am really afraid now. I should concentrate on my physical surroundings and try to survive, not to be lured into mental squabbling. I am losing it, which is the worst, if there could be anything worse.

I am drowning. It's me I am seeing lying there, my heart flapping, my body incapacitated, my mind blurred.

Slowly I lift my head against tons of water and open my mouth. I say a simple prayer: 'Please, don't let me die, please.' I have another vision, that of Jusus of Ghent's *Communion of the Apostles* where Jesus offers the piece of bread to the mouth of a gaping disciple. I wouldn't know who he is. Perhaps Peter, perhaps Judas. I wonder why bread and not fish. In Greek the word for fish, *ichtus,* contains the same letters as Jesus Christos Theou Uios Soter, which means Jesus Christ, Son of God, Saviour. It's so simple and close to the heart, what Jesus does, what he preaches: LOVE. Where is my love, my love for myself? I start to cry, but my tears can go only inwards, since there's so much water around me that it repulses them.

Suddenly I am light and relaxed. I realise that I have never been closer to nature and to the universe. It's a funny feeling that fills me with pride and a prelude to happiness. I am numb, but I start to laugh. I see Jan Steen's *Beware of Luxury,* that little dog on the table gobbling up a bake while the family lives it up . I have always been sorry for the lovely cookies scattered on the floor within reach of a snorting hungry pig, who is ignoring them for pearls, satisfying the painter's taste for proverbs. Yet here it is; I think of the pig alongside the other pigs, the long pigs.

Then I ask myself, what are the odds that I stay alive? I admit: little. I slowly come to terms with that gnawing thought, and as I do it activates me to start moving, crawling, sliding, rolling. Soon I disappear among the lush greenery of the Amazon jungle.

FORTY-TWO

My friend Norm likes to say that the Earth is a whirling dervish.

The moment I lift my head it starts spinning like...well, like a whirling dervish. My menstrual blood continues to run freely out of my body. My mouth, eyes and ears are full of water; I am so soaked, my bones are probably not full of marrow anymore but slime and mud. The only good news is that the torrential rain gives signs of subsiding. In the situation I am it doesn't help much, but it looks like the straw grasped by the drowning man.

I find a huge hollow tree and try to use it as a shelter but regret it immediately. What seems like hundreds of small insects are disturbed by my intrusion and fly away with a cry, run away with a snort or crawl on top of me. I scream. Something that looks like a scorpion, only because it is a scorpion, lands on my bared breast close to my heart. I try to remain motionless—not easy with other crawlies trying my patience. A gang of mosquitoes start to work on my face and I understand how people's hair goes white in a fraction of a second.

I must have been naïve to consider the combination of the scorpion and the mosquitoes as the worst scenario. A few minutes into my enduring motionlessness I feel a sneeze coming. Stretching my luck I feel around me with both hands, operating them only from the wrists in search of two sticks. The idea is to lift the tail of the scorpion with one stick while using the other to whack it away.

Then I touch something with my right hand that makes my hair stand on end. My brain registers all the properties: slippery, cold, rope-like, subtly rippling and scaly. My brain processes the data and announces its impartial conclusion: snake, a big one. Coming from Australia where nine of the most venomous species in the world live, I have been raised with the belief that snakes are harmless creatures unless you provoke them. I remember once stepping two inches away from a red belly snake. He remained calm and undisturbed, perhaps because I also calmly continued my parallel trajectory, which was no threat to him.

That was long ago and I wasn't on my last leg. I wasn't alone, a fugitive in a jungle where the arm of the law is a chimera.

I stop breathing.

Under my hand I can feel how slowly, very slowly the snake shows an interest in my presence. My brain forgets minor perils like scorpions and mosquitoes. I haven't got much to lose; it's only my life that's at stake. I grab the scorpion in a lightning strike and hurl it away, jump to my feet and start to run back to where the jeep is. With both palms I squash some mosquitoes before I trip on a root system and fall, hitting my head.

I must have lost consciousness. When I open my eyes the snake is all over me. A brown constrictor, thick as my two arms together.

Suddenly I feel high. I can hear my mother playing Chopin in our suburban house in Everton Heights. I'm going for a walk along the streets, absorbing the life of this area. The whinging of a spoiled brat. Couples having dinner with in-laws. A glimpse of a garage with clotheslines of rainbow washing. A square of dim glow behind a curtain; nobody knows what drama is about to be staged—he is sleepy, she's hysterical. A late chat around a car, someone is leaving, for good? Kitchen landscapes with china plates arranged on stands like frozen daisies. The dog across the street is suspiciously quiet despite the occasional cars. A triangle of grass like a patch of pubic hair divides two streets with a common dead end. A late skateboarder shredding the quiet evening is soon accompanied by a whistle, a laugh, water flushed in a toilet. Potted plants like hanging gardens, the smell of fried fish. An empty chair on a deck with the halo of human warmth. That noise of the skateboard again.

The noise of my cracking bones.

FORTY-THREE

I see myself from above. I float and circulate light as light. I am in a state of subtle bliss when I see myself wrapped in a sliding coil. There's nothing dramatic about it. It's not a Laokoon. It's me crossing the threshold between two worlds. I even have some fun thinking that I am slowly turning into one of the mummies Dr Belloc was talking about, but with a living bandage. A piece of art. A piece of cake. Whatever.

I see that the rain has stopped and the water now soaks deeper into the ground, vanishing under roots, leaves and branches. There are still puddles mirroring the canopy high up where I am floating. Seeing my reflection in a puddle, I think of the theory of the coacervate drop as the first cradle of life.

Now that I am on the other side I can perceive all this with detachment, as Professor Enescu recommended, without any emotional engagement. The snake is beautiful, perfect. His belly is lifeless yellow, almost beige, and blends with his brown back decorated with black ripples. The elegance of his movement while constricting me matches this beauty, an aesthetic delight equal only to watching Van Gogh's *Sunflowers*, my all time favourite painting. This here is lacking a bit in vibrant, insane yellow, but the insanity comes from a different source so it's still compelling to watch how I shrink more and more in the grip of my last lover.

I keep thinking of a certain woman I used to know, Sandy, what was her name? She was good at getting high on danger, challenge, recklessness. A kind of carefree, careless facets of behaviour and life, a spirit painfully determined to express its freedom away from the beaten path, foreign to animalistic traits like instincts of self-preservation or survival.

No dream for this woman of a quiet living and security. A stone cast into still waters to disturb, a slap across death's face with that casual approach. She treats life as a game of Russian roulette because she knows, this Sandy, that fear is a pair of bats she wears as clinking earrings half hidden in the night canopy of her hair. Because she knows fear doesn't stand between her and death. I love this Sandy girl. I love the bloody bitch and I want to show how I feel, but I can't. My feelings have been surgically extracted, though I don't feel emptiness, just relief.

I know it's time for me to go, so I say good-bye to Sandy and wish her luck. She might need it.

I am feeling even lighter when I see him. A small dark man, totally naked with the exception of a machete he is holding next to his body, which glistens like it has been soaked in crude oil. It's Venezuela after all; the chances of being soaked in crude oil are higher than they might be somewhere else. The man approaches cautiously. It's not out of fear, as I first presume, but over calculating his next move. I close my eyes, detached but still not in a hurry to see my own head chopped off. After all, I am not Marie Antoinette, or am I?

The little fellow lifts the machete above his head and strikes.

I fall into darkness.

FORTY-FOUR

Far, far away I want to go and partake in a masquerade, changing personalities, my face, voice, harmless vice, dumping stagnant thoughts, clogged bursting feelings, trading in an expired existence rolled in perverted solitude and clumsiness. I want to be free again, borrow new names, new identities, be anyone, anything but me.

Now that I am so close to the stars, floating between these enormous gas whirlpools, I meet a tree whose bark I hear, fish allergic to water, birds with a fear of heights. I see other beings inhabiting those spaces and I am happy because it's proof of what I have always thought: we are not alone. There is life on different planes. This is where my soul belongs.

My body now is the haunt of ghosts. The dead live inside me. My words are tiny crumbs from their dinner table.

I was is future tense.

FORTY-FIVE

The first tingling I feel is around my eyes. I feel my eyelashes, each coarse hair, each root, the tantalisingly slow growth. It takes time for me to feel the next tingling, around my heart. It pumps slowly. The quietness between pumps scares me; this feeling of fear, this emotion makes me think that I am alive. This theory is backed up by the next tingling, the latent growth of my pubic hair, which over the years I have trimmed, blow-dried, shaved, dyed, waxed, plucked, and frizzed. Then my nose comes to life. The air tastes of champagne, bringing back nostalgia for the time when Frank was still an expectation, anonymous, unidentified by place and time, something in the air due to happen.

I try to move my fingers, then my toes. I can't. I feel annoyed about it, but the annoyance doesn't do me any good and my brain shuts down again. I sink into semi-consciousness, hearing distant voices, sounds I can't understand. It's a language unknown to me, another reason to get annoyed. Somebody pours a burning liquid into my mouth and I convulsively react by throwing up and sitting up at the same time, as if a spring has clicked in the small of my back. I feel my heart pumping like crazy. My blood resumes circulating, rushing to the remotest corners of my body so even my nails get enough warmth. Then I collapse back onto the ground, looking up at some trees with creepers so thickly knitted I can only see the sky as if through a mince machine.

A small fellow bends over me; he is wearing a feathered band in his hair and strings around his neck, mostly made of big rattling seeds; one string I identify as made of teeth. Human teeth. I don't know whether I should be grateful for being brought back to life. The guy is still working on it with such a concentration and authority that I sink into his spell and start to cooperate.

The shaman, because there's no doubt that this is a shaman or a medicine-man, starts to leap around me, occasionally jumping over me and then bouncing his knees against his bent forehead. He brandishes a carved ward and fans me over with a whole bird wing of black and vitriolic green colours, reminding me of certain eyes. My head is still not functioning, so I can't connect them with a face.

The man stops jumping, squats and feels inside a bundle. He produces a small, two-sided drum on a stick with two loose seeds attached by strings and starts to whirl it in a howling rhythm, occasionally correcting it. Once happy with the sound he starts to accompany it by producing low deep-throat animal-like barks. My mind is clearing now, tuning into his chant. First I look around, then at myself. I am a mess. I don't know how I am in one piece, my arms are twisted and my legs look like they have been kept in bottles for ages. My feet look like they belong to a Chinese girl, a century ago when they kept them bound in wooden shoes, crippling them so they wouldn't grow, thus satisfying the sexual demand of the time. For a moment I think whether I can use this to my advantage. The idea brings a smile to my face, a smile that hurts. I fall into complete darkness again, but the chanting somehow pierces my conscious and I feel my body responding to it on a physical and chemical level. I also start to hear cracking sounds inside me accompanied by more pain, and this time I black out and remain totally numb.

When I open my eyes again the surroundings have changed. Now I am lying in front of a strange house that looks like a beehive. On a branch in front of me hangs a familiar snake. They have cut off its head and tail and skinned it, and the skin is hanging motionless in the windless heavy humidity, its scales reflecting the sieving sunbeams toiling their way through the wild, aggressive flora. Snakes have scales like fish, I think, and try to remember why I am here. Perhaps another location for shooting one of my TV series on cooking, the one entitled 'Unexpected Encounters.' A tantalising aroma gives me hunger pangs as strong as an appendicitis attack.

Over to one side I can see the figures of some small people gathered around a fire. There are seven of them: two men, three women and two kids that could be any age. They are all naked and wear it like expensive evening outfits. For a moment I feel my own clothes like an old skin. I am expecting them to peel me like they did the snake. Then I realise that I am also naked; what I take for clothes is a layer of caked mud mixed with plant matter. I start to like it here. I have done culinary tourism, sex tourism, but I have never lived in a nudist colony.

I try to get up and eventually succeed. My body feels funny, a stranger's body, like a borrowed car with a coded computerised mode of operating which I have yet to learn to drive. I manage to put my foot forward, but can't complete a step and fall. That draws the attention of the women. They look at me and one of them comes over to me and disappears past my legs into the house. She comes back to check on the food cooking (Janette might also be interested in it) and after a while the shaman appears. He drags me fully inside the beehive house and blocks the hole with a palm leaf. He then brings fire—from the oven outside, I presume—and starts smudging me with herbs whose fragrance is so overwhelming that I feel nausea. I try to tell him that I am hungry and have to eat something to boost the glucose in my blood. He doesn't pay attention to my desperate pantomime. I fall asleep, light-headed with the smell.

When I open my eyes it's day again, but somehow I know that it's not the same day I fell asleep. I feel so good that I stretch and give a yawn. I am moderately hungry, thirsty actually. There's no one around so I get up and walk on my fours out of the beehive house. I see them all gathered around the earthen oven. They all look up at me and smile to return my smile. One of the men gets to his feet holding a machete like a cross against his naked body; for a moment I think that one of the spells of the crucifixion is that Jesus is nailed almost naked on the cross. That breaks every woman's heart. Small wonder there were and are many brides of Christ.

Then it happens. The image of the man with the machete bursts my amnesia. Everything floods back to my memory and I scream. The man stops in his tracks, reprimanded by the women who show him to leave the machete behind. I look around, but I don't see the shaman. The man slowly approaches me, perhaps expecting new outbursts of hostility or fear. I stand still, overwhelmed by the return of my memory and the events of the last few days. My hunger, however, is stronger than my fear so I look towards the women and ask them in English, then in Spanish, then in gesture language whether I can join them for the meal. They point at the man. I haven't noticed that he is also carrying what smells like a piece of roasted meat wrapped in a palm leaf. I run unrestrained towards him; he instinctively backs off a couple of steps, then smiles and lays the leaf on the ground in front of me. I sit quickly and start to devour the succulent food.

The kids don't take their eyes off me. The women giggle. The men nod their heads approvingly. I want another piece, but they don't oblige. Instead I am handed a primitive clay jar with cool water to drink. I start to sing the shepherd's tune from the *Pastoral*, thanking the universe, my mother, and these people. I now know that it's been a miracle to bring me back to life and to patch me up. I get up and make a low bow. They can't interpret it but the kids start to mimic me. We bow to each other for a while and it's a relief to know that life now has different dimensions.

A couple of hours later I am scrubbed squeaky clean with the help of the two women. My body is bruised black virtually everywhere; that I belong to the Caucasian race is something I can't prove right now. My joints hurt, my muscles are sore, but I mentally repeat: *it's a miracle, it's a miracle, Sandy, that you are alive. Enjoy*. But I am never satisfied. Once fed and cleaned I start to think about getting out of here.

Then comes the shaman. This time it's not for a healing session. Very aloof, he touches my nipples, then kneels and sniffs between my legs. He nods approvingly and orders me with gestures to follow him.

Before we depart I ask the men with gestures if I can have the snakeskin and see the surprise in their eyes. It's not dry so it is easy to fold and tie up with a piece of liana.

FORTY-SIX

The shaman and I walk for more than an hour, until I am at the end of my magically reclaimed strength. The shaman is understanding. He walks in front of me and clears a path with a machete, often stopping to give me water, which he collects by shaking some leaves over each other. Sometimes he also cuts a liana above his head and gapes his mouth to meet the gushing water stream, then letting me do the same.

In a small clearing he stops and shows me to lie down and have a rest. He speaks some Spanish so I get the idea that he wants to leave me for a while. I become hysterical. He turns his back to me, but I throw myself at his feet and ask him not to leave me alone. He misunderstands me. A huge, lustful smile turns his chiselled face into a papier-mâché mask. He pats me on the buttocks with a moist, surprisingly gentle hand. *Luego, luego*, he says, after, after. *Tu mi mujer*, you my woman.

Not that I haven't suspected what's going on, but the brutality of the revelation hits me hard. After all, in fairy tales princesses always marry the good guy who saves them from the dragon. I shouldn't be so bloody ungrateful. I try to talk sense to myself: he dug me out of the grave. One man, more or less, who cares. I am alive and I have to celebrate. Easily said.

First I have to deal with my panic attack. I don't want to be left alone and he is not going to stay. Suddenly an idea comes to my mind. I grab the two-sided drum from his medicine bundle, catching him off guard, and start to whirl it; the two seeds go mad, bouncing, rattling, beating the shit out of the tiny musical instrument. He makes a furtive attempt to retrieve it, but the destructive rhythm works faster than his magic-based defences. Perhaps because of them he is more susceptible. My wrist hurts and I am about to drop the drumlet, but I persist, silently blessing Dr Nicholas, and promise myself that if I get ever out of this jungle, I will visit him and buy him a coffee at that place by the lake where the owner had bushy brows and knew how to make real coffee.

Once the shaman starts to look like a zombie I have enough sense left to stop drumming. He is my only lifeline to the world and I don't want to lose him. I collect the contents of his bundle and stuff them back inside; when I hand it over to him, I bend and kiss his hand, hoping the message of this simple gesture is universal. It might be because the shaman remains still and quiet for a while, then looks at me thoughtfully and utters: '*Sagrada, sagrada, mujer sagrada.*' Sacred woman. Next he kills a bird for its wing. The feathers are the same black and bright green colours like those of his fan. It's dripping blood, but I receive it without making a big fuss. Now that my own bleeding has stopped I can afford to carry the horrendous fan around.

Soon we are on the move.

FORTY-SEVEN

I am thirsty. My lips are sealed by glue that must have been my saliva not long ago. Frida Kahlo's still life *Viva la Vida,* a Jewish six-pointed star configuration of watermelons, dances in front of my eyes. In the centre is the dark green globe of the fruit and the six points are created by six watermelons in different stage of consumption. All cut pieces show bloody red pulp, and I want to bury my face in the painting and suck them dry.

I promise to myself to bury my face in a cooled watermelon once I am out of here.

Out of the no man's land.

Out of nowhere.

Finally I can't walk so the shaman throws me across his shoulder. I wonder how he does it, since he is such a small man. His face is fat and flat and he smells of oil that's been reused many times for frying chips.

Not only am I thirsty I have a craving for chocolate to lubricate my brain and give my wrecked body a shot of energy. I wouldn't mind a good piece of meat either. I am no vegetarian. I love my buttered chicken, my sweet and sour pork, my meatballs in tomato sauce. Yet every winter I cook at least once a disgustingly cheap meal that people disregard over its plainness without knowing the benefits. For it I buy a bag of bones with as much marrow and cartilage as possible and boil them on low flame for several hours until they almost disintegrate, adding occasionally a piece of celeriac, a carrot, and a potato which all disappear in the bouillon. I tell you there's nothing more nutritious and more simple to get your minerals and to lubricate your body parts. Anyway it tastes better than the chicken feet at the Chinese restaurants.

I am still torn about the shaman; I wouldn't have gotten anywhere without him, but I am still uneasy over his previous possessiveness of me. And where is he taking me?

We take a break under a tree whose fruit he collects and invites me to try. It's not much, but I suck on the stringy, shrivelled, rotten-pear-tasting fruit. I thank him. He could have been a good husband and it's silly that we are conditioned by our upbringing in different civilisations.

I hear again the noise and ask him: '*Que es esto?*'

He points to the sky.

I already know that the sky is full of small aircraft, but this noise definitively comes from nearer ground level. I'm sure he knows this perfectly well but is reluctant to admit it.

It's a long shot, but I try it. '*Coche?*' I shout, and he looks kind of scared. *Car*?

I am not that stupid to presume a car is wandering around in the thickness of this plantation kingdom. Yet the noise gets under my skin and I tremble with excitement. Perhaps Tamati or Dr Belloc have organised something to find me. Perhaps it's the Australian government, alerted that a citizen got lost in the jungle, sending a platoon of well-trained Special Forces to track me down. I always cry when I see people rescued from impossibly dangerous situations just because they are Australians. The spirit of mateship has been institutionalised on every level, no matter the cost and effort. I have tears in my eyes. That must be the case.

I plant a big kiss on the shaman's face, say good-bye and thank him, then turn my back and rush towards the noise, which grows louder and louder. I trip and fall, and run and slip and fall again. I must be numb to pain because I don't feel anything but the revs of an engine somewhere in front of me.

Then I fall and hurt myself really badly and I can't get up any more. I hear the noise getting more and more distant and I sob with despair. Then I see them, the two parrots. One red and green, the other turquoise and yellow. It can't be that they are the same ones, I say to myself. And I black out. It must be the defence mechanism of the exhausted brain and body giving themselves a chance to recharge.

When I open my eyes it's almost dark and the shaman is by my side. I take his moist, smooth hand in my palm and tap into the knowledge. I know that he has guided me back to where I belong, the last stepping stone to the civilised world in the outskirts of the Amazonian selva. I love him for that and he receives my love SMS through the tips of my fingers. That makes him close his eyes and start chanting. He chants something that sounds like a lullaby, swaying his body. Then he feels in his bundle and comes out with an ointment which he lavishly spreads on my sore and bleeding feet. Helping me up, he supports me until we reach the familiar dirt road. In the distance I can see Ingrid's German restaurant. I am in such shock that I almost collapse again, but the shaman rubs an herb under my nose and its pungent smell keeps me alert.

'*Adios*,' he says and adds softly. '*Sagrada*.'

'*Adios*,' I echo and add, 'Thank you, *gracias*.'

He turns and disappears beneath the canopy.

I don't wait but start walking along the road. Suddenly I am aware of my nakedness. The snakeskin is still wrapped around my waist, but I can't extend it to cover my top half. It's not a Versace dress, but it has to do.

Then I hear the engine from behind me. That's it. The jeep! The one I didn't wreck. Somebody with a safari hat on, perhaps Dr Belloc, is driving towards me bumping like crazy all the way.

He catches me with the long lights and I remain still like a hypnotised hare. He gets out of the jeep, comes with the light like a Greek god, perhaps Apollo, or Zeus heralding the end of my ordeal. I run against him and fall into his arms.

'Hello, Ms Cornelius.' There they are: eyes of vitriolic green, staring at me close-up.

Enescu pushes me back gently and gives me a quick overall look. 'You look remarkably well for someone lost in the jungle for over a week.'

His hands handcuff my wrists and we stand facing each other like a pair of ice-skaters waiting for the music to start dancing. My mind is bursting, analysing my new situation (lose-lose) and calculating options (none). A whole range of useless thoughts and ideas.

'Please, don't get any ideas this time. And you have forgotten your crocodile.' He takes out of his pocket the wooden artefact and hands it over to me. If I come to think it looks like one of those souvenirs the boys in the Juvenile Centre carve under the Norm's instructions.

Enescu leads me to the jeep and, helping me in, he notices the horrendous bruises.

'Oh, Sandy,' he says, 'you shouldn't have done this to yourself. You deserve better.' His voice is soft, soothing, sympathetic, and it makes me burst in sobs.

I hope I am not going to faint. I wonder but don't ask whether they have found the jeep I ran away with, or the papers. But I ask the only question I am interested in.

'Cloning is the future,' he answers. 'We are obliged to be there when the biotech revolution happens. It won't be a glamorous one, I tell you. We are going to reproduce ourselves in other galaxies but we'll be crippled by agoraphobia of the spiritual space. Only the poor will remain on Earth, like a ghetto numbering billions over billions, killing and eating each other for mere survival. I see young people turn more and more to martial arts, carrying weapons to protect themselves and their families. The survival instinct will test every virtue and morality standard. But that's the future. The rest is past.'

'Who are your clients for cloned humans used in ritual cannibalistic killings?' I ask.

He remains silent looking at the moon rising above Salto Angel.

'Why Michael?' I ask grasping at air, emotions gnawing on my vocal cords.

'Michael,' he repeats the name dismissingly. 'It could have been anyone, but Michael was a good shot at the target and the target was you.'

'Why me?'

He remains silent.

'How about Beverley?'

He answers with a question to my question. 'You remember the catacombs of Rome? There Christianity germinated, an underground movement accused of all the deadly sins: bloody orgies and eating the flesh of the dead. I started to ask myself why Nero put Rome to the torch while fiddling on the roof of his palace, as the legend goes. And this answer contains the answer to your question about our clients.'

Behind Professor Enescu, a shadow has sprung up like

a folding knife. It's the shaman and he is not alone. At least ten small dark men stand motionless with machetes dripping moonlight.

FORTY-EIGHT

I shut my mouth to prevent a scream.

A flickering flame of suspicion appears in Professor Enescu's eyes, and he breaks off his monologue. He is ready to drive, hand on the wheel, the other on the knob of the gear stick, when he *senses* them. First he is not sure and shifts uneasily for a moment. Then he turns abruptly away from me and sees them. I have to give him credit. There is no emotion on his face. I don't know how he achieves it, but it's impressive by itself. What actually surfaces on his face is curiosity. He envelops them all with a glance and exclaims, 'The Zhingro men!'

'Who?' I ask feebly, my heart palpitating like crazy.

'The only living cannibals. Described by a half-eaten survivor from the depths of the Amazonian jungle.'

'What do you mean half-eaten?' I get so jittery, my teeth chatter.

He raises his eyebrows at me. 'Have you seen a shark victim, Sandy?'

Coming from Australia, I have an idea of what he's talking about. 'But we aren't in the depths of the jungle, are we?'

'No, we are not. But I have been travelling in their lands trying to spot them, to no avail.'

He is still composed and analysing, not a muscle twitching on his calm, totally detached face. I hate him for this, at the same time I can't help but admire him. Trying to measure up to his cold-bloodedness I ask, 'You've got a gun or a cell phone?'

'You don't want to provoke them, do you?' he responds.

'I don't want to look like a shark victim, that's for sure.' In a fit of vanity I toss myself over the wheel and press the horn.

The men, like hunting jaguars, jump inside the jeep and drag us out. In the confusion we get entangled in a knot and I can feel the warm athletic body of the professor against mine. I feel his blood pumping, almost bursting the banks of his jugular, and I know he doesn't want to die. As stupid as I am, I start to feel sorry for him.

But what about me?

He put me in this position. I must be crazy to take pity on him. But it's human nature to be compassionate, and somehow I sense what is going to happen. The presence of the shaman tells it all in the subtle, wordless way of energy waves.

I watch, feeling guilty and cowardly as they literally scrape Enescu off me and take him into the darkness of the jungle. He does not resist. He walks straight, impossibly handsome, and the moon seems to shower him with more light than any of us.

It's too much to bear. I look at the shaman, my eyes are blind with tears, but I perceive his answer. Sometimes justice is done on nature's most primitive level. I remember Frank telling me that what we do, all of it gets recorded on magnetic field strips girding the planet. These strips absorb and send information at the same time, from and down to earth and from and out to space. He told me that runes were meant to explore this information, as is I Ching and Tarot cards and so many other tools for divination.

I want to believe that the Zhingro men having seen Professor Enescu wandering around their habitats, came to know about his interest in them and are now inviting him as a guest. I even want to follow them, but a force outside me keeps me rooted beside the jeep. I hope that Professor Enescu will turn his head for a farewell, but it doesn't happen. After they all disappear, I can still hear soft rustling and I know it comes from his steps.

The shaman does not turn his head either. Nor does he call me *sagrada* again. Suddenly I feel something falling over my feet and I look down in terror. It's the wooden crocodile.

FORTY-NINE

I am so engrossed with their noiseless departure that at first I don't notice the lights coming from the direction of the restaurant.

I find Ingrid and the pilot inside; they nearly drop dead at the sight of me. Ingrid brings a piece of linen and I wrap myself up. She suggests running a hot bath for me but I don't feel up to anything. They might suspect me of killing Enescu and dumping his body in the jungle because they don't know what to make out of what I tell them.

'Zhingro tribe, never heard of them,' says Carlos.

Soon they both kind of start to believe my story, my bruises speak for themselves. Ingrid suggests that I should rest, but I don't want to hear any of it. I think of Herr Tommler and his bimbo Maria and I want to go back to Caracas, back home. I've had enough.

They tell me that Dr Belloc and his colleagues left after several unsuccessful attempts to find me, but Carlos was hired to fly back and wait for news about me for another couple of days, just in case. I presume Dr Belloc also wanted his conscience clean along with the documents. The documents of Herr Tommler.

'What about Tamati?' I ask.

'Ah, Tamati,' says Ingrid and smiles meaningfully. 'The black hunk, Dr Whititika. He flew back with the rest of the doctors.' There's typical woman's spite triumphing on her face when she sees my obvious disappointment.

Even so, she fixes a nice German meat-and-potatoes meal for me with sauerkraut and sausages on the side. Then she suggests that I do have a bath and a good sleep. Carlos will fly me to Caracas the following morning. Meanwhile she will call Dr Belloc and advise him of my happy ending and Professor's Enescu's unhappy one. She still casts unpleasant glances at me when she talks about Enescu. I feel uncomfortable; I am not at all sure she won't call the police in Caracas so they can press homicide charges.

I can't eat much. I keep drinking gallons of water and soaking myself in the lake filled with Salto Angel waters. My body is so sore that I cry silently and pray for a quick recovery.

I must be desperate, mad to cross continents and oceans hunting evil. Too many people paid with their lives. Michael, Fernando, the Nigerian refugee, Beverley. Beverley who hated her husband for the same reason she once married him. I used to watch how she dressed him in a wedding gown slowly, savouring each step, seeing him humiliated to the degree where he wouldn't care whether he was humiliated or not.

I am dozing on a deck chair by the lake when I hear voices. Ingrid and Carlos are speaking German, and the only word I pick out is *schade*, it's a pity, pronounced by Carlos.

Pity. That's what can characterize my life in one word right now.

FIFTY

The following morning I feel really crook after spending the night on the deck chair. Not even the two parrots can cheer me up.

Ingrid is surprised that I have remained outside with the mosquitoes. I have been bitten, it turns out, but with my numb, bruised flesh I wouldn't know the difference. I am wearing a dress with patterns of the Acropolis and the Parthenon, which makes me nostalgic about another time and another life, when I was a sex tourist chasing Frank all over the world. It's Ingrid's dress, of course, and it's quite large and makes me look like Marylin. But it covers most of my bruised body and has to do for the time being.

Ingrid makes a decent omelet for me and brings a bowl of fried sausages for Carlos. I notice that his 'soft drink' continues to be white wine, but I don't want to stir up trouble by asking who will fly me back to Caracas.

Instead I ask about my documents. Ingrid smiles and says they are already in the plane. I take my wooden crocodile and go to say good-bye to the lake full of heavenly waters.

In ten minutes I am boarding the plane, which perches lonely on the tiny strip. Carlos is checking the instruments and invites me to sit next to him in the cockpit, which is constructed of transparent material. I gladly join him in anticipation of the flight, but Carlos is not in a hurry. He takes his time checking things and I praise his professionalism before I understand that his delay and mucking around is due to a different reason.

Ingrid, dressed in a frock with patterns of the pyramids of the Pharaoh Egypt, also boards the plane. She first throws in a big grocery box, then a bundle and finally a voluminous bag. I follow her movements with questioning eyes, but Carlos says nothing. He helps Ingrid arrange her luggage and comes back to the pilot's seat, bringing the sliding door into place.

'A bit of shopping will help,' says Ingrid after taking a seat and buckling her belt. She smiles at me and adds: 'A last minute decision.' Then she shrugs her shoulders and shifts her glance towards the window next to her.

I fasten my belt but feel uneasy. It doesn't sound right. One doesn't go shopping with full bags. Anyway, I decide to dismiss the growing premonition in my heart and concentrate on Carlos and his expert maneuvers.

Once airborne I forget all my concerns.

Venezuela is an extremely beautiful country. Nature matches her dashing women. Yellow, red, black, and green rivers cross the savanna, rivers that take on the colours of the metals in the ores they wash along their way. From above it's like looking at a detail from a Miro painting through a magnifying glass.

The jungle is no man's zone. On the other side of the border, in Brazil, they cook *fejuada*, called also the meal of the poor slaves: leftovers from the boss' table (salted pork or veal, chorizo sausages, ribs, tongue) mixed in black beans with rice.

On the other side of the jungle, life is marked by a coexistence of religion and paganism, and people know the meaning of *saudades*: nostalgia, melancholy, unexplained sadness—something that I am experiencing right now with one only difference: mine is an explained sadness.

The feeling is so compelling that by the time I notice that we are curbing the *selva,* we have already turned back and fly over it again. 'Why are we flying back?' I ask.

'We have a surprise for you.' Ingrid speaks loudly, trying to drown the noise of the engine with her voice.

I need little to turn aggressive.

'Why don't you bloody well tell me what the fucking game is?' I shout back at her, ready to jump out of my seat. Then I turn to Carlos, who keeps looking straight ahead undisturbed.

'We are taking you to see my diamond mine.' Ingrid smiles as if she is doing me a big favour.

'I don't want to go anywhere. I want to fly back to Caracas, you bloody idiot.' Unfastening my belt I grab Carlos by his forearm and shake him. 'You are hired to take me there, not to visit diamond mines.'

I might be foaming at the mouth. I can't stand the thought of delaying any longer, mucking around in this unhealthy place. 'You are hired,' I repeat, appealing to his professional moral standards. But Carlos shakes me off his arm and smiling at me says: 'Sorry, Ms Cornelius, but Mrs Ingrid rehired me.'

I can't believe my ears. It just can't be happening. Not again.

'I'll pay you more, Carlos,' I start to negotiate. 'Tell me your price.'

'A plane full of diamonds.' He is a jolly fellow.

'Turn the bloody plane around.' I try to tackle him.

He fends me off, amused. Between my efforts and Carlos' mirth, the plane starts to jerk around. Carlos keeps laughing. He is so drunk his breath puffs wine vapours the way a dragon puffs fire. I feel dizzy. In my state I can't even kill a fly, which is pity. *Schade*. I remember the German word. Why would he say it?

I wonder why Ingrid hasn't come to tackle me. I turn around and see her sitting frozen as an ice-statue. There's a gun pointing at her right ear and a dark-skinned hand holding it tight.

Tamati.

'You better turn this wheelbarrow around, bro,' says Tamati in such a venomous voice that even I feel chills crawling down my back.

'Yes, sir!' echoes Carlos, still laughing and leering drunkenly. 'Sorry, ma'am,' he addresses Ingrid. 'I've just been re-rehired.'

'You can't do this,' Ingrid protests.

'Yes, he can!' snaps Tamati.

I am amazed, however, at the certainty in her voice. Carlos stops laughing and peers uneasily to his right. Following his gaze, I see that a big, dark cloud has appeared out of the blue, heading our way.

Carlos sobers in a split second. 'I am afraid, sir, we have to try an emergency landing if we care to remain alive.'

'What's going on?' asks Tamati, still ignoring me.

'The rainfall takes down planes like ours, sir.'

I remember the rainfall when I was escaping in the jeep, like a million hammers, choking, suffocating, drowning me.

Tamati turns to look where Carlos is pointing, enough for Ingrid to try to be brave. She reaches for her gun, but Tamati is quicker and whacks her on the head. She collapses with one arm hanging outside her seat, her head nested on her shoulder. She looks like Marat in the bathtub from Jacques-Louis David's painting *Death of Marat*.

When I look up in the sky again there's no cloud; instead the whole sky is murky and spelling trouble.

'There's no time to beat the fucker and get out into the flat,' says Carlos. 'Believe it or no, sir, our only chance lies with the landing strip at the diamond mine.'

Tamati who has his hands free from Ingrid, turns his attention to Carlos. 'Listen, you stinking alcoholic shit, you have two choices: die in a crash or by my gun. It's your funeral.'

Carlos doesn't hesitate long. The plane swirls sharply and heads for the eye of the darkness spilling from the sky.

For several minutes nothing happens. We can see the line where the clutter of trees finishes and the savanna begins. Tamati stands behind my seat, his hands on my shoulders. We haven't exchanged a word, and I don't want to be the first to say something because the last thing we need now is more tension.

'Sir, find a seat, fasten the belt,' snaps Carlos.

Tamati gives my shoulders a squeeze and seats himself.

Right then it starts. The sky opens in a ferocious downpour as if a thousand steam hammers are banging on the tiny craft. We quickly start to lose height. The turbulence is such that I feel all my bones go into a loose state again and I scream out in piercing pain.

Carlos misinterprets it as a display of fear and finds time and heart to comfort me: 'Carlos good pilot. We *tres hermanos*, three brothers, all pilots, one civil, one military. All die. Carlos good pilot.'

I'm not comforted. It's like being in a cocktail shaker. We fly so low we occasionally touch the tops of trees. I don't know where I find the strength to grasp the arms of the seat, but my knuckles are white. Now we see nothing but a mass of water like a huge, merciless surf crashing over our fragile craft, trying to turn it into splinters.

We crash.

It's not much different from flying at this point. Perhaps there's a bit more pulling on the seat belt.

Carlos declares that he has landed the plane safely and reaches for the bottle. 'It was a close shave.' He smacks his lips and takes another generous slurp of rum.

Anger always brings a tide of energy to me. I scramble out of my seat and confront Tamati: 'You,' I stutter with pain and suppressed emotions, 'you fucking idiot, we could have been killed.'

Then I see that he is motionless, his forehead bleeding. 'Oh, no!' I sag on the floor and embrace his legs; my head rests against his knees.

Everything smells of rum. There's as much rum as rain around me and my hair and my nose are soaked in rum. I lift my head and see Carlos pouring his precious liquid over Tamati's bleeding cut and into Tamati's mouth.

Both to good effect.

Then we all hear it. In the weird silence after the deluge it's a distinct *mechanical* sound. A clock waking us to the idea that we are not out of the woods.

'Bomb.' Carlos words the collective feeling.

'Bomb?' Ingrid comes to her senses and plunges for the door struggling with its heaviness.

'Time bomb.' Grins Carlos, his macho thing thrilled.

The door is stuck with the landing and Ingrid can't do much about it.

'Give me a hand, quick.' She doesn't address me in particular but I am the only one who joins her efforts.

Carlos grabs the big dangling cross and gives Jesus a drunken kiss.

Tamati remains still, his head to one side listening. Then he slowly starts to move towards the direction of the ticking sound.

The device happens to be wired right under the seat that has been occupied by Ingrid. Seeing it she loses it. Her screams hit harder than the rain but I have to take it. It's not the time to express dislikes. Our luck is that the explosive hasn't gone off prematurely with all the bumping and shaking.

While Carlos prays to his Madonna, Ingrid screams, still pulling on the door along with me, Tamati starts to *work* on the bomb, separating coloured wires. Then he produces a folding knife.

'Please watch, these are not tonsils!' I stop breathing. There's fresh stain of blood on his knife.

Sensing my new scare with instincts of an animal, Ingrid shuts up and snuggles against me. We both drop pulling the stuck door waiting for Tamati's result.

They say time doesn't exist but in our minds. For some people time passes quickly by hence *tempus fugit*, for others times drags annoyingly slow. When I am with Frank in bed for a week, it could have been only a morning or a short siesta. In between our meetings time tends to drag, that I know.

Right now, in a split second, time plays tricks on me. Listening to the bomb clock, my heart giving arrhythmic kicks against my chest, in my mind I watch deja vue-s.

I see myself creating drawings on breath-fogged windows, things I find difficult to express in words. Objects, moments, people as beautiful as trees abandoning their roots to travel, like that Botero character listening to Albinoni. Even killers like those hunters slaughtering a herd of elephants for piano keys while their wives chop a piano for firewood. I am in a hurry to imprint the image before the breath-coated patch shrinks and disappears. These are the only drawings I am good at. This is my only artistic connection with the old masters. Frank is impressed. He is still in bed, keeping it warm for me to return to so we can resume what we are here for: sex. Persistent, wild marathon sex that makes me lose those extra pounds and be more attractive than ever for him. Honestly, I lose track of where we are, and that can be annoying. Sometimes I have no idea what language I am expected to speak when I get out of our hotel room, what currency to use or what wardrobe to carry around. It actually doesn't matter because wherever we are we spend our time experimenting to create the first successful merging of two humans. The blender we use is that simple atavistic urge to love and be loved. We are aware that there's nothing new in it and that millions have tried before us the way billions will try after us. There's no record of a couple having achieved it, but this hasn't discouraged anybody and certainly it doesn't discourage us.

We might have been in Bali. In that bungalow in the middle of a rice field overlooking some of their one thousand Hindu temples, in a hot, humid evening when the gamelan music attacks your ear drums: chack, chack, chack from the men performing the Frog dance.

Chack, chack, I don't know, is it still the bomb ticking or...? I have closed my eyes and we stand there with Ingrid, two pathetic entangled figures, that could carry a title like Friends in Death or Caramelised Mustard for Your Funeral. I start to think of all the goodies pharaohs, emperors and kings take to their grave chambers so they don't starve in their afterlife, this euphemism for death. Vessels and amphorae full of wheat, honey, rice, figs and dates, palm wine, olive oil, seeds to last for the eternity along with humans. Humans, servants, solders, wives, concubines, children, sacrificed. As companions or as lasting meal in time when there were no refrigerators? So what would I take with me if the bomb goes off? *Bian*? A concoction of male organs in chicken stock? Ingrid is too old to pass for a chicken.

Chack, chack.

Silence.

Then the sound of a snap and Tamati rips the seat together with the wire.

This time the silence is deep, mixed with distrust, even more scary then the ticking.

'You did it! Tamati, you did it!' I react first. Going back to my real feelings I give Ingrid a punch in her armpit, a nasty spot, you can kill like this, but then so what, and throw myself towards Tamati for a congratulation kiss. Actually throwing is a bit overstated since the device ticking or not, still produces respect in me.

'Tonsils, ah?' With a grin the size of a cutting board, Tamati is not in a hurry to forget my sarcastic remark. He looks sweaty and is panting, quite understandable under the circumstances.

Due to the permanently jammed door we can't get rid of the explosives and it's a worry. Carlos is convinced that his prayers to his Madonna saved us and also wants a congratulation kiss. I have to sacrifice myself by giving him one while repeating 'Carlos good pilot, Carlos good pilot!'

Ingrid has erased herself like a bad smell treated with apple cider vinegar. She sits invisible and mute and nobody hears anything about diamond mines.

For a while we all stay like this, then start to get moving.

The old plane, despite the crash landing, is still flyable once the rain lets us up. When after lots of maneuvering and additional hazardous situations we take off I start to think that Carlos is, indeed, a good pilot.

FIFTY-ONE

That night we stay again at the Anauco Hilton. A man appears at our window on the sixteenth floor of the twin building. He is not a burglar but a party in adultery and runs for his life. We let him into the room and he escapes through our door into the corridor, clutching a shoe like a ceremonial gourd to his masculine attribute. Life is not short of suspense for us, not even for a minute.

We have room service, since none of us feels like a restaurant. I order lots of fresh juices and some aggressive protein like cold pork, beef and turkey rolls fumed and stuffed with allspice and black pepper. I also order comfort food like chips, Lindt chocolates, strawberries in cream, hazelnut mousse. I ask for a pot of black coffee for me, a newspaper for Tamati and champagne for both of us.

There's no love night scheduled. Not only because I look like an eggplant moussaka leftovers but because I find it a bit overwhelming to sleep with a mercenary.

Mercenary.

That's what Tamati has finally told me he is in this puzzle. Privately hired to track down one of the last Nazi criminals alive and finish him off.

'Did you do it?' I ask then remember the blooded knife and I know Herr Tommler is no longer an international tribunal issue. That gives me the answer why I am still alive and out of the jungle where I was at his mercy.

'How about that bimbo, his bodyguard Maria?'

Tamati purses his lips, 'A bit of waste there but we don't want witnesses, do we?'

With Enescu out of the way and Herr Tommler liquidated by *a mercenary*, Dr Belloc was in a hurry to go back to civilisation and redeal his cards independently.

The following morning Dr Belloc comes to see us at the hotel. He says he was concerned about my fate and wishes me a quick recovery. I don't answer, neither do I succumb to my anger, advised by Tamati to play it safe until, ah well, until we leave the country.

Dr Belloc treats us to a coffee and inquires about the wooden crocodile. I respond that it looks all right, at least better than me.

'I am so sorry, what can I do for you, Ms Cornelius?'

I can't believe it, the bastard pretends that he's never been part of the game.

'I want...' Tamati gives me a friendly kick under the table before I finish:...to strangle you with my bare hands. So I finish instead: '...to send you my new book with an authograph, Mr Belloc!'

'I love writers,' he says drinking his *macchiato* with a poker face.

It all looks like a worldly chat between colleagues. Tamati tells him that we refused an invitation to see a diamond mine in the Amazonian jungle. He doesn't specify by whom.

Dr Belloc approves that we haven't accepted the invitation. 'Once you go there nobody ever finds you again. For the rest of your life you'd be forced to dig or fry bananas for the diggers. Every day small aircraft fly from the jungle with their load of precious stones to the sea where boats wait to load the gems, and then they vanish north to the States. The police are busy combing the sky for the pirates; when they spot one they attack the smugglers and make them land, then confiscate the gems. But the smugglers know the police just can't catch them all. The odds favour the pirates so they keep trying to fulfil their dreams of becoming fabulously rich in no time.'

Dr Belloc expresses his gratitude for our interest in his pursuits. He talks to me as if I have also given a lecture at his creepy institution.

'Dear Sandy,' he says. 'It was pleasure to get to know you. I like audacious young women, and beautiful at that. We do have small differences in our approach to what might be the new millennium's hottest subject. Man tries more and more dangerous and forbidden things. You see the deadly sports he's involved in these days? In his pursuit of new tastes he is eager to trespass any boundaries in sport, sex and life. Next on the agenda is the revival of cannibalism. I hope we'll see you again, lovely Ms Cornelius.' Saying this, he kisses my hand and remains bent over it for a while.

I have the creepy feeling that he is having a good sniff of my flesh.

The only fight I generate is with Tamati.

'I want home,' I scream at him when I find out that he has bought tickets to Oslo. 'I want Brisbane. I want to lie in the sun for days and do nothing. I want to soak in the ocean and heal my bashed body. I want to find myself a real lover and fuck my head off.'

'Sandy, everything is coming to you,' says Tamati.

We head for the airport accompanied by Mr Belloc. Surprisingly I already start to feel nostalgic about Venezuela.

Passing through the streets I again admire the iron-wrought grilles that protect the windows in Caracas. This time I see Rubens-like curves of ornaments: vine leaves, flowers, animals, fantasies, improvisations. Flamboyant colours borrowed from the Incas painting their faces to warn off death or celebrate life. Patterns of handcuffs or Jack Ketch knots, bisons' horns, or constrictors like the culprit of half my misfortunes.

'The real artists are the thieves,' says Dr Belloc, seeing us off with a bottle of wine that smells of papaya. 'The thieves are the real architects of our homes here.'

I want to forget him so I quickly proceed towards the customs officer, a young man with the local greasy and curly hair, and a face like a grain of dark red grapes good for cabernet. He vigorously rummages through my hand luggage, and Dr Belloc comes to see what the problem is and offers his help. I have no idea what help I need. Tamati waits in the line behind the mark, shifting uneasily from one foot to the other.

Suddenly Dr Belloc casts a triumphant glance at me and grasps a stack of papers rolled among my belongings. 'I hope you don't mind that I keep these papers, Ms Cornelius. You are possessing them illegally.'

Who am I to mind?

He turns to the officer who shows a small smile as greasy as his hair. 'These documents are stolen and Ms Cornelius has nothing against it that I keep them, unless she is curious to hear what the law advises for theft of secret information. Here, officer. I am Dr Belloc.'

The officer takes the papers and gives them a quick look, a grimace changes his greasy smile. '*Esta seguro, Doctor Belloc?*' Are you sure? The officer looks back at the papers and this time his brows arch in the shape of horseshoes.

I don't move. What's the difference if they put me in jail for possession of planted drugs or illegal possession of documents? I wouldn't like it either way. Tamati breathes heavily behind me. I try to give him a mental message not to interfere.

Finally Dr Belloc retrieves the papers from the officer and nervously puts on glasses that I've never seen him wear before. His hand is a bit shaky and he almost pokes in his eye with the metal frame. Once his eyes armed he starts to examine the papers. First he can't believe it and turns them around and upside down. Then he looks at me with such venom that I jump back and almost step on Tamati's toes.

Dr Belloc grunts something and throws the papers at my feet; then he straightens his backs and walks away.

I bend and pick my scattered papers. Tamati helps me and reads some of them. *Menu of the Gala Evening of the IX International Congress on Obesity. Starters: coated prawns on green salad and lemon mayonnaise, spinach croquets, ham in melon injected with vodka...*

FIFTY-TWO

It's a relief to hang in the air in a big, powerful, British Airways machine that doesn't even wink when there's turbulence. Quite a difference from Carlos' dishwasher. I still feel like a heavyweight boxer after the thirtieth round and still wearing that hideous cotton Acropolis-patterned frock. I'll have to do some shopping at Heathrow airport where we have a four-hour stopover unless I want to snuff it—from pneumonia this time.

Soon after we are airborne Tamati orders a couple of whiskeys for a palate-cleanser. He is preparing for a confrontation, but I am not in a hurry to talk. If I start, I have to go to the core of what I want to say and something tells me that it's not the time or the place.

I wonder when it will be the right time and place for me to patch up my life and move on, throwing a stone behind my back so that the bad forces from the past can never catch up with me again. I am not sure what kind of a belief it is, but I desperately want to try and see whether it works.

It's so fresh and painful, in the literal meaning of the word, that every revival brings agonising memories I'd rather try to forget or at least sweep under the carpet for the time being. Any word referring to our hellish jungle experience would be like rubbing salt on open wounds.

I give Tamati a sideways glance. His eyes are like ice-cream scoopers in action, he can't have enough of the willowy hostesses, his thumb on the service button. He orders peanuts, then orange drink, then beer, then peanuts. Soon he calls them all by their names.

Perhaps he thinks that by ignoring me I haven't got much of a chance to attack him. Why should I actually?

Carlos, Ingrid, Professor Enescu, Her Tommler, Dr Belloc, Laura, Dr Brankovic, Dr Nicholas: they are all part of a past I am never going back to. Some of them, like the professor and Her Tommler, were trying to play God, but I am not responsible for all the weirdoes on this planet. The only thing to remind me of them from now on will be the wooden crocodile, which I clutch in my hands as evidence of the ordeal I've been through.

Yet it's not easy to knock the whole bloody thing out of my mind. I start to think in terms of law and realise that the cloned people are not protected. They don't exist; their births haven't been registered anywhere. Cloning them as spare parts is already on the borderline of jurisdiction. Cloning them for supplying cannibalistic rituals is as criminal as it can get. Yet in order to wipe out this heinous project in one night and close down the abattoir, mountains of evidence would be necessary. All I have is a sign on a door and a snitched document both unfortunately only in my memory.

Manifesto of the Cannibals reads the creepy document, yet it sounds more like the Ten Commandments. 1. Declare yourself free to experience the most natural food wrongly declared taboo. 2. Declare yourself a free spirit ready to incorporate another spirit along your journey on this planet. 3. Cleanse yourself accepting with your body the blood of another human body as a sacred offering. And so on.

As everything of a suspicious nature the document contained lots of holy terminology.

I can't but think again of Diego Rivera who said: 'I believe that when man evolves a civilisation higher than the mechanized but still primitive one he has now, the eating of human flesh will be sanctioned. For then man will have thrown off all of his superstitions and irrational taboos.'

The beautiful and filthy professor Enescu, that piece of constipated shit, was only too happy to initiate me into his sick doings. But thanks to the Amazonian Zhingro tribe, I couldn't get the main information about who his clients were, who put in orders for catered cannibalistic orgies, as if they were wedding or kids' birthday parties. I have been worrying over his last words, that the answer is related to the early Christians, Nero putting Rome to the torch.

My thoughts return to the text of William Wyatt Gill: 'The body was cooked, as pigs now are, in an oven specially set apart, red-hot basaltic stones, wrapped in leaves, being placed inside to insure its being equally done. The best joint was the thigh.' I hope it's not what Professor Emescu has been through. My problem is to find out why Nero set Rome on fire.

'Tamati,' I say nonchalantly, 'why do you think Nero put Rome to the torch?'

If I had punched him in the mouth he couldn't have been more surprised. People are helpless when you don't perform inside their boxed and labelled expectations.

'Nero,' I repeat. 'In case you don't know there was a Roman emperor who liked to party and fuck around in disguise. He set Rome on fire...'

'I know, I know.' Tamati is back in total control, even a bit aggressive, as if *I* had taken *him* to the other side of the world to play hide and seek with snakes, nuts and real cannibals. 'He blamed it on the Christians so he could have public opinion on his side when exterminating them.'

'Tamati,' I look straight into his eyes, 'why, you fucking A-grade arsehole, did you put me through all this?'

Tamati winces. 'I meant well, Sandy, cross my heart. I thought we could establish ourselves as moles in Dr Belloc's research premises and lay out hands on some valuable information. I think we both did well, didn't we?'

'Tamati, have you met Professor Enescu before?'

'No, I haven't, but I have heard his name mentioned a few times by Dr Belloc. By the way, Sandy, it was *arranged* that he approached me with the offer to become his consultant a couple of months ago.'

'Arranged?'

'Yes, arranged. You know, money paid in a bank account, no questions asked.'

'Like they paid you?'

'Yes, Sandy,' he nibbles on his peanuts. 'Normal. A money transfer.'

'Who are *they*, Tamati?'

'Jacobsen is not the only one after the Cult.'

'But you mentioned something about Nazi criminals. Uncle Willie told me about Herr Tommler but he wouldn't know that he was hiding in the jungle of Venezuela, nor that he was actually up to his old gut-wrenching tricks.'

'Your uncle? Walter Kretz is your uncle?'

I turn towards Tamati with all my body. A Molotov cocktail of feelings, dominated by horror and shock explode inside me.

Of course, Tamati has been part of the game all along but now I smell another rat. I start to wonder which of the Renoir's *Nudes* have paid the whole mission. Mission of justice or revange? Mission, in which people killed and got killed.

Suddenly I feel empty. Empty and small. There are big games out there and I burnt myself by thinking that I, Sandy Cornelius, can make difference in this world. I should have kept to myself doing what I can really do well: cook, fuck, hang out with friends. I have no words to mince through my teeth, no questions to ask.

Tamati also remains silent, chomping on his peanuts. I know he can't say more. He has already told me too much.

They all have used me. *They*, forces anonymous, organised, serving different ideals, all behind the flag of humanity.

'So you acted impromptu, taking me with you.' I finally say, my words all soaked in bitter herbs.

'I don't know what impromptu is, Sandy, but you never know when the last missing segment of the puzzle will come to you.'

'Tamati, there's not one, but hundreds of missing segments; and the puzzle remains the same enigma as it's been all along since I saw myself sprawled across Beethoven's grave presumably having taken my own life.'

His body language shows he doesn't share my opinion.

A hostess serves plastic containers with meals and pours tea and coffee, but neither of us touches our meal.

'I am so sorry,' he says and that's it. Sorry.

'I'm not,' I say, and the weird thing is that I want to comfort him.

He gives me a look of a puppy that has wetted the Persian carpet and expects a newspaper spanking for a punishment. He even takes my hand and kisses it and repeats: 'I am so sorry.'

'I don't know. We can't undo things, that's for sure. After all, it could have been worse.'

'Worse?'

'You could have been accompanying a metal casket, you bloody idiot. How about Ingrid? Wasn't she part of Herr Tommler's game, too?'

'I don't think so,' says Tamati seriously. 'Just an ordinary business woman, you know.'

'Yes, I know, a restaurant in the jungle, a diamond mine, greedy for slaves.'

'Come on, Sandy, remember? Not all Germans are bad.'

He reaches for his orange juice. But I still feel far from emotionally spent and snarl, 'How about introducing me to cannibalistic practice? Tonsils, pfu, I don't even want to think about it.'

His eyebrows go up, and then he laughs. 'Sandy, I swear, they were giblets, all right? I wanted to tease you.'

'I never know when to believe you and when not.'

'Let's give it a try. If I say Sandy you are the best lay in the world, would you believe me or not?'

And we laugh. He spills his orange juice and orders whisky. I get rid of the microwaved chicken drumstick and produce a tiny bottle. I am happy to have found it in Caracas.

I fight the foul smell of my brew and have a gentle slurp, then wait for its effect to tune me into what's called divine wisdom.

Ayahuasca. The shaman drink.

Soon I hear the voices of the savannah inside me as if interpreted by the best guitarist of Latin America. I see the python embracing my boneless spiritual body, jaguars playing with gold and crystal models of celestial objects. I float in those images and the images float in me. Then I ask questions without dressing them in words. Questions like: is Frank really in love with me, does the Earth also breathe, what is a better bed for Moroccan pork—rice or couscous, who my father is?

Soon I do see Frank in shiny gilded clothes. He tries to warn me about something but I am also trying to say something to him. Our voices meet and create a dead sound point.

You can see your future in the pan while frying onion, that's what I say to Frank.

The tiny cuttings form golden brown shapes, broken hearts, anchors, old-fashioned homes with fuming chimneys, figures, faces familiar and unfamiliar, prompt what events are coming your way. Those small onion pieces form the landscape of your life. Good and not so good, they are all part of life. They even form the soulscape of your spirituality. I called this way of clairvoyance *onionmancy*.

I tell Frank that I also often use the method called bibliomancy to answer my questions. I usually use cookbooks. I sit in lotus position on the floor and lift my head, my face drinking the refreshing universal juices coming down from the sky, the sun, the stars, the clouds or the moon. I take a cookbook that corresponds to my mood.

If I am melancholic I take one related to the ocean. Lots of seafood preparation is going on within the hard covers; usually there is a red crab on the front, a fact that makes me feel very important as it's my zodiac sign. Then I whisper my question as I gently rock my torso, imagining I float 'as a weed flung from the rock on ocean's foam to sail,' as Byron says.

Finally I hear Frank. 'Bullshit,' he says.

'Bullshit,' I repeat and open my eyes, the effect of ayahuasca gone.

I jump to my feet and go to the middle row where Tamati is sleeping stretched out over four free seats.

I shake him awake. 'You bloody bastard, you tricked me about Frank, too, didn't you?'

His smile runs all over his face like a soy sauce spill. Then I ask another question I already got an answer to in my ayahuasca dreaming. 'How about the fuss that Dr Belloc made at the airport? Was it a show-off, too?'

Tamati lifts his lovely torso into a seating position, rubbing his eyes with fists, the power of sledge-hammers. Fists of a mercenary. 'He has to cover his ass,' says Tmatai with the simplicity of those physical creatures that somehow could combine odd professions like rugby, medicine, killing. He pulls me to him in a breath-taking embrace and whispers into my ear, 'Like everybody else, Sandy. Like everybody else.'

I also whisper, his warmth brushing against mine, 'Tamati, how about your medical ethics of saving lives, how about the Hippocratic oath you are supposed to be committed to as a physician? Never do harm to anyone, never prescribing a deadly drug?'

'The Hippocratic oath, Sandy, also says, *But I will preserve the purity of my life and my art*. The purity of my life to save other lives, you understand this?'

'Yes, I do,' I murmur and my head bumps against his, courtesy of a moment of turbulence.

'So don't be concerned about my ethics.'

'I am not.'

'Then don't use this ayahuasca stuff any more! It's dangerous.'

I fish in my pocket. The little bottle is gone.

'I hate you,' I say and fall asleep in his arms.

FIFTY-THREE

In Loeten Tamati delivers me *franco porta* at Frank's house and disappears, mumbling something about finding a hotel room in Hammer.

At first glance Frank doesn't recognise me.

'You need a doctor,' he says, stating the obvious.

'It can wait until I go home,' I say stubbornly.

'You are home here, Sandy,' he says, overcoming his fear to approach and touch me. I must be looking worse than I think.

'Frank.' That's all I can utter. My throat bursts like an Aswan dam wall, spilling tons of suppressed sobs, pains, curses, and complaints, all soaked in tears, spit, and snot. My tears sink into his skin and make their way to his heart. His big reassuring hands stroke my hair, my back. His lips whisper something into my ear, I don't understand what.

My hysterics culminate in a wail that any dingo on Fraser Island could be proud of.

'Frank,' I utter again, making an effort to take control of myself and show that speech is not lost to me; but I fail. Soon I give up and just stand there, hanging on his strong arms, my face buried in the dent between his shoulder and chest. He leads me to a sofa where he lets me sag among the cushions, leaving to them the task of supporting me and soaking up the excess of my emotions turned liquid.

'You are a brave girl,' he says lovingly—enough to spark the anger inside me. Another, bigger dam wall bursts and I flood him with my bitterness because I already suspect his role in my trip to Venezuela.

He doesn't deny anything. He doesn't object. He just listens to me the way a shrink would listen to his patient on the brink of a breakdown.

That annoys me. I want to cause him a fraction of the pain I've been through, but somehow he looks aloof and untouchable.

'You bastard!' I yell at him and dig my nails in his smooth, big hands. 'I could have died there! Are you aware I could have been dead?'

'But you are not,' he says calmly and pulls his hands away without fuss.

'While you were sitting here enjoying good food and life, perhaps even screwing your wife, I—'

'It's finished, Sandy.' He continues to be calm; my nails might have scratched his skin, but not his self-composure.

It stops me in my tracks. Finished? We are finished? I knew it. If he cared about me he would never let me out of his sight. Now I can swear I had the premonition that it was coming the moment we were left alone. Something was different between us.

The closeness, the intimacy were missing.

'Finished,' I repeat almost automatically. This is more than I can bear because it's not a pain, it's death itself engulfing me.

I sit mesmerised, knowing I've only got myself to blame. Men don't like being treated as waste-paper bins for emotional clutter. And maybe Frank shouldn't have let me out of his sight, but all I did from the first moment was run away from him. I sober up from my momentary intoxication at seeing him again.

'Finished,' I repeat again as if to convince myself that this exact word has been lobbed like a snowball between us, leaving me cold and wet. I wonder whether I am entitled to farewell lovemaking.

'Yes,' he nods and a vague smile flickers on his mouth like a sunray caught in a mirror. It's not exactly a smile, and if it is it looks more like a motherless smile to me, a smile that begs to be adopted and cared for.

He called me a brave girl, didn't he? So I have to be brave no matter what. I try a smile, but it's a useless effort. I lift my palms to meet my falling head. I don't want to hear or to see anything more.

'Sandy?'

He has to call my name several times before I spread my fingers and look at him, waiting for the blow delivered by his statement.

'Sandy,' he says matter-of-factly, cupping my hands and face with his palms. 'My divorce papers arrived. My marriage is finished. I am single.'

We spend the night touching each other with words of love. First I don't want to expose my bruised body, but finally I succumb, and when he sees me he kneels and cries and begs me to forgive him.

'The way a dying mother wants to protect her child from the shock of a life-changing loss, and deliberately behaves weird, even nasty, might even tell the child she doesn't love her—I had to assume the same pattern and make you believe that I had betrayed you so you could be free to go and follow your pursuit. I had to remain here.'

'With Jacobsen?'

'Yes, with Jacobsen.'

Now that the initial high tide of surprising revelations has subsided, I suddenly feel cool and empty. This sentimental, even pathetic parallel between him and a dying mother might be catchy, but not with me.

I can't make much of love either, which contributes to my cranky mood. A tiny orgasm costs me so much pain and discomfort that I give up. He is also reluctant to screw a body that looks fresh out of the morgue.

Single.

I munch on the notion, but there's not much juice in it, as if half of his sexual attraction has evaporated along with my subconscious urge to grab the forbidden fruit. That he is available now is kind of a cold shower for my libido. As we lie in bed and I think with a huge amount of bitterness about the joy his announcement would have brought me only a week ago.

He gets out of the bed.

Perhaps he also feels the temperature dropping between us because he goes to the bathroom and runs a tub full of hot water for me to soak in, filling it with aromatic salts and arranges candles. He throws some drops of my nutmeg perfume, too. I hop in and cover myself in bubbles.

I might not feel like Aphrodite being born out of the sea foam, but when he starts to massage my feet, for the first time in days I start to feel good. It's not unlike Bangkok.

Then I sleep.

For how long I don't know.

He appears now and then and brings me things to eat. He even cooks beer soup for me. It's a weird delicacy, which I try for the first time. The beer has to be flat when it's added to browned sugar and flour in melted butter, then a bit of lemon juice and peel, and cinnamon. Beaten eggs are stirred in while cooking. I also notice that my lovely Viking sweetens everything, even the beans-and-ham soup he prepares for me. I try to hide my surprise when he feeds me with sausages floating in strawberry preserve.

When I have had enough sleep, I call him and ask him in a business-like tone to tell me all details, which he does on the condition that we can take a dip in the hot tub.

'The Nigerian asylum seeker told us about arranging a meeting with you. After he was killed we knew that you would be off to Venezuela. Jacobsen contacted his partners in Caracas. They sounded concerned when they knew that you were off to the jungle; it's a difficult zone for police operations.'

'There are no police operations at all there,' I interrupt him. 'The jungle is outside the reach of the law. That's why Herr Tommler, Dr Belloc and Professor Enescu have chosen to establish their human farm there.'

'Jacobsen sent people to arrest Dr Belloc on the day after your departure from Caracas.'

'On what accusations?'

'Tamati sent us information that allowed us to use a hacker. He penetrated Dr Belloc's secret data files. Besides,' he stops to accentuate the effect, 'we couldn't find you, but we found the jeep and something in the glove compartment.'

I am triumphant.

'Do you know the names of the clients?' I hold my breath waiting for his answer.

He gives me a queer look and says, 'The Confraternity of Our Lady founded in the cathedral town of Den Bosch, otherwise known as the Brotherhood of the Swan.'

'Oh shit! That doesn't mean anything, Frank. I don't need you mocking me. Who are the members of *this* Brotherhood?'

'Jacobsen is working on it.'

'Working on it?'

'Any moment he will crack the names. Perhaps Dr Belloc will start to sing, too.'

'I'm not sure. Dr Belloc might be of no help when it comes to the clients. It was obviously Professor Enescu who was the mastermind behind the supply of cloned human beings for cannibalistic rituals. How terrible it sounds! Yet it's Her Tommler, the father of the experiments with history, behind them.' And I tell him what I know from Uncle Willie.

He listens carefully.

We both fall into silence for a while.

'Frank,' I say gloomily, 'sometimes I do think that the whole of mankind is sailing on a Medusa raft. No compass, no direction, no hope. Toys in the hands of evil personified by Professor Enescu and the like.'

'Well, it's not entirely hopeless,' Frank says matter-of-factly. 'Tamati has also collected some evidence.'

'Tamati! I want to strangle him.'

Here Frank bursts in laughter. 'You are no match for him, Sandy, and you know it. The guy is desperately in love with you; he followed you everywhere risking his skin.'

'Are sure we are speaking about the same guy? Tamati? The big dark bloke who continues to look like a rugby player even now that he is a medical doctor and cuts tonsils?'

Frank nods. There is still this mocking smile on his lips. 'After all, you shouldn't be surprised at inflicting feelings in the guy. Look at yourself. A Goddess. In any culture, Maori or Viking.'

I look at myself, lounging in the spa with tall cocktail glasses sweating along the edge. Rose petals float on top of the gentle foam and I feel the subdued jets reaching for me, pushing the water mass like a programmable love machine.

I look at myself in the ceiling mirror. The only new thing about me is this eggplant bruise colour, which makes me much sexier if one likes black leather and whip cracking.

I look at both of us. We look good together. It feels right.

'Tamati.' I continue to chew on the name. It's so physical, it's almost like having a threesome. This satisfies my promiscuous nature. 'I thought that for him women were only numbers.'

'It will kill his macho ego to admit that one particular woman has got hold of his heart.'

I hope this is not a new Frank's fantasy.

'Frank,' I say in the grip of a romantic seizure, 'I want to take you to Fraser Island and watch how the dingoes chew on your leather shoes.'

Soon I am covered all over with his fingerprints, eyeprints, lipprints.

'Let's honour your zodic,' whispers Frank. My zodiac is Cancer and the symbol is 69.

We get out of the water and honour my zodiac sign by making French love, posture *soixante-neuf*. Or, let's use the popular name: we gave each other a head.

I let it go. I feel the woman in me meet the man in Frank, and the woman in Frank meets the man in me. The woman in me meets the woman in Frank, the man in Frank meets the man in me.

The pain surfaces once the game of infinity is over. I hurt. I hurt so much I want to die.

Frank goes to his writing desk and opens a drawer. He comes back to me carrying two pieces of paper with rune symbols on them. He hands them over to me.

'Sandy this is your name and my name written in the symbols of the runes. Sandy and Frank. You can read the interpretation of each name. Yours starting with the symbol for Sun and the power of the Sun. Each symbol has its meaning. What I want to draw your attention to is that we share two symbols: *Anzus* for A and *Nauthiz* for N. The first one stands for god, deity. The second, for necessity.

That means that we both need to believe in a deity or in something that has a status of deity. There is another interpretation however. *Anzus* can also mean mouth and *Nautiz* can mean also pain. That leads to the conclusion that we both share the urge to cause pain through mouth, that is through words.'

It sounds sad.

'Frank, I appreciate that you have tried to read what's behind our names,' I say, and I mean it. Then I look at him and grab his hand. 'Frank, what did you say was the second interpretation? Inflicting pain through the mouth? Can't you see?'

'What?'

'We have been gathered together for a purpose. To pursue the trace of those inflicting pain through *mouth*, the cannibals, Frank, who else?'

Frank is flabbergasted. 'What did you say?' He looks at me as if he sees me for the first time and says the last thing I expect. 'The mission is accomplished. Does it mean that our paths separate from now on?'

'It's not accomplished,' I snap. 'But our paths do seperate.' An aggressive defence, a hedgehog rolling in the comfort of its own spikes.

Then I remember that I haven't taken the pills for days. I must have lost them in the jungle of Venezuela when fighting my menstrual Amazon river I didn't need them. I hope I won't be responsible for the future birth control among pythons.

The realisation about the pills sends chills up my spine.

Then I calm down.

The worst scenario would be that I'd conceive a tiny cute cannibal that will suck on my blood for nine months and then milk me for good. Somehow I like the idea.

'Elephant terrible,' I say to Frank, paraphrasing the French *enfant terrible*. Then I add, 'The Greek Goddess of the Hearth Hestia, the kitchen goddess of the Olympians, she was immune to the spells of the Goddess of Love Aphrodite and she never wed.'

'Nobody was out of his mind to marry her,' he snaps. 'I should have never ever taken care of your bloody laptop.'

FIFTY-FOUR

When my aunt and uncle show up at the Oslo airport they are surprised not to see Frank with me but tactfully do not ask questions. Neither I mention my categorical refusal to be accompanied by someone who is not part of my life any longer.

'Sandy, why don't you leave Australia and move to Europe? We want to look after you,' says Aunty Susan. 'Especially now after what happened to you. You can stay with me at the hotel. Lugano is beautiful at this time of the year.'

She tells me she has sold her favourite painting, Renoir's *Nude,* to meet the growing expenses of her business. I don't want to hear more. I don't want to know whether she is also into hiring mercenaries.

'She can stay on the yacht with me,' volunteers Uncle Willie. 'I can play the piano for her as I used to do when she was a little girl.'

He is wearing a three-piece made-to-order suit and smells tantalizing. A long Italian shawl hangs casually over his shoulders. His accent is cosmopolitan. He grows stubble under his nose that could pass for a miscarried moustache. Mr Big Money one can spot in a VIP waiting room, Casino or a Grand hotel foyer going through *Financial Times* or *Newsweek.*

I look at him, then back to Auntie Susan. Then I say it, just like this. Something that I have suspected, but never dared to formulate as a simple question.

'He is my father, isn't he?'

'Sandy!' It's Aunty Susan. 'It's not what you might think. Willie has always been faithful to me.'

'I beg your pardon?'

'I mean, Margherita and Willie, they never...'

'They never screwed each other? It's hard to believe. After all, why should my mother escape all the way to Brisbane if everything was okay between the two sisters?'

She takes my hand. Suddenly she is an old woman without the stamina to pretend she is not. Uncle Willie keeps his distance, eating with his eyes a couple of Asian hostesses who cross his horizon.

'Well,' says Aunty Susan finally, taking a deep breath. 'Willie donated sperm for Margherita's egg.'

'I beg your pardon?' I feel I am starting to repeat myself. Come to think, reducing me without any ceremony to an egg and a couple of sperm cells that have nothing to do with the Sperm of God.

'In a tube, in vitro?'

She nods. 'In vitro. Margherita desperately wanted a child.'

'How about you?'

'Never. But we thought that we could share you.' She purses her lips.

'What happened?'

'She tricked us by taking you away to Australia. You had to be hers only. It wasn't fair.'

'Funny,' I say. 'I remember travelling with Uncle Willie to India and to other places when he was performing.'

'He could take you with him very rarely and after endless scandals between me and Margherita.' She purses her lips again.

Finally I find the strength. I slowly turn to *the man* lingering around with a poker face.

'So *you* are my father?'

'Yes and no,' he answers promptly without taking his eyes off a young, high-bottomed passenger.

'What do you mean yes and no?' I regret having started to unravel this family secret, since there can't be any winners there, at least from my perspective.

'Yes, I donated sperm, and I am your biological father,' he says loudly, attracting unwanted attention and remaining undisturbed about it. 'But no, I am not your father. I didn't raise you, and you never looked to me as a father figure.'

Uncle Willie throws in his iron logic: 'There are thousands of guys doing it for living. Many guys make a living as sperm donors, and they don't know who their kids are. Something more, they have no right to know.'

'So what?' I say aggressively.

'Nothing, Sandy, nothing.' Uncle Willie looks distracted again.

But I know what he means and it makes me sick. In a matter of hours I have lost a father just found.

I look at Aunty Susan for support but get no response. I suspect she is secretly triumphant over his slippery behaviour. It must suit her as a post-mortem revenge over Margherita.

'You know what?' I tell her. 'My mother has always been the better looking one between the two of you.' I nod at Uncle Willie. 'He was aware of it, wasn't he? He wouldn't miss it. Perhaps you made it impossible for her to remain in Lugano.'

I am looking Aunty Susan straight in the eyes. 'And you sent me to Elsinore with that stupid riddle about Hamlet because you had wrong information that his yacht was there while he was in Copenhagen.'

'Sandy,' she says more warmly than I would expect, 'I know, kid, that you've been through a really tough time, so I accept this as overreacting.' She takes my free hand and squeezes it gently. 'Don't forget I am the only family you've got and that I am always here for you.'

This simple truth is so depressing, it makes me cry—just as they announce my flight.

'What's the matter?' asks a genuinely intrigued Uncle Willie. 'Why are you crying?'

'I don't know what to call you,' I say, feeling my weakness exposed to the limits.

'Why don't you call me simply Willie, Sandy-babe?' he says gently and takes me in his arms.

'I love you,' I say desperately through streaks of tears.

Almost inaudible he whispers into my ear: 'I love you, too! You are my heritage! You rebuilt the bridge for my father's avange!'

No one mentions the name of Herr Tommler but it's hanging there between us like a rusty butcher's cleaver.

Then he drops me back under the scrutinizing eyes of Auntie Susan. I lose balance and a trolley full of luggage passing by saves me from falling. I excuse myself to the man pushing the trolley.

When I turn back my father, the man who I am supposed to call *Willie,* is talking to his wife. She is adjusting his long Italian shawl with that unmistakable authority of a spouse that makes me cringe. A sudden urge to be able to do such things overwhelms me.

Then they leave: my aunty and her husband, my father who is not my father because he is not supposed to recognise me in case I am just one of his many sperm cells donated on one January morning thirty six years ago in a Lugano clinic.

I have enough time to ponder on the Moso tribe in Tibet, who say that the woman was born with foetus inside her. The man simply waters her like a plant. There's no word for *father* in Moso language.

Yet I feel that the bond between me and Uncle Willie (it's easier for me to keep on calling him like this) is stronger than blood, it's the bond of conspiracy.

FIFTY-FIVE

It smells of undercooked macaroni and mouldy, acidy tomato sauce.

I am in my den in Everton Heights and Marylin is taking over. She brings me a bowl of macaroni. I am quick enough to stop her pouring the tomato sauce over it. Instead I sprinkle finely powdered parmesan.

Spaghetti in bianco (without sauce) could be a beautiful meal in Italy. But the comparison is not fair for Marylin, who is trying her best to support me in this difficult moment in my life, not least due to my dysfunctional separation with Frank. Whether separation is dying or dying is separation, I don't know but what I know is that it has something to do with the reason why my mother Margherita gave up on her career as a performing musician.

I feel hungry and recover satisfactory. At the Royal Brisbane hospital they had problems tracing my bone scars back to their original fractures. Of course, I don't say anything about the shaman. He is my secret.

Marylin comes in to take my bowl away, happy to see that I have polished the macaroni clean off. Like a real butler she carries a letter on a small tray and leaves it next to me. The envelope shouts with its stamps that it's from Europe so she backs off silently and closes the door.

Scanning the envelope, I see that it's not from Frank. I want to call her back, but then I have second thoughts.

The envelope contains a postcard with nine tiny images of my mother Margherita's country, Switzerland. One of the images, of course, is the lake of Geneva with that high orgasmic squirt of a fountain. I turn the card over, wondering why Aunty Susan would bother to send a postcard in an envelope; then I see that it contains a delicate issue. It's signed by Uncle Willie *your loving father*.

It's still a secret around here that I have found him, the man I was so anxious to discover.

Aunty Susan's postcard announces that the buyer of her Renoir's *Nude* is *my father*. Now the *Nude* is hanging in his sailing yacht. It is an invitation to follow the *Nude*, writes Aunty Susan, sounding quite cheeky for someone who thinks that sex is not for people over seventy. I hope for her sake that she'll never find out that what hangs in uncle Willie's yacht is a replica of her Renoir's *Nude*.

'I'm going to take a wild guess and say it's from Frank.' Marylin bursts in.

'It's not,' I say curtly, then regret being cross with Marylin, who has left her daughter Wendy in a house across from the cemetery to look after a cranky woman like me. 'Sorry,' I add.

'I understand,' says Marylin. 'It's been a bit too much for you. Besides you have bad vibes in your house. There's something necrophilic about keeping so many books around. It's like a graveyard, books for gravestones with the chiselled names of the authors.'

I have to see that she doesn't go any near my special book, which Aunty Susan returned to me at Oslo airport.

Marylin still insists on cheering me up and announces, 'I will cook eggplants for you.'

My prayers go with the eggplants.

She tries to tackle them for the best part of the afternoon.

When Marylin brings the tray with my dinner, what I get is stew with big onion and eggplant chunks, overcooked and over seasoned. Yet I find it so good that I ask for two more helpings and my friend is happy.

'Marylin, I have a debt to pay,' I say dunking some bread in the sauce. Aunty Susan's card makes me feel uneasy. I want to send her the money I *borrowed* in Lugano. I want to feel honest again. 'Where is my chequebook?'

'You better first make some money, love,' answers Marylin carefully.

'What happened? Don't tell me I am broke or something?'

Marylin doesn't want to meet my eyes. Then I look at her dress she has changed into for the evening. It has nothing to do with her usual multilayer rags she stuffs herself into. A classy frock in black and white, label shoes in which her feet don't look like skateboards any more.

'Marylin, is there anything you want to tell me?'

And then she cracks: angry, accusing me, defending herself, 'You'll be rich anyway, Sandy Cornelius. Either you'll cash in on all your adventures or your aunty will kick the bucket leaving you a hotel in Switzerland. You've always been the lucky one of us two.'

'So?' I feel edgy and sad.

'So, I thought I might as well use some of your money. Not that I expect you to pay me for looking after you.'

Swallowing hard I work to quell my reaction. 'It's okay, no worries.'

She can't be happier. 'If you want I'll take you for a night ride in the car.'

'What car?'

Marylin has never had a car.

'The one you I bought with your money. You forgave me, remember?' She gives me an inquisitive look and finishes impertinently: 'Come on, we are going for a *joy* ride?'

It is nine o'clock in the evening and I am sure she has had one glass too many of her vinegary wine she loves so much. Yet I say yes and get off the sofa I lay on most of the day.

I wait in the cool of the night for Marilyn to get the car (a third-hand apple-green sedan) out of the garage. The whole manoeuvre is accompanied by noises of rolling, bumping and bouncing, by hiccups of the engine and rattles of gears. Finally Marylin pulls out onto the driveway, lit by the jaundiced light of the moon. In unison with the spooky atmosphere, the car appears half covered in a sheet dragged from the clothesline. Marylin tries to open the door for me, but it refuses to move.

'Okay,' she smiles, 'open the back door and then climb to the front.'

I open the back door and can't let go of it, since it is held only by one hinge. Clutching the door, I slide in and fall, hitting my nose while my knee bumps against a spring protruding out of the gnawed tapestry of the seat. Forgetting about new bruises, I pull myself up to the front seat where I have to find a spot among napkins treasuring stale pizza leftovers, batteries and two shrunken balloons from someone's birthday party.

We drive south to Wynnum, where the ocean is friendly and quiet. At roundabouts Marylin goes in circles three or four times before exiting them, a real whirling dervish.

At one such roundabout I say to her: 'You know what, I will never ever again mention the word *cannibals*.'

'Cannibals?' snorts Marylin, circling for a fourth time. 'I am also into cannabis these days.'

'Marylin,' I ask her. 'Have you any idea when these experiments *in vitro* actually began?'

She is again the belligerent feminist. 'Of course I do. We protested against it at its twenty-fifth anniversary a couple of years ago. Exactly when my cat died.'

'Then it can't be true!'

Marylin cuts a corner and forgets to ask what it is that can't be true.

'I can't be an *in vitro* baby, can I? If I was born a decade before the experiment started?'

Now I have her attention. After I spill the whole story Marylin has only one comment: 'The bastard.'

I try to defend Uncle Willie because I feel I am obliged to experience unconditional love for my only living parent, but Marylin interrupts me. 'I mean your Aunty Susan, she's the bastard.'

'You better save that name for Frank, Marylin.'

FIFTY-SIX

They all keep calling to ask how I am doing.

Norm tells me how much he loves me and I tell him that I want to return to the Juvenile Correction Centre. I feel so guilty about Michael that I have started to change my feelings about Norm's students. I no longer think of them in terms of cats' throats slitters, old women bashers, rapists and killers. I want to try to heal their anger and aggressiveness through cooking a special meal for those misplaced boys. It should be a white meal, cleansing the spirit, cleansing the soul, cleansing the mind, cleansing the body. Milk, salt, water, flour, garlic for the gravy. Whiting fish boiled or baked, white light, white thoughts.

I think of my profession in relation to myself.

I am one of those thousands of TV cooking gurus with an unmistakable air of arrogance, part of a presumed elite of initiated individuals in possession of knowledge inaccessible to other people. I play God when I say that one should grate and not chop the carrot for the zucchini schnitzel.

Cooking has always had the quality of a shaman's ritual.

There is always power and multifaceted significance in the way you mix ingredients into the pot. Never poison it with black gloomy thoughts. Allow only cheerful ones while you are cooking.

Norm says this sounds all right but is suspicious that I am rehearsing my new TV series. Yet he wants to know what I think of him and me as an item.

My cell phone rings and I excuse myself.

Someone, tone-deaf, is singing *Fifty Ways to Leave Your Lover*.

It's Frank.

'I need your help,' he says bluntly.

'You bloody bastard,' I scream, remembering that we reserve this name for him.

'That will do,' he says and I can hear his orgasmic groans.

I can't believe it. The narcissistic, amoral, borderline personality bastard!

Suddenly I burst into a chuckle that threatens to choke me.

Marylin hears me and comes with a glass of water. She sits on the sofa next to me. Her red chilli hair covers her fleshy ears like a veil, her full firm face showing a determined opinionated person. I feel the sweaty temperature of her body moving inside the layers of her usual clothes. She has caused me much grief over the years but I still love her. Actually I have no choice.

When I tell her what's happened, she says lovingly, 'You are healing, baby.'

Then she gives me a daily paper.

I might be healing but I am not healed. It's hard to bring myself to open a newspaper without risking a panic attack. I still expect to see myself dead and decorating the front page. I know that Marylin is trying me so I reluctantly pretend I am interested in it. Suddenly I see: a branch of the Brotherhood has been exposed.

They have raided some houses in London after months of surveillance. There were some gruesome findings: human body parts, mainly hearts. Jacob Jacobsen continues to do a good job.

When David rings I end up with a second offer for a book. 'Make it sound really great, Sandy. You are capable of inventing a title that will sweep them off their feet. Something like "The Sex Life of Cannibals" for example.

I pretend I don't know he's been teaming up with Beverley. 'But David,' I protest meekly, 'I've never seen what their sex life actually is like.'

'That's the beauty of it,' says David seriously. 'You couldn't have seen it because they cooked and ate you, didn't they?'

Eh well, who am I to disillusion him?

'Don't hesitate to call me if you need help. Anytime. By the way, a cheque is coming your way. We are talking exclusive rights here, and I am talking a fat cheque.'

I am speechless but manage to mumble something that sounds like thanks.

'I think you mentioned something like quitting.' Marylin teases me, 'Don't tell me you changed your mind, I wonder what made you did so.'

'Money,' I say simply. 'Money is everything as Aunty Susan says and who am I to contradict her?'

Janette van Haren, my TV producer, calls last. The conversation with her is no different from the one with David. She also has a title ready for my new series: '*Omate* fork and *tanoa* drinking bowl' (whatever that means).

The idea is that I present my new cooking programme from places with history. Like picking a location on one of the Fiji islands where cannibalism has been practiced up to the end of nineteenth century: bodies from the battlefield were dragged to the spirit house and offered to the war god, then roasted and eaten on his behalf. While doing so the men performed the death dance, *cibi,* and the women an obscene dance, *dele,* through which they sexually humiliated dead bodies and war captives. Then the surroundings of the spirit house were adorned with trophy bones, sexual organs and fetuses.

This time I refuse, under the approving eye of Marylin.

'People can't stomach that crap,' I say, and I mean it.

'Bull,' says Janette. 'Since *Big Brother* people can stomach any crap.'

I say I will give it some thought. I am the one negotiating terms these days.

FIFTY-SEVEN

A week later I am on the deck constructed by a bunch of ex-rugby players with bits and pieces from demolished fences.

I bask in the sun, suppressing my cannibalistic urges. Sometimes I puncture the tip of my ring finger and suck on my blood to close the circle.

Still, I am a humble pupil.

No one can be a bigger man-eater than life.

Everton Heights is proud of me because I have brought them the story of resurrection. They know I was dead and now they see me in the garden chasing crows.

What nobody knows, however, is that I plan a manuscript about food-related themes in music and the cannibalistic messages one finds there. The good thing is that they are coded so deep in notes and polyphony that it won't be easy to catch their abstract meaning.

I will try again to write about the Brotherhood, mythical or not as it may be, because it's time the truth came out. The truth that mankind of the twenty-first century is like the stranded sailors of *The Medusa Raft*, drifting with no direction, no compass, no captain, drifting with no food, but a few drops of wine and man flesh to satisfy the hunger. Mankind climbing on a pyramid based on half-gnarled human bodies, yelling for help in the vast water desert, in the womb of the universe. Drinking blood turned into wine, eating bread made of bodies.

I try to find why Nero set Rome on fire.

So that he could rebuild Rome to his liking, suggests the historian Tacitus, who was a kid at the time of the fire.

There was also a prophecy in 64 AD that Rome had to pay for throwing Christians to the lions in gladiators' fights, which Nero observed using an emerald eyeglass. Nero himself had to pay for illuminating his garden parties with Christian-human torches. Perhaps someone set the fire to make sure the prophecy came true.

Or, perhaps, the prophecy itself turned out to be true.

I put on the Beethoven's quartets and touch Margherita's tiny gold cross that I wear on a chain these days. I am a bit disappointed that Beethoven is not my father but I forgive her. I also pat the woodcarved crocodile Dr Belloc bought for me in the Amazonian jungle. The bastard!

I think of myself as a half pagan, half spiritual being. I also think of a young hunk by the name of Jesus who knew human nature and tried to address it on both these levels, offering himself as a sacrificial food.

Of course, I can't be sure.

Life is a flower, a bird, life is a breath. Life is you and you are life. It is the way it is.

I hear the shaman's message with my heart and thank him. He is a good mate.

Taking of flowers, I found my African violet dead after so much watering and care. As for the geranium, it comes to life from a dried stem shortly I resume looking after it.

I brew myself coffee and drink it on the terrace.

In the garden I see Marylin having a leak standing, and I know that she is also a good mate.

Suddenly it's not Beethoven but the invigorating pounding rhythm of *Ka mate, ka mate, ka ora, ka ora* (I die, I die, I live, I live) whirls around me. I run back into the house and see Tamati poking his tongue, stamping his feet, his arms outstretched to embrace me.

And suddenly I know it has been all in vain trying to forget him and the love and passion we had. It's been as impossible a task as trying to forget Rotorua.

I know why Nero set Rome on fire.

Not because he was such a determined estate developer and wanted a terrain for his palaces but because he had a dream, a clairvoyant dream, that Rome would one day become the centre of Christianity.

He knew he would not be there to set the lions on the followers of Jesus whose flesh we eat and whose blood we drink in hope of eternal life.

Slowly I walk to meet Tamati, my heart pounding, my skin tingling with blood rushing, almost surfacing, through my pores, my sexual appetite like a monstrous wave. With every step I anticipate, pretaste, degustate Tamati's body, falling in his aura, sucking on his healthy animal smell, hearing his juices hissing in the claustrophobic enclosure of his physical entity.

'Coming back home, baby,' I say and whether it's for him or for me I am not sure.

He looks at me with his eyes like marbled eggs, cracks all over the shells, marinated in tea leaves that the Chinese love so much.

He smiles a smile just like a pork rib rolled in plum sauce, and it's so mouth-watering.

I melt, already savouring him, and close my eyes, barely hanging in the air, my feet coming off the floor, my body hesitating, tricking gravity for a moment of unforgivable deception. It took me a series of death scares, several weeks and three continents to understand that it's Tamati that I love with all my heart and sexual drive. That it's Tamati I have to thank for the raw feeling of being alive and sharing the wilderness of dreams again.

Good-bye, pretence that I am over the moon with the fact that I am part of the statistics of sexy, successful, single women over thirty with nothing better to do but brag about how good they feel about this.

'Welcome home,' I repeat, and my eyelids flicker over tears.

Tears of happiness. Complete and total bliss.

I better let him see the tears, I think, and push my flickering eye-lids up a bit enough to see him heading towards me. The disturbance of the air he pierces sends ripples all over me.

Then he is gone.

I don't see him. I don't feel him.

I only hear him saying a soft hello.

I turn in time to see Marylin falling into his arms, that are quick to encircle her generous torso and pull her against him.

They kiss.

FIFTY-EIGHT

It feels like I am having my own personal Waterloo these days.

Must be something in the cards or in the stars. Yet somehow my experience with the shaman has made me understand that life is not what happens around me, life is what happens within me.

I can enjoy the simple beauty of the night, leaning on the railing of my shaky terrace, looking into the garden, where frog-mouth owls sit among the branches.

It's quiet, nothing moves.

I pick up my laptop and go again through all the files Beverley had left for me after she stole my manuscript to pass it on to David Hall as hers. I read again recipes for cooking the long pig called Sandy Cornelius.

'The small and tender palm muscle just under the thumb is arguably considered a delicacy. Arguably because some say the thighs are the real thing. When it comes to a specimen like Sandy Cornelius it could even be hips. Her hips would provide the finest protein, highly digestible and succulent.'

I am not flattered one bit. I hate Beverley; she deserves to be where she is, stitching wedding gowns for the dead.

I am about to shut down the program when something catches my eye. The word *succulent* is highlighted. I hesitate, considering whether I should open the editing tool and read the comment. I'm not sure I can take any more of this graphically explicit description of me and my body like in a butcher chart for beef portions. Yet something stirs my curiosity.

I open Beverley's comment.

What I read next makes my heart sink, my whole world turns around.

'Dear Sandy, I have always admired you and I always will, no matter what. I wanted to attain your standard as a cookbook writer, a philosopher of the palate, and become one myself. I like to hang out with you, breathe your air in an attempt to snitch a small idea that you wouldn't bother to use and develop it as my own. Soon destiny offered me more than I bargained for when I agreed to look after the African violet and the geranium and submerge myself in the coffee-scented atmosphere of your home. Believe me, I had no intention to go through your writings at that time.'

I stop reading because I can see Beverley's eyes of lapis lazuli colour as if she is looking straight at me. I can hear her voice reaching me through the gates of another world of dissipating energies. Then I collect myself, drink some coffee from the jar on the kitchen bench and continue.

'On the first day of your absence the telephone rang when I was at your place measuring the moisture in the pot of that capricious African violet. On a spur of the moment, something that I deeply regretted afterwards, I pretended to be you on the phone. The man became agitated and insisted that he meet with you as soon as possible. I arranged to meet him in the garden late that evening since he said he could only come when it was dark. A bit before nine a slim, tall man appeared out of the blue and stood by me, which was quite scary. He had glassy blue eyes, a young aged face, if you know what I mean. A very wide-brimmed grey hat gave him an old-fashioned and gracefully dangerous appearance.

'*Ms Cornelius*, he addressed me and I was already sorry to have pretended being you. *We are aware of your interest in the old books revealing strange appetite for human flesh. When I say we, I mean the Masters, the very few on this planet with real blue blood in our veins coming down from our out-of-Earth ancestors. Coming down from the stars. We are race within race. We look like you but we are not you. So when we put human meat on our table, that doesn't make us cannibals. For us it is the same as if you enjoy a beefsteak, a pork chop, a lamb rib. And it is a lot different from what your presumption might have been when you followed artists enlightened by our presence on this planet. Because we are coming down from the stars.*

'Dear Sandy, I was standing there and believe me I didn't want to hear more. But he continued. *The Brotherhood of the Masters can't be harmed, it harms. It's just a friendly warning, Ms Cornelius.* Then he disappeared into thin air the way he materialized. I felt a damp cold creeping all over me and ran back into the house. I drank from your glass, I drank from your filtered water. My hands were shaky and I dropped the glass; then I collected the sharp pieces with your brush. I found your coffee and made a full mug of aromatic *Belvedere* and I soaked my stunned soul in it and it was great. Finally I was not only you, I was more you than you.

'Sandy, I am in possession of the real truth and I am going to make it work for me. I'll contact your publisher David Hall first thing in the morning. This time he is going to sign with me. Soon it will be me on the TV screen dancing in a grass skirt around an *umu* oven. I am sick and tired of stitching wedding gowns using that insignificant, small-pricked Paul for a model. I deserve better. Ciao. Your Beverley. I love you Sandy.'

I love you, too, I say to a rare photo of the three of us, *best friends*: Marilyn, me, Beverley.

So it wasn't that Beverley's life was taken by accident and instead of mine. They have killed her because between the two of us she was the vicious hound chasing the truth while I was fucking around.

I love you, I say to nobody because there's nobody to hear it.

It proves wrong.

Footsteps cautious as if belonging to someone approaching the bed of a sick family member echo gently in the house. Footsteps full of care and concern, tiptoeing, afraid to disturb, draw attention or stir an emotion that could be too strong and claim a life. Footsteps like notes on a Beethoven's sonata, romantic, promising, heart-nourishing. Footsteps like drops of boiling syrup dripping down from a ladle onto paper, my all time favourite thickness check. Footsteps, light like a water spider's. Footsteps, I turn to.

Finally he is here.

'Oh my God! Sandy!' he says and I run to him, my head soon resting on his non-existing shoulder of a rice-cooker torso.

I sob and cry and yell and talk, uncontrolled fits of long suppressed emotions surface threatening to tear me apart. But he, as always, is there for me, comforting me, taking onboard the heavy ballast I am carrying so I don't sink, don't go mad, don't think that *friend* is a dirty word.

Norm is here.

'I was so worried,' he says wiping my tears with his fingers.

'So was I,' I sob. 'About you. What they did to you about Michael? Do they press charges for a supervisor's negligence or something?'

'They can't prove anything,' he pulls away from me. 'I was worried about you! That jerk Frank dumped you as I expected and you are alone.'

'Thank you,' I manage to utter. 'It was the other way around: I dumped him. Actually,' I confess, 'I am not sure who ditched who but at the end of the day it's the fact that matters: we are not together any longer.'

Norm smiles encouragingly. 'Freedom, new opportunities, who wants to stay in the same relationship for donkey's years?'

He goes to the trolley bar and fixes himself a drink. 'You want some?'

I nod. 'I better have a glass myself.'

'Any preferences?'

'Vodka, top it with espresso. There is a jar on the kitchen bench.'

He pours the vodka in a cognac goblet and I make a grimace, which doesn't escape him. He brings me the glass and leaves for the kitchen to look for the espresso.

'Norm, you remember Marylin's obsession with that crocodile hunter?' My voice trails through the kitchen door.

'Yeah,' he says. I hear him rattling with the jar unplugging it. 'What about crocodile hunter?'

'Marylin scared the hell out of him.'

'How?' He appears in the doorframe, a jar full of beautiful super quality espresso, the aroma hopping, bursting out of the jar like a toddler explosive with energy, not listening to his mummy's pleas not to jump into puddles.

'She told him she'd feed his crocodiles with the man responsible for my miseries.'

He drops the jar. I don't mind the carpet, yet such a waste of super quality espresso made of ripe healthy coffee beans makes me feel worse than having to drink vodka out of a cognac goblet.

'Don't worry, Norm,' I say matter-of-factly. 'It's very in to hate Frank. And I'll clean the carpet with baking soda.'

'Where's the book?' He stands there rooted to the threshold, looking at me full blast.

'What book? Don't tell me we'll be having a poetry reading about stars. I am a bit divorced with my senses right now.' Saying this I am suddenly aware that the nose-poking aroma of quality coffee starts to fade giving way to another powerful smell.

Smell of danger.

He slowly walks towards me, his dough-colour eyes with yeast of madness ready to leaven.

Quicker than a computer my mind starts to run details and data, patches of information, blank spots, words, meanings, significant and *insignificant* events, impressions, confusions, misunderstanding, comprehensions, overlooked links in a chain still around my neck, still trying to strangle me, because I suddenly know he is here to kill me.

To kill me but not before he gets the book. The book that triggered a series of misfortunes around me. The book written by my grandfather after a miraculous survival in a Nazi Death camp witnessing the bizarre, gut-wretching experiments of a 'scientist' called Herr Tommler. The book printed in a single copy as heritage and then duplicated, a book Uncle Willie left with the woman he loved and had a child with. The book meant for me to inherit as a burning memory.

'The book belongs to me,' says Norm breathing in my face. 'My mother's maiden name is Tommler. I am a Tommler and we all come down from the stars.'

They come down from the stars.

It's still hard to believe.

'You killed Beverley? You planted the capsule with poison in her jacket? You stole and put those horrendous files on my laptop and then 'returned' it to me?'

His madness takes a break, he permits himself a short barking laugh. 'Beverley was my mistress. You see, you didn't like me but she knew when she got onto something worthwhile. She did what I told her to do, from copycatting you, breathing down your neck, to stealing your laptop and installing that lovely reading about the *long pig* Sandy Cornelius. Then she returned it back to you to read it.'

They come down from the stars.

What an idiot I've been. No matter what she did, Beverley tried to warn me but I failed to read behind the text of her comment.

'Don't tell me Beverly posed for that collage of a picture on Beethoven's grave!'

He grins.

'You killed Michael, too!'

'He was very close to exposing me. The kid was street-smart and I felt threatened by him questioning my orders.'

'Orders?'

'Everyone has to acknowledge our supremacy! The supremacy of those coming down from the stars. We used you as a decoy to see who wants to track down the Brotherhood and how they would do it. But your beloved Frank also used you, as did that buffoon Jacobsen. He couldn't have done much of a decent job if not for you. You're a smart cookie, Sandy, and beautiful at that but I have to kill you.'

'How about the book?' To bargain for my life has become as natural as breathing.

'I'll find it. It can't be far away. Your aunty gave it back to you at the airport.'

'Your copy, bound in human skin, is with Dr Nicholas.' I try to keep him busy talking.

'What the young lady tells you is correct, Norm,' says a familiar voice behind me. 'I have *that* book bound in human skin, a piece of art!'

The old creep is also here. I am in a good company.

I turn a bit only to see that Dr Nicholas holds a gun pointing at me. That's what I expect. What I don't expect is to see that in his other hand he is holding a gourd threaded around with human vertebrae. He rattles it gently.

'What are you doing here?' I ask nervously.

'Giving *him* a taste of his own medicine,' he answers gently.

'What are *you* doing here?' I ask again.

'I told you—' starts Dr Nicholas.

'I am not asking you,' I say, looking behind him at the giant figure filling the terrace door.

'She's asking me, *Dottore*!' The giant figure is covering Dr Nicholas with his own gun.

I turn back to Norm.

The rattling sound behind me tunes me in to remember Tamati's lessons. I throw the glass with vodka up in the air, ducking at the same time behind a chair, taking down with me an avalanche of books.

Like lightning Norm also produces a gun.

Three shots.

A split second later, *four* shots, tumbling of furniture, thundering of bodies. Then it's quiet, totally quiet besides the gentle rattling of the gourd rolling in front of my eyes, covered in blood.

I lie face down, buried in books, not daring to lift my head, waiting for some noise prompting me what the situation is.

I hear a moan, a hollow grumbling moan, then a moan drowned in the soft gurgle of a table fountain. It comes of the direction of Norm.

I cautiously shake a volume of Alexander Dumas' *Dictionary of Cooking* off my head and steal a look around from under the chair.

The first thing I see is Norm lying on his back, a black stain on his baggy shirt spreading with the speed of octopus ink. Blood, I think, bloody blood!

'Norm!' I scream forgetting the last ten minutes of my life, going back to the time when he was a friend to hang out with in the *Café on the Park* or covered in sawdust teaching stars and galaxes in the Juvenile Correction Centre. I cry and I spring on my feet and run to him tripping on books. 'Norm!'

'Hi gorgeous!' he utters with that same gurgling sound. I see the streak of blood surfacing in his mouth with bubbles. 'Remember I have always loved you...it was that I had to be...to clean...family name...' His words drown in blood.

'Norm, tell me that you were not using me like all the rest. Tell me it's not true that...' And I stop, for I don't know any longer what's true and what's not. I don't even know who has shot him. Whether the bullet was meant for me or for him. Now that I have exposed myself, it's too late to be afraid so I turn to face the other two participants.

I don't see Dr Nicolas. What I see, though, is a blond giant with saffron hair blocking the exit to the terrace, clinging to the frame, swaying, his eyes out of focus, his knees giving in. His is a slow motion fall following the collapse of the terrace, which has finally had it. The noise deafens me. I reach for my cell phone, which has rolled out of my bag, half squashed under...Ah well, under Dr Nicholas.

I am about to faint, to prevent it I instinctively start to scream.

Frank!' I yell. 'Frank!' And I run down the stairs and into the garden only to see Tamati bent over Frank, gently inspecting him for injuries. I feel Frank's pulse. He doesn't look good. He hasn't been shot but he'll be lucky if he hasn't broken a leg in the fall. The ex-player for the kiwi *All Black* scoops Frank in his muscle arms and carries him upstairs laying him on the sofa. Then he brings water and pours it over Frank's face. Frank moans and tries to open his eyes.

I haven't forgotten Dr Nicholas. He is going to kill me. Why doesn't Tamati do anything? I start to scream again.

'Don't make a fuss, Ms Cornelius,' Dr Nicholas suggests politely. He has gotten up and finds his gourd, he wipes the blood off it on my velvet cushion and again starts to rattle it. 'You better say good buy to your friend.'

'Norm,' I whisper and turn to see him, his face changing colours, from flour white into tortoise shell grey.

His lips move and I put my ear down against them to decode his breath wheezing in the bubbles of blood.

'Billie...'

I hear it almost clearly. Billie, his husky.

'I'll look after her, Norm. I'll look after her.'

He thanks me with his eyes, the last thing he does in this life. His body judders a couple of times.

Then he is gone.

I cry. I cry to the soothing rhythm of the rattling gourd. Suddenly I am aware that Norm is lying in a puddle of coffee and blood like Beverley. Beverley who posed for the montage picture showing me dead on the grave of Beethoven.

Dr Nicolas looks unharmed. Perhaps I should run or at least feel fear, but I am too exhausted for any of it. I stay there, my hand touching Norm's, still giving me warmth.

'Don't grieve for him,' says Dr Nicolas. 'And don't be afraid of me.'

'How come the change of heart?' I ask feebly. 'And what actually happened? And shouldn't I call the police?'

'Your friend has already done it.'

Then I see that Marylin is also here busy on the phone.

'They thought they had me.' Says Dr Nicholas. 'Strange enough you were the one to help me turn the tables. The flying object, it's a first-class defence lesson.'

I accept the compliment, giving credit to Tamati.

'Then I was a second time lucky. Targeting me and you, they didn't realise that they remained facing each other the moment you and I ducked for our lives.'

'I am absolutely sure he didn't target *me*!' I say still holding Norm's hand. But I am talking about Frank. Then I realize that Tamati has killed Norm.

'It's your choice to select what you want to believe.' Dr Nicolas sighs and stops rattling the gourd. He leaves it next to me. There is a feeling of vibrant life coming from it, compared to no life coming from Norm. I drop his hand and grasp the gourd.

'It's easy to cross boundaries, Ms Cornelius, boundaries between good and evil, when you are an obsessed collector of sinister musical instruments. It's easy to let bad people manipulate and make use of you for their hideous beliefs. But then, through your collection you get in touch with strange entities that show you the path to follow to be decent again. Good-bye, Ms Cornelius, it was pleasure meeting you. You are always welcome to Campione d'Italia. Perhaps you'll help me burn the book, the one bound in human skin.'

He pauses. 'And now when it's time to say good buy, I have to admit that I am here to collect the ring.'

'The ring?'

'The ring you snitched off Fernando in the hope that you could find one day more truth along the road. The truth was always under your nose when you first visited me in Campione d'Italia, you never picked it. The book, bound in human skin. Beverley, oh Beverley she was clever. I played on their weak spots and they responded perfectly. I opened Norm's eyes about his monstrous ancestor and Beverley would do anything to get into your shoes of a kitchen goddess. Oh god, Sandy, can't you think of a more sophisticated professional name? Like maestro of gourmet decadence or wizard of the velvet palate?'

Saying this Dr Nicholas, Fernando's rich lover, picks up the wooden crocodile, gives it a tap on the back and the huge ruby ring falls out onto his hand. 'Thank you,' he says and goes, leaving me the gourd.

Tamati is already outside meeting the paramedics and the police. Dr Nicholas himself goes inside one of the police cars.

I sob and moan. I feel like a widow.

'I am sorry,' I say kneeling by Frank. 'Sorry to leave you like this, sorry for a relationship that didn't work?'

'You think so?' He suddenly grunts in my ear.

'Oh Frank, you are alive!' I throw myself over him covering, cleaning the debris so I can get hold of him and plant a kiss on his lips. 'You are back baby! I thought I lost you for good!'

'You stupid old girl. Why you think I travelled across the world? Luckily I was on time.'

'On time to save me!'

'On time for our marriage, stupid!'

'Frank!'

I feel subdued and quiet. My body quivers under the invisible touch. Warmth like a baby animal pulsates through me and I know that the shaman will always be there for me. My fingers search for his like on that famous Michelangelo's fresco on the ceiling of the Sistine Chapel. Our hands meet across meridians and oceans, across cultures and language barriers. They meet across galaxies and the Sun God Himself does our palm reading because we all are His children.

Three weeks later I am the new Mrs Syversen.

My father, Uncle Willie, takes me to the altar. Tamati is our best man. I know he is filthy rich but his present for the wedding is only a rice-cooker. Yet he pays for the catering, which is a replica of the extravagant menus of *The Brotherhood of Swan*, whose member was that cheeky bastard Hieronymus Bosch, the artist of *Table of the Seven Deadly Sins*. Everybody is there for the ceremony. Marylin, her daughter Wendy; Mimi and the other doctors, housemates of Tamati, along with the ex-rugby players who rebuilt my terrace snitching more fence timber; Jacobsen and the boys, wanna-be chefs from the Juvenile Correction Centre; Paul and Billie, the husky, whom he adopted; Aunty Susan and Lilly whom she is about to adopt. All pushed around by Janette for the footage she shoots with the cameraman, footage for our new series *'Til Death Do Us Part*.

Needless to say, I am wearing one of Beverley's wedding gown creations, all lace and ribbons with real pearls. As for the wedding cake, we use one of her recipes and it's a two-story monster with candy figurines: a bridegroom looking like a chimneysweep and a bride like a hooker. The flowers are courtesy of David; the party is at the *Café on the Park* with an ocean view and tortoises stretching their necks, reminding me of walking penises.

Finally I settle down. No more adventures, no more stray sex fantasies. The music of Mendelson's wedding march fills the church and I say yes to Frank, in bandages and stitches, and good-bye to my dualistic existence as a spiritual pagan being.

Suddenly I hear drumming. Not loud, but distinct, it drowns the music in the background. The drumming comes out of me. It creates a vortex and drives me into semi-consciousness. Soon I don't resist it but submerge into a trance. In my mind's eye I see a black caiman; its phallic symbol sends waves of guilt and pleasure through my body. A python curls around me. A nervous macaw rests its neck on my bare feet and a butterfly walks in the grove of my lips reminding me of Goya's obsession. A school of piranhas nibble my worries away and strip me down to a nature child. I feel the breath of the shaman, it's the breath of ayahuasca; it fills the space around me with visions of a serpent copulating with the crescent moon. The vine of the dead blends with the aged aroma of Brazilian coffee, coffee like Beethoven's music: velvet violin-toned or machete-sharp on the senses, helping me along my own metaphysical escapades, opening a door to a spiritual cosmos where knowledge does not come in words.

I recline on the thick compound scent as on a floating carpet and close my eyes. Heaven and underworld meet tuning into each other's mystic channels. For the first time I am not scared to get close to the living energy inside me. It feels like a small sturdy thing, warm and pulsating, hairy and rough like a coconut. I am not afraid to feel it, to play with it, to explore it. I am not afraid to be in touch with the core of my essence as a being. I realize that I have spent most of my life suppressing that natural merging of a planetary god force and shameless juicy flesh of a long pig. My apprehension that I might go mad, crack and commit cannibalistic suicide no longer exists. I am no longer a feather in the wind of events; I have my own grounding center. I don't resonate events; I produce them. I am full of myself, of that unique substance called Sandy Cornelius. No longer an empty vessel waiting to be filled with food, sex, success, art, money, friends, relationships. I am no longer a pursuer of dreams about missed identities. No longer asking, who am I? I am what I am and that's plenty for a lifetime to live with. Of all relationships the most important is the one with myself.

My body is torn by sensations so strong I nearly die, sensations induced across continents and oceans, across astral planes.

My secret knowledge is that of the shaman making love to me across life and death.

Made in the USA